RIBBON OF MOONLIGHT

Sometimes the past is our future...

When her beloved grandfather dies in 1958, Polly Merton is forced to share her home with a woman she scarcely knows: the mother who abandoned her. Sadie Merton, glamorous and selfish, has her own set of morals and Polly is appalled by her scandalous lifestyle. Ashamed and resentful, she takes refuge in her friends and her college studies. Then Polly's love of France takes her to Paris, at a time when the tragic memories of wartime are at last giving way to new hopes and dreams, and where a chance encounter means her life will never be the same again.

RIBBON OF MOONLIGHT

For
all my writing friends

RIBBON OF MOONLIGHT

by

Margaret Kaine

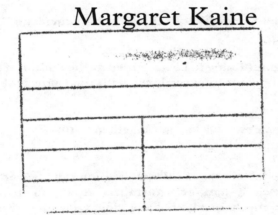

Magna Large Print Books
Long Preston, North Yorkshire,
BD23 4ND, England.

British Library Cataloguing in Publication Data.

Kaine, Margaret
    Ribbon of moonlight.

    A catalogue record of this book is
    available from the British Library

    ISBN   978-0-7505-3069-9

First published in Great Britain in 2008 by Hodder & Stoughton Ltd.

Copyright © 2008 by Margaret Kaine

Cover illustration © Condé Nast Archive/Corbis courtesy of Hodder & Stoughton Ltd.

The right of Margaret Kaine to be identified as the author of this work has been asserted by her in accordance with the Copyright, Designs and Patents Act, 1988

Published in Large Print 2009 by arrangement with Hodder & Stoughton Ltd.

Magna Large Print is an imprint of Library Magna Books Ltd.

Printed and bound in Great Britain by
T.J. (International) Ltd., Cornwall, PL28 8RW

Acknowledgements

As always I am grateful to my wonderful
writers' workshop for their invaluable
constructive criticism and to Biddy Nelson
who is so generous with her time.

My appreciation to Laurence Caplat for her
patience in answering my questions about
France, and to Margaret Cullingford and Peter
Nelson for sharing their knowledge of Paris
during the 1960s. My thanks to Karen Baker,
Librarian at the National Railway Museum,
Mary Hudson at the RAF Air Historical
Branch, to Anita Chadwick and to Liz and
Ron Rockett. And my gratitude to
Kevin Saunders at the wonderful
Château de Villars for his interest
and advice.

And to the late Stewart Walker.

'Memory is a diary that we all carry with us.'

Oscar Wilde

1

Polly was a nut-brown wren. At least, that was what her grandfather called her at the age of three. And as she grew older, Polly was destined often to remind people of that familiar small bird, so eminently sensible, so welcome in everyone's garden, but hardly decorative. It wasn't that Polly was plain. Her brown hair was silky, if straight, her large eyes a soft brown, her body curved in all the right places and she even grew to a medium height. But as soon as the sun shone then her skin, no matter how she tried to prevent it, would turn a warm, nutty shade. And Polly longed to be an English rose, with a fair and delicate complexion. But her female vanity, her dissatisfaction with her looks, paled into insignificance against the fact that the grave, kind man who had so accurately described her, the man she adored, was taken away. In 1958, when Polly was seventeen, John Merton died suddenly in his sleep as quietly as he had lived, and in the following year she would often rail against a God who had so deprived her. Because Polly knew with absolute certainty that her life would have been very different if her grandfather had been alive.

Polly could see daylight beneath the brocade curtains, but she lay quiet and tense in her comfortable bed, listening warily for soft footfalls on the thickly carpeted landing. It was a long time since that traumatic day when they had paused

13

outside her room, but Polly had learned never to get up while any man her mother might have brought home was in the house. And so it was another hour before Sadie, sitting in the warm kitchen, turned as the door opened and her daughter, fully dressed, came in.

'You needn't look at me like that!' Sadie, still in her pink quilted housecoat, looked at her daughter with ill-concealed irritation.

'Like what?'

'With that blasted look on your face! Why didn't you phone and say you were coming home last night instead of today?'

'I did. But I missed you.' Polly lifted the tea cosy from the teapot and peered inside. 'I see all the tea's gone.'

'Well, you should get up earlier.' Sadie crossed her legs and, blowing a nonchalant ring of smoke, narrowed her eyes. 'They don't bite, you know!'

Going over to the sink, Polly refilled the kettle. 'Who don't?'

'The male species.'

'I'll take your word for it!' She switched on the grill to heat for toast, took a loaf out of the white enamel bread bin, and began to slice it.

Sadie gazed morosely at the young girl before her. Maybe it was better that she *did* keep out of the way. The sight of Polly, in the first flush of womanhood, might make a man look more closely at her mother, and that, Sadie decided, stubbing out her cigarette, was not something she was willing to risk. 'And what, may I ask, are your plans for the day?'

'I'm not sure. I might drive into Stafford.'

14

'What for?'

'Do I have to have a reason?' Polly, waiting for her toast to brown, turned round. 'I expect you'll be out again tonight?' Even as she asked the question, Polly guessed what the answer would be.

'Yes. Jerry's picking me up.'

'And how long have you known this one?'

'A couple of weeks.'

Polly bent down to the grill. 'Did you get any marmalade?'

'What? No, I forgot. There's some honey in the larder.'

'I don't want honey,' Polly said, beginning to spread butter on to her toast. 'I've told you, I like marmalade.'

'Well you'd better buy some, then. I'm off upstairs.' Sadie got to her feet. 'I don't suppose *you're* out tonight?'

Polly shook her head. And thanks for the welcome home, she thought.

As she left, Sadie turned, tightening her lips at her daughter's rigid, disapproving back. 'You don't know how to enjoy yourself, that's your trouble!'

Ignoring the familiar jibe, Polly, taking her toast and tea with her, went into the breakfast room and slumped into an armchair at the side of the fireplace. She stretched out her toes to the warmth of the fire, listening to the steady tick of the old mahogany clock on the wall. She loved sitting in here, with its brown painted frieze and darkening cream textured wallpaper. No matter that the pattern on the square Axminster carpet was fading, to Polly, this cosy room, more than any other in the spacious if old-fashioned house,

15

represented home, love and security. Yet frighteningly, since her grandfather's death, that security he'd striven so hard to provide seemed to be slipping away from her.

Sadie's disturbing presence had changed everything. The perfume she wore and her – Polly searched for the words and guiltily came up with – 'sluttish behaviour' were insidiously eroding the respectable atmosphere of John Merton's home. And Polly, even now she was almost twenty, didn't know how to prevent it.

Her breakfast finished, she glanced up as the clock in sonorous tones chimed eleven times and, getting up, went back into the kitchen to clear away the clutter that Sadie and Jerry had left. Once again the morning was almost over, and with bitterness Polly realised that at these times she was almost a prisoner in her own bedroom. A self-imposed isolation it might be, but she knew that unfortunately it was the only means she had of distancing herself from the way her mother chose to lead her life. At first, when Sadie had moved in after the funeral, Polly had tried so hard to understand, remembering how her grandfather had made excuses for his daughter-in-law.

'It's not that she doesn't love you,' he'd told her, when as a growing child she'd questioned him about her mother's absence. 'It's just that she can't have you to live with her – it wouldn't be suitable – and she wouldn't be happy living here.'

'Why not?' Polly had asked, wide-eyed. Surely anyone would be happy living in this cosy house with lovely old Barney, their golden retriever, and the glorious sheltered garden.

'Because, my pet, our way of life isn't her way of life.'

Polly had pondered on this, but had never reached a satisfactory conclusion. However, having implicit faith in her grandfather's wisdom, she'd reluctantly accepted his reason. But that hadn't prevented her from staring with curiosity and bewilderment at the high-heeled, platinum-blonde young woman who, on her infrequent visits, would sweep Polly into a hug of scented face powder, and shower her with unsuitable presents. Sadie would sit at the dining table, cross her shapely legs in their sheer nylons, and smoke one lipstick-stained cigarette after another. Polly never knew quite what to say to her, she would sit mesmerised by the sight of Sadie's milky-white cleavage, uneasily aware that none of her friends' mothers would display their bosoms in such a way. John Merton's expression, however, was usually impassive. He merely, as always, listened politely to his visitor gossiping, answered her questions, and offered ham sandwiches, fruit cake and cups of tea.

'I suppose it's no use asking you for a gin and tonic?' Sadie would say archly.

'I'm afraid not,' John would reply.

Polly wondered why they went through this pantomime each time. But then she would catch a glimpse of merriment in Sadie's eyes, and realise that her mother was just teasing. And a ghost of a smile would hover around her grandfather's mouth. But it was all too fleeting, and once again she would see the familiar strain appear in his eyes, and empathise with his almost audible sigh

17

of relief when her mother left to return to London.

And so Polly had grown up without a mother, or at least without a 'normal' mother. And if there were times when she felt wistful for what she knew was missing in her life, she'd been a happy child. John Merton had made sure of that. His discipline was fair, balanced with affection, and he'd treated this unexpected girl child in his home with the same respect he accorded his friends and business associates.

Now, as the first days of her Easter holiday stretched ahead, Polly could only be grateful that although her training college was only in the next county, Sadie's scant knowledge of geography meant that she didn't question why her daughter never came home at weekends.

And the next day followed the same pattern, except that the man Sadie brought home – probably this Jerry – left earlier. And, because it was one of Mrs Booth's 'days', her mother was fully dressed and already downstairs by the time that Polly got up. She could hear raised voices even before she descended the wide oak staircase. 'As I've said from the start, I have me principles. And there's no way I'm setting foot in that bedroom of yours, let alone cleaning it!'

'Oh yes? And who said you could pick and choose. I don't see why I should keep a dog and bark myself.' Sadie's voice was so shrill that Polly winced.

'Yes, well as we both know, you aren't the one that keeps me, are yer?' In the short silence that followed, Polly sat on the bottom tread of the stairs, a grin spreading over her face. If Sadie thought she could get the better of Mrs Booth, it would be the first time anyone had in the last twenty years!

'I think you forget yourself,' Sadie said icily. 'And that's been said before!'

'So has my refusing to clean your room. I've always been a respectable woman and I intend to stay that way! So you're wasting your breath!'

'Oh, for heaven's sake, how narrow-minded can you get?'

Polly scrambled up as her mother flounced out of the kitchen. 'It's time you got rid of her,' Sadie said through gritted teeth. 'That woman's getting above herself.'

Polly stood aside as Sadie went back upstairs, and then going into the kitchen shook her head reprovingly at the cleaner. Doris looked shame-faced. 'Sorry, ducks, she just rubs me up the wrong way!'

'How do you two get on when I'm *not* here?'

'We avoid each other. But I'm not setting foot in her bedroom, no matter what she says. I've seen it – all pink satin and flounces. Glory knows what goes on in there!'

Although the inference both hurt and embar-rassed Polly, this woman with her flowered cross-over overall, lisle stockings and hairnet had been so much a part of her childhood, that she hadn't the heart to be cross with her. 'How are you?' she said. 'How's all the family?'

'Well, Ernie's got himself into trouble again,' Doris Booth sniffed, 'but what do you expect, the time he spends in that pub!'

Polly smiled. Ernie Booth's drinking habits were

a constant topic of conversation. 'What's happened this time?'

'Only knocked a bobby's hat off, didn't he? Up before the beak he was, and damn lucky to get off with a caution!'

Polly laughed. 'Go on, you know you think the world of him!'

'Oh, do I? Fat lot you know!'

Leaning against the kitchen table, Polly watched as Doris opened the cupboard under the sink, and took out a couple of yellow dusters and a tin of beeswax polish. 'How's everyone else – all right?'

'They're fine. I've got a bit of good news. Our Shirley is getting married. And about time – I was beginning to think she'd never find a husband, fussy madam!'

'She can't be that old!'

'She's twenty-three this year! And I always say that if you're going to have kids, better before thirty than after.' She glanced slyly at Polly. 'How about you – have you got anything to tell me?'

'Nothing in that direction, anyway I'm too busy studying.'

'You've only got another year to do at college, haven't you? And then you'll be a qualified teacher! My, your grandad would have been that proud!' Doris looked searchingly at the young woman before her. 'What will you do then? Get a job, local like, and go on living here?'

'I don't know, Mrs Booth, and that's the honest truth.'

Doris studied her for a moment, then said, 'Ah well, there's plenty of time to decide.' She jerked her head at the ceiling. 'Has she said anything?'

Polly shook her head. 'The subject's never discussed.'

'Mmn,' Doris muttered darkly. 'She'll take some shifting, you mark my words!' Polly turned away feeling, as always, uneasy at discussing her mother in this way. But Doris was the only person she *could* talk to about the unusual situation. Seeing that the cleaner was anxious to 'get on', as she called it, Polly wandered into the large hall, glancing at the heavy front door with its surround of stained glass, to check if there was any post. There wasn't, and pulling her cardigan closer against the chill, she went into the drawing room. Impressive in size and gracefully proportioned, it had hosted many dinner parties, mostly connected with her grandfather's business life, but not nowadays. Sadie, of course, delighted in showing it to her men friends, probably hoping, Polly thought with resentment, to impress them.

With a sigh, she went to look out of the large bay window overlooking the formal garden. But the house, with its long circular drive and set behind a tall yew hedge, was almost invisible from the lane, so there was little to distract her. Going over to the elegant rosewood sideboard, she paused, and then picked up the silver-framed photograph of the father she'd never known. Gazing at the good-looking RAF officer, at the keen intelligence in his eyes, she wondered yet again how any man raised by John Merton could have been foolish enough to not only get involved with, but to actually marry a woman like Sadie. And how, she thought grimly, would either man feel if they knew, as Polly had recently discovered, that The Gables, the home they'd both loved so much, was beginning to gain a reputation as a 'house of ill repute'?

2

Sadie, still resenting what she called the cleaner's 'insults', sat before her triple-mirrored dressing table, and decided to sort out its drawers. She would go downstairs only when she was sure that Doris was on the other side of the house. It was 'bedrooms' morning, and the woman would insist on cleaning all of them, not only Polly's, but also the other three – despite the fact they were never used – while Sadie, to her annoyance, had to look after her own. Despite the ruched net curtains, the pitiless morning light poured in through the window, and she averted her eyes from her reflection, painfully aware that her complexion was beginning to show signs of fine wrinkles. When she'd first moved into The Gables, she'd been furious not to have John Merton's large bay-windowed bedroom at the front of the house. But Sadie didn't know then how implacable her daughter could be. Polly had simply refused.

And so, Sadie had settled for this spacious room at the back, which, she realised now, was actually more practical. For one thing, it was some distance from her prudish daughter, for another it wasn't visible from the front of the house, and essentially, she'd been allowed to redecorate it to her own taste. The restrained furnishing of what had been a spare room had been replaced with silken curtains, a pink satin counterpane with a frilled valance, ivory and gilt bedside lamps, and pink-fringed lampshades. The plain oak headboard to the double bed was replaced by a velveteen arched one, the serviceable brown and beige carpet had gone, and the floor was now covered with a cream one scattered with pink roses. Being able to stamp her personality on this room had been, in a small way, one of the highlights of Sadie's life.

Now, she took out a pile of lingerie, examining the lace, discarding and refolding. Then tucked into a corner in the bottom of the drawer, she picked up a pair of peach camiknickers she rarely wore, and felt the familiar hardness of the small photo-frame wrapped inside. Slowly she withdrew it, and gazed down at the face of the man who had fathered Polly, the only man she had ever married.

They had met in a London nightclub in January 1941, where Sadie had recently begun working as a hostess. 'These lads deserve a bit of light relief,' her boss had told her when he'd taken her on. 'Make them smile, help them to forget their troubles,' he said. 'Remind them of their sisters, their sweethearts and the gentler side of life, what they're fighting for.' Billy Fraser was a man full of admiration for the armed forces and was bitterly disappointed that he was too old to be a part of the war. He could at least, he thought, give them all a good time when they were on leave. Nothing tacky, of course, but he knew a man's needs. To Sadie, eighteen and 'man-mad', it was a job straight from heaven.

The club had been fairly quiet that Saturday night when the small group of RAF officers came in. They had obviously been drinking elsewhere, and their noisy arrival in the smoky basement room enlivened what had promised to be a dull evening. Sadie sidled forward to their table, hips swaying; her mouth curving in the smile she practised before her mirror. 'Hello boys!'

'Hey, you're a smasher!' one said. He was a pilot – by now she was adept at recognising insignia. 'Look at her, André, even you must admit that!'

The tall, thin officer, with a navigator's wing on his tunic, smiled thinly but only gave her a fleeting glance. Instead, he stood up. 'My turn, I think?' When his friends nodded with enthusiasm, he walked silently past Sadie to the bar, and miffed, she stared after him. Miserable sod!

But then the officer who'd first spoken said, 'Don't mind him, sweetie, he's a bit down. His mother died a couple of weeks ago – it's hit him hard.' She lingered by the table, laughing and flirting, enjoying the men's admiration and suggestive glances, the heady sensation of knowing they fancied her. With the exception of André, of course, whose disregard when he returned with a tray of drinks both irked and challenged her.

'Hey, you didn't bring a drink for Sadie!' the pilot said. 'What'll it be, sweetheart?'

'I'll have a gin and tonic, please.' She glanced up at André from beneath her sweeping eyelashes. When she'd first come to work at the club, she'd drunk gin and orange, but soon realised that it was considered 'common'.

André Merton looked at her properly for the first time, and thought how young she was to be working in such a place. Not that the club wasn't fairly respectable, but this girl must be still in her teens. 'Sorry,' he said, realising he'd been impolite, and momentarily startled by the warmth of her answering smile, he went back to the bar.

One of the men went to fetch a chair for her, and Sadie joined them; asking their names, encouraging their badinage, knowing that her presence, in her daringly low-cut blue cocktail dress, contributed enormously to their enjoyment of the evening. Any physical contact, such as the occasional touch of her hand, her bare shoulder, her knee, she accepted with good grace. Billy didn't approve of 'goings on', as he called it, at least not on the premises. But it was her job to keep the customers happy, and if a slight stroke of her skin gave them such pleasure, Sadie certainly had no objection – in fact, she enjoyed the attention. Sometimes she even felt inclined to give one or two more intimate pleasure, away from the club – and that, she considered, was nobody's business but her own.

But when André returned from the bar to sit beside her, Sadie turned to him with particular interest. He seemed different from the others around the table, whose laughing faces disguised not only their bravery but also, she suspected, their fear. This man, with his narrow face, dark hair and intense expression, filled her with an unusual excitement. Perhaps it was his disinterest in her, something Sadie rarely experienced, but suddenly it became essential that she should coax a smile out of the brooding face, and leaning forward, she brushed her arm against his. 'Penny for them?' she said softly.

André, who had been quietly drinking his beer, turned to her. 'I don't think they're worth sharing.'

'Perhaps not, but maybe I could provide some distraction?'

André, gazing into Sadie's china-blue eyes saw both gentleness and sympathy there, and an offer he couldn't mistake. Normally he kept his distance from what his father would call 'loose women', but there was something about this blonde girl that appealed to him. André found it difficult to place her in such a category; she seemed so young, so unspoiled. He drained his glass, uncaring that he was already over the normal limit he set himself for alcohol. What the hell does it matter, he thought in despair. What does anything matter? As if it wasn't enough watching your friends, men you've trained and fought with, die in this bloody war, you even go home and ... but the pain of his loss was too raw, and André struggled to close his mind against it. He knew for the sake of the aircrew, that he had to emerge from the black mood that was threatening to envelop him. And so with an effort, he tried to relax his taut muscles and he suddenly realised how very pretty the girl at his side was.

'Maybe,' he said slowly, 'maybe you can.'

'How about another round, chaps?' This time it was Sandy McBane, the wireless operator, who got up to fetch the drinks, and glancing over her shoulder Sadie caught the eye of another girl, a brunette, who promptly came over to join them. 'Is this a private party, or can anyone join in?' she quipped.

'More the merrier, as far as I'm concerned,' the pilot officer reached out and, taking her hand, pulled her willingly on to his knee. 'I'm known as Kelly,' he grinned, ''cos my first name's top secret!'

She laughed down at him. 'From the Isle of Man?' she said, quoting an old music-hall song.

He grinned. 'Not me. I'm a Londoner, born and bred. Now let me guess your name.' He put his head on one side and pretended to consider. From behind the girl's back, Sadie mouthed, 'Babs.'

'You look like a Barbara, to me,' he declared.

Babs twisted round. 'Hey, did you hear that?' Then she saw Sadie laughing, and playfully cuffed Kelly's head. 'Oh, you teaser!'

Even André smiled, and he found himself beginning to relax for the first time in weeks. The light-hearted atmosphere was infectious and as the club became more crowded, and full of laughter, alcohol and cigarette smoke, he found he was beginning, just beginning, to enjoy himself. After all, wasn't that why they'd come, he and the rest of the crew? To escape from the terrible scenes that kept replaying in their minds. Not that the chaps talked about it, the way they coped was to put on an air of bravado, but André suspected that, like himself, they had their dark moments and vivid nightmares.

And as the rounds of drinks kept coming, with music from the piano tinkling in the background, André found the edges of his unhappiness slowly becoming, blurred. Knowing that he desperately needed distraction after the hell of the past few

27

months, he saw again the tempting offer in Sadie's lovely eyes, and with despair thought – why not? Only a fool would refuse. If he'd learned one lesson in his twenty-six years, particularly since this blasted war started, it was that there was no point in waiting for that elusive tomorrow.

Now, Sadie, wrapping up the photograph with a sigh, dwelt for a moment on that night so long ago, when she'd taken André back to her cheap bedsit. With the gas fire flickering they'd sat in the cramped room, he, at her insistence, in the one shabby armchair, Sadie at his feet, her head resting against his knees. And as they smoked their cigarettes he had talked in a low and strained voice, while she had listened and felt a growing tenderness for this sensitive man, a respect for his grief, and admiration for his undoubted courage. He told her that before the war, he'd taught French at a local grammar school, a far cry, as he put it painfully, from carrying out raids that he knew were necessary, but which resulted in so much death and destruction.

When eventually she'd led him to the bed and they'd made love that first time, André's passion and consideration had been a revelation. He'd treated her as if she was someone special, not merely used her for sex as other men did. And in response, Sadie had, for the first and only time in her life, fallen hopelessly in love. So much so, that in the hope of seeing him again, for six long, lonely weeks, she didn't sleep with anyone else. And that was how she knew without a shadow of a doubt, that Polly was André Merton's daughter.

3

As the summer term drew to a close at the Cheshire Training College, Polly found herself dreading the next two and a half months. 'You're so lucky,' she said to her closest friend, Ruth. 'It must be lovely to have a proper family.'

'Oh yes?' Ruth said, with a grin. 'And how would you like to share your bedroom with two squabbling fifteen-year-old twins? Or to have them pinch your make-up, ladder your nylons, and ask embarrassing questions?'

'Sounds wonderful to me,' Polly's voice was wistful.

'I don't really understand your problem.' Ruth glanced sideways at the other girl. They were so different, she and Polly, and yet they'd been inseparable from the first day they met. Ruth was tall and thin – painfully so in her own view – with a flat, narrow chest, a bony nose, and dark hair so coarse and springy that it frustrated all her efforts to control it. Her homely features were, however, redeemed by an amazing pair of intelligent green eyes. 'I mean, you've never really said a lot about your mother, except that you find her difficult to live with.'

Polly looked down. She knew she was secretive about her life at home. 'Yes, well,' she said hesitantly, 'perhaps it's because she didn't bring me up.'

Ruth frowned. She'd known that, of course, and it was certainly odd. I mean, she thought – what sort of mother dumped her kid on an old man? 'Is she bad-tempered, miserable, I mean?'

Polly said, 'No, not at all. In fact, she's one of those people who take life as it comes. For my mother, life is all about the froth, not the substance.'

Ruth looked at her with surprise. 'My, that sounds disapproving. It's not like you to be so judgmental.'

'Sorry, I don't mean to be!' As Ruth turned away to speak to another student, Polly walked slowly on along the winding path, thinking back to the morning a few days after her grandfather's funeral, when she and Sadie had sat in the solicitor's office. The room was large and square, with tall windows overlooking a quiet street. There had been a bird perched on the wide ledge outside, fluttering its wings before it flew away, a secretary quietly bringing in a tray of tea.

Cedric Black, an elderly bachelor, had been John Merton's closest friend and was the chief executor of his will. Now, with his bald scalp gleaming in the dusty sunlight, and seated next to the solicitor, he gazed with some perplexity at the two anxious faces before him. At the pretty, blonde woman, the mysterious Sadie, of whom Cedric had heard much, but had until now, never met. At Polly, who reminded him so much of Emilie, her French grandmother, with whom, to his shame, he'd been a little in love. With a sigh, he forced himself to smile at Emilie's granddaughter with encouragement, despite his misgivings about the information he knew the solicitor was about to impart. Fifteen minutes later, two pairs of eyes gazed back at him. The brown ones, belonging to Polly, were wide with incredulity. The startlingly blue ones, belonging to Sadie, showed both surprise and apprehension. Cedric's plump fingers drummed uneasily on the table. John Merton had always been generous to his daughter-in-law; certainly without his monthly allowance she would have found it difficult to support herself in the comfort he knew she enjoyed in London. But now, if she obeyed the conditions of the will, Sadie was going to find herself an even wealthier woman, at least for the next few years.

'You mean,' Polly was saying slowly, 'that although The Gables belongs to me, it was my grandfather's wish that my mother should come and live there?'

The solicitor nodded. 'As next of kin, both The Gables and all his assets, which I might add are considerable, are left to you in trust until you are twenty-one. An income will be paid at regular intervals to cover the costs of running the house, and also your personal needs.'

'And me?' Sadie leaned forward.

'If you are willing to leave London and move to Staffordshire in order to provide care for Polly, then under the terms of the will, you will receive a considerably more substantial allowance.' He named an amount that made Sadie's eyes widen.

'But what,' Polly said, 'if my mother doesn't want to leave London?'

Cedric regarded her for one long moment and then turned to Sadie. He raised his bushy eyebrows in query.

She shook her head vigorously. 'I'm quite willing to take on my responsibilities.'

Polly and Cedric exchanged glances. Both suspected that it would have been a different answer if John hadn't provided the necessary financial incentive. Then Cedric composed his features into a more suitably legal expression, and seeing the mutinous flash in Polly's eyes, said, 'You must remember, my dear, that when this will was drawn up, you were only fourteen. Your grandfather naturally felt he had to make provision for you, at least until you came of age.'

But that, Polly thought in despair as she heard Ruth hurrying to rejoin her, won't be for another eighteen months. She turned to her friend and smiled, but Ruth, seeing the strain in Polly's eyes, didn't respond. Instead she said gently, 'Look, you can trust me, you know. It's no good bottling things up, Polly. I've known for some time that there's something worrying you. Don't you think it's about time you told me?' Ten minutes later, seated with cups of tea in a quiet corner in the almost deserted refectory, Ruth leaned forward, propped her elbows on the Formica table, and waited for Polly to begin. And slowly her eyes began to widen with shock, until the exclamation burst from her, 'Mary, mother of God!'

Despite herself, Polly had to smile. No one would ever mistake Ruth for anything but a Roman Catholic. Her conversation was littered with such expressions. She had even, although born in England, absorbed a slight Irish accent from her parents. 'Are you telling me that she...'

32

Polly, feeling acutely embarrassed, nodded.

'And while you're in the house?' Ruth was astounded.

'Sometimes. Although not as often as she used to. To be honest, I think she does try and make an effort when I'm there.'

'What is she? A nymphomaniac?'

Trust Ruth to go straight for the jugular, Polly thought, feeling the colour rise in her cheeks. 'I suppose she must be in a way.'

Ruth studied her. 'Well, don't go worrying in case you've inherited it, cos I can tell you right now, there's no chance!'

Polly, despite her anxieties, felt a giggle rising within her. It was Ruth's constant complaint that Polly never showed any interest in any of the male students.

'In fact, now I know all this, I reckon you're in denial!' Ruth looked at Polly with concern. 'You'd better watch it, girl, or you'll end up an old maid.'

'No one could say that about you!' Polly retorted. Ruth, who had a keen sense of humour, was enormously popular, despite her assertion that she looked like a scarecrow.

'Ah well, love 'em and leave 'em – that's my motto!' Then Ruth added hastily, 'And I don't mean in the same way as...'

'My promiscuous mother,' Polly ended the sentence for her.

Ruth sat back and stared at her. 'Can't you just tell her to sling her hook?'

Polly shook her head. 'Apparently not; I'm stuck with her, at least until I'm twenty-one!'

'What about that executor chap? Have you

been to see him?'

'Yes, I made myself go, a few months after she moved in. Oh, Ruth, can you imagine how I felt – talking about my own mother like that?' Even now Polly hated the memory. 'But although he was very sympathetic, appalled in fact, it seems there's nothing he can do as there's no clause in the will regarding my mother's behaviour.' Although I didn't tell him everything, she thought with an inward shudder.

Ruth was thoughtful. 'Do you think your grandfather knew what she was like?'

Polly shook her head. 'I shouldn't think so, not for a minute. He told Mr Black that she was "a bit fast" – you know – liked parties and gadding about.'

'I just wondered,' Ruth said slowly, 'whether he suspected. Which is why he kept you with him?'

'But then,' Polly said, 'he wouldn't have appointed her my sort of "guardian".'

'No, I suppose not. What sort of person is she?' Ruth said curiously. 'Apart from all this, I mean?'

Polly thought for a moment. 'I can see why men find her attractive. She's not hard-faced or anything like that, or even "tarty".'

'Do you like her?' Ruth's blunt question caught Polly unawares, and forced her to face her feelings. She looked away, unable to find an answer.

'Come on, you must know how you feel about her?' Now Ruth's voice was gentle. 'She is your mother, after all. I'm trying to help here, Pol.'

'I just don't know, Ruth. There are times when I feel drawn to her. She can be very funny and perceptive about people sometimes. I was a bit

34

inside myself, you know, just after my grandfather died, and couldn't relate to her at all. Now, we just seem to snap at each other all the time.'

'Maybe she's picked up on your disapproval?'

'Oh, she's in no doubt of that!' Polly's tone was so sharp, that Ruth glanced at her in surprise. But Polly looked away. A few seconds later, she added, 'To be honest, I think she finds me a great disappointment.'

Ruth stared at her in amazement. 'What makes you think that?'

'Well, for one thing, we bear no resemblance to each other. She's blonde with blue eyes. I take after my French grandmother – she died before I was born. Sadie must look at me and wonder where I came from. And for another, as you say, I probably do give off an air of disapproval all the time, and that hardly helps to play happy families.'

'I notice that you refer to her as Sadie – you don't call her Mum, then?'

'I did when I was little, but the first thing she said when she moved in, was that I should call her Sadie. Better for her image, I suppose,' Polly said with some bitterness. 'It makes her seem younger.' She pushed away her cup and saucer, and glanced at her watch. 'Come on, that's enough about me. The traffic will be quiet now so it's probably a good time to leave.'

They went to their rooms to collect their suitcases, and minutes later, with them loaded into the boot of John Merton's old Humber, Ruth settled herself into the leather passenger seat. Polly, who had passed her driving test at the earliest opportunity, switched on the ignition and

35

drove slowly out of the college entrance, away from Alsager.

Ruth remained quiet, gazing out of the window at the passing scenery, thinking of the situation facing her friend. There had been times, to her slight shame, when she'd envied Polly, who was obviously much 'better off' than she was. The other girl's clothes were what Ruth's mother would call 'quality', unlike Ruth's, which were usually bought from Hanley indoor market. Ruth's mum was a great bargain hunter – she needed to be with four children. Sean, her husband, worked as a slip-maker at a local pottery factory, known locally as a potbank. Sending Ruth first to high school, and then to train as a teacher had meant huge sacrifices, but both her parents were inordinately proud of their clever daughter and Ruth was determined not to disappoint them. Now, as she compared her own warm, chaotic family life, albeit with few luxuries, and the lonely one of the girl driving, Ruth knew that she was the lucky one. Mum's right, she thought suddenly. Money doesn't buy everything.

Eventually, Polly was approaching the Potteries and the small district of Abbey Hulton, and pulled up outside the modest, semi-detached house on the council estate where Ruth lived. A freckle-faced boy was swinging on the gate and grinned, while a ginger tomcat lay sunning itself in the middle of the narrow front path. The door was slightly ajar, and within seconds, Ruth's mother, a plump smiling woman, came bustling out. 'There you are! I was beginning to wonder...' She held out her arms even before Ruth was out

36

of the car, and after giving her daughter a warm hug, turned to greet Polly. 'Will you be coming in for a cup of tea?'

Polly shook her head, and smiled. 'Thanks, Mrs Donovan, but I'd better push on.' She got back into the car, waved, and then watched Ruth and her young brother follow their mother into the house. With a sigh, Polly drew away from the kerb to begin the rest of her journey home. I don't suppose for a minute, she thought with some sadness, that there will be a welcome like that at The Gables.

4

When Polly turned into the large circular drive of her home, the sight of the mellow, graceful house, bathed in sunlight, softened her mood. Despite everything, it was wonderful to be back. Parking before the entrance, she got out of the car and retrieved her luggage from the boot, let herself in and put her case down on the black and white tiled floor. She'd anticipated silence, as Sadie was in the habit of having a nap in the afternoons, but instead there was the sound of loud music coming from the drawing room where the door was ajar. Polly was furious. She had specifically written to say what day she would be arriving, and yet Sadie was obviously entertaining one of her men friends! Polly turned to escape upstairs, but then suddenly stopped. Why the hell should she? After all, it was *her* house! And so, walking quietly to the drawing room she angrily swung open the wide door, only to halt in surprise.

Sadie was alone and, with complete concentration, dancing to Cliff Richard singing 'Living Doll'. Polly gazed with grudging admiration at her mother as she twisted and turned, her skirt flaring around her shapely legs. Polly loved the song herself, and was suddenly tempted to join in. Almost involuntarily she began moving to the catchy tune, and when Sadie turned and saw her, the look of astonishment on her face made Polly giggle. Together they danced in their individual style all too briefly until the record ended, and then Sadie went over to the radiogram and switched it off.

For a moment they faced each other in an uneasy silence, then Polly smiled. 'He's great, isn't he?'

'Absolutely,' Sadie said, and gave a tight smile back. 'Did you have a good journey?'

'It was fine, thanks.' Polly hesitated. 'I'll just take my things up.' Well, that's the first time we've shared *anything*, Polly thought, going up to her room and lifting her case on to the white flowered counterpane. She noticed with surprise and affection that Mrs Booth had placed a vase of pink carnations at the side of her bed. Bless her, she thought. And then with a bemused smile at the memory of the scene that had just taken place, she went first to the bathroom, and then downstairs to the kitchen.

But when Sadie greeted her with the words, 'You've finished, then?' Polly noticed there was the usual edge to her voice.

'Yes, until September.'

Sadie shrugged. 'It seems a long holiday to me! What will you do with yourself?'

Polly stared at her. 'The same as you do, I suppose,' she said, 'Well, not *exactly* the same, of course!'

'Do you ever let up?' Sadie snapped. 'I've told you before, I'm a grown woman, and perfectly entitled to live my life as I choose!'

'And as I've told you, maybe you are – but do you have to get The Gables a bad name?'

Sadie flushed. 'Nonsense.'

'It isn't nonsense,' Polly protested. 'I heard it from a very reliable source.'

'Oh yes, and who was that? The sainted Mrs Booth, I suppose!'

'No, it wasn't, as it happens. And I'm not telling you who it was, so you needn't ask.'

'Narrow-minded old biddy – I bet it was a woman!'

But Polly wasn't going to give her the satisfaction of an answer. Instead, suddenly weary of all the bickering, she said, 'Do you think we could both make an effort to get on better, Sadie? Otherwise the summer's going to be unbearable.'

Startled, Sadie looked at the young girl before her, and then silently poured out a cup of tea and put it on the table. 'I suppose we might,' she admitted. 'We used not to be like this, not at first.'

'That was before...' But Polly didn't want to finish the sentence.

'I've told you, that wasn't my fault!'

'*You* brought him here!'

'And I sent him packing, just as soon as I found

39

out. What else could I have done?'

Realised just how upset I was, Polly thought with weariness. Instead of which, you just made light of it and made me feel like a hysterical kid!

'Look,' she said, determined to try and offer an olive branch. 'We both know what happened, and there's nothing we can do to change it. Can't we just put it behind us?' Although it won't be so easy for me, she thought grimly, as the treacherous memory threatened to surface. But what alternative did she have? At least, if there was to be any chance of normal life in this house!

'I've always been prepared to,' Sadie said, 'you're the one who's never been able to let it go.'

'Well, I'm going to now,' Polly said. 'So? Is it a deal?'

Sadie looked at the flushed and determined face of her daughter, and recognised that she was being given a second chance. 'It's a deal,' she said quietly.

'Good!' Polly gazed up at her mother. Then in a deliberately lighter tone said, 'I don't suppose there's any cake?'

Sadie reached up to the cupboard and took out a round tin with a picture of a crinoline lady on the lid. Since coming to live at The Gables, she'd become quite good at baking, and with a feeling of pride she took out a large fruit cake and, cutting a slice, handed it to her daughter.

'Mmn, that looks nice.' Polly bit into it with appreciation. 'One of the things I might do,' she said, when she'd finished, 'is to invite Ruth to come and stay for a few days – maybe in August.'

'Ruth? Oh, yes, I think I've heard you mention

her before.' Damn, Sadie thought – I'll have two of them looking down their noses at me! I suppose she'll be another sobersides like this one!

'And,' Polly continued, 'there are a few of my old school friends I want to catch up with. I thought they might come over and we could play a few records, that sort of thing.'

Sadie raised her eyebrows. Well, that'll be a first since I've been here, she thought. She really is trying to make a fresh start.

'Hello, there!' Polly held the front door open, and the two young women waiting outside came into the hall. 'Wow, Hazel, you look fabulous!'

The tall redhead, her high heels clacking on the tiled floor, smiled. 'And you're the same, got a tan to die for as usual!'

Polly laughed, and turned to the smaller girl behind her. 'Anita, what's this I hear – that you've got engaged?'

'Sure have. His name's Andrew. He's the brother of one of the girls on my course at uni. He's a surveyor.' Anita, a curvaceous brunette, laughed and waggled her left hand.

Polly duly admired the diamond hoop and exclaimed, 'I might have known you'd be the first!'

'Sheer sex appeal!' Anita said loftily.

'Take no notice,' Hazel said, 'She's just got a swelled head, that's all.'

'No, honestly you'd like him, Pol,' Anita said.

'I should hope so! Oh, it is good to see you both. Come on into the drawing room – I've got a great selection of records. And I'm dying to hear what you've been getting up to.'

41

'We can guess where Anita's concerned!' Hazel winked at Polly, and she grinned.

'Yes, well curiosity killed the cat!' Anita retorted. 'I always did like this house,' she said, sitting on the green leather chesterfield. 'It's ages since I've been. Not since...' her voice tailed off.

'My grandfather died,' Polly said. 'No, I know. I'm sorry about that. Still,' Polly said in a cheerful tone. 'Things are different now.' She saw them exchange embarrassed glances, and guessing what they were thinking, added in an innocent tone, 'You haven't met my mother, have you?' They both shook their heads. 'Well, you will. She's promised to supply us with tea and cakes later.' Polly saw their astonished expressions and thought – if they're expecting a femme fatale, they're going to be disappointed. At least I hope they are! She suddenly had an alarming image of Sadie dressing for the part and appearing in a low-cut, clinging cocktail dress, plastered with make-up and twirling a cigarette holder! She's capable of it too, Polly thought in panic. It's just the sort of thing that would appeal to her sense of humour, *and* it would give her a chance to show her contempt for what she calls 'provincial prudery'.

'It must have been quite an experience, her coming to live here,' Hazel said, and was immediately nudged sharply by Anita.

'Yes it was,' Polly said. 'Never a dull moment, if you know what I mean!' She made her tone light, amusing. Not for one minute was she going to give them anything else to gossip about. Good friends they might be, but Polly wanted to subdue the rumours, not add to them. 'Right,' she

42

said, 'who likes Elvis?'

Sadie, making sandwiches and collecting food together in the kitchen, couldn't hear anything of the visitors at first, but after the first half-hour, one of the girls came out to use the cloakroom, and on returning to the drawing room, left the door slightly ajar. And as Sadie heard laughter, high-pitched voices, and above them music, she began to hum along with the hits of Adam Faith, the Everly Brothers, and Michael Holliday. This is more like it, she thought – a bit of life in the place! And she was pleased to see another side to this prissy daughter of hers. Dressed in a white pleated skirt, and green and white striped jersey-knit blazer, Polly had not only looked wonderful, but was without that set expression that Sadie had become used to. The girl even seemed animated! Certainly, the last two weeks had seen a vast improvement in their relationship. And I hope Polly realises the sacrifices I've made, Sadie thought with a touch of resentment. Staying in every night wasn't her idea of living, and if she didn't get a bit of male company soon... Eventually, she laid the table in the dining room and, satisfied with her handiwork, went upstairs to quickly change. Going down to the hall, she checked her hair in the ornate gilt mirror then gave a light tap on the drawing-room door and went in.

Polly was sitting on the floor surrounded by record sleeves. One girl had kicked her high-heeled shoes off, while the other lay sprawled on the settee, blowing not very successful smoke rings. At that moment, Frank Sinatra began singing 'The Lady is a Tramp'.

'Tea anyone?' Sadie said in her sweetest tone.

Polly glanced round, then her eyes widened. Scrambling to her feet, she turned to the others. 'This is my mother, Sadie.'

As each girl got up, Polly introduced them by name, seeing with amusement their astounded faces at the sight of Sadie wearing a white frilly apron over a sedate dress, her make-up discreet, her lipstick a demure pink. Polly, hugely relieved, had to struggle not to giggle. Doris Day eat your heart out, she thought, struggling to keep a straight face. And once all the girls were seated in the dining room, Sadie even discreetly disappeared.

'Wow, what a spread,' Hazel said, looking at the dainty sandwiches, sausage rolls, scones and Victoria sponge. 'Did you make these, Pol?'

'Good heavens, no,' Polly said. 'If I had, the sponge would be as flat as a pancake.'

'My cakes always sink in the middle,' Anita complained.

'You'd better put that right!' Polly teased. 'You know what they say about men and their stomachs!'

'Don't remind me,' Anita said. 'You should hear my future mother-in-law go on about, "My Andy likes his bacon crisp," and all that sort of stuff.'

'I don't see why it should be women who have to do all the work,' Hazel declared. 'When I get married, I'm going to start as I mean to go on; particularly if I keep on working.'

'How do you like it at the bank?' Polly asked – her mouth half full of a cucumber sandwich.

'Boring.'

'Why do it, then?'

Hazel blushed, and Anita chimed in, 'Because she fancies the assistant manager, that's why!'

'What's he like, then?' Polly leaned forward. 'I must come in and have a look.'

'You keep your hands off!' Hazel said. 'Actually, he's a bit like Dirk Bogarde.'

'Gregory Peck's my favourite,' Polly said, getting up to cut the sponge cake. 'Has anyone seen *The Big Country?*'

Later, as Polly saw the girls out, she waited until Hazel drove them away in her father's Austin Cambridge, and then went to find Sadie. Her mother was sitting in the breakfast room, having a cup of tea, a cigarette, and leafing through the latest issue of *Vogue*. 'Thanks,' Polly said awkwardly.

'I take it I passed muster, then?'

'More than that!' Polly began to laugh. 'You should have seen their faces when you came into the room!'

'Actually, I did,' Sadie said drily. 'I don't know what on earth they expected.'

'A cross between Marilyn Monroe and Jane Russell, I think.'

'Pity I didn't wear a basque, then!' but now Sadie's lips were twitching, and soon they were both laughing.

'I just hope it works, that's all,' Polly said, when they'd calmed down. 'Maybe people will think it was all malicious gossip.'

Sadie looked at her and raised one finely plucked

eyebrow. This was the first time since what she thought of as their 'agreement' that Polly had referred to the wretched subject. 'But we know different,' she said in a tight voice, 'and you still can't handle that, can you?'

'Do you think any daughter could?'

Sadie said wearily, 'I've told you, it's just the way I am.'

Polly stared at her, wanting desperately to ask the one question that constantly burned inside her. *Why* was her mother 'that way' as she called it? There were so many questions – so much she desperately needed to know. But their relationship was still too new, too fragile, so instead Polly remained silent, while Sadie flicked over a page of her magazine.

5

A week later, Polly and Sadie sat in a sunny position by the window in the restaurant of the Crown, a first-class hotel in the picturesque small town of Stone. John Merton, who had appreciated so much Emilie's flair for cooking, had booked a regular table for Sunday lunch after his wife's funeral, and the weekly visit had become so much a part of Polly's life that she'd simply continued. Lately, of course, Sadie's blue Ford Anglia was often to be found in the evenings in the hotel car park; a fact that hadn't gone unnoticed and had led to the comment that upset Polly so much.

'You'd better watch it, Pol,' Hilary, a girl Polly had always disliked, whispered at the tennis club. 'I hear The Gables is getting a bit of a reputation. You don't want to be tarred with the same brush!' There had been more than a hint of malice in her eyes, and Polly, incensed, had been livid when she failed to beat her in the next set.

Now, enjoying the roast lamb, Polly reached for the serving dishes and helped herself to more buttered new potatoes. Sadie watched with envy. These days she had to be careful with her figure, having recently developed a tendency to put on weight. She sighed, and then placed her knife and fork together on her plate, and gently put the white damask napkin to her lips. André had first introduced her to what she considered civilised society, and Sadie had learned the correct way to behave simply by following his example. She debated the wisdom of having a pudding, but eventually succumbed to temptation, and it was while they were both enjoying Bakewell tart and custard that the interruption came.

'Polly! I don't believe it! I thought you'd left the country, it's so long since I've seen you.'

Polly's face lit up. 'Mark! It's been ages!'

'I know.' The tall young man, who had come over to their table, gazed down at her with pleasure. 'How's training college?'

'Fine, and how's Oxford?'

'Brilliant.'

Suddenly Polly realised that she hadn't introduced him, and turned to Sadie, 'Sorry, this is Mark Eldon, we used to...'

'Go out together,' Mark grinned.

47

'And this is my mother, Sadie,' Polly finished.

Sadie said with surprise, 'I'm delighted to meet you, Mark.' And she was. Not only was she relieved that her daughter had at least *had* a boyfriend, but Mark was tall, dark and handsome and such company was always welcome. 'Would you care to join us for coffee?'

Polly stared at her mother, who had somehow managed to make a casual invitation almost enticing. Sadie's skin was slightly flushed, her eyes raised to Mark, and Polly glanced swiftly up at him. He seemed bemused, then said hurriedly, 'Thank you, but I can't really, I'm here with my father.'

Sadie glanced across to the table he'd indicated. The sole occupant had his back to her, but the height of the man sitting there was promising, as was the fact that there were only slight flecks of silver in his dark hair.

'Then why don't we all have coffee together in the lounge,' she said gaily. 'You and Polly must have lots to catch up on.'

'That's very kind of you,' Mark said, and looking down at Polly, raised his eyebrows in query. She nodded. 'It's fine with me, Mark.'

'Good, that's settled then!' Sadie rose from the table, and after speaking to a passing waiter, gracefully led the way to the hotel lounge. Polly followed her, feeling slightly stage-managed. 'There,' Sadie said, 'that's a good spot.' She settled herself in a corner of the room, where there was a comfortable leather sofa and two armchairs surrounding a Queen Anne coffee table. 'Won't this be nice – a bit of company for a change?'

Only because it's male, Polly thought. At least, where her mother was concerned. But it was good to see Mark again. She used to be really keen on him. They had gone about for a bit together, but John's death had coincided with Mark going up to Oxford, and somehow he and Polly had drifted apart. But then, Polly reflected, she hadn't been bothered that much – she'd been so traumatised by her bereavement, that it had taken her ages to pick up the threads of normal life again. But now Mark and his father were approaching, and Polly suddenly felt her mother, who was sitting beside her on the sofa, tense. Hearing her sharp intake of breath, Polly glanced at her with alarm, then swiftly up at the middle-aged man standing before them. He was still handsome, even distinguished looking, and was to Polly's dismay, staring at Sadie with acute embarrassment. Oh no, Polly thought with rising panic and horror, she can't have ... not with Mr Eldon? Not with Mark's father?

'Hello, George.' Sadie's voice was light, casual.

'Sadie,' Mark's father looked sheepish, 'good to see you again.' He turned to Polly, 'And you, Polly.'

'So,' Mark sat in one of the armchairs, 'I see you've already met Polly's mother, Dad. Where was that, then?'

Polly saw a quick exchange of glances between George and Sadie, then her mother said with a bright smile, 'It was at that charity do, wasn't it, George?'

'Yes,' he said with a look of relief. 'That's right.'

In an effort to distract Mark, Polly said, 'How's

49

your mother these days? Is she any better?' His mother had been an invalid for years, and that, Polly supposed – trying to be charitable – might in some way excuse his father's behaviour. And then she gave herself a mental slap on the wrist. She really must stop being so judgmental!

'Not really,' Mark said, his face clouding over. 'She's not too well, I'm afraid. Is she, Dad?'

George shook his head. 'No,' he said quietly, 'not well at all. It's kind of you to ask, Polly.'

'Well, isn't this cosy,' Sadie said, turning as a waitress brought in their coffee.

There was silence as she served them, and then once she'd left, Mark said, 'Have you got any plans for the hols, Pol?'

She shook her head. 'Not really. I've got a friend from college coming to stay but apart from that, nothing.'

'Great. We must fix up for some tennis.' He turned to Sadie. 'Do you play, Mrs Merton?'

'Sadie, please. No, unfortunately I don't. It's something I've always wanted to take up, though.'

'Dad could give you some coaching, couldn't you, Dad?'

George hesitated, looked uncomfortable, then said, 'Yes, of course. I'd be glad to.'

'That would be wonderful,' Sadie breathed, and once again Polly looked at her with both amusement and bewilderment. Her mother's eyes were luminous, her lips slightly parted, and with a shock, Polly realised that both father and son were fascinated by this woman in her late thirties. An image of the fabulous Marilyn Monroe flashed into Polly's mind, the film star's sexual allure with

50

its subtle hint of vulnerability and innocence continued to intrigue her fans. And suddenly Polly realised that this was Sadie's secret. She *was* sexy; she *did* love men's admiration, their attention, and yet somehow she also portrayed this same aura of simplicity and innocence. Intrigued, Polly watched as with charm and wit, Sadie eventually coaxed George to relax, while Mark seemed content to be passive, simply enjoying his coffee and chocolate mints.

'Why don't we all go back to The Gables?' Sadie suggested. 'There's a good selection of records, and then later we could have afternoon tea? I made fresh scones this morning.'

Polly, who found it irritating to hear Sadie act the part of hostess – after all, *she* didn't own The Gables – hurriedly interjected. 'I think they'll have to get back, Sadie, because of Mrs Eldon.'

'It would be okay, wouldn't it, Dad?' Mark said. 'Granny's looking after Mum.'

George hesitated and then saw his son's eager expression. 'Yes, I don't see why not. I can always ring and explain.'

'Great,' Mark said, then once their bills were settled and they made their way out of the hotel, murmured, 'Sundays are always so boring, don't you think, Pol?'

'Depends if you're religious,' she laughed.

'Don't remind me! I had to sit through the most mind-numbing sermon this morning.'

'At least being Church of England, you're not expected to go that often! I don't go to Mass every week now,' she confessed. 'Most of the time it was only to please my grandfather, anyway.'

51

Mark lingered before going to the other side of the car park. 'It's funny that when he was a Protestant you should be brought up a Catholic."

'That's because of my French grandmother. And because it was what my father would have wanted.'

'And what about your mother?'

Polly shrugged. 'She's never expressed an opinion.'

The journey to the village of Brandon, situated between Stone and the busier county town of Stafford, took only a short time, and Sadie was soon turning into the circular drive of The Gables. George, in his Jaguar, drew up behind her, and Polly and Mark went straight to the drawing room to browse through the records.

Sadie invited George to stroll in the garden, and they walked along a winding path to a colourful rose bed. For a few moments, they both admired the blooms in silence then she said quietly, 'It's good to see you again.'

'You too.'

'But not in your son's presence, I take it?'

George shook his head. 'No, you have to admit it's not an ideal situation.' He paused, 'You do understand why...'

'I haven't heard from you? Of course – I told you at the time it was just a bit of fun. That and two lonely souls comforting each other.'

George looked down at her, thinking how feminine and sexy she looked in her coffee-coloured tailored skirt and flimsy cream blouse trimmed with lace. 'You're a woman in a thousand, Sadie.'

'A million, actually,' she said lightly. 'I didn't

realise you knew Polly. You never said.'

He shrugged. 'It didn't seem quite the "thing" to talk about the children – not in those circumstances.'

His voice was tight, and Sadie glanced quickly up at him. 'Don't be too hard on yourself, George. Your wife is a very lucky woman, believe me.' She hesitated then said, 'You did say that you knew my father-in-law?'

'Yes, but only in a business capacity at the Rotary and suchlike. And as you know, I never met André, because we didn't move here until after the war.'

Sadie looked up at him, seeing the lines of strain around his eyes. 'What exactly *is* the situation with Felicity?'

'Just between ourselves, it's only a matter of months now.'

'I'm so sorry.'

Inside, Mark and Polly were relaxing; he sprawling on the sofa, while she sat curled up in a winged armchair. The radiogram was playing at high volume, while they hummed and sang along to the latest hits. Then Polly got up to change the record. 'This was one of my grandfather's favourites,' she said. 'I really like it.'

For a few moments they listened to the haunting tune of 'April in Paris', then Mark suddenly said, 'How would you like to go?'

'What? Do you mean to Paris?' Polly gazed at him with astonishment.

'Yes. I've been thinking about it for a few days, but it's no fun on your own. I'd enjoy it much better with you.' He grinned at her, 'No strings

53

attached, separate rooms, I promise!'

'Spoilsport,' she laughed.

'No, honestly, Pol, we always had a good time, didn't we? Even though we've split up, I don't see why we can't remain friends. What do you think?'

Polly looked at him, at his thin, intelligent face, and why not, she thought? Why shouldn't they be friends, spend time together? 'I agree,' she said, already feeling excited at the prospect. She'd always loved going to France. As a small child, John Merton had often taken her to visit her great-grandparents in Montpelier. They had died several years ago, but she had many happy memories of holidays there.

'What – to the trip to Paris, or...?'

'Both! But I pay my own way,' she warned. 'After all, you're not my boyfriend any more.' Would she like him to be, she wondered? She wasn't sure.

Mark looked at the girl before him, recognising that Polly was now a very attractive young woman. He'd been too keen to leave behind familiar sur-roundings and people when he'd gone to uni-versity, to be drawn into the heady experience that was Oxford. Certainly he had a slight sense of guilt that he hadn't been more supportive when Polly was bereaved. All he'd done was to send a short note of condolence. 'Maybe in Paris – the romantic city and all that?' he teased.

'I wouldn't bet on it,' she laughed. 'But yes, I'll come.'

'What about your mother?' Mark asked with a frown. 'Will she be all right about it?'

'Sadie,' Polly told him, 'doesn't believe in what

54

she calls "stupid conventions", so there won't be a problem there!' And, she thought grimly, if there is she couldn't possibly justify it.

6

Sadie, as Polly expected, had little comment to make about the proposed spree in Paris, apart from the dry comment, 'Lucky you! I don't suppose you'd like company?' At the alarmed expression on Polly's face, Sadie laughed. 'Don't worry, I was only kidding. When are you thinking of going?'

'As soon as Mark can arrange it.'

After Polly had gone upstairs, Sadie wandered into the drawing room. Going over to the sideboard, she picked up the photograph of André and gazed down at his familiar smile. Even seeing the RAF uniform brought back so many poignant memories of those wartime days. Of those anxious weeks when she'd first discovered she was pregnant, of her desperation and indecision. And then, when she was at her lowest ebb, André had come back into her life.

He and his crew had come again to the club one Saturday night and it had been Babs who saw him first. 'Guess who the cat's brought in!' she hissed. Sadie turned, and with sheer joy saw André's tall figure. He glanced across at her, smiled and then went to sit with his friends at the same table as before. Sadie, who was standing at the bar

55

drinking with another customer made an excuse to leave, but the man, an army major and on his third pint, was persistent, reaching out to catch at her hand. She shook her head, and glanced wildly over at André, who within seconds was at her side, saying with perfect charm, 'Excuse me, do you mind if my sister comes over to sit with me? We don't often see each other these days?'

Flustered and embarrassed, the officer had immediately withdrawn his hand, and trying not to laugh Sadie followed André, with Babs joining them ten minutes later saying, 'This is just like old times, boys!'

But it wasn't exactly like the first time, because one of the crew, a quiet lad called Chalkie, had 'bought it' over the English Channel. One stray bullet, one hit, was all it had taken to bereave his parents of their only son. The plane, although damaged, had managed to return to the airfield, with its men shaken but undeterred. 'Bloody Jerries,' was their only grim comment, knowing how lucky they were to have escaped a similar fate.

And Sadie and Babs, only too aware of the men's need to blank out what they had been through, and what was before them, tried to lighten the atmosphere, encouraging them to buy drinks, trying with smiles and jokes to bring some gaiety to the evening. Sadie was glad she was wearing her favourite cocktail dress. The green silk clung seductively to the curves of her body while its low back and slender straps displayed her shapely shoulders. André, apart from that first chivalrous action, seemed preoccupied, content just to smoke his cigarettes and observe the others, although at times he would turn to her and give a small, intimate smile.

Sadie, her stomach almost painful with nerves, was longing to be alone with him. With the overwhelming relief she'd felt on seeing him, had come the fervent hope that he would know the name of a shady doctor, one prepared to defy the law and secretly perform an abortion. Everyone knew such people existed and Sadie thought, with some bitterness, that if she'd been one of those rich society women, her problem would have been solved weeks ago. But her only choice, now that the gin hadn't worked, was either being butchered in some filthy room in a backstreet, or her whole life ruined, not to mention that of the kid. Bastards, at least in the district of London where Sadie had grown up, were constantly taunted in the playground, their mothers treated with scorn and considered unfit for decent people to associate with. Well that wasn't going to happen to her! André was a decent chap – surely he'd help her, would give her the money she needed? Yet Sadie hated to ask him, hated the thought of how humiliated she'd feel. She'd thought about him so much these last few weeks, hadn't been able to bear the thought of being touched by anyone else. And now, glancing at him, seeing again his good looks, his long, sensitive hands, she knew that her feelings hadn't changed. And she sensed that he wanted to be with her, to sleep with her again. The next couple of hours seemed endless, with the pianist in melancholy mood, playing such haunting tunes as 'Smoke Gets in Your Eyes' and 'Moonlight Serenade'. Then André turned to look

57

at her, and said softly, 'May I see you later?'

'Of course,' she whispered.

For one brief moment their eyes met, before Babs called across the table, 'Hey, Sadie, tell the boys the story about that army chap. You know, the major with the lah-di-dah voice who boasted he could drink anyone under the table!' She turned to Sandy McBane, the wireless operator. 'Well, there was this navy lieutenant on the next table, and an RAF warrant officer on another one nearby – go on, you tell it, Sadie...' Minutes later the table was in uproar, as Sadie, who was a born mimic, gave her account of that unforgettable evening.

But later, as she unlocked the front door to her shabby, but tidy bedsit, Sadie's heart was hammering against her ribs. Now, she thought with panic, I've got to tell him! And what was filling her with terror was the very real danger that André wouldn't believe that the baby was his. After all, she thought miserably, as she crossed the room and drew the blackout curtains before switching on the light, why should he?

But this time, unlike the first, André's need was physical and urgent, there was no companionable talking, no opportunity for Sadie to confide, although even then his lovemaking made Sadie feel special and cherished. This man respects me, she thought with wonder, as afterwards she curled up contentedly in his arms. She looked down with tenderness at his head resting on her breasts. He was sleeping lightly, his muscular body and limbs relaxed. And this, Sadie told herself with some sadness, is what happened last time. She'd stayed close to him, instead of getting up and performing her usual vinegar douche. As André hadn't come prepared she'd been the one to supply a French letter. Sadie wondered if there was any truth in the rumour that a tiny percentage of them had, by law, to be made faulty? Whatever the cause, she'd ended up pregnant. At least she didn't have to bother to get up now – the damage was already done.

But when André began to stir, she realised that she couldn't postpone it any longer. Any minute he could be dressed and out of there, and who knew if she'd ever see him again? Now, she thought, I'll tell him now, while we're lying close together, all warm and intimate. André, raising himself on one elbow, looked up at her, and then lowered his head to gently kiss the pink tip of her nipple. 'You're beautiful, do you know that?' She smiled, and he levered himself up the bed, and leaned against the wooden headboard. 'Cigarette?' She nodded, and he picked up a pack of Senior Service and his lighter from the floor. Sadie waited a few moments as they both inhaled, and gathered her courage. But André was turning towards her saying, 'You know, we only talked about me last time. I don't know a thing about you, where you were born, about your family, that sort of thing.'

Sadie knew he was wondering how she'd become the sort of girl who would bring an airman home, or any man for that matter. It wasn't the first time she'd been asked. Usually, she amused herself by spinning a yarn. Sometimes she was a victim, her virginity taken by an unscrupulous family friend, or she painted a picture of a good-time girl who simply liked men – a bit near the truth, that one – and she'd once told a Yank she was the daughter of an earl who had been disinherited! But there would be no teasing, no fabrications with André. He was too special to lie to.

'Well,' she began slowly, 'I'm a Londoner, I'm eighteen and I was brought up in a council flat in Hammersmith.' She glanced at him, and added, 'Brace yourself! My dad was a dustman, and my mum cleaned a block of offices.'

'Both essential jobs,' André said quickly.

She smiled. 'I know. And my dad was a lovely bloke. Believe it or not, he used to write poetry.'

André stared at her, then his mouth split in a grin. 'You're joking!'

She shook her head. 'I'm not. He was a huge chap, strong as an ox, wouldn't hurt a fly. But he just loved poetry. Self-taught, of course. He was always down at the public library.'

'Did he ever try to get it published?'

She shook her head. 'He died when I was twelve. After that,' she gave a slight shrug. 'Well, Mum – who was a bit of a looker – went off the rails a bit. You know the sort of thing, one boyfriend after another.' And that, she thought, was an understatement.

'Not much of an example, then.'

'I suppose you could say that.' Sadie turned to face him. 'But I'm not making that an excuse. André, I just want you to know, to understand. I don't want to pretend, not with you. I'm not a prostitute or anything like that. No' – she put her finger to his lips – 'don't say anything, not yet. I just enjoy sex. I like male company, and,' she

60

admitted, 'I like the way men make me feel, knowing that they find me attractive. And I've learned a lot from them, listening to their experiences and everything. Believe me, I'm a different girl from when I first started at the club. But I want you to know that there haven't been many. And I'm very choosy.'

'I was lucky, then?'

'No, André. I was the lucky one,' she said softly. And Sadie knew that now the time had come. 'But I'm afraid that our night together last time did leave me with a problem; one that I need your help with.'

André frowned. 'In what way?'

'There's no easy way to tell you this. I'm nearly three months pregnant.'

Stunned, André could only stare at her. Pregnant? What did she mean, she was pregnant? And what was she saying – that he was the father? But...

'I'm sorry,' Sadie said with desperation, 'I don't really know how it happened. But it's true, André. And before you ask, I know the baby's yours, because I haven't slept with anyone else since, and you were the only one since my period.'

André, his mind still reeling with shock, repeated with incredulity, 'You haven't slept with anyone since?'

Sadie looked at him. 'No,' she said quietly. 'Somehow I couldn't. Not after that night.'

André gazed at her, and saw to his amazement that in those incredibly blue eyes shone not only anxiety but also something that looked sus-piciously like love. He suddenly realised that this girl had fallen for him. André had often thought

61

of Sadie since that night, of her femininity, her humour, how she had listened to him, her softness after they had made love. But he had never imagined that he had become someone special to her. Although, when the crew had at last got a weekend leave, he had been swift to suggest they came back to the same nightclub, hoping that he would see her again. And then suspicion flared. How could he be sure of what she was saying – that the child was his? But then he remembered clearly her insistence that they should 'use something', and also recalled with shame that he'd been drinking heavily. It had probably been his fault, fumbling idiot!

Just then the gas fire began to splutter, and with a silent curse, Sadie got out of bed and began to search in her handbag for coins. But André was quicker, picking up his trousers, fishing in the pocket, and was at the meter before her. He inserted as many coins as he could find, and said, 'I'm having the warmth, it's only fair I should pay for it!'

Sadie smiled, knowing he was trying to save her embarrassment. Sensitive as always, she thought. Because there was one rule she strictly enforced. Never would she accept money off any man, not for sex – after all, she had her pride. Then suddenly she saw that André had begun to put his clothes on. He couldn't be leaving? In panic, Sadie grabbed her dressing gown and went over to the small curtained alcove in one corner, which concealed her tiny cooker and old porcelain sink. She filled the kettle and took two cups and saucers from the overhead shelf. 'I'll make you a cup of tea,' she called frantically, hoping that this would delay him.

'No, don't!' André said, and twisting round, she saw that he was moving towards the door. His expression was set, his jaw rigid, and Sadie felt a sickening lurch in her stomach. He couldn't just be going, walking out of her life! Apart from the despair she felt, she still hadn't asked him for the information and money she needed. And it was only right he *should* help her, she thought, anger flaring that he believed he could escape so easily. But the door was closing, with André simply throwing over his shoulder, 'I'll be back – I just need a bit of time.'

It was the longest hour in her life. Sadie did make herself a cup of tea, although her hand was shaking so much that the cup rattled on the saucer. What would she do if he didn't believe her, and wouldn't give her the money? There was no way she could have this baby. She could hardly work at the club when she looked like a barrage balloon, or anywhere else for that matter! What would she live on? There was nobody she could turn to for help; she had no family, no one. And with misery, Sadie couldn't face the thought of being tied down with a kid before she was twenty, being condemned to a life of struggle and poverty. She wanted to have a better way of life than that of her parents. In any case, how could she bring up a kid in this cramped bedsit – it was hardly big enough for one person, never mind two. The thoughts whirled round and round in her mind, and she was desperate by the time she heard a light tap on the door. She flew to open it, and stood aside, as André, his dark hair damp with rain, came in.

'I'll have that cup of tea now, if that's okay,' he said, and with her throat closing with tension, she went to the alcove and reboiled the kettle.

André took off his wet coat, and sat in the armchair. He felt unutterably weary. What a bloody mess! He turned and took the cup and saucer from Sadie, sipping the hot liquid gratefully. 'Sorry about rushing off,' he said. 'I just needed some time – you know, to think.' He looked across at her, seeing her troubled expression, the strain in her eyes. In her pink dressing gown, her hair still ruffled from their lovemaking. She'd told him she was eighteen, but he suspected she was younger.

'What do you want to do?' he said quietly.

Sadie handed him a cup and saucer. 'I can't face a backstreet abortion, André! They're too risky – although if you hadn't turned up, I might have had no choice.'

'And now?' his voice was tense.

Sadie took a deep breath. 'If you can afford it, I thought you might pay for a proper one. There are doctors who will do it, even if it is against the law. I'm sure we could find someone.'

André stared first at her, and then into the flickering flames of the gas fire. An abortion – just two words, and yet they meant the taking of a life, a life he and Sadie had conceived on that one night. Could he destroy a child of his? Did he even have the right to? He thought of his parents. This would be their grandchild, and he knew that Emilie, with her French Catholic upbringing, would have been appalled at the thought. She would never have forgiven him. And John Merton too, a man who was proud of his name, of the respect his family had earned, would have been against it. I've seen enough death over the last couple of years, André thought grimly. How could he callously destroy another life before it had even begun?

'There's always adoption,' he said with despair. 'That's one alternative.' He glanced swiftly at her. 'I'd support you until you could work again.'

But as far as Sadie was concerned, adoption wasn't an option. She wasn't prepared to waddle around for the next six months and submit herself to the agony of childbirth, only to give the baby away! And the orphanages were crowded with kids, since the war began. The chances were it would only end up living in an institution.

Listening to her sharp refusal, André felt his spirits sink. Again he stared into the gas fire. He'd had ambitions for his future, had made plans, but it was more than likely that, as with thousands of other young men, he wouldn't live to see them come to fruition. Hitler had seen to that. So he asked himself, as he had on his lonely walk, why not? This might be the last decent act he would ever do.

'No, Sadie,' he said, 'no dodgy doctors. I have a better solution.' He paused. There was a short silence, then André said in an unsteady voice, 'How would you feel about getting married? I can't guarantee surviving the war, but if you're willing to have the child, at least you'd both have some security.'

Now, Sadie, recalling her euphoria and disbelief, smiled at the memory. As she replaced the

65

photograph she couldn't help wondering, as she had so often over the years, whether if André had lived, she would have led a normal life, would have been a faithful wife, a loving mother. But then, on hearing Polly's quick steps across the hall, Sadie turned swiftly away from the sideboard, and went out to face with a bright smile the brown-haired girl she always thought of as André's daughter, rather than her own.

7

When the telephone rang a few days later, Polly hurried from the breakfast room to answer, hoping it would be Mark. She was full of impatience to go on the trip to Paris, and had thought of little else since he'd suggested it. Eagerly she picked up the receiver.

'Polly?'

'Mark! Any news?'

'You bet. Can you be ready to go at the weekend?'

'No problem.'

He kept the conversation brief, simply giving details of the travel arrangements, and afterwards Polly went to find Sadie. She was in the garden, cutting some roses for the drawing room, and looked up as her daughter, youthful and carefree in her white and green summer dress, came down the winding path towards her. I was like that once, Sadie thought suddenly. Never so carefree, but certainly glowing with health, that wonderful gift of youth; her skin silken and smooth, her stomach flat. Yet she'd taken it all for granted. It was only now, when she was beginning to detect subtle changes in her body, that she began to appreciate what she had lost. And Sadie was finding that very hard to accept.

'You look as if you've had good news,' she said, clipping a crimson damask rose and placing it into her basket.

'I have. Mark's just rung and guess what? We're off to Paris on Sunday.'

Sadie felt a swift pang of envy. 'Fine,' she said. 'Are you all organised, got your passport and everything?'

'Yes. Grandad often used to take me to the continent.'

Sadie stood for a moment, watching her walk back into the house, and sighed. How could she ever have anything in common with this privileged girl? In Sadie's case, a day trip to Southend had been the best her mother could manage. And over the years, when Sadie made those lightning, awkward visits to The Gables, she'd seen her daughter develop the easy assurance that only money and a private education can bestow. Sadie shrugged and returned to her task, then winced as she caught her finger on a thorn. Just like life, she thought wryly, there's no pleasure without pain. And at the thought of pleasure, her lips curved in an anticipatory smile. With Polly away...

Polly was still full of her news when Mrs Booth arrived the following day. Her reaction was swift. 'Going to Paris? What do yer mean – just the two

67

of you?'

'Yes,' Polly told her, as she made the cleaner a cup of tea. 'You remember Mark, don't you?'

'Of course I do, and I'm not saying he isn't a nice lad, but...'

'Hardly a lad any more, Mrs Booth, he's twenty-two.'

'Old enough for a lot of things,' Doris muttered. She glanced darkly at Polly. 'I don't think yer grandad would have approved, I can tell you that!'

Polly grinned at her. 'We're only going as friends, for heaven's sake, he's hardly likely to rape me!' Doris stared at her, profoundly shocked. 'I'm only joking,' Polly said hastily. 'I just meant...'

'I know you were joking. But that's not a word to use in polite conversation, young lady!' Doris frowned, as she stirred two lumps of sugar into her tea. She'd thought as much – living with that fast woman was definitely a bad influence. 'Try to be a lady,' she said quietly. 'That's how you've been brought up. How long are yer going for?'

'Five days.' Long enough for Lady Muck to be up to her tricks, Doris decided. And if that woman thinks I can't tell when she's had a man here, she underestimates me. She finished her tea and said, 'Now go on – out of me way, love, I want to clear the larder out.' As she cleaned shelves and wiped tins, Doris wondered what Ernie would think about all this. Not that he paid that much attention to what she said; he'd always got his head stuck in that blasted racing paper. But one thing she did know, when their Shirley was nineteen he would never have let her go gallivanting off to a foreign country with a man she wasn't married to! Well, she thought grimly, let's hope it doesn't all end in tears.

The small hotel in Paris was near the Left Bank, retaining its post-war shabbiness, and full of that indefinable French character that Polly loved. After their late arrival Mark ushered her into the antiquated lift cage, and whispered, 'Why do they always wear black?'

Polly winced as the door clanged behind them. 'Who?'

'The concierges. At least, the women do.'

Polly smiled up at him. 'I think they're quite often widows.' A few seconds later, they were in a narrow corridor and Polly opened the door to a small, but adequately furnished bedroom. As Mark followed her in, she darted over to the long casement windows and flung open the shutters. Then she stepped out onto the narrow balcony and took a deep breath of sheer joy. 'Just listen to it!' She breathed in deeply. 'I've dreamed of these smells; the coffee, the cigarette smoke, French cooking. There's nowhere like it, is there?' She turned with excitement to Mark. 'This is Paris!'

'Well, I didn't think I'd brought you to Amsterdam!' Mark laughed at her. 'I'm next door, so just knock on the wall if you get lonely or scared.'

'Oh, yes, and what will you do?' Polly teased.

'Sneak round in my pyjamas, of course.' With what he hoped was a wicked grin, Mark disappeared, humming to himself. It had been a cracking idea to invite Polly, he thought with satisfaction. She was much more fun these days. He used to find her a bit on the serious side,

69

which wasn't surprising when she'd grown up with only her grandfather for company.

The following morning, as they bit into warm croissants, Polly said through lips sticky with crumbs and strawberry jam, 'I wish we could get these at home.'

'What do you want to do while we're here? Sightseeing?'

Polly nodded. 'But not the usual things like the Eiffel Tower and Notre-Dame. I've seen all those, and I'm sure you have.'

'Absolutely.' Mark leaned forward. 'One thing I really want to do is to find a bookshop. I want to get *Lady Chatterley's Lover*.'

'Mark Eldon – you're disgusting!' But Polly was laughing. 'All I can say is – pass it on to me when you've finished!'

'Okay – but I warn you, I'm expecting to take a long time to read it!'

'I can't think the book can be that bad,' Polly said thoughtfully. 'After all, D. H. Lawrence is a good writer. I've read *Sons and Lovers*.'

'So have I. But how about you? Is there anything you particularly want to do?' Polly drained her coffee cup and dabbed at her mouth with her napkin. 'I'd like a wander round the Louvre, and,' Polly paused, and then whispered, 'I want to go to the Moulin Rouge!'

Mark spluttered with laughter, causing other guests to glance across at them, then said quickly, 'Polly Merton, you're a bad influence on me.'

'Rubbish,' she said. 'I bet you've been before.'

He grinned. 'I went last year with a friend from Oxford. Believe me, it won't be any hardship to go again!'

'I thought not!' Polly pushed back her chair and stood up. 'Right – I'll just go up to my room and then I'll meet you in the lobby in ten minutes.'

Mark lit a cigarette and waited. He couldn't help thinking that not only was she a good travelling companion, Polly looked especially attractive this morning. Of course, there was always that slightly foreign look about her that she'd inherited from her French grandmother. He'd been a fool to let her drift away, although his lack of ties *had* given him more freedom to sample the joys of student life! But now he was keen to get through his finals, and to begin his career. He was going into the family legal practice, of course. He'd never questioned that. What was the point, when a lucrative income was waiting? When his father and grandfather had worked so hard to build it up? Besides, for him not to do so would break his father's heart, and Mark was only too aware of the tragedy looming over them both. He'd hesitated about this trip, but his mother had urged him to go. 'If you don't,' Felicity, wan against her pillows, told him, 'it will only make me feel guiltier than I do already. My illness has affected all of us far too much, for far too long. I want you to go, and if Polly goes with you, so much the better – she'll keep you out of mischief!'

I'm not so sure about that, Mark thought, as he watched Polly approaching. 'What first?' she said eagerly. 'Can we just wander about a bit today, you know, take in the atmosphere, and sit at pavement cafés; read a newspaper?'

And that's exactly what they did. After an hour

71

or so strolling in the warm sunshine, Mark bought a newspaper from a kiosk, and they climbed the hill to settle at a pavement café near Sacré-Coeur. Mark stretched out his long legs, his coffee before him, content just to watch the artists paint on the easels they had set up on the street, while Polly read *Le Monde*. He glanced across at her. 'Your French is much more fluent than mine,' he said. 'I can get by, but you speak it like a native.'

'I did have a French nanny and spend lots of holidays in Montpellier when I was small.' She frowned, looking down at an article in the newspaper. 'The Algerian unrest still goes on. You tend to forget how worrying it is for people here. Did you notice all that graffiti about?'

'I could hardly miss it, or the fact that the police are armed with machine guns,' Mark said. 'The whole situation is a powder keg waiting to explode, if you ask me.'

But they were on holiday, and the day was too good to dwell on serious matters. After they'd had a long, leisurely lunch of escargot followed by Normandy sole, and luscious fresh peaches, Mark went to find his bookshop, while Polly decided to go to the Louvre. In the evening, they wandered down the Rue de Rivoli, and after eating at a bistro on the Place de la République, they strolled along the banks of the Seine, not talking much, just absorbing the sounds and odours of Paris. Eventually they crossed over the narrow road to a bar on the other side that Polly fancied because she liked its burgundy-red awning, and sat outside in the warm evening air where, after he'd ordered their drinks, Mark told a joke so funny that she exploded into laughter.

Neither noticed a man passing by them on the pavement come to a sudden halt. He stood motionless for a few seconds, then turned and stared back at Polly, his expression one of utter bewilderment. She laughed again, a deep throaty laugh, tilting back her head. And the man, tall and thin, with a dark, close-cut beard, put a hand swiftly to his right temple, as if in pain. He hesitated for a moment then, drawn as if by a magnet, moved slowly in their direction, choosing to sit at a table near the back, one that gave him an unobstructed view. 'Cognac,' he said tersely to the waiter who came out, and when it was brought to him, he drained the glass swiftly, glad of the fiery liquid bringing him warmth and strength. Watching the girl closely, seeing her brown straight hair, her tanned complexion, he could still sense something hovering, shimmering on the fringes of his memory. Puzzled, he struggled without success to recall whether he'd met someone like her in the past, or could it be simply that the girl reminded him of someone? Mystified, he ordered another cognac, but this time sipped it slowly. The young man, he mused, was probably English. The girl, however, dressed in a simply cut blue linen dress looked so chic she could easily be French. But although his gaze never left Polly's face, although he watched every expression, every smile, every frown, the almost painful flash of recognition that had pierced his mind, had halted him so suddenly, eluded him.

Jules Giscard remained at the café until the young couple left, and it was much later in a state of some perplexity, that he made his journey back to the tree-lined street where he lived. He was still shaken by what had happened. The experience had been powerful enough to make him feel, at least for several minutes, quite ill. What on earth could it mean? Jules smote one fist against the other, cursing his stupidity. He should have followed them, discovered where these people lived or were staying! Perhaps tomorrow or another day, that startling recognition might come again. And if it did, then he would approach the girl, find out something about her. But foolishly, he'd let the opportunity pass. And this, to Jules, was an affront to his pride, to his intelligence, reflecting, he thought grimly, how deeply the episode had disturbed him.

Over the next couple of days, Polly and Mark continued to explore Paris and went to the Café de Flore in St-Germain-des-Prés. 'It's hard to imagine, isn't it?' Mark said with wonder, 'that we could actually be sitting in the same seats that Sartre and Simone de Beauvoir used to.'

Then on their last night, Polly got her wish and they went to the first show of the evening at the Moulin Rouge. They had seen the show advertised on a pink, white and beige poster as *La Revue Japonaise*. And Polly, loving the water ballet and thrilled at the spectacle of the tightrope walkers, drew a sharp intake of breath when she first saw the naked geishas. But it was the music, the colour, and the superb vitality of the cancan that made it an experience she knew she would never forget. 'It was so exhilarating,' she en-

74

thused, as they threaded their way through the animated crowds after leaving the theatre. 'I can't get the music out of my head.'

'Fancy having a try when we get home?' Mark teased. 'I could get the record and you could give me a private performance. Mind you, you'd need one of those skirts with frou frou petticoats and black stockings...'

She twisted round to face him. 'Do you think I've got the legs for it?'

'You, my love, have got the rest as well!' Mark bent his head and, regardless of other people around them, suddenly kissed her full on the lips.

Taken by surprise, Polly kissed him back, and then pulled away, 'And what was that for?'

'Oh, I just couldn't resist it – you looked so glowing, so happy.' He took her hand as they began to walk away from Montmartre, and told her that earlier he'd managed to phone home.

'How's your mum?'

'She sounded weak, but was putting a brave face on, as she usually does. She's been *so* brave, Pol.'

'Leukaemia is a terrible thing,' Polly said. 'And there's not much they can do about it, I believe.'

'Not yet,' Mark said with despair. 'And I'm afraid if they can, it will be too late for her, anyway.' He tightened his lips and made a determined effort to push the image from his mind. 'Come on, don't let's spoil the evening with talking about it, she'd hate that. Let's talk about your mother instead.' They divided to allow a family to pass, and Polly swung sharply round to face him. 'How do you mean?'

'Well, it must have taken some getting used to,' he said, 'her coming to live at The Gables, I mean.'

'Oh that!' Polly relaxed. 'It did a bit, and that's putting it mildly!'

'I couldn't believe it when I saw her – she's so glamorous.'

Polly smiled, and let him take her hand again. 'I know what you mean. And don't think I didn't notice you eyeing her up and down.'

'Come off it, she's old enough to be my...' Mark broke off.

Seeing the flash of pain in his eyes, Polly tried to lighten the moment. 'Some young men like an older woman,' she said. 'They think they can learn from their experience.' And they could certainly learn a lot from Sadie's, she thought!

'Nope, not for me.' Mark looked down at her, and whispered, 'I like them young and virginal!' Polly laughed, and he said, 'You know, you've got a very sexy laugh, Polly Merton; very seductive in fact.'

'Oh, hoping, are you?'

'That would be telling.' Mark paused at a café, but Polly shook her head, saying she didn't like the colour of the tablecloths. 'I want red checked ones,' she said, 'and somewhere with more atmosphere.'

With the mention of Sadie's name, Polly, as they continued strolling, began to wonder what was happening back at The Gables. Would Sadie have taken advantage of her freedom? She'd made a huge effort since the beginning of the summer holidays – in fact she'd behaved almost like a conventional mother. But Polly had no illusions;

76

Sadie would almost certainly seize the chance to have 'a bit of fun' as she called it. It could even be that Mark's father was with her at this very moment. Although she knew she should despise him for his infidelity, Polly knew from experience that George loved Felicity, was a caring husband, infinitely patient with her long illness. And gradually, Polly was beginning to see things not simply in black and white; it seemed that a man's need for sex was almost a physical necessity. But surely women were different? At least, that was what she'd always understood. Until Sadie had moved in, that was. Yet again, as she had so often over the last couple of years, Polly wondered if she would ever understand her mother.

'Here we are,' Mark said suddenly, 'does this meet with madam's approval?'

Polly looked at the small café, which was so typical of the French way of life she loved, and nodded. She looked up at the sky, detecting the first few drops of rain, and so they went inside and once they were seated, she smiled so brilliantly at the waiter that he forgot his habitual scowl and took their order with good humour. She looked around with satisfaction at the antiquated mirrors and dark, slightly shabby décor. 'You know,' she told Mark, 'my friend Ruth would love all this. She's never been abroad.'

'Why is that?'

'The fact you can even ask that question shows what a rarefied environment you live in at Oxford. It's because she can't afford it, you idiot!'

'Is she the one who's coming to stay?'

Polly nodded, warily watching a gendarme walk

slowly past the café. She could never get used to the European police being armed. Our English bobbies seem able to manage with truncheons and their helmets, she thought. Unless, of course, Mrs Booth's husband is about! She told Mark how Ernie had ended up in court.

'I bet she gave him what for – she used to terrify me.'

'She didn't approve of me coming away with you at all,' Polly laughed. 'She thinks you've got evil designs.'

'And how do you know I haven't?'

'There hasn't been much sign of it so far,' she retorted.

'That can always be remedied.' Mark glanced up as the waiter approached with their coffees. 'Particularly if we have another couple of drinks later,' he whispered. 'After all, it is our last night.' Wearing a white shirt dress, with its buttons undone to reveal a delicious cleavage, Polly was a young woman any man would find attractive. When he'd invited her to come to Paris with him, it had been as friends, and he hadn't wanted to renege on that, but tonight – well, it would only take one subtle hint...

However, that hint wasn't in Polly's soft brown eyes as she gazed at him and merely smiled. But later, as they walked for the last time by the Seine, he slipped his arm around her waist. 'We might as well look the part,' he whispered, nodding at a couple closely entwined in front of them, 'this *is* supposed to be the most romantic city in the world.' As they neared the same café with the burgundy-red awning that she'd liked, Mark said

78

again, '*Do* you fancy a last drink before turning in?'

For one wild moment, Polly was tempted, but the words, 'Oh, why not?' died on her lips as an image of Sadie flashed into her mind, followed by panic. Was this how it had begun for her? 'Best not to,' she said, avoiding his eyes, 'I need to pack when we get in, and we've got an early start in the morning.' There was a flash of disappointment in Mark's eyes, and then he turned swiftly as her voice rose. 'Glory, look at this lot!' A small cluster of tourists was coming towards them, the one leading the group, a large florid-faced man, proclaiming loudly in English that this was the famous river Seine.

'I think they could have guessed that!' Mark muttered, and to avoid the chattering crowd, he and Polly squeezed by on the inside. A few minutes later, they crossed over the bridge and within ten minutes were entering their hotel and bidding goodnight to the concierge

'Do you think she'll smile, just once before we leave?' Polly whispered, as they went up in the lift.

'I doubt it,' Mark shrugged. 'I don't think it comes with the job.'

That same evening, at the café with the burgundy-red awning, Jules Giscard was sitting at a small round table near the pavement. He only vaguely registered the noisy group of tourists on the opposite side of the road and hardly paid them attention. All his senses were keenly attuned to watching people passing by the café, hoping desperately to see two particular young people or, to be more exact, one laughing, brown-haired girl. People tended to have favourite cafés, even if they were on holiday. If only, Jules thought with bitterness, he had previously sat where he could overhear their conversation. But from his table at the back – shakily chosen so that he could observe without being seen – it had been impossible. Now, he could only wait.

Slowly, interminably, the hours passed, but with determination Jules remained at the café, occasionally drinking coffee or anis, just as he had every evening since that first night. The memory of the girl's laugh, her face, her silky brown hair, were still burning in his mind. But despite all his efforts, he'd been unable to think of an answer to the mystery. Most men, he knew, would have dismissed the episode. But then, he thought grimly, *most* men didn't have his traumatic history. It was not until midnight that Jules, with a sigh of resignation, turned to the young man by his side. 'I am not prepared to give up,' he said. 'Not yet. I shall simply come again.'

8

Since Polly had been at college, her visits home had simply meant an unwelcome interruption to Sadie, one she had accepted with resignation and not much pleasure. So it was with surprise that she found herself feeling ambivalent about Polly's expected return from Paris. And it was a glowing

Polly who arrived later that day. Mark simply dropped her off at the front door before driving swiftly away. 'He wants to see how his mother is,' Polly explained.

'Not too good, I'm afraid.'

So Sadie *had* brought George back to The Gables, Polly thought, and Sadie, seeing her daughter's tightened lips said hastily, 'Nothing like that! I just happened to meet George in the High Street. I'm sorry, Polly, but it seems it's only a matter of days now.' Even I, Sadie thought, wouldn't sleep with a man when his wife was on her deathbed.

'Mark's going to be devastated,' Polly said, her elation from the Paris trip rapidly evaporating. 'He'll think he shouldn't have gone away, I know he will. I don't suppose there's anything we can do?'

Sadie shook her head. 'Not yet, but maybe we can help them to pick up the pieces afterwards.' She glanced at Polly, wondering just how close she and Mark had become on the holiday, and then led the way into the kitchen. 'Come on; tell me what you've been doing.' Or at least, she thought with amusement, the bits you want me to know.

Felicity Eldon died ten days later, and Polly, but not Sadie – who didn't think it appropriate – went to the funeral. It took place at St Mary's, a twelfth-century church in the centre of Stafford, and every pew was full. George was not only a respected lawyer; he had married the daughter of a judge. As he stood at the front with his only son by his side, George was grateful that his marriage had, on the whole, been a happy one, marred only by these last four years of illness. Mark was pale and rigid in his dark suit and black tie. He could hardly bear to look at the highly polished oak coffin before the altar, and when the congregation began to sing 'The Lord is my Shepherd', he was almost unmanned. Unable to join in, fighting tears, he stared straight ahead.

For Polly, sitting at the back of the church, listening to the same traditional hymns and the same vicar's sonorous tones, Felicity's funeral brought back poignant and painful memories of the service for her grandfather. And it was with understanding and sympathy that she watched Mark with his father walk slowly back down the aisle in the funeral procession. And then they were all out of the dim interior of the church and into bright sunlight, with gleaming black funeral cars waiting to take the chief mourners to the cemetery. Polly followed, giving a lift to two elderly spinster sisters, who had known Felicity as a child. Later, Mark managed to find a few moments to speak to her. 'Thanks for coming, Pol. Are you joining us back at the house?'

She thought for a moment and then shook her head, feeling it would be an intrusion. 'No, I won't, thank you, Mark.' A middle-aged couple, their expressions ones of commiseration, approached, and with an apologetic glance at Polly, Mark turned away. Slowly she left, casting a backward glance at the newly turned earth surrounded by wreaths and flowers. Then pausing for a moment beside her grandparents' headstone, she made a mental note to bring some fresh roses from the garden.

'How did it go?' Sadie asked when Polly let herself in the front door.

'As they do, I suppose. The church was full.' She looked at her mother. 'It reminded me of Grandad's funeral – same hymns and everything.'

Sadie's eyes shadowed. 'It must be a comfort to actually have one – to be able to say a final goodbye. I never had that with your father.'

Polly stared at her. This was, unbelievably, the first time Sadie had ever directly referred to him. And Polly suddenly realised that they had never talked about personal things, or the emotions that a mother and daughter would normally share. 'It must have been awful for you,' she said awkwardly. 'When the telegram came, I mean.'

'It was; and for your grandfather too.' The moment passed as Sadie moved away, and said, 'I'll make a pot of tea and there are some fresh scones.'

'Oh, lovely.' Polly was ravenous and soon demolished two scones thickly spread with strawberry jam.

'Lucky devil,' Sadie said. 'I used to be like that. I could eat anything and never put on an ounce.'

Polly wiped her sticky fingers on a napkin and poured out the tea. 'Don't forget that Ruth is coming to stay next week.'

'I haven't forgotten.' Sadie looked thoughtfully at her daughter. 'What's she like?'

Polly considered. 'She's clever, in fact very clever. Not a dull academic, though. She can be really funny. I thought I'd invite the other girls round again on one of the days. What do you think?'

'Why not?' Sadie said, brightening up at the thought of some vitality coming into this sedate house. Comfortable it might be, but it was far too quiet for her taste.

When, on Sunday morning, Polly turned into the council estate at Abbey Hulton where Ruth lived, it struck her afresh just how different their backgrounds were. Warily, she slowed down as she saw a lone German shepherd dog sniffing on the grass verge near to the road, half expecting it to suddenly lope out in front of the car, while nearby a small child sat on the kerb of the pavement, playing with warm, sticky tar. Two mothers were chatting in the sunshine by their single wooden gates, one with her hair in curlers, the other nursing a baby. Further on, two men were tinkering with a car parked on the road, their transistor radio blaring out *Family Favourites*. The Gables, quiet and dignified behind its high hedges, seemed part of a different world.

Polly drew up outside Number 35, switched off the engine, went up the narrow path, and knocked on the door. The small boy she remembered seeing before opened it, his smile beaming through his freckled face. Mrs Donovan appeared behind him, 'Come on in, Polly.' She gave her son a shove. 'Go on, Michael, tell Ruth her friend is here.' As Polly went into the tiny hall, he scampered upstairs. 'She's just finishing her packing. Will you have a cup of tea after your journey?'

'Thank you, Mrs Donovan, I'd love one.'

'Well, you come and sit yourself down; I'll have the kettle on in no time.' She turned and shouted up the stairs, 'Are you two ready for Mass yet? Don't think Father O'Malley won't notice if you go in late! The rest of us went to the eight o'clock,' she explained, 'but those young monkeys like their bed too much.'

Polly smiled. 'They're just at that age. I remember needing lots of sleep when I was fifteen.'

Once in the sitting room, she looked curiously at her surroundings. The room, which was larger than she'd expected, had floral wallpaper and a narrow skirting board, slightly scuffed and painted in a sort of mushroom colour. There were a few toy cars on the floor, copies of the *Universe* and the *People* lying on the black vinyl settee, a cardigan flung over the back of a shabby armchair and a pair of men's check carpet slippers by the hearth. Polly noticed a pipe rack and a container of spills. On one wall was a rather lurid picture of the Sacred Heart, on another a smaller one of the Virgin Mary, and inside the door, a small font on the wall filled with holy water. A strong Catholic home, she thought, and certainly Ruth's mother was a good housewife. Even Mrs Booth wouldn't have found fault with the room's cleanliness. Polly immediately felt horrified. For heaven's sake what had she expected – that because people could only afford to live on a council estate that meant they would be scruffy? Feeling ashamed, she turned as Michael appeared in the doorway. 'She says you're early!'

'Yes, I know. That's because I wanted to catch her snoring!' She laughed at his astounded face and said, 'I'm only teasing. There just wasn't much traffic, that's all.' Mrs Donovan came in, carrying

85

a tray covered with an embroidered cloth. On it was a china cup on its saucer, a milk jug, sugar bowl, and a matching plate with a selection of biscuits.

Michael was staring at the tray. 'Cor, that looks posh!'

Mrs Donovan glared at him, and Polly suppressed a smile. She offered him the plate. 'Only one, mind, I don't want you spoiling your dinner,' his mother said sharply, as Michael took the chocolate one from the centre. 'And you should have left that for our guest, have ye no manners at all?' She looked at the mahogany clock on the tiled mantelpiece and tutted. 'Those dratted twins!' She went into the hall and called up again, 'It's twenty to eleven, and you'll be going in after the offertory at this rate!'

'That'll mean they'll have missed Mass,' Michael informed her, 'and me dad'll skin 'em alive. He always takes the collection at the eleven o'clock.' He added with importance, 'I'm goin' to be an altar boy next year.'

'Are you,' Polly said. 'Wow, I am impressed.'

Just then there was a stampede of feet down the stairs, and two girls so alike it was almost impossible to tell them apart, burst in. Pretty and, unlike Ruth, curvaceous, they oozed vitality.

'I can't find my mantilla,' one wailed, and began to rummage in a sideboard drawer.

'She only wants to wear it, because she thinks it makes her look like Maureen O'Hara in *The Quiet Man*,' the other one complained. 'Have you got it? Right – come on.'

They both glanced hurriedly at Polly, and chorused, 'Oh, hello, sorry we can't stop.' Two minutes later, the front door banged behind them.

Polly laughed. 'Which is which?'

'The one looking for her mantilla is Teresa, the other one's Maria. And the good Lord help us when they get a bit older. At least I've got one sensible daughter,' she added, as Ruth came in and dumped her suitcase on the brown patterned carpet.

'Sorry, Pol, not to come straight down but I wanted to finish off me packing while I was organised.' Ruth glanced at her friend and grinned. 'Does that make sense?'

'Sort of,' Polly said, thinking how good it was to see her again. 'I've been getting to know the rest of the family.'

'Poor you!' Ruth smiled at her mother, whose dark springy hair, despite its grey streaks, so resembled her own. 'Do you want me to help with the veg before I go?'

'No, love, you get off, and Michael will set the table for me.'

He looked up from his comic and pulled a face but his mother ignored him. 'Have a good time, now,' she said.

'At least,' Ruth grinned as after their farewells she got into the car, 'she didn't say – be sure to behave yourself!' As they drove away she added, 'How are things? You know, between yourself and Sadie?'

'Better, thanks. I took your advice and made more of an effort. And she has as well. So don't worry,' Polly reassured her, 'you won't be walking into a battlefield.'

Ruth was dying to meet Polly's mother. Sure, she thought, and isn't she going to be the exact opposite of my own? No one could ever describe Mrs Donovan as a 'scarlet woman', which Ruth knew would be her mother's contemptuous words for someone like Sadie. She hadn't dared to even hint at Sadie's lifestyle, knowing that Mrs Donovan would have been so scandalised she would have forbidden her daughter to set foot in The Gables, never mind spend a whole week there. Whereas Ruth was not only intrigued, but feeling hopeful of seeing some scandal at first hand.

9

Polly drove directly to Stone and saw with relief that Sadie's blue Ford Anglia was already in the Crown's car park. She turned to Ruth, 'I'm starving, I don't know about you.'

Ruth got out of the passenger seat, closed the car door, and nervously smoothed down her skirt. Her pale green dress, bought specially the week before from C&A, was straight, with short sleeves and a matching belt. Demure and neat wasn't her style, but she had never been to a posh hotel, and was anxious to 'fit in'. So instead of her normal gypsy earrings and jangling charm bracelet, she wore only a wristwatch and her mother's pearl studs.

They went into the main entrance, through the reception area with its deep red and gold carpet and domed chandelier, and into the bar, where

Sadie was waiting; a gin and tonic before her. She rose with a welcoming smile as they approached. 'Hello, Ruth, so nice to meet you.'

'You too,' Ruth said, rather disconcerted. Sadie, in her cream dress and jacket, didn't look at all like a woman of 'loose morals'. In fact, even though her blouse was a bit revealing, she could have been any middle-class woman who could afford to dress well. She was, however, satisfactorily glamorous.

'I'll get us a drink,' Polly said. 'Do you want another one, Sadie?'

Sadie shook her head.

'Is it half a shandy for you, Ruth?'

'Yes, please.'

When Polly went to the bar, Sadie asked, 'Do you know this part of Staffordshire, Ruth?'

'Not really. I've never been further than Trentham Gardens.'

'Actually,' Sadie said. 'I've never been there or as far as Stoke, although of course I know it's famous for its pottery. You live somewhere called Abbey Hulton, Polly tells me. What a lovely name, it sounds like a really picturesque village.'

Ruth was saved from having to reply, as a middle-aged man paused by Sadie's chair. 'Hello, there. I haven't seen you in here much lately.'

'I've been rather busy,' Sadie said serenely, and Ruth stared in fascination at the man's fleshy face, adorned with a greying moustache. Was this one of her lovers? Her imagination running wild, Ruth stared from one to the other, embarrassed to feel the colour rising in her cheeks, and was vastly relieved when the man shrugged and moved on. Sadie, who considered him to be one of her rare mistakes, drained her glass, and glancing up as Polly came back, wished she'd ordered another gin and tonic. 'Journey all right?' she said.

'Fine.' Polly glanced around the room. 'Any sign of Mark?'

Sadie shook her head. 'Too soon after the funeral, I would imagine. In any case, I expect George's mother is still there.'

When they went into the restaurant, even to Ruth's inexperienced eyes it was obvious that their table was one of the best in the room. She looked down at the array of cutlery, at the crisp white tablecloth and napkins, thinking that the rich certainly knew how to live. For a few moments there was silence as they all studied the menu, then, 'Roast beef for me,' Polly announced, 'and I'll just have a fruit juice.'

'I think I'll go for the lamb,' Sadie said, 'and the tomato soup.'

Ruth hesitated then decided to have the same as Polly. She glanced down at the puddings, but realised that the others weren't choosing those yet. Impressed by how at ease her friend was, Ruth realised that gradually, over the last year, the other girl had changed a lot. At first when they'd begun at college, she'd been quiet, withdrawn even, but towards the end of last term, she'd begun to relax, and with this new vitality Polly had become a very attractive girl. 'I've got some friends coming round in the week,' she was saying, 'and maybe we could go dancing at Trentham on Saturday.'

'Really? Maybe I should go,' Sadie said with interest, causing the two girls to glance at each other in alarm. 'Perhaps not on a Saturday night,'

Polly said hurriedly, 'but they do have the big bands sometimes. I went to see Joe Loss once.'

Sadie visibly brightened. 'I love to dance,' she told them. 'I used to go to the Hammersmith Palais at least twice a week.'

'Is Hammersmith where you used to live?' Ruth asked.

Sadie nodded. 'I used to go to the Windmill Theatre, as well. You know, the one that "never closed" during the war?'

Both girls stared at her in undisguised envy. 'Did the nudes really stand perfectly still, in a tableau?' Polly said, while Ruth tried to imagine such a shocking scene.

'Yes, they had to, because of the Lord Chamberlain's rule,' Sadie explained. 'And the variety acts were fantastic – real vaudeville. Lots of famous comedians started there; Harry Secombe for one, and Tommy Cooper and Tony Hancock.'

The meal passed in much the same way, easy chat among the girls, with Sadie listening, interjecting, and finding to her surprise that she was enjoying herself. And being with the two girls reminded her of her own friendship with Babs from the nightclub days. She was now living in Hereford, and although they hadn't met for several years, they wrote sometimes, and exchanged Christmas cards. Sadie suddenly felt a keen urge to see her again. It would be wonderful to reminisce about the old days in London during the war. I could invite her to stay, Sadie thought – after all, there's plenty of room. But she decided to wait until after Polly went back to college. Babs, Sadie recalled fondly, although great fun was terribly indiscreet. For instance she was bound to prattle about André. And Sadie wasn't sure she wanted her daughter ever to know how casually she'd been conceived. How could the girl possibly understand what it had been like in 1941? No one who hadn't lived through it could imagine the sheer horror of war, the fatigue of shortages; the desperation for distraction, for release from the constant trauma. Servicemen on leave, with the fear of imminent death always with them, would find themselves turning to alcohol to blur the awful reality of their lives. And then there would be the temptation to sleep with a girl, any girl. For some young lads, tragically, it would be the first and only time. It would be good to chat about old times, Sadie reflected. I shall definitely write to her at the beginning of September.

To Polly's delight, Mrs Booth and Ruth were immediately comfortable with each other. 'My cousin Eileen lived in Meir,' Doris said, on learning that Ruth was from the Potteries. 'I used to go and stay with her sometimes, and we'd go to the Broadway cinema and arrange to meet lads on the front steps. That way,' she added with a broad grin, 'they paid for us to go in.' Both girls stared at the cleaner. With her greying perm imprisoned in an 'invisible' hairnet, it seemed inconceivable that she'd ever been young and flirtatious. Doris raised her eyebrows. 'Yer needn't look so surprised, I wasn't always this age, you know!' She sipped at her mug of tea. 'So, what are you two doing today?'

'We're off into Stone this morning,' Polly told

her. 'Then Hazel and Anita are coming round later.'

Stone, the nearest small town with its pleasant streets and mature trees, delighted Ruth. 'It's got sort of a peaceful atmosphere, don't you think?' Polly said. She was very fond of Stone. 'And we've got some really good boutiques.' Ruth thought they seemed rather expensive, and would have liked to go to the factory shop at Lotus Shoes on the outskirts, but she didn't say anything. She'd always known that Polly lived in a different world, but it was only since seeing The Gables that Ruth realised just how different. To her disappointment, she hadn't caught even a glimpse of Sadie's sinful boudoir, because the door was always closed, but the drawing room alone was bigger than the whole of the ground floor of the Donovans' house. The solid and expensive furniture, the rich fabric of the lined curtains, the high ceilings and deep skirting boards, even the way her feet sank into the pile of the wool carpets, were all new experiences. Polly hadn't a snobbish bone in her, but already Ruth was beginning to feel anxious about meeting her friends.

And when they arrived, her fears seemed justified. Talking gaily, the two girls swept into the house, their perfect vowels making her conscious of her own flat ones. It wasn't that any of the Donovan children had adopted the Potteries' dialect, but they did have the area's distinctive intonation, even if it was with an Irish lilt.

'Ruth went to St Dominic's at Hartshill,' Polly told them, once they'd all settled.

'Really? But it's strange how the St Dominic's

school in Stone is fee-paying only, and that one takes scholarship girls,' Hazel commented.

'Well, it's a good job as far as I'm concerned, as I *was* a scholarship girl,' Ruth said, suddenly deciding she wasn't going to pretend to be anything she wasn't.

All Anita said was, 'It must have saved your parents a fortune.' She began to take off her cardigan. 'Gosh, it's warm in here. Can you open a window, Pol?'

Polly did so, saying to Hazel, 'How's the assistant manager?' She explained to Ruth, 'Hazel works at the local bank, but she's on holiday this week. He's her current heart-throb.'

'Not any more!' Hazel's slightly freckled face reddened. 'He's only gone and got himself engaged, hasn't he? And she's as plain as a flaming pikestaff!' They all laughed. 'How about you, Ruth – do you have a boyfriend?'

'Not me! I like variety,' Ruth began to relax. 'Don't I, Pol?'

'She gets it, as well.'

'You'd never think it to look at me, would you?' Ruth said. She looked disparagingly down at her small breasts. 'It's certainly not because of my physical attributes!'

Anita laughed and turned to face Polly. 'Come on, Pol, we're all dying to hear what happened with Mark in Paris.'

'Nothing happened,' Polly said firmly. 'No, honestly, we're just good friends. Anything else is in the past.'

'Do you think it's possible to have a platonic friendship between a man and a woman?' Anita said with a frown.

They all looked expectantly at Polly, who bit her lip. 'I'm not exactly sure.'

'There you are!' Anita's dark hair brushed her face as she leaned forward with excitement. 'I knew something had happened!'

'Oh, all right, maybe there was a friendly kiss, but that's all!'

'Not even an attempt at seduction – and in a romantic setting like Paris?' Hazel raised her eyebrows in disbelief.

'I'm ashamed to say not!' Polly laughed at their incredulous faces. 'Maybe if it had been one of you...'

'Chance would be a fine thing!' Anita said. 'But if that Hilary at the tennis club ever got her claws into him, he wouldn't stand a chance – she's been after Mark for years.'

'Oh, I think he could handle *her*. I tell you what,' Polly suggested, 'why don't we all have a game tomorrow morning?'

'I can't,' Anita told them. 'I'm going to London to see Andrew.'

Hazel turned to Ruth. 'I take it you play? Did you bring your racquet?'

'I certainly did.'

'Well, let's hope Hilary isn't there. She always makes a beeline for a newcomer, just so she can show off.'

'Good player, is she?' Ruth's tone was casual.

'She thinks she's Wimbledon standard,' Anita said with sarcasm. 'But unfortunately, the answer's yes.'

And later that evening, when they mentioned

the tennis to Sadie, she said, 'I wonder whether Mark will be there? Life has to go on, and the sooner he picks up the threads the better.'

'I hope so,' Ruth said promptly. 'I'm looking forward to meeting him.'

Sadie regarded them both, envying their youthful optimism. She'd been sorely tempted to join the girls earlier; particularly when she'd heard them playing Ella Fitzgerald, but common sense had told her that her presence wouldn't be welcomed. After all, she was Polly's mother, not another girlfriend. Sadie hadn't found being excluded amusing at all, and it made her even more determined to write to Babs. But for now, she decided to go to bed. At least there, she thought ruefully, even if she had to sleep alone, she could indulge herself with a romantic novel and a box of Black Magic.

10

The tennis club, a couple of miles from The Gables, was a popular meeting place for players in the surrounding area. It had six hard courts, and a green-roofed wooden pavilion, which was spacious enough to contain a large if slightly battered table. It was around this that members would sit and chat while waiting for a court to become vacant.

'The weather's perfect,' Polly said, as she parked the car in the lane outside. And it was, with a blue sky, warm sunshine, and a slight breeze.

She glanced at other cars drawn up by the grass verge, and noted that Hilary's was one of them. Hazel was already there, her expression lightening as the two girls entered the pavilion. 'I didn't think you were here yet,' Polly said. 'I didn't see the car.'

'No, Mum needed it for herself, so she dropped me off.'

Polly turned to where Hilary, the only other person in the room, was sitting opposite Hazel. 'Hilary, can I introduce Ruth, a friend of mine from college?'

'Hello, Ruth,' Hilary said without much interest.

Ruth looked at the slim blonde, noting her strong shoulders and tanned muscular arms. 'It's nice to meet you, Hilary. I hear you're a good tennis player.'

'Passable,' Hilary said, her gaze flicking over the other girl in such a way that Ruth immediately became conscious that her well-worn white Aertex blouse and shorts were in sharp contrast to the expensive tennis dresses the other girls wore.

'Ruth's from Stoke,' Polly said, 'she's staying with me this week.'

'Oh, yes?' Hilary said. 'Which tennis club do you belong to?'

'I'm not a member of any club,' Ruth told her.

Hilary's pale blue eyes narrowed. 'Where do you play, then?'

'At Hanley Park. The public courts are quite good, actually.'

'Really? You do surprise me.' Polly felt anger rising as she saw Ruth flush at the patronising tone. But then her anger was replaced by revengeful delight when Hilary added, 'I think a court will be free shortly – how about Ruth and I having a singles, while we can?'

Polly said swiftly, 'Good idea. As a visitor, Ruth,' she explained, 'you can only play when there aren't members waiting. But that's okay with us, isn't it, Hazel?'

Hazel gave Polly a bewildered glance, but said, 'Of course.' There was a short silence, then Hazel asked Hilary, 'Have you seen Mark here lately? Only my mother was asking. She was really cut up about Mrs Eldon, they were good friends.'

Hilary shook her head. 'No sign of him so far.' She glanced at Polly. 'That was a bit off, wasn't it, that he should be in Paris with you, when the end finally came?'

'She wanted him to go,' Polly said shortly, 'and he was back ten days before she died.'

'Even so...' Hilary raised one finely plucked eyebrow. 'Still,' she continued, 'I suppose being willing to go away with him like that, is one way of getting your boyfriend back.'

Polly's expression hardened. 'Sorry not to satisfy your curiosity, Hilary, but I really think that's between me and him, don't you?'

'Well, *I'd* never have gone. But then, I suppose living with a mother who has, let us say, rather "liberal" views on morality, does make a difference.'

For a moment Polly was stunned, but Hazel flashed, *'You'd* never have had the chance, Hilary.'

Polly said in a tight voice, 'Times are changing. You need to move with them, Hilary.'

The blonde girl just gave a supercilious smile, and Ruth, who had listened to her spite with growing fury, silently got up from the table, and went to look out of the door. 'They're coming off one of the courts,' she called over her shoulder. 'Ready, Hilary?'

'Certainly.' They both picked up their racquets and balls, and Hilary, with a smug glance at the other two girls, followed Ruth out on to the tennis court.

'Bitch!' Hazel said. 'But hey, Polly, what are you up to? You know what Hilary's like. She'll just love humiliating Ruth.'

'Watch, my child, and learn,' Polly grinned. 'Shall we go out and spectate?'

After their 'knock-up', the two girls spun for first service and Ruth won. Hilary strolled back in a relaxed manner and turned expectantly. Ruth's first ball whistled through the air at such high speed, that Hilary's attempt to return it only landed the ball in the net. The shock on her face was visible even to the two girls sitting on a wooden bench behind the green wire. Then Ruth served again. This time Hilary was forewarned. She placed the return ball on Ruth's backhand, but the shot that came back was not only strong, it was so expertly placed that the ball dropped neatly just over the net. 'Thirty–love,' Ruth called and, expressionless, she walked back to serve again.

'You dark horse,' Hazel whispered to Polly. 'She's fantastic!'

Unable to break Ruth's powerful service, Hilary only managed to win three games in the first set, and lost the second with a humiliating score of 6–2. By this time, a few other members had drifted out to watch, and relished seeing the unpopular girl trail off the court devoid of her usual triumphant air.

Just then Polly felt a light touch on her shoulder, and turning, exclaimed, 'Mark! I didn't know you were here.'

'I think we were all involved in the match,' he said. 'Who's the dark girl?'

'Ruth. You remember, I told you she was coming to stay.'

'Oh, yes, of course.' He turned to Hazel. 'Hi.'

'Hello, Mark. I was so sorry to hear about your mother,' she said gently.

'Thank you.' He gave a quiet smile, and then one or two other members drifted towards him and began offering their condolences.

Polly had gone to meet Ruth who, looking hot, was coming along the path. Hilary had already swept past her without a word. 'Well done!'

'She's good, though,' Ruth admitted.

'But pure poison. Never mind her, Mark's here, you'll be able to meet him.' But seeing he was still talking to a couple of people, Polly said, 'Later – come on, you need a drink, and you can meet some of the others instead.'

'Hang on – is that him – the tall one?'

'Sure is.'

Ruth stared. 'Lucky you!'

'I've told you, we're just...'

'Good friends – that's what they all say!' Both girls laughed, and then they were entering the pavilion to hear a fair-haired youth say, 'It makes a change for you, Hilary – losing a singles match.'

'Good for the character,' Hazel said, her lips twitching.

Slumped in her chair, Hilary ignored them both, so Polly said, 'Mark's here.'

The blonde girl sat up, 'Really? I must go and offer my sympathy.' She jumped up and hurried out.

Hazel raised her eyebrows. 'Anita was right – she does fancy him.'

'Don't all the girls?' the fair-haired youth said glumly.

Polly looked with sympathy at his poor complexion, with its oily skin, and pimples. 'They will you, Adrian, in a couple of years.'

'I should live so long,' he grumbled, and then smiled revealing a set of white even teeth.

'She's right,' Ruth said. 'Sure and won't it be worth waiting for? You should see the lad who lives next door to me. A fright he was for years, and now isn't he fighting them off!'

'Sounds wonderful,' Adrian grinned, 'and thanks for comparing me to a "fright".' They all laughed, and it was into this laughter that Mark came, followed closely by Hilary.

'Mark? Come and meet Ruth,' Polly said.

'Hello.' He smiled. 'I've heard quite a lot about you. But not what a smashing tennis player you are.'

'Thank you,' she smiled. 'But I bet I've heard a lot more about *you!*'

'You don't want to believe all that Polly says.'

'Really?' Hazel murmured, glancing slyly at her friend.

'Now look what you've done,' Polly told him.

'Thanks a lot!'

Mark grinned, and she was glad to see it. Sadie was right, life did have to go on, and on an impulse Polly said, 'If you and your father aren't busy, would you like to join us at the Crown for lunch on Sunday?' The moment the words had left her mouth, she regretted them. It's not up to me to invite George, she thought with horror. Suppose Sadie doesn't want to see him, or even more importantly, suppose he finds it embarrassing to see her? She added quickly, 'Ruth will be there too. I'm not taking her back until afterwards.'

'That's kind of you, Polly. I'll mention it, although you might find it difficult to get a bigger table.'

'You're right.' Thanks, Mark, Polly thought; if Sadie's not keen, that will be a good excuse. 'Anyway, let me know, and I'll check.'

More people began to wander into the pavilion, and going to look out of the door, Hazel said, 'Two courts are free.'

'Singles, Mark?' Adrian suggested.

'Sure.' The two young men collected their racquets and left.

'How about doubles?' Polly said to the others. 'Hilary,' she offered with reluctance, 'do you want to partner Hazel?'

When the two girls got back to The Gables, they were in high spirits.

'First,' Polly told her mother, 'Ruth soundly beat her at singles, and then we managed to win the doubles, as well. You should have seen Hilary's face!'

'A triumph all round,' Sadie said, who could never understand why people got so competitive about sport; although out of all its forms, tennis was one she'd rather like to try. But that was mainly because she fancied cutting a dash in a tennis dress, and, of course, having the chance to see and meet good-looking men in shorts! Perhaps, she thought, as Mark had once suggested, his father might eventually give her some coaching. And it was while she was thinking of George, and as Ruth left the room, that Polly told her about her impulsive invitation. 'We can get out of it,' she suggested, 'if you'd rather not.'

But Sadie had no hesitation. She liked George, had respect for him. 'No,' she said. 'If they want to join us, it's fine with me. And as Ruth will be with us that will stop any gossip.' She saw Polly's surprise and said, 'I'm thinking of George, with it being so soon after the funeral.' A pity you don't think of such things with regard to yourself, Polly thought grimly.

But early on Saturday afternoon, their plan to go dancing at Trentham had to be shelved. Polly, on a trip to the bathroom, found her period had started two days early, and an hour later was doubled up with stomach cramps, slumped in an armchair, and clutching a hot-water bottle. From experience, she knew the rest of the day was one simply to get through. 'Sorry, Ruth,' she said with a grimace, 'I'm afraid I'm not up to driving or dancing.'

'You do have a bad time, don't you?' Ruth sympathised.

'Always have. God knows how I'll manage

when I have to stand in front of a class of kids!'

'Our Maria's just like you. She's been raving about some new tablets she's got. I'll ask her what they're called.'

On Sunday, Mark and George joined them at the Crown. 'Good idea of yours,' Mark said in an aside to Polly. 'Gran went back yesterday, so it would have felt a bit awkward at home. This will ease things a little.'

Polly looked at him with sympathy, seeing the strain in his eyes, and Ruth watching, wondered if there *was* anything between them. She glanced again at Mark, seated opposite her at the table, liking his dark good looks. Just at that moment he looked up, and as their eyes met, Ruth – wearing the same pale green dress she'd worn on the previous Sunday – felt her colour rise. For heaven's sake, she told herself as he smiled; he's not going to be interested in you, a girl from a council estate! And remember, this is only an interlude – in your real life you'll be behind the sweet counter at Woolworths for the rest of the summer.

Polly hadn't told Ruth of Sadie's intimate relationship with George, and with Mark still being unaware of it, the lunch passed in a pleasant, if rather quiet manner. When they all got up to leave after having coffee in the lounge, George murmured to Sadie and Polly, 'Thank you. It was very thoughtful.' He turned to Ruth. 'Goodbye, Ruth, and good luck with your studies.'

Mark just smiled. 'Keep Polly in good order, won't you? When she gets back to college, I mean.'

'You can rely on me,' she said, her eyes briefly meeting his.

And then it was Sadie's turn. She leaned forward and kissed Ruth lightly on the cheek. 'Goodbye, my dear. It's been lovely to have you stay at The Gables.'

Ruth glanced at Polly, guessing that she wouldn't be happy about her mother adopting the role of chatelaine. And Ruth was right, but Polly was also reminding herself that the following year she would be celebrating her twenty-first birthday.

11

It was not until October, with Polly safely away at college, that Sadie wrote to Babs. And almost by return of post came the reply.

Dear Sadie,

You're a lifesaver. Your letter came just at the right time – Jimmy dumped me three months ago, for a twenty-four-year-old redhead. So much for nineteen years of marriage! And I swear I've never even looked at another bloke. The kids are devastated, but at least they're old enough to understand. Anyway, they're back at boarding school now, so I'd love to come up, and I promise I won't cry on your shoulder. I've done all that. Now I'm just effing furious. When can I come?

Three days later Babs arrived in her green Morris Minor. She got out of the car, straightened, and stared up at the imposing frontage of The Gables. Sadie, who had been hovering before the large bay window of the drawing room, hurried into the hall, opened the door and went out to greet her. The two women gazed at each other with nostalgic delight. Babs was the first to speak. 'Lord, you hardly look any different!'

'Neither do you!' Sadie linked arms with her old friend. 'Come on in, we can get your case later. You must be dying for a cup of tea.'

'Anything stronger?'

Sadie laughed. 'Oh, Babs, you don't change! Gin and tonic do you?'

'Make it a double! It's quite a drive.'

'Yes, I know.' Sadie led the way into the drawing room and went over to the sideboard. Babs looked around her in admiration. 'Wow, Sadie, you landed on your feet here.'

'You didn't do so badly – kids at boarding school, indeed!'

Babs flung herself down on the sofa. 'It was only because Jimmy's parents pay the fees. He was never much of an earner. The house is okay, but nothing to compare with this.'

'It's not mine,' Sadie told her. 'The old man left it to Polly.'

Babs seemed about to say something, but instead stretched out her hand for her drink. She looked reflectively around the room, and when she saw the photograph of André, said quietly, 'Gosh! That brings back memories.'

Sadie followed her gaze. 'Yes. It all seems so long ago, now. In some ways, that is, and yet in others...'

'I know what you mean.' Babs put her glass down on the coffee table and got up. 'Sorry, I'll have to go to the little girls' room.'

'There's one downstairs, the first door on the left.'

Sadie, admiring Babs's still-slim figure in her navy pleated skirt and pink twinset, watched her leave, wondering how Jimmy could be such a fool. Babs had fallen for the fun-loving young army captain the first time he'd come to the club, and from that moment had never been interested in anyone else. And Sadie looked again at the photograph of André. In a strange way, Babs being there seemed to make its presence even more evocative. He had liked Babs, she'd made him laugh, and in those days laughter had been something to be cherished. It's going to be so good having her here, Sadie thought. Just seeing someone from my old way of life has cheered me up. And that thought surprised her, because she hadn't consciously been aware that she needed it. But it was true; her spirits had been a little low lately. Was she missing Polly and the company of her young friends? A possibility surely, and yet Sadie knew that it was probably the usual reason. It had been, as far as sex was concerned, a long, arid summer. Even during the week that Polly had been in Paris, when there had been the opportunity to meet someone, nothing had happened. Maybe I'm becoming *too* fussy, she thought, but George had been her last lover, and that had been months ago.

She turned as Babs came back. 'Shall we get your things, and I'll show you to your room?' she suggested. 'Then you can unpack while I cook us a late lunch.'

'Brilliant,' Babs said. 'I confess I'm starving. It must be all the strain of driving.'

107

'It affects me in the same way.'

But although over their meal of grilled lamb chops, Babs continued to be cheerful, Sadie could, in an unguarded moment, detect the pain behind her smile. And tactfully, she didn't ask any questions regarding Jimmy. Afterwards she gave Babs a tour of the house. John Merton's bedroom and Polly's were simply referred to, but it was with pride that Sadie showed her friend her own sumptuously furnished one. 'Remember, Babs, what my poky little bedsit in Maida Vale was like?'

'I certainly do, you couldn't swing a cat in it.' Babs paused, and looked around, at the pink satin headboard, the cupids on the wall. 'It's a far cry from that but, if you don't mind my saying so, perhaps a bit over the top?'

'I know, but I don't care. You should have seen the cleaner's face when she first caught a glimpse of it. She went away muttering it was like a tart's boudoir!' Sadie turned to laugh at Babs and was startled to see a look of shock on her friend's face. 'Oh, come on, Babs, you always knew what I was like!'

'Then, yes. But surely not now?' Babs stared at her, wide-eyed.

Sadie shrugged. 'When I get the opportunity, yes!'

'Well, I'll say one thing for you – you never made any secret of it,' Babs admitted, as they went down the wide staircase.

'And you,' Sadie said lightly, with a grin at her friend, 'were always just a tease.'

'But how do you manage it, with Polly in the house?'

'Now therein lies a tale,' Sadie admitted, as they went into the kitchen. She turned on the taps and as she began to stack the dishes in the sink, Babs picked up a white Irish linen tea towel. 'And, my old friend,' Sadie added, 'is something best talked about over a bottle of wine.'

'Amen to that,' agreed Babs, 'a good old confab, just like old times.'

'But not tonight,' Sadie said with concern. 'You look tired.'

'I am,' Babs yawned. 'An early night, I think.'

'Absolutely – a bit of television then a warm bath. Anyway, we'll have lots of time to catch up later.'

The following morning, Sadie told Babs they were going into the county town of Stafford. 'Out of old bootface's way,' she explained. 'Or should I say, Mrs Booth, the family retainer. Well, actually, she's just the cleaner, but try telling her that! You won't believe this, but she refuses to clean *my* room. It offends her morals, or some such rubbish.'

'Don't you mind, Sadie?' Babs looked at her old friend in puzzlement. 'Not that you have to do your own room, but someone thinking that about you? I think I would.'

Sadie turned to her. 'I don't let it bother me. You saw *Coronation Street* last night. Remember Ena Sharples? Well, Mrs Booth could be her sister. So you can imagine how narrow-minded she is!'

Babs didn't say anything, simply drained her cup, and then offered to help with the breakfast dishes. 'No, leave them,' Sadie told her. 'She'll be able to tut about lazy women!'

109

'Your tiny revenge?'

'Exactly.'

And so ten minutes later, Sadie drove them into Stafford, which, to her initial surprise, she had discovered she liked; finding it not only historic but also charming. Babs was quick to agree with her, and as they strolled by the river that lay at the bottom of the town, she said, 'You know, Sadie, there's nowhere quite like London, but I do think the rest of the country has a lot to offer.'

'You've liked living in Hereford, haven't you?'

Babs nodded. 'I think I'm happier in a quieter environment – how about you?'

Sadie didn't answer immediately then she said thoughtfully, 'I think maybe I could be, in the right circumstances.'

'Which are?'

'Oh, my own place, I suppose; and the right man. But God, Babs, I get bored stiff in that great house on my own.'

'Not always on your own, from what you say!'

'Maybe not, but that's only now and then, and even less frequent recently.' Sadie paused to look at a pavement artist. 'I miss London like hell at times,' she confessed.

'Then why not get a job? You always worked before. You were at Derry & Toms for ages.'

'I know. But I don't need to now, at least not while I'm living at The Gables. The will took care of all that.'

'Then do voluntary work!'

Babs's voice was sharp, and Sadie looked at her in surprise. 'Do I detect a note of censure?'

'Sorry,' Babs looked discomfited. 'It's just that

110

I'm not used to this "lady of leisure" stuff. It seems such a cop-out somehow.'

'Thanks very much!'

Babs grinned at her. 'Well, you know me, feet first!' She glanced curiously at her friend. 'Have you made any friends up here?'

Sadie shook her head. 'Not a one!'

'So when Polly's away at college, you don't see anyone?'

'Not unless you count Mrs Booth – and we avoid each other. The only time I have any social life is when I go out and find it.'

'And I suppose that's male?'

Sadie nodded. 'I gather,' she said with sarcasm, 'that I've acquired a bit of a reputation, so I don't suppose women would be interested.'

'Well, you can hardly blame them, particularly if they're married!'

Sadie stared at her in shock, and then suddenly realised how painful this conversation must be for Babs. Damn, she thought, I should have had more sensitivity. 'Come on,' she said gaily, in an effort to change the mood, 'let's go and have some lunch. Afterwards, we could go to see a film? I've read smashing reviews of *Breakfast at Tiffany's*. What do you think?'

Babs, already regretting the way she'd snapped, said, 'Great idea. Come on, you're right – let's eat.'

So later, fortified by their lunch of steak and kidney pie, followed by Neopolitan ice cream, they went to the cinema. Three hours later, at the end of the programme, they emerged, Babs feeling bemused by the elfin beauty of Audrey Hepburn, while her character of Holly Golightly was one

111

that Sadie had delighted in. 'As for George Pep-pard,' she declared with relish, 'he could come home with me, any day!'

It was later in the evening, after a couple of gin and tonics, and with a bottle of white wine on the coffee table between them, that Babs began at last to talk. Slumped in one of the leather arm-chairs with her stockinged feet resting on a pouffe while Sadie reclined on the chesterfield, Babs poured out her heartbreak, her disillusion-ment, and her anger. 'I just feel so betrayed,' she said, and Sadie could see her fighting back tears, 'and stupid! Because I thought our marriage was okay, that we were happy. At least, as much as most people are.' She paused, and Sadie waited in silence. 'Okay, I admit I'm not that brilliant in the bedroom – but did I ever refuse him? Not once in nineteen years! So why in God's name did he have to go out and find someone else? We were always good friends, bickered a bit maybe, but nothing major.' Babs drained her wine glass and after refilling it, looked pleadingly at Sadie. 'Sorry, I promised I wouldn't do this, but if I could just understand where I went wrong!'

Sadie gazed at her with profound sympathy. It was a story she had heard countless times. A man could love and respect his wife, not want to leave the mother of his children, but all too often his needs, his physical needs – which, as one man told her, 'are as instinctive as hunger for food' – were neglected, often because they were simply not understood. Sadie was always amazed how couples could live together yet never talk about such fundamental problems in their relationships.

Most women were brought up to believe that sex was something private, secretive even – certainly not to be openly discussed. And it had been the same for generations. Sadie had read that at one time 'nice women' weren't even supposed to enjoy it! But just wait until this contraception pill is readily available, she thought; then their lives will change.

'What do you mean, exactly,' Sadie said quietly, 'when you say you're not brilliant in the bedroom?'

Babs shrugged with some embarrassment. 'You know, not very adventurous.'

'So it was always the same routine?'

She nodded. 'And even then I wanted it to be over as quickly as possible.'

Poor Jimmy, Sadie thought – no wonder he strayed.

Babs said, 'To be honest, Sadie, I've never been able to understand how you could do it ... you know ... with so many different men. *Why* you did – what you could see in it?'

'I just enjoy sex,' Sadie said, 'it's as simple as that.'

'What – always? Even though you don't love them?' Babs looked at her with incredulity.

'Oh, I can sometimes make a mistake in my choice. But it doesn't happen often. To answer your question, Babs, for me it's just a physical thing, a fleeting attraction, no strings on either side; a bit of fun. And I can tell you one thing – I feel a damn sight better when I'm having it than when I'm not!'

'And it doesn't bother you if they're married?'

Babs's tone was bitter.

'I don't ask. Sometimes they tell me, sometimes they don't. But I can tell you one thing, I think women like me can sometimes strengthen marriages rather than sabotage them.'

'And how the hell do you make that out?'

As Babs's voice rose in anger, Sadie leaned forward, picked up the wine bottle and refilled both their glasses. 'Because we provide a safety valve. A man can talk to someone like me, a woman he may only see a few times and then never again, without any emotional hang-ups or the worry of being judged.' Sadie shrugged. 'I suppose I'm just a receptacle, really.'

They both stared at each other and then spluttered with laughter. 'Rather an unfortunate choice of phrase,' Babs was laughing so much that she had to wipe her eyes. 'Oh, Sadie, I'm so glad I came.'

'So am I.' Sadie leaned forward intently. 'But let's get this right, Babs. What I don't do, have never done, is build up a relationship with a man I know belongs to someone else. And I don't steal other women's husbands.'

At the last sentence, Babs's mood changed. 'I wish everyone else thought like that – I'm glad to hear you've got *some* morals!'

That's my girl, Sadie thought, never misses a chance! But smiling, she remained silent. She'd long become accustomed to such criticism.

Babs persisted. 'So why are we so different? Is there something wrong with me or something wrong with you?'

'Where does the word "wrong" come into all

this?' Sadie said. 'As you say, we're just different. We're all as we're made, Babs, and we have to live our lives accordingly.'

Babs stared at her for a moment, and then capitulated. 'I suppose you're right,' she said sulkily. 'But it doesn't seem fair.'

'Life isn't!' Sadie yawned. 'I don't know about you, but I'm ready for some beauty sleep. Come on, I'll clear these things away in the morning.'

Babs uncurled herself with some reluctance, and picked up her shoes. 'What are we doing tomorrow?'

'Tomorrow, my friend, you are going to meet my daughter!'

Babs looked up at her in astonishment.

'I had a phone call earlier while you were in the garden,' Sadie explained. 'Polly's decided to come home for the weekend, there's a dance at the tennis club or something. What's more, she's bringing a friend. So,' Sadie turned to Babs as they went into the hall, 'she's bound to ask you about André, and I want you to be very careful what you say. Polly has no idea how we met, or how she was conceived, and I want it to stay that way.'

Babs nodded. 'I promise.'

And just to be sure, Sadie thought grimly, I'm going to remind you of that promise in the morning.

12

On Saturday morning, after driving Ruth to Abbey Hulton, Polly found herself once again waiting in the Donovans' sitting room. Maria, her dark hair in rollers, was sitting on the black vinyl settee silently filing her nails, while Polly could hear Michael pestering his mother in the kitchen. 'Mum, where's me football boots?'

'Go and look in the coalhouse. I might have put the mucky things in there – they were covered in mud the last time I saw them.'

'Aw, Mum...' There was the sound of the back door slamming.

Ruth had gone upstairs to rummage through her wardrobe. 'I haven't got anything to wear,' she'd complained to her mother when they'd arrived.

Mrs Donovan merely raised her eyebrows in exasperation. 'You come and sit down, love,' she said to Polly. 'She'll soon sort something out.'

The decision to go home for the weekend had been a sudden one. It wasn't until Friday morning that Polly got the letter from Mark, saying that he was coming home.

I'm going to try and get back as often as I can in these early months. I've just realised it's the tennis club dance on Saturday. I don't suppose there's any chance you might be going?

Polly, who hadn't given it much thought, casually mentioned it to Ruth, and had been surprised by her enthusiastic reaction. 'If you do – any possibility of my coming with you?'

'Of course,' Polly said. 'But don't tell me you want to see the horrendous Hilary again?'

Ruth laughed. 'Hardly. But I wouldn't mind going.'

'In that case, we will. I'll ring Sadie and let her know.'

Initially, Polly had been alarmed when her mother told her she had an old friend staying, but then Sadie had laughed – a tinkling, young-sounding laugh – one which Polly later realised she hadn't heard for some time. 'Before you get any wrong ideas,' Sadie said, 'her name is Babs!' Well, that's a relief, Polly thought, but then followed a rising sense of panic. Goodness, I hope that doesn't mean there are two of them 'at it'. She glanced at the small crucifix on the wall at the side of the tiled fireplace, and thought with discomfort how shocked Mrs Donovan would be at those words.

The front door opened and seconds later a heavily built man came into the room, halting as he saw Polly sitting in the armchair. She stood up, guessing that this must be Ruth's father. 'Hello, I'm Polly, Ruth's friend.'

'A pleasure to meet yer,' he said, holding out his hand.

Polly shook it, feeling hardened skin against her own. 'Ruth's upstairs packing,' she explained. 'We're going to a dance near where I live, so she's going to stay overnight.'

117

'A tennis club dance!' Maria smirked. 'Our Ruth's getting above her station.'

'You watch yer lip,' her father said. 'Jealousy will get you nowhere, miss! Where's yer sister?'

'Gone to confession,' Maria said sulkily.

'And why haven't you, may I ask?'

'Don't need to.'

'That's a matter of opinion.'

Polly glanced up at the square-shouldered Irishman, unsure how to react to his blunt manner, but he was already moving away into the kitchen, where she heard him ask, 'Is dinner nearly ready?'

'It won't be long.' Mrs Donovan sounded weary.

'What're we having?'

'Chips and egg.'

'Do me some peas as well and plenty of bread and butter, love. Me stomach feels as if me throat's cut. Where's our Michael?'

'Out the back, putting some dubbin on his football boots.'

As he came back into the room, Ruth came clattering down the stairs. 'Hello, Dad!' She leaned into his arms for a hug. 'All right?'

'Fine. Now, 'ave yer got enough money?'

Ruth nodded. 'I'm okay, thanks. Bye, Mum,' she called.

'See you tomorrow, love. Have a good time.'

As the two girls left, Polly heard Mr Donovan say, 'Get yerself up and give yer mother a hand in the kitchen, Maria.'

'She can peel these potatoes for a start,' Mrs Donovan called. It fascinated Polly, how the family could converse from different rooms. It was so unlike The Gables with its thick walls, which

118

meant that each room was self-contained and private. Her home was also so large compared to Ruth's, that a megaphone would be needed! But, she thought wistfully, living in such close proximity must bring families closer together. She and Sadie, although they were getting on a lot better, could often go for hours without much contact. That would be impossible in the Donovans' house.

'Sorry I was so long,' Ruth said, as they got into the car. She'd had a sudden panic, realising that they would probably be going to the Crown for Sunday lunch. Eventually she'd packed her best red jumper and a new charcoal grey pencil skirt she'd been saving for Christmas. Then that had meant deciding on which court shoes and another pair of nylons; it would be just her luck to ladder the ones she planned to wear at the dance. Her heart was already humming with anticipation at the thought of seeing Mark again. And tonight would prove whether her attraction to him was merely a fleeting one, or whether, as she suspected, she really had 'fallen' in a big way. But what if I have, she thought with despair? I'm a conceited idiot to think he'll even remember me. And if a miracle happened and he liked her, there was the complication of Polly to take into account. Ruth wasn't sure she believed the story that they were only friends.

Polly, of course, had no idea what was passing through Ruth's mind. Her own thoughts were concentrated on what she would find at The Gables. An old friend, Sadie had said. That could only mean someone she'd known in London. But would that be fairly recently, or, and here Polly's pulse quickened, someone who might have known her father? Sadie never talked about him, and so far Polly felt too embarrassed by her mother's promiscuity to even mention his name. But she longed to know how they'd met, the details of their wedding. There wasn't even a photograph. The reason her grandfather had given was that it was difficult to get films during the war. But Polly had seen other such photographs, with the bridegroom and often the best man standing proudly in uniform. It seemed inconceivable that the couple couldn't have found someone, anyone, to record the happy event. She'd asked John Merton if he'd been there, but he'd shaken his head. 'Petrol,' he said briefly, 'you couldn't just travel around the country in those days.' And that, Polly thought, didn't add up either. A man with his influence would surely have organised something.

Maybe, she thought, as she turned into the circular drive and drew up outside the front door, if I steer the conversation back to those war years, I might learn a bit more. And she found herself profoundly hoping that Babs was indeed a *very* old friend.

Earlier that morning, Sadie, while Babs watched with amusement, had been busy making cakes.

'I can't believe it, Sadie! You, of all people, doing the little housewife bit.'

'Oh, shut up and pour us a glass of sherry.'

Babs, with another amused glance at Sadie's apron, flour-covered fingers and absorbed expression, went into the drawing room and returned with two full glasses. She sat at the table and propped her chin on her elbows. 'Seriously though, it hardly goes with your – how shall I put it? – "courtesan" image.'

'If only,' Sadie laughed. 'Now that would have been my ideal profession – they led a very privileged life, you know. But unfortunately, nobody from the royal family has ever crossed my path!'

'I'm glad to hear it,' Babs said with indignation. 'And I hope even you would have drawn a line there!'

Sadie pulled a face at her, then said, 'It's only since I came up here that I've begun to enjoy cooking. It's such a lovely kitchen, with an Aga and everything. All I had in the flat was a Baby Belling – a bit of a difference. The only problem is my waistline's beginning to suffer!'

She lifted a round of pastry and placed it over a dish of apples while Babs said, 'Can't say I've noticed – well, not much anyway.'

Sadie grimaced. 'Thanks a bundle.'

Later, the kitchen cleared, they went to relax in the drawing room. 'At least that's lunch organised,' Sadie said with relief, 'all in order for when my prissy daughter gets here.'

'Is she? Prissy, I mean?' Babs looked at her with surprise.

'Well, I suppose that's a bit unfair. But when I first got here, and in the months following the funeral, believe me it was like living with a waxwork! You could sense her resentment even in the way she walked.'

Babs gazed at her then, glass in hand, slowly swirled the pale liquid of her second sherry.

'Don't you think that's understandable?' she said awkwardly. 'You know, after you...'

'Abandoned her, you mean?' Sadie's voice suddenly became hard, as she snapped, 'Go on – say it, Babs. I know you've always thought it. But it was hardly abandoning the kid, leaving her in a place like this!' She waved a hand at the comfortable, almost opulent room.

'I've never understood how you could do it,' Babs said. 'After all, she was only twelve months old.'

But Sadie didn't have a chance to reply, because just then there was the sound of a car drawing up outside. They both jumped up and went to the bay window. 'Which one?' whispered Babs.

'The girl with the straight brown hair,' Sadie said, and turning led the way into the hall.

'You look well,' Sadie said, as Polly dumped her case on the floor.

'I'm fine, thanks. Hello, Babs.'

'Good to meet you both,' Babs said, but she was staring with undisguised curiosity at Polly.

Sadie laughed. 'Not much like me, is she?'

Babs shook her head. 'Who does she take after, then? I can't see much of André, either.'

Polly's spirits lifted. So this friend *had* known her father! 'I'm supposed to be like my French grandmother. There's a photo of her in the drawing room.'

Babs smiled. 'I must look at it more closely.'

'It smells as if someone's been baking,' Polly said.

'Always hungry, this one,' Sadie said. 'Yet she never puts on an ounce. Anyway, lunch will be ready in half an hour.'

Babs moved aside so that the two girls could take their cases upstairs. 'Not exactly lovey-dovey, are you?' she commented, as she followed Sadie into the kitchen.

'How do you mean?'

'Well, no hug. Not even a kiss on the cheek. I thought you said you were getting on better.'

'We are,' Sadie said, 'compared to before. But we haven't quite reached that stage yet.' She went to the refrigerator and began to take out the ingredients for a salad. 'Something happened,' she said quietly. 'But I'll need a few drinks, before I can tell you about it.'

'Tonight, then?'

Sadie nodded. 'Once they've gone out.'

The annual tennis club dance was held at a small hotel situated some distance outside Stafford. It was an intimate affair, with the number attending being small, but, as Hilary was known to comment, 'very select'. And it was interesting, Polly always thought, to meet other members' wives and husbands. She and Ruth arrived fairly early, and were glad to see that Hazel was already there.

'Anita's not coming,' Hazel said. 'Apparently there's something on at the university.'

'You're looking very glam!' Polly commented.

Hazel looked down at her peacock blue cocktail dress and grinned. 'I've got my eye on someone, haven't I? Look – over there in the corner – the tall one with fair hair. He's a new member.' The other two girls glanced over. 'But you can keep your greedy hands off him, he's mine!'

123

'You hope!' Polly laughed, and then turned as she saw Mark come in. She went to greet him, and Ruth saw them hug each other.

Mark followed Polly back to the two girls and after greeting Hazel, said, 'Hello, Ruth.' He smiled, and as her eyes met his direct gaze, her heart did a somersault. 'Are you staying with Polly again?'

She nodded, and Polly said, 'Mum's got a friend staying too. Babs, her name is – someone she used to know in London.'

'Gosh, I bet there's a lot of gossip going on with four of you there.'

'You, Mark Eldon, are a male chauvinist pig. I suppose the word would be "discussion" if we were four men?'

'Naturally!'

'Well, you can just take Ruth on the floor for that,' Polly retorted. 'She'll soon sort you out, won't you, Ruth?'

Startled, Ruth entered into the teasing. 'Just leave him to me,' she said, 'I scare everyone!'

'You don't look very scary to me,' Mark said. 'Come on, it's a waltz.' He ushered her on to the tiny dance floor, and as he slipped his arm around her waist said, 'Jolly nice dress, by the way.'

Ruth felt a warm glow. Green had always been her colour, and the silky finish of the fabric made it feel really feminine. Also, to her gratification, the bodice was cut in such a way that her breasts seemed much fuller than they actually were. Although, she thought with some guilt, that could be because of the new Wonderbra she was wearing. Whatever the reason, Ruth knew that seeing

124

Mark again had dispelled any doubts she had. He was tall, he was dark, he was handsome; in fact, he was the image of the Mills & Boon heroes that the twins were always swooning over. More importantly to Ruth, he was an intellectual, soon to be an Oxford graduate, and that exactly matched her criteria. I've got to find out, she thought with desperation as the warmth of his arm, his firm clasp of her hand all intensified the emotions sweeping through her. She decided to be direct. 'What's the situation with you and Polly, then?'

Mark looked down at her with surprise, noticing again those marvellously intelligent eyes. 'How do you mean?' he countered.

'Come on, Mark, everyone's been asking her. I'd just like to hear your version.'

Mark grinned down at her. 'We're illicit lovers!' he whispered.

'Pull the other one. You wouldn't be telling me if you were,' Ruth laughed, and he said, 'I should hope not!' The music stopped but he made no move to lead her from the floor.

'So,' she persisted, 'there's nothing between you? Serious, I mean.'

'Well, I could be tempted,' he admitted. 'We get on really well, Polly and I. But the truthful answer to your question is, no.' He gazed down at her, a quizzical look in his eyes. 'Why the interest? Is she employing you as a spy?'

Ruth laughed. 'No, nothing like that.' Relief flooded through her – that's all I wanted to know, she thought. The band struck up again and as the vocalist, blonde and glamorous in a strapless gold lamé dress, began to sing 'Mr Sandman, bring me a dream', they swept into a quickstep.

Mark murmured, 'Have you got a dream, Ruth?'

'I most certainly have. I want to run my own school. You, Mark Eldon, are dancing with a future headmistress.'

'Gosh, I'm quaking in my boots already!' He expertly guided her to avoid another couple. 'Actually, I can just imagine you. I saw how ruthless you were on the tennis court.'

She smiled up at him, 'I have my romantic dreams too.' Their eyes met in a long, considering look, and with delight Ruth saw interest in Mark's eyes. Perhaps, she hoped, even more than that.

Polly, meanwhile, had been dancing with Adrian, who unfortunately, because of his terrible complexion, rarely found a partner. As the music ended, she stood watching her two best friends walk towards her, and suddenly saw the light in Ruth's eyes, the softness of her smile. So that was why she'd been so keen to come! Now, am I jealous? Polly wondered. And in all honesty, she wasn't sure.

13

Once the girls had left for the dance, Sadie and Babs made themselves comfortable in the drawing room. 'Music?' Sadie offered, and began to search among the collection of records. Eventually she extracted one, and seconds later the strains of 'A String of Pearls' filled the room.

'This will bring back memories for both of us.'

'Such a shame, what happened to Glenn Miller,' Babs said. 'They never discovered the truth about his plane disappearing, did they?'

'No. Another decent man's life lost,' Sadie said with bitterness, going over to the sideboard. 'Drink?'

'I'll have a gin and tonic, please – although I thought you mentioned opening a bottle of wine. Remember, you were going to tell me something?'

Sadie turned. Babs, looking rather pretty in a pale pink cardigan over her white blouse, was looking at her expectantly.

'I am, but there's no reason we can't start off with G&Ts.'

'Oh, I see. Going to be one of those nights, is it? Suits me!'

Leaving Babs listening dreamily to the music, Sadie poured them both a generous measure of gin, and then went to the kitchen to slice a lemon and fetch ice. A few minutes later, she handed Babs her glass, and taking her own drink, sat in the armchair opposite.

'This is such an impressive room,' Babs said, looking around. 'I still can't get over how you've landed on your feet.'

'It's not permanent, though.' Sadie explained in detail the unusual terms of John Merton's will.

'Phew, that's a stunner. When is she twenty-one?'

'Next November.'

'And?'

Sadie shrugged. 'I've no idea what will happen.'

'Would you want to stay up here? Permanently, I mean?'

Sadie hesitated. 'I'm not sure, and that's the truth, Babs. Part of me would like to – I mean I'd be daft to want to give up all this. But I've got to be realistic. I don't suppose Polly will want me here, and in any case there's always the possibility she might meet someone and want to get married.'

'I suppose you had to give up your flat?' Babs drained her glass, and put it on the coffee table, then leaned back in her chair, crossing her slim legs. She was looking, Sadie noticed, far more relaxed than when she'd arrived.

'I had no choice. It was only rented.'

'At least,' Babs said with relief, 'I'm okay to stay in our house while the children are of school age.' She looked reflectively at Sadie. 'I wonder about you and André – whether, if he'd survived the war, *your* marriage would have lasted.'

'What you really mean,' Sadie said with a wry smile, 'is that you wonder whether I'd have been faithful to him!'

'Well, you can't blame me.'

'I like to think I would,' Sadie said. 'I certainly hope so.'

'You really think one man would have been enough for you?'

Babs's tone was disbelieving, but Sadie said quietly, 'If that one man was André, then the answer is yes.'

'Has there never been anyone else – not in all these years? I mean,' Babs said, 'surely there must have been one or two who were special?'

Sadie smiled. 'Of course, in a way.'

Babs persisted, 'But you've never been tempted to get married again?'

Sadie shook her head, getting up and stretching out her hand for Babs's empty glass. 'Another?' Babs nodded, and Sadie went over to the sideboard. As she mixed the drinks, she considered. *Had* she ever been tempted? There had been a couple of proposals certainly, serious ones, from men she'd become fond of. James, a businessman from Manchester, witty, charming and an experienced lover, had been really keen. And so had Eric; a quiet, rather bookish man. But she hadn't loved them. And Sadie wasn't willing to give up her independence, her freedom, for anything less.

'I've had my chances,' she said over her shoulder, 'but no, not really.' She took the drinks over, and went to change the record. 'What do you fancy? Frank Sinatra?'

'Oh, yes, please. God, that man knows how to sing.'

'It's the inflection in his voice, the way he puts a song over,' Sadie commented.

'Whatever he does, he makes me go all soft inside.'

'Pity we haven't got a couple of fellas here, then!'

Babs laughed and agreed. Later, Sadie opened a bottle of Sauternes, and they talked, at times with Babs becoming emotional, of their lives over the previous years. Then eventually, as a silence fell, Babs said gently, 'Okay, Sadie, we've avoided it long enough. Isn't there something you were going to tell me? With Polly, I mean?'

Sadie looked down, feeling momentary panic, but her need to tell someone, *anyone*, was too

129

strong to resist. There had been very little in her life that she was ashamed of, but what had happened in The Gables that night still lay heavily on her conscience. And, she thought, Catholics seemed to set great store on the benefits of confession, of unburdening themselves. Babs was no priest – but she *was* the oldest and closest friend Sadie had.

And so, haltingly, with Babs gazing at her, Sadie began to try and explain how someone with her experience of men could have made such a dreadful error of judgment. 'I was so lonely, Babs. Three months I'd been up here, with a daughter who was so withdrawn she was like a zombie. I didn't know a soul. I missed the buzz of London so much, that and my job and my cosy little flat.' She leaned forward, pouring herself another glass of wine, and took several sips. 'Also,' she said flatly, 'although I know you won't understand this – I missed my sex life. Anyway, one night, after yet another silent, boring day, I just flipped. I went out in desperation, met this chap in a bar, and brought him home. I knew Polly would be in bed, and thought if we were quiet, he'd be gone by the time she woke up, and she'd be none the wiser.' She paused, while Babs, wide-eyed, silently waited. 'Unfortunately, he'd had a fair amount to drink, and at a certain moment, had to go to the bathroom. But when he came out,' and now Sadie found her voice faltering. She took a deep breath. 'He blundered into Polly's room by mistake.'

'Oh, my God!' Babs covered her mouth with her hand in horror.

Sadie could only stare at her helplessly. 'Can

you imagine it, Babs? At the age of seventeen, having led a sheltered life, waking up to find a naked, middle-aged man clambering beneath your sheets? I'll never forget her screams,' Sadie said, shuddering as the painful memory flashed before her. 'She must have thought he was an intruder about to rape her! But that wasn't all. This man, this *stupid* bastard, once I'd pulled him away from her, tried to turn his mistake into something else – started muttering about a mother *and* her daughter. Even someone as naïve as Polly could guess what he meant.'

'Bloody hell, Sadie!' The shock on Babs's face was palpable. 'What sewer did he crawl out of?'

'I don't know. I must have been insane. Where I got the strength from I don't know, but the sod ended up on the drive with his clothes thrown after him!'

'And Polly?'

Sadie winced, remembering how she'd returned to Polly's bedroom to find her sitting up in bed, still trembling and swathed protectively in her eiderdown. Sadie had never been able to forget the expression of disgust and contempt on her daughter's face. 'She shut herself in her room. Wouldn't let me in, wouldn't even talk to me.'

'But...' and Babs almost stammered over the question. 'She was all right? I mean he...'

'He didn't get a chance, not with the racket she was making, and I was there in seconds.'

'The poor kid!' For a moment Babs, her face pale with shock, was silent. 'What happened after that?'

'Well, no matter how much I apologised, she just froze me out. So eventually I thought – what the hell! I decided that if I was going to be stuck up here for the next few years, I was going to lead the life I wanted.'

'Which meant bringing men back?' Babs was staring at her with disbelief.

'If I wished to, yes!' Sadie's voice was defiant. With a sick feeling of emptiness she got up and went over to the window. She drew back the heavily tasselled brocade curtains, and said in an effort to change the subject. 'Look at the sky, Babs. Don't you think the stars are mysterious?'

'They're not nearly as much of a mystery to me as you are!'

Stung by the sharp tone, Sadie turned round. In a shaky voice she said, 'You must think I'm a terrible mother.'

Babs, looking down at her hands, didn't – or couldn't – answer.

For a few moments there was silence, then Sadie said in a tight voice, 'Time for bed, I think.' Silently, they both collected the glasses and debris from the coffee table, taking them into the kitchen. When a few moments later, they began to climb the wide stairs, she said in a tense voice, 'Babs, please don't ever utter a word about what I've just told you – not to Polly, not to anyone. I'm not asking for my sake, but for hers.'

'I promise,' Babs said, but her tone was decidedly cool. Seconds later, Sadie, going into her bedroom and closing the door behind her, leaned wearily against it. Instead of a feeling of peace, of a burden shared, her confession had simply

132

tarnished their friendship. Perhaps I was wrong, she thought. Perhaps the presence of a priest was essential after all.

14

The following morning, while the girls slept in, Sadie and Babs sat opposite each other in the breakfast room. Sadie, cigarette in hand, black coffee before her, watched Babs pop the last morsel of her thickly buttered toast and marmalade in her mouth, and begin to pour herself a cup of tea. The atmosphere between them was palpably uneasy, and suddenly Sadie couldn't stand it any longer. 'About last night...' she began

Babs interrupted her, 'What about it?'

'I wish I'd never told you.'

Babs gazed at her for a moment. 'What you forget, Sadie, is that I'm a mother too. And I have a teenage daughter.' She held up a hand as Sadie began to speak. 'No, let me finish. I know you feel awful about what happened, but do you know what really gets to me? That you carried on taking the same risk. You went on bringing these men back here, to the house that Polly grew up in, to what should be her one safe refuge in the world. How on earth do you think she feels about it?'

Sadie stubbed out the butt of her cigarette on the glass ashtray. 'As any daughter would, I expect. But the damage was already done. The following morning we had a massive row, and the next thing I knew there was a locksmith here putting a lock on her bedroom door.' She shrugged. 'So after that, what did I have to lose?'

'The small matter of her trust?' There was a wealth of sarcasm in Babs's tone.

'Oh, you're as bad as she is,' Sadie snapped.

Babs tightened her lips. 'Well, if that's your attitude, there's no point in discussing it any further.' She got up from the table, and began to pick up the dishes.

'Leave them,' Sadie said shortly. 'The papers are in the drawing room. I think we need a bit of space between us, don't you?'

Babs moved away, and then turned at the door and said with an obvious effort, 'Still, things seem to have settled down now, with Polly, I mean. I didn't notice a lot of animosity between you yesterday.'

Sadie went past her into the kitchen, turned on the taps and squirted washing-up liquid into the water. 'Oh, eventually, I think we came to understand each other better. And I've compromised. I no longer "indulge" myself when she's at home.'

'A pity you didn't behave like that from the outset!'

'For God's sake, Babs, you sound like a vicar's wife. To be honest, I don't think I need you or anyone else to tell me how to live my life!'

The two women faced each other, Sadie's expression one of hurt and anger. But before Babs could leave, the door opened and Polly, still in her pink quilted dressing gown came in, yawning.

'Good morning, Polly,' Babs said, while Sadie dried her hands and picked up the kettle. 'Tea?'

'Good morning. Yes, please.' Polly reached up to a cupboard, and taking out a box of cornflakes shook a generous amount into a bowl, then took it into the breakfast room. She picked up a jug of milk, poured it over, and began to eat.

Babs followed her in. 'Did you have a good time?'

'Yes, fine, thanks. I think Ruth's still asleep.'

'No, she isn't.' Ruth came through the door, but unlike Polly, she was fully dressed. 'I meant to ask – sorry to be a nuisance, Pol, but what time's Mass?'

Polly put a hand to her mouth. 'Oh, gosh, I forgot. There's one at eleven and if we hurry up, we can just make it. What do you want for breakfast?'

'It's okay, I can get myself some of those cornflakes.' She glanced at her watch. 'I've just time if I want to go to communion.'

'How do you mean?' Babs asked.

'We have to fast for one hour before.'

You will, Polly thought. I won't be able to go, because I haven't been to confession. And realising just how much she'd allowed her religion to lapse came as a slight shock. Why, she hadn't been to church since she'd made her Easter Duties! But she hadn't got time to linger, and after a gulp of the tea that Sadie brought in, Polly hurried upstairs. Ten minutes later she reappeared, dressed in a warm tweed suit, and carrying a headscarf.

'Ready, Ruth?'

'Sure am.'

'We'll see you both at the Crown,' Polly called over her shoulder, and seconds later they were gone.

135

Sadie and Babs finished clearing up, and then went into the drawing room to look at the Sunday papers. Despite the coal fire in the grate of the ornate mahogany fireplace, the atmosphere between them was distinctly chilly. At last Sadie said, 'Come on, Babs. We've known each other too long for this.'

Babs put the newspaper down on her lap and looked a bit sheepish. 'I'm sorry, Sadie,' she said. 'I didn't mean to go all stiff-necked on you. After all, you were just the same in the old days. It's me who's changed, I suppose.'

'Not that much, Babs. You were always what people call "respectable". Just...'

'Less judgmental?' Babs sighed. 'Yes, I know. It comes of getting older, I suppose.'

'Still friends, then?'

Babs nodded. 'Still friends.'

It wasn't until after they'd returned to The Gables, after an enjoyable lunch, that Polly had a chance to be alone with Babs. Ruth had immediately run upstairs to pack her bag, while Sadie, pleading a headache, had gone to lie down. Babs was in the drawing room, leafing through an issue of *Staffordshire Life*, and glanced up with a smile as Polly came in.

'I was hoping to catch you,' Polly said, suddenly feeling a little shy.

'Oh?' Babs waited, and encouraged by her friendly tone, Polly went to sit opposite. She cast an uneasy glance over her shoulder, aware that time was short. 'It's just that there's so much I want to know – about my father, I mean. You knew him, didn't you?'

'Yes, I did.'

Polly hesitated. 'It's just that Sadie rarely mentions him, and I don't like to ask. I mean, I don't want to upset her.' It was a sentence she'd previously rehearsed. After all, she could hardly tell Babs the real reason. And Polly wasn't even sure what that was.

'And you think talking about him might?' Babs studied her, and Polly saw sudden sympathy in her eyes. 'It is twenty years ago, you know. I don't think you need to worry too much about that.'

'But I hardly know anything,' Polly persisted. 'How they met, for instance?'

'Your grandfather never told you?'

Polly shook her head. 'He said all he knew was that they'd met in London, at some sort of party. That they got married down there, and he couldn't be at the wedding because of petrol shortages. And Sadie never talks about the past.' For a moment Babs was silent, and Polly noticed her eyes narrow slightly.

'Were you there? When they met, I mean.'

'I certainly was.' Babs became reflective. 'I can remember it so clearly. André arrived with the rest of his aircrew. They'd obviously been somewhere before, and were a good-natured bunch, if a bit noisy. All of them, that is, except André. I can see him now – he looked so handsome in his RAF uniform. But then,' Babs gave a nostalgic smile, 'so many of them did. Anyway, although he'd obviously been drinking like the rest of them, he was withdrawn, quiet. In fact, the others were worried about him.'

137

Polly's eyes widened. 'Why?'

'Because he'd become sunk in depression. "Gone into a dark place," one of them told me. It's difficult to explain to someone who didn't live through those times,' Babs said. 'So many of the servicemen we met were traumatised by what they'd seen, what they'd done. But with André, it was losing his mother so unexpectedly that had knocked him off course. It was one death he couldn't cope with, not on top of everything else.'

Babs paused, and Polly said, 'I know he was very close to my grandmother.'

Babs nodded. 'Don't get me wrong. The other chaps said he'd always been the strong one, someone the others turned to. And that's why they were at a loss to know how to help him. But then,' Babs leaned forward, 'then,' she repeated, 'he met your mother. And Sadie turned him around. Make no mistake; she was the one who brought him out of it. You should always be grateful for that, Polly. Anyway, she went and fell for him, didn't she? Like a ton of bricks. There was never anyone to touch André after that.'

'And so they got married. Were you there? Did you go to the wedding?'

Polly's voice was eager, and Babs smiled. 'I was a flaming bridesmaid. Literally – in a red dress!' Seeing Polly's startled expression, Babs said, 'You don't know the half of it. What it was like, I mean. Sadie wore a blue two-piece. No clothing coupons,' she explained. 'We didn't have any left, so we just had to make do with what we'd got. And we didn't have much time...'

Suddenly her voice faltered, and Polly said

quickly, 'How do you mean?'

Babs recovered herself. 'Well, André got a special licence and it all happened in about three weeks. People couldn't plan ahead like they can now, nor get leave when they wanted it, not with a war on.'

'So they saw a chance and took it?'

'Something like that, yes. It was a nice little church – Catholic of course, André insisted on that.'

'Had they known each other long – before they got married, I mean?'

Babs shook her head. 'A matter of months. But that was by no means unusual, not in those days.'

'But why are there no wedding photos? I've always wondered. My grandfather said it was because people couldn't get films, but...'

Babs smiled. 'That was true, but most managed to record their weddings, for heaven's sake. Sandy was in charge of those. Sandy McBane – he was a wireless operator. Anyway, he certainly took some, but unfortunately there was an air raid that night, and he forgot to take the camera to the shelter with him. The place he was staying in got a direct hit – and that was the end of your mother's wedding photographs.'

'Oh, that's awful! Was anyone killed?' Polly stared at her in horror.

'No, luckily they'd all got out in time. But I'm afraid poor Sandy did get killed a few weeks later – he was shot down over the Channel.'

Shocked, Polly was silent for a moment, and then she said, 'My father wasn't with the same squadron when he was killed, was he? Grandad said something about him being transferred to another unit, to Intelligence?'

'That's right, quite soon after the wedding. I remember Sandy telling me about it.'

They both turned as they heard a clatter in the hall, and Babs said quickly, 'You know, Polly, you should talk to Sadie. You should take your questions to *her*.'

Before Polly could answer, Ruth popped her head around the door. 'I'm ready if you are.'

Polly reluctantly got up. 'Fine,' she said. She went over to Babs, and after warmly kissing her cheek, said, 'Thank you, Babs. I'm so glad to have met you.' She turned and said to Ruth, 'I'll just nip up to my room, I won't be long.' Once there, before collecting her things, she went to sit for a moment on the velvet chaise longue by the window. Listening to Babs talk about her father, her revelation of his grief and depression had moved her deeply. Her grandfather had referred in the past to the strong bond between his beloved Emilie and her only son. And Polly's heart went out to the young RAF officer, embroiled in a bitter war, exhausted from combat, only to come home to the funeral of his mother. She stared out of the window at the garden, at the trees, which although their leaves were beginning to fall, still retained enough of their glorious autumn foliage to give colour and charm. This was a view that her father must often have gazed at, just as she was now. And again, as she had so many times before, Polly wished with all her heart that she could have known him.

Not once during the next few days did Babs refer to her conversation with Polly. Sadie drove Babs around the area, showing her the colourful barges on the Trent & Mersey canal that flowed through Stone. And they both, rather guiltily in Babs's case, spent a considerable amount of money shopping. On a couple of evenings they went out to dinner in Stafford, although Sadie, not wanting to risk any embarrassing encounters, was careful to avoid any of her usual haunts. And, by keeping their conversation light, they spent the remainder of Babs's visit renewing and enjoying their old friendship.

And so it was with mutual regret that they sat for the last time in the breakfast room. As always, Sadie just had black coffee and a couple of cigarettes, while Babs fortified herself for the journey ahead.

It was not until they'd finished, that Babs said, 'Sadie?'

'Mmn.' Sadie tipped back her head and blew a perfect smoke ring. 'See that – I haven't lost my touch.'

Babs laughed. 'Don't ever change, Sadie. You know, I don't think you'll ever be middle-aged.'

Sadie shuddered. 'Don't even mention the word! Sorry, what was it you wanted to say?'

There was a moment before Babs answered. 'There's something,' she said, 'that I thought I should tell you.'

Sadie heard the hesitation in her voice and her hand became stilled.

She lowered it and stubbed out her cigarette. 'This sounds serious.'

'It is, in a way.' Babs floundered for a moment, and then said, 'It's just that Polly came to see me, just before she left. I got the impression that she'd been waiting for a chance to find me on my own. It was after we got back from the Crown,' she explained. 'You'd gone for a lie down, and Ruth was packing.'

'I see.' Sadie waited, anxiety rising within her. Had Babs blurted out something? Was that what she wanted to confess? Her voice was tight as she said, 'What did she want?'

'To talk about André.'

The alarm Sadie felt must have shown, because Babs said quickly, 'Don't worry, I didn't let you down. She said her grandfather had told her you and he met at a party, and I left it at that.'

'Thanks.'

'It's just that I wondered why you never talk to the girl. About André, I mean? To be honest, Sadie, she shouldn't have to come to someone she hardly knows. After all, she is his daughter.'

Sadie got up abruptly, and going over to the sink, stared out of the window. Then, aware that Babs was waiting for an answer, she struggled to compose herself before she turned. 'I can't,' she said simply. 'I daren't let down my guard, give Polly a chance to get too close.'

Babs stared at her in bewilderment. 'Why ever not?'

'Because,' Sadie said painfully, 'I know that once I do, once she feels able to, she's going to ask me why I left her. Why I didn't stay, like any normal mother, and bring her up myself.'

'And you don't think you could make her

understand.' Babs's words were a statement rather than a question.

'I've failed with you, and you're not emotionally involved. I can't risk it, Babs. As you've seen, we've established a fairly decent relationship, at least on the surface. Perhaps,' Sadie gave a wry smile, 'in your opinion, more than I deserve.'

'She's never thrown it at you – during a row, for instance?'

Sadie shook her head. 'Not yet, she's never said a word.'

Later, after watching the green Morris Minor leave the circular drive, Sadie turned to go back indoors. Suddenly the prospect of all those empty hours to fill, ones when because of the weather she couldn't even garden, was dispiriting. She wondered whether Babs was right. She certainly didn't need the money, but maybe she should think about finding some sort of part-time job. 'And wouldn't that be one in the eye for Mrs Booth,' she murmured as she went back into the drawing room.

15

Paris, October 1961

The bedroom, large and old-fashioned, was still in darkness when Jules Giscard awoke. He lay still, instantly alert. Instinctively he knew it was vital not to let the dream elude him, to slip away,

143

and somehow, by sheer force of will, he managed at last to succeed. Jules turned over, closing his eyes. It was the voice that lingered most – a woman's voice. Soft and tender, she'd been singing to him, a song all schoolchildren in France learned, the lilting 'Sur le Pont d'Avignon'. And there had been an image too, an image of a woman. Her brown hair had been swept up into a chignon, her large eyes dark and gentle. There had been such warmth, such happiness in her expression that he'd wanted to stay within the dream for ever. And with a feeling of loss, it was some time before he gradually drifted off to sleep again.

The following morning was damp, with a keen wind as Jules walked to the pâtisserie to buy fresh croissants. The chill was beginning to make his leg ache, and he was limping slightly as he returned across the small square, noticing with regret that the trees were already beginning to lose their leaves. Shivering slightly, he let himself into the apartment where he had lived for so many years, and went into the kitchen, welcomed by the aroma of freshly brewed coffee.

'Good morning, Papa.'

'Good morning, Nicolas. It's very cold outdoors.'

'At least it's Saturday, and we don't have to go to work.' Nicolas, his dark hair damp after his shower, turned to smile at him.

Jules smiled, but was thoughtful as he put the croissants on to a blue and white china dish, and carried it to the table. Already there was a selection of jams, a slab of yellow butter, napkins and plates. 'You forgot the knives,' he said absently, and going over to the heavily carved French dresser, took out from a drawer what they needed.

Nicolas glanced at him. 'You seem a little *distrait.*'

'Distracted,' Jules automatically corrected him. It was a firm rule that only English was spoken between them. As he had explained to Nicolas many years ago, if he wished to become bilingual it was essential to use the second language on a regular basis. 'I'll tell you later,' he said. 'Come, enjoy.' Both men ate in companionable silence, and it wasn't until they were drinking their coffee, and Jules had lit a cigarette, that he began at last to speak.

'I had a dream last night,' he said. 'It disturbed me.'

Nicolas looked at him with concern. 'A nightmare?'

Jules shook his head. 'No, not a nightmare – it was more of an emotional experience.'

'Can you remember it? Tell me.'

Slowly, choosing his words, Jules explained what had happened, how much it had affected him. 'She was so beautiful,' he said in a wistful tone.

Nicolas raised an eyebrow, and Jules said, 'Not that sort of dream at all, young man!' He paused for a moment. 'The strange thing is that she looked very much like that girl. You remember – in July, when we went to the café and tried to see her again?'

'The one with brown hair? The one you heard laughing?'

'Yes.'

'That could explain it, then,' Nicolas said. 'Maybe you were simply dreaming about *her*.'

Jules shook his head. 'No, it isn't as simple as that. Although there was a likeness, this woman was definitely older, I think possibly in her mid-thirties.'

Nicolas frowned. 'And in the dream, is that all you can remember – that she was singing?'

Jules nodded. 'But she was singing to me, just me, and the way I felt – I remember there was an emotion I can only describe as love. But not the sort of love a man feels for a woman.' He shrugged. 'I find it difficult to explain.'

There was a moment's silence, then Nicolas said, 'You think there is some significance in this, don't you?'

Jules gazed at him, his eyes shadowing as he said, 'I don't know. But I admit I'm curious.'

It was four weeks later, when Jules dreamed again. As before, he woke suddenly and saw from the luminous dial of his alarm clock that it was 5.30 a.m. Hauling himself up to lean back against the wooden headboard, he reached out to his bedside table and, with a shaky hand, lit a cigarette in the darkness, and inhaled deeply. The fear, the horror of the dream was still with him – the roar of the large car; its ghostly image grey in the darkness as it hurtled round the bend. There had been no headlights, no time to evade, and even now he could feel the force of the brutal impact and, as he was thrown against the verge of the road, excruciating pain as his head smashed into a rock. His breathing still shallow and ragged,

146

Jules lifted a hand to his scalp, touching and exploring the areas of puckered skin. Then slowly, he let his fingers wander down his face, tracing the familiar scars beneath his beard. It had always been assumed that his injuries had been caused in a road accident, but there had never been any proof, any evidence. Had this just been revealed to him? Was it possible that a dream could reveal the truth? For a long time Jules remained deep in thought, and then suddenly became very still when he remembered the date.

And when he told Nicolas the following evening, the tall young man became thoughtful. He poured red wine to drink with their evening meal, and said, 'You know, this is all very strange. As for this dream occurring on the anniversary of the actual event, if it was portraying that...' He shook his head in puzzlement. 'And why now, after all these years – you have never dreamed like this before. Why not at the beginning, when you told me you tried so desperately to remember?'

'I don't know.' Jules frowned as he began to spoon from a large rustic dish of succulent lamb and herbs. 'This smells wonderful, Madame Caplat has surpassed herself.'

Nicolas grinned. 'I told you she was a good cook.'

'Yes, well you had inside information, didn't you, having romanced her daughter.' Jules shot him a sharp glance. 'I take it that's all over now?'

Nicolas shrugged. 'There were no hearts broken, Papa. We were just good friends, that's all.'

'No such thing for a Frenchman,' Jules retorted. 'A pretty girl and friendship only?'

Nicolas laughed, and then began to eat with relish. 'You're right. This is good. How was your day?'

'Quiet,' Jules admitted. 'Which was just as well – I'm afraid I found it difficult to concentrate.'

'Thinking about the dream?'

Jules nodded. He gazed at the young man opposite. With his thin, intense face, high cheekbones and unruly black curly hair, his resemblance to his mother was at times almost a painful reminder. Jules picked up his glass and swirled it thoughtfully. 'Something is happening, Nicolas. I feel it.'

'Do you think losing Maman so suddenly could have contributed?'

'Perhaps,' Jules said. The bout of pneumonia that had taken Gabrielle had been sudden and swift, and the shock had affected him deeply. He felt his heart twist with anguish. No man ever had a more loyal and affectionate wife. He was silent for a few moments, then admitted, 'You could be right. After all, it was shortly after the funeral that I had that experience with the girl.'

'I should watch how you put that!' Nicolas smiled affectionately at him. 'Don't go saying it to anyone else, will you?' Jules laughed, but his expression became serious, his conversation abstracted. Eventually Nicolas lapsed into silence until he said, as he began to clear away their plates after they had finished, 'I believe that shock can affect people in quite dramatic ways. Maybe Maman's death will prove to be the catalyst you needed.' He turned away, not wanting the other man to see how even referring to her loss still had the power

148

to upset him.

'And wouldn't that be a tragedy,' Jules said grimly. 'If it had to take something like that to...' he didn't complete the sentence. But, he thought later as he got up to fetch a ripe Camembert, he was absolutely convinced of one thing. Something *was* happening. Could he dare to believe, that he was, at last, after all these years, on the verge of a breakthrough?

16

Since her grandfather died, Christmas had been a rather subdued affair, and this year Polly was determined to change things. So she tentatively suggested they might forgo their Christmas Day lunch, and instead go to help out at the church hall, where a festive meal was being prepared for local parishioners. Since Ruth's visit, Polly had been making an effort to attend Mass more regularly, and on her first weekend home had seen a notice in the church porch appealing for helpers. 'It's for people who would otherwise be alone,' she explained. 'Elderly people or those in poor health who haven't any family.'

She and Sadie were in the drawing room, decorating the fir tree that stood majestically in the bay window. Sadie frowned, as she hooked a golden bauble on to one of its wide-spreading branches and stood back to study the effect. Polly was gazing down at a tiny white and silver doll with a china face and gossamer wings, remembering how, as a small child, she'd thought it was a real fairy. 'But only if it's the two of us,' she said, standing on a chair to perch the doll on the top of the tree. 'I don't want to leave you here on your own.'

Sadie felt a sudden ache in her throat. It was a simple sentiment, and yet there was a thought, a kindness in the words, that wouldn't have been there the previous year. And the fact that she'd been affected by the words revealed how much their relationship had improved. But Polly's suggestion didn't appeal at all. I can just imagine it, she thought with dismay. All those worthy matrons; having my hands in hot dishwater for hours ... and then she glanced at Polly and saw the eagerness in her eyes. 'Okay,' Sadie said with reluctance. 'I'll come with you. But,' she warned, 'I'm not wearing one of those hideous crossover overalls for anyone, not even you!'

Polly laughed. 'That's brilliant. I'll let Father Doyle know tomorrow.'

'And,' Sadie warned, 'I shall expect to spend Boxing Day in splendid sloth. That means chocolate, booze, cigarettes – the lot. You're not going to the hunt out at Woore, are you?'

Polly shook her head. 'Not me. I don't agree with hunting. I agree with Oscar Wide, "The unspeakable in full pursuit of the uneatable." How can anyone call it a good day out, when the sole purpose is to chase a terrified animal and kill it? Maybe foxes do have to be culled, but it's hardly sport!'

'That's one thing we do agree on,' Sadie said. 'Anyway, why do you ask? It's quite a drive.'

150

'I was invited to go, but I refused.' Sadie saw the suspicious look in Polly's eyes. 'Yes,' she said, 'you're quite right. It was a man, someone I met in Stafford. And, before you ask, there's no danger of him coming here. I don't do that any more, not when you're at home.'

'Well, that's something, anyway.' There was an edge to Polly's voice, and Sadie mentally cursed herself for bringing up the subject.

Polly, as she continued decorating the tree, was hoping that Father Doyle hadn't heard any gossip about Sadie. Certainly there wouldn't be too many people able or willing to leave their homes and families on Christmas Day. But Polly needn't have worried. Her offer of help was accepted with enthusiasm.

She went to Midnight Mass and then on Christmas morning, after a breakfast of bacon, eggs and warm oatcakes, they relaxed before a crackling log fire in the drawing room and began to unwrap their gifts to each other. To her delight, there was a cream cashmere scarf for Polly, and Sadie, who adored perfume, was delighted with her bottle of Chanel No. 5. Polly also received a box of chocolates from Ruth, Liberty hankies from Anita, and a generous book token from Hazel. A few days before, the postman had delivered a small parcel from Hereford, and Sadie had managed to resist the temptation to peep inside. Now, she tore off the Christmas paper, and found a journal diary. With it was a note.

Write in it each day your feelings about Polly, about being a mother, about having her as your daughter.

151

Then at the end of the year, you'll be able to see just how far you've come. Regard it as a challenge!

Love,

Babs

Sadie smiled; that was just like Babs, a subtle reprimand wrapped in tissue paper!

At eleven thirty, Sadie drove them both down to the church hall. Carefully, she and Polly took two cardboard boxes filled with home-made mince pies out of the boot, and carried them in. The sound of 'Jingle Bells' met them, coming from a red Dansette record player on the stage, and the small hall was lavishly decorated with colourful paper chains and home-made streamers, which must, Sadie thought, date from before the war. But there were balloons too, and she had to admit that everywhere looked very festive. A long trestle table was set up down the middle of the room, and on its holly-patterned white paper tablecloths were forty place settings, red paper napkins, paper cups, and gaudy Christmas crackers. Small glasses of fruit juice were already set out as a starter.

They took the boxes through green swing doors into the kitchen, where several women were bustling about, to be met by the appetising smell of cooking. A massive turkey, donated by a local butcher, its skin crisp and golden, was resting by the side of the stove, large saucepans full of carrots and Brussels sprouts were simmering on the hob, while potatoes were already roasting in the oven. There was an atmosphere of camaraderie, laughter and not a few curious glances as Polly and Sadie came in.

'Merry Christmas, everyone,' Polly called.

'And you, love. Are those the mince pies?' A buxom grey-haired woman, her round face perspiring, turned towards her.

'They certainly are, Jean. And this is my mother, Sadie. She's the one who made them.'

'Well, I'm sure we're very grateful, aren't we, ladies?'

There was a murmur of agreement, and then Jean said, 'As you know, you're both down for serving. And if you could greet and welcome people when they come in?'

'It'll be a pleasure,' Polly said, and added, 'you look all organised in here.'

'I think so. Betty?' Jean called. 'Don't forget you're watching the Christmas puddings. Don't let them boil dry.'

'I won't, Jean. Stop fussing. How about a glass of sherry for the workers?'

Sadie brightened up at this suggestion. 'Shall I pour them out?'

Jean nodded over to a cupboard. 'Good idea. The glasses are in there. I brought Bristol Cream, everyone. Is that okay?'

'Ooh, lovely,' came the chorus. Sadie poured out the drinks and began to hand them round. She suddenly realised that she'd worn the wrong thing. Her smart red dress and court shoes seemed somehow incongruous with the other women, who were – as she'd imagined – all wearing crossover pinafores. But then, they had been busy peeling vegetables and cooking. Sadie glanced at

Polly, who, in a grey pleated woollen skirt, and a white polo-necked sweater, with flat shoes, looked smart, but comfortable. While I, Sadie thought, look much too formal.

But then one of the women, called Dora, said, 'Don't you look nice, Sadie. You'll brighten the place up no end. We've got our glad rags on, haven't we, girls? Underneath, I mean.'

'Yes, well you can ruin your best dress if you like – my overall stays on 'til the Queen's speech!' a thin woman with tightly permed hair declared. She was sipping her drink as if it was vinegar.

'She can't *see* you, yer daft bat,' Jean said.

'Maybe not, but I'm not wearing a pinafore when I'm listening to Her Majesty, and that's that.'

The others laughed and then Jean, glancing at her watch, said, 'Right, Mass must be finished by now. All hands to the pumps!' She leaned forward and with a swift movement and loud clatter, raised the shutters to the serving hatch.

Polly and Sadie quickly finished their sherry and then rather self-consciously went into the hall to stand by the door. Within minutes, bringing the cold air in with them, people began to arrive. Polly was the first to move forward with a smile to greet an elderly woman, wearing a green velour hat, firmly fixed with a lethal-looking hatpin. 'Merry Christmas! Would you like me to take your coat? I'm Polly.'

'Yer can call me Mrs Bates,' the woman said, taking it off. 'And I'll keep me hat on, thanks.'

'Oh, right!'

Sadie was already moving towards the table,

with an elderly man clinging to her arm. Trust her to find a man, Polly thought with an inward giggle, and then the hall was filling up, with warm coats and scarves being removed, much indecision about where to sit, calls to acquaintances, and within minutes there was a queue for the toilets. Polly and Sadie went along each side of the table; making sure people were comfortable, lifting jugs of orange squash and pouring them into the paper cups. One woman, her hair blue-rinsed and carefully set, sat primly at the end of the table, staring silently ahead, and Polly bent down to her. 'Hello, I'm Polly. Do you know any of the others?'

She shook her head. 'Hello, dear. I'm Mrs Corbishley. I don't know why I've come really. I hardly ever come to church. It was the St Vincent de Paul people. They came to the door and invited me.'

'Well, it's better than being on your own.'

'I have got a family,' she said defensively, 'but they live a long way away, you see, and petrol being so expensive...'

'Of course,' Polly sympathised, 'it must be very difficult.' She turned away, but not before she'd seen the hurt and loneliness in the woman's eyes.

Then Father Doyle bustled in through the door, calling 'Merry Christmas, everyone!'

Back came the unanimous chorus, 'Merry Christmas, Father.'

He went over to the serving hatch. 'Are we about ready, ladies?'

'We certainly are, Father.'

Smiling broadly, the priest, middle-aged and balding, walked over to the head of the table. 'Shall we say grace?' Obediently forty heads were

155

lowered, and there was silence as he made the sign of the cross before saying, 'Bless us, O Lord, and these Thy gifts, which we are about to receive from Thy bounty, through Christ our Lord, Amen.'

The answer came, 'Amen.' And then crackers were pulled, and with much merriment among some, and obvious embarrassment among others, paper hats were put on, and Polly almost exploded with laughter when Mrs Bates put a yellow crown on top of her green velour hat. Mrs Corbishley left hers at the side of her plate. 'She doesn't want to spoil her hairdo,' Polly whispered to Sadie, and went over to the serving hatch. 'What's next, Jean?'

'Take these trays, and when they've finished their fruit juice, collect up the empty glasses. We're going to start dishing up.'

A few minutes later, Polly and Sadie went to and fro with steaming plates of roast turkey, stuffing, roast potatoes, carrots and Brussels. Father Doyle strolled around the table, having a word with each of his 'guests'. 'Do they do this every year?' Sadie whispered.

Polly shook her head. 'No, this is the first time. A good idea, isn't it?' Polly was hovering, uncertain whether to offer to help some of the more infirm people, as despite trembling hands, and frailty, they clung fiercely to their independence. Eventually, seeing him struggling, she bent to cut up an old man's turkey, and smilingly did the same for a woman whose knuckles and fingers were badly deformed.

'It's rheumatoid arthritis, love,' she explained.

Sadie, watching, saw with some surprise how much at ease Polly was. She's so good with these

156

people, Sadie thought, and realised with a slight shock, that there was still much to discover about this daughter of hers.

After the Christmas pudding and mince pies, it was time for cups of tea, and as Dora poured from a large urn, Polly and Sadie distributed the hot drinks. Sadie, finding her name called, went over to a tiny woman with hennaed hair. 'Who made the mince pies, duck?'

'Actually, I did.'

'They're bloody good, ain't they, Freda.'

Freda, plump and having problems with her dentures, snapped, 'Don't swear, Annie. Father will hear you.'

Annie cackled. 'I bet he's heard worse.' She looked up at Sadie. 'And who are you, when you're at 'ome? I 'aven't seen you afore.'

'I'm Polly's mother.'

'Nice lass, is Polly. A bit posh like, but she can't help that,' Freda said.

'Where are you from, Annie?' Sadie said. 'You talk differently from the others.'

'She talks Pottery, that's why,' Freda said.

'I come from Neck End, that's Longton, to you,' Annie informed Sadie, then seeing her bewilderment, added, 'in Stoke-on-Trent – yer know, the Potteries. Glory, it ain't that far away! I came ter Stone ter live with me daughter five years ago. Only she's in 'ospital.'

'Oh, I'm sorry to hear that. I'm not from round here, either. I'm a Londoner.'

Annie stared at her in disbelief. 'Yer don't sound like it.'

Sadie leaned down, and said in a low voice, 'I

bleedin' well do come from London! Me plates o' meat are killing me in these blasted shoes, and I'll be glad to get up the apples and pears ternight!' She smiled, 'Is that better?'

The two women burst into laughter, and so did Sadie. Polly glanced across, wondering what her mother had said. The day was going far better than she'd ever dared to hope. Sadie had worked so hard, first by baking all the mince pies, and today in the hall. Yet she still looked elegant and un-flustered. And people had seemed to like her. Certainly Sadie's light-hearted banter had teased a smile out of even the grumpiest old man. Almost grudgingly, Polly realised that for the first time, she felt not just unashamed, but even a tiny bit proud of her unconventional mother. I wonder, she thought, just what else I'll discover about her!

17

Christmas Eve found Jules and Nicolas, as always, enjoying Midnight Mass at Sacré-Coeur. Jules was moved almost to tears as the pure voices of the choirboys soared above the congregation, and he was still in an emotional mood as they left the church amidst shouted greetings of, *'Joyeux Noël!'* On the way home he thought of how, earlier in the evening, he and Nicolas had eaten their traditional meal of roast turkey with chestnuts and apple sauce. 'Gabrielle loved Christmas Eve,' he said. 'Do you remember how the whole house smelled wonderful; the spices, the cooking and baking – her excitement about the whole thing?'

'I do.' Nicolas smiled. 'She made it such fun for us.' His voice suddenly became sombre. 'It's not the same, is it, with just the two of us.'

Jules glanced at him swiftly. 'Life goes on, Nicolas. And just think,' he tried to lighten their mood, 'when you get married, and the babies start arriving, that will change everything, you'll see.'

'Marry? Me!' Nicolas began to laugh. 'There are too many beautiful girls out there. I can't imagine restricting myself to just one.'

'You'll feel differently when you fall in love. Real love, I mean...'

'As you had with Maman?'

'As I had with Maman.'

Eventually, they neared their small square, and Jules began to search in his pocket for his key, but Nicolas was quicker and, going ahead, was already opening the front door. As they went into the apartment, he suggested, 'A cognac before bed?'

Jules nodded as he switched on the lights in the sitting room. He glanced at the now unused sewing machine near the window where Gabrielle had loved to sit; the whirring of the needle had been a familiar sound in all their lives. Maybe, Jules thought, it was such a painful reminder that they should part with it. With a sigh, he went to sit in his favourite armchair and mentioned his idea to Nicolas. 'Madame Caplat might find it useful,' he said, 'she's been such a godsend, preparing our meals and generally looking after us.'

'I'll ask her in the New Year.' Nicolas handed Jules his glass and settled in the chair opposite,

159

stretching out his long legs.

After a few moments Jules looked across at him and said quietly, 'When we were in church, I had this strange compulsion to go to the house again.'

Nicolas, who had been gazing into his brandy glass, glanced up. 'You mean to the address that was on your identity card?'

Jules nodded.

'Do you want me to come with you?'

'Thank you, Nicolas, but no. It's not as though you haven't been before,' Jules added reflectively, 'as did your grandfather. He did everything he could to find out something about me. It was a terrible winter, but he even struggled to Paris through the snow and bitter cold. But when he found the address, nobody knew of me or, if they did, they weren't saying. But during the Occupation people were, and with just cause, deeply suspicious of strangers. They kept themselves to themselves; it was safer that way.' Jules paused and then went on, 'I'll never forget Jean-Paul returning, how exhausted he was, how difficult the trains had been. Either they were cancelled without notice, or didn't run on time. And he hated the frequent checks by German soldiers. I remember him saying, "Me, a true son of France, having to prove my identity in my own country!" If only,' Jules continued, 'I'd been well enough to go – but then you know my circumstances...'

Nicolas nodded. All this was a familiar story to him. He looked at Jules with sympathy. 'After the dreams,' he said slowly, 'you must be feeling impatient. I can understand that. But don't be disappointed if yet again the house means nothing to you.'

Jules knew that not even Nicolas could imagine how desperate he was becoming. For another dream, a flash of intuition, even to see the brown-haired girl again. Always, throughout the long years, he'd clung to the hope that one day... He finished his brandy and hauled himself to his feet, wincing at the pain in his now tired leg. 'Come,' he smiled, 'to bed – it's Christmas Day, and you don't want *Père Noël* to catch you awake.'

'How did you know I still believe?' Nicolas grinned, and Jules placed an affectionate arm around his shoulders as, immersed in their own thoughts, they went to their respective bedrooms.

It was not until Saturday, two days afterwards that Jules travelled on the Métro to a quiet, shabby district of Paris. It was one he rarely visited, and the narrow tree-lined road where, according to his papers, he had lived at Number twenty-eight, was deserted. He walked slowly along the pavement, trying as always to feel a sense of familiarity. But there were no memories, only the knowledge he'd gained from his previous visits. The house, he noticed, which always before had worn an air of dejection, was now looking smarter, with a fresh coat of paint on the shutters and a new front door. Jules stood and stared up at the second floor, but the house, the street, meant nothing.

Another wasted journey, he thought, and with a shrug, turned to leave, moving politely aside to let an old woman carrying a shopping basket pass by him. But she didn't. Instead she came to a halt, glared at the house, and muttered, 'All the paint in the world will never take away *your* sad history.'

Her tone was bitter, angry, and Jules said, 'What do you mean, madame?'

'My friends lived here,' she said, 'Henri, Maurice and Nicole. Some bastard collaborator betrayed them.' She spat on the pavement; her lined face a mask of fury. 'I saw the Boche take them away!' She turned to point to the other end of the street. 'I stood there with my bicycle, I was their courier – we were all working in the Resistance.' Jules saw in her eyes an unbearable sadness. 'They were never heard of again. I'll never forget – never!'

Jules, listening to her story with growing anger, looked up at the house, imagining the German uniforms, the terror and despair of the three people as they were arrested. 'Of course I couldn't stay after that,' she said, 'it was too dangerous. I left Paris the same night and managed to join my sister in Lyon.' She went on to tell Jules that she'd settled there, and had come to spend Christmas with her cousin. She was going home the next day.

Jules said quickly, 'Madame – tell me. Which apartment did your friends live in?'

'One on the second floor – Number 3.'

Jules felt the blood drain from his face. That had been the address on his identity card! This woman, in 1941, had actually known the people who lived there. With his throat tightening with tension, he said, 'Did you ever know or hear of a man called Jules Giscard?'

She hesitated, searching her memory, then slowly shook her head. 'Not that I can recall. But then many in the Resistance used a code name. And only Maurice would have known the identity of anyone "passing through". It was safer that way. I'm sorry.'

Jules struggled to hide his disappointment. 'Thank you, madame, and I too am sorry – about your friends.' She glanced up at him, nodded, then began to continue down the street; her small erect figure dressed entirely in black. A brave woman, Jules thought, as he watched her, because she wouldn't have been young, even then.

'So it *was* a "safe house"!' Nicolas, having sat spellbound throughout Jules's account of his visit, leaned forward intently. 'I know you've always thought that was a possibility.'

Jules, still thawing out after his cold journey home, gratefully sipped the coffee Nicolas had given him. 'It would be one reason why no one was willing to talk about it. But don't you see, Nicolas, this means that I *could* have been working for the Resistance when the accident happened! And knowing me as you do,' Jules lowered his cup, his expression hardening, 'can you believe that I *wouldn't* have been involved?'

Nicolas shook his head. 'I have no doubt of it.'

Jules's expression became grim. 'I still feel, you know, that I didn't do enough. Living as we did on the farm, we were quite isolated. But at times we sheltered people, helping refugees to flee – a small link in the chain. I lost count of the number of Jewish children who came, poor little souls. But I often wonder if I should have come to Paris then; been more "in the front line", so to speak.'

Nicolas ran his fingers through his hair in exasperation. 'I don't know why you torture yourself.

163

It would have been' – he searched for the right word in English – 'idiocy – and dangerous for others.'

Jules grimaced. 'You're right, of course. But that doesn't prevent me from regretting it.'

'It was hardly your fault you suffered such terrible injuries.'

'But who would have thought,' Jules said grimly as he lit a cigarette, 'that the effects would be so long lasting? Twenty years is a large part of anyone's life.'

18

In England, Polly, after the success of Christmas Day, suggested to Sadie that they should hold a New Year's Eve party. 'That's unless you've already got plans?'

Sadie shook her head, so Polly began to make a list, 'It's a bit short notice, but I thought Hazel and Anita, and Ruth of course, and possibly her twin sisters.' She glanced at Sadie and said quietly, 'They could sleep in my grandfather's room. I think it's time we began to use it again.'

Sadie, who had never approved of the large bedroom being treated as some sort of shrine, felt a sense of relief. Polly went on writing down names. 'Mark,' she paused, 'and his father – if that's okay with you?'

'Perfectly.' Sadie hesitated, wondering whether to confide that she and George had been seeing each other. She had nothing to hide – so far it was all completely innocent. They merely met for lunch or dinner; always somewhere quiet and discreet. But, unsure of Polly's reaction, she decided against it.

'Then there are some people from the tennis club,' Polly continued, 'Adrian for instance, and a few others, but definitely not Hilary!' She paused, 'Who would you like to come?' Her pencil poised, Polly's stomach began to churn with anxiety in case her mother invited any of her 'men'.

Sadie shook her head. 'As long as George is there, I'll be fine.'

'Is there no one?' Polly asked with a frown. 'Surely you must have made some friends?'

'Not really. Of course, if I'd gone ahead with my idea of getting a part-time job, I might have done. I didn't tell you about that, did I?'

Polly's eyes widened. 'No, you didn't! Although I can't say I'm surprised you want to do something. It must be very quiet for you here, all day on your own. What sort of job – in fashion, the same as you were at Derry & Toms?'

'Probably, but then I thought of the build-up to Christmas and the hectic sales afterwards.' Sadie shuddered, 'Never again!' She laughed. 'You can see how lazy I've become. It's amazing how not needing to earn a living can give you choices. But I'm definitely going to look around for something soon. But to come back to the party – I'll be fine if George comes.'

It was with satisfaction that on the morning of New Year's Eve, Polly counted up the final numbers. 'Probably about twenty,' she said. 'Ruth rang last night after she got my letter, and I said I'd go over and fetch them this afternoon.'

'I think we're pretty organised on the food front,' Sadie said. 'And you say you've checked on the booze?'

Polly nodded. 'And the records are all sorted. So it's just a question of what to wear.'

'Oh, glammed up, surely? After all,' Sadie said, 'the house looks wonderful, the holly and mistletoe are still fresh, there's the tree and everything, so why not go to town?' Then, seeing the sudden alarm on Polly's face, she laughed. 'Don't worry – I'll be careful what I choose. No cleavage – I promise.'

Polly breathed a sigh of relief. Sadie's taste in clothes did tend towards the 'provocative'. And as most of the guests at the party hadn't as yet met her...

The journey back from Abbey Hulton was, for Polly, one of hilarity. She was hardly able to keep a straight face as Ruth, sitting beside her, sent over her shoulder a stream of orders to Teresa and Maria who, on the back seat, were glowing with excitement. 'Now don't you two show me up; there must be no making pigs of yourselves with the food and if I catch either of you at the punch or drinking alcohol, you're for it!' Ruth glanced at Polly and muttered, 'You should see what they're going to wear – they look about eighteen! If Mum knew they'd unpicked the lace modesty vest from beneath their frocks, she'd have a fit!'

'You didn't tell her?' Polly whispered.

Ruth grinned. 'I've been fifteen myself.'

166

And later, as Teresa and Maria came self-consciously down the wide staircase, Polly, who was on her way to the drawing room, saw exactly what Ruth had meant. They were wearing identical emerald green shot-silk, with plunging necklines, and 'made up to the nines'. When Ruth saw them, she offered up a prayer for any young man likely to come within their orbit. Sadie, however, thought the two girls were wonderful, and declared she couldn't tell them apart. 'I bet you have some fun with the boys.'

Teresa nudged Maria. 'We're beginning to, aren't we?'

Maria giggled then said politely, 'This is a lovely house, Mrs Merton.'

'Oh call me Sadie, everyone else does.' She laughed at their astonished expressions and said, 'Come and meet some people.'

Ruth stood in a corner, glass in hand. There was only one face she was looking for, and when she heard Mark's deep voice in the hall, she felt almost shivery with anticipation. It was a few minutes later that he saw her, and after threading his way through a cluster of people, was at last smiling down. 'Hello, Ruth. Polly said you were coming.'

'Were you glad?' She looked up at him, and saw a teasing gleam in his eyes.

'What do you think?'

'How am I to know, unless you tell me?'

Mark bent to whisper in her ear. 'Then, yes, I am.'

'And why is it a secret, tell me that?'

He threw back his head and laughed. 'I love that hint of Irish in your voice.'

167

And I, Mark Eldon, love *you*, Ruth thought. Polly, busy looking after her guests, glanced over to where they were standing, and felt a swift pang of jealousy. Not exactly about Mark liking someone else; that was her own fault. No, it was their growing closeness that she envied. I'd love to meet someone and fall passionately in love, she thought wistfully. She suspected that Ruth had, and knew that her own feelings for Mark, however affectionate, had fallen far short of that.

Sadie, having been introduced to Mark's grandmother, settled her in one of the armchairs, while George stood at her side, surveying the other guests. 'Who are the twins?'

'Ruth's sisters, Teresa and Maria. Pretty, aren't they?'

'I'd guess a bit younger than they'd like to be thought?'

'You, George, are too observant for words.'

'It comes of sitting in a courtroom.'

Sadie laughed and then moved towards the hall as the doorbell rang. She opened the door to find a sheepish-looking young man with acne, behind a tall, sharp-faced blonde girl whose lip curled slightly as she gazed at Sadie. 'You must be Polly's mother,' she drawled, and Sadie disliked her instantly.

'I certainly am,' she said, but her tone was deliberately cool.

'I'm Adrian,' the young man smiled showing even, white teeth. 'This is Hilary.'

Is it indeed? Sadie thought. I don't believe you were invited, miss! But she moved aside to let them enter the hall. 'Let me take your stole,' she

168

said and as she did, stroked the fur. 'Not a bad imitation!' Hilary glared at her, and then followed Adrian into the now crowded room. Sadie almost laughed aloud as from the radiogram drifted the strains of 'Don't Bring Lulu.'

Polly was horrified when she turned and saw Hilary, elegant in a close-fitting black dress, hovering behind Adrian. 'Hilary – what can I get you to drink?'

'A gin and tonic, please,' Hilary said, her gaze sweeping around the room. It came to rest on Mark, who was still talking to Ruth, and her eyes narrowed.

'I'll have a beer if you've got one?' Adrian said.

'Of course, they're in the kitchen.' Polly swivelled her eyes, indicating that he should follow her, and once there she hissed, 'What did you bring *her* for?'

'Sorry.' Adrian went red with embarrassment. 'I had no choice. She nabbed me in Woolworths and asked me if I was coming and who with. Before I knew it, she'd offered to give me a lift...'

Polly took a bottle of beer out of the fridge and handed it to him. 'The opener's over there, and the glasses,' she said, but was unable to remain angry, knowing he wouldn't have stood a chance against Hilary's scheming.

'Well, don't get landed with her,' she told him. 'There are two super-looking girls here, just dying to meet you.'

'Really?' Adrian brightened, and Polly noticed with some relief that his complexion had improved considerably. 'I'll get Her Highness a gin and tonic, and then introduce you,' she said. And a couple of minutes later, it was with no surprise that she found that Hilary had joined Mark and Ruth in the corner.

'One G&T,' Polly said with forced gaiety. 'Now, Hilary, you must circulate, you know. Come and meet Andy, Anita's fiancé.'

With ill grace, Hilary followed her across the room, and Ruth said, glancing up at Mark, 'You do know she fancies you, don't you?'

'Hilary? Good Lord, I'd rather kiss a tarantula!'

Ruth laughed. 'But I suppose we too should circulate a bit?'

'If we must,' Mark grumbled. He glanced down at her and said, 'But don't be too far away at midnight, will you?'

Ruth flashed him what she hoped was an enigmatic smile, 'You'll have to wait and see.'

But Mark had seen the answer in her eyes, and his pulse quickened as he watched her, lithe in a red sheath dress, move across the room. This quick-thinking, intelligent girl had often been in his thoughts during the past few weeks, and he suddenly realised just how delighted he was to see her again. He watched her bend down to his grandmother, seeing her answering smile, and when Polly approached with Teresa and Maria in tow, he said, 'I know all about you two. I've been talking to your sister.'

'Don't believe a word of it,' Maria said with alarm.

Polly laughed. 'Mark, would you introduce them to Adrian for me? The lad's dying to meet them, but you know how shy he is.'

'Ah, let's go and put him out of his misery.'

Ushering the two girls before him, Mark guided them past other guests to a corner where Adrian was talking to another boy of a similar age.

For the next hour or so, Polly and Sadie, in between socialising, were kept busy with offering drinks and replenishing the buffet table. 'Your vol-au-vents are popular,' Polly murmured. Sadie, on her way to take Mark's grandmother some cheese and pineapple on sticks and a sausage roll, smiled with satisfaction. Later, with the music drifting through the open drawing-room door, one or two couples, including Mark and Ruth, began to dance on the tiled floor of the hall. Polly noticed Hilary watching them, her face like a sour lemon, and smiled to herself, but that smile faded as she saw Hilary then glance over to where George and Sadie were talking earnestly. For one split second her expression was unguarded, her eyes almost glittering with spite. She's going to say something, Polly thought with panic. She's going to tell Mark about Sadie, I can sense it. And he's not daft – he's bound to wonder if that's how she and his father met. He shouldn't have to cope with this, she thought with sudden fury, not so soon after losing his mother. So seconds later, when she saw Hilary make her way over to the hall and tap Ruth on the shoulder, saying, 'An excuse-me, I think,' Polly was already behind her.

'Sorry, Hilary,' she said tersely, 'there's some-one in the kitchen wanting to talk to you.'

Hilary frowned. 'Are you sure?'

Mark tightened his arm around Ruth's waist, and threw Polly a grateful glance. With Polly's hand firmly beneath her elbow, Hilary had no choice but to retreat, and reluctantly be escorted into the empty kitchen. She turned round with irritation. 'I thought you said someone…'

'I did!' Polly snapped. 'It was me. I'm on to you, Hilary. Don't deny it – you were about to tell Mark of the rumours about Sadie! Weren't you?'

Hilary's face hardened and she shrugged. 'So? Don't you think he deserves to be warned? Before she gets her claws into his father.'

'You nasty piece of work!' Polly was incandescent with rage. 'How dare you come to my house and talk about my mother like that. I'd like you to leave – right now!'

'And what reason will you give?' The insolence in Hilary's tone made Polly's palms itch to slap her.

'*I* won't,' she said through tight lips. '*You* will. You can go into the drawing room, call goodnight and say you're promised at another party. And if you don't, and if I ever hear of you tittle-tattling about something that's none of your business again, I promise you'll regret it.'

'Oh yes,' Hilary drawled, two red patches of anger now burning on her normally pale cheeks. 'And what can *you* do?'

'I'll tell you what I can do,' Polly said through gritted teeth. 'I can tell everyone the truth about that so-called "holiday" you had when you were seventeen. Remember – the one when you went to stay with your auntie in Wales, and then were supposed to have appendicitis?'

Although she saw the pupils of Hilary's eyes dilate with shock, Polly was relentless, 'Unlike you, I don't believe in blackening people's characters. But I warn you, Hilary, one word against my mother, and I'll do a bit of whispering myself. Two can play at that game, you know!'

'I don't know what you're talking about!'

'Oh, but I think you do.' Polly's voice was quiet, yet full of threat.

For one long moment Hilary stood perfectly still, then without another word, she turned and went back through the hall to join the others. Moments later, during a lull in the music, she called out, 'Bye, everyone – another party to go to. What it is to be popular!' She brushed unsmilingly through the dancers in the hall, took the stole Polly was holding out, and seconds later was gone.

Polly went slowly back into the kitchen to find Sadie waiting for her. Silently, she offered Polly a glass of white wine. 'I think you need this,' she said. 'I was in the larder!' She indicated several packets of potato crisps now lying on the table. 'I heard every word.' She gazed steadily at her daughter. 'Thank you, Polly. Has she gone?'

'That's okay, and yes, she has.'

There was an awkward silence, then Sadie said, 'I'm sure someone will run Adrian home. As a matter of interest – how did you find out about this so-called "holiday"?'

'I didn't,' Polly confessed, with a sheepish grin. 'I've always wondered, but never knew for sure. It worked, though, didn't it?'

They returned to the party, to see Teresa dancing with Adrian, while Maria was gazing up entranced at the red-haired son of a member of the tennis club. Polly looked around the room, wishing there could have been just one person there to set her own pulse racing. As midnight

173

neared, and from the radiogram came the sonorous chimes of Big Ben, Mark whispered, 'Happy New Year, Pol,' and after bending to give her a brief and affectionate kiss, turned to where Ruth was waiting. As she saw the intensity of their embrace, Polly had to look away. She glanced over to where Anita and Andy were wrapped in each other's arms, and Hazel kissing her latest boyfriend. Sadie, she noticed, was circumspectly offering her cheek to George. And then suddenly Polly pushed all thoughts of envy away. After all, it was now 1962. She would not only be twenty-one in November, but who knew what this year might bring? And then laughingly, she too was swept into a deluge of hugs and kisses.

19

'I assume you have plans for later?' Jules smiled as he sat at the heavy mahogany dining table. He glanced down at his plate. 'This foie gras looks good!'

'Yes, it does.' Nicolas poured them each a glass of Sauternes. 'And to answer your question, yes of course!'

'I shall take a stroll along the Champs Elysées myself,' Jules said, and raised his glass. 'To 1962. Who knows what it will bring?' As they began to eat they listened to the wireless and the haunting voice of Edith Piaf singing, *'Non, je ne regrette rien'*.

'Do you?' Nicolas asked, as he spread his toast,

'regret nothing?'

Jules gave a grimace. 'Nothing I can remember.'

Nicolas smiled. 'You're in a fortunate position, do you know that? Many would envy you.'

'You think so?'

'Sorry, that was a stupid thing to say.'

'How about you – do you have any regrets?' Jules raised a sardonic eyebrow.

Nicolas laughed. 'Not me, I haven't lived enough yet.' He dabbed his mouth with his napkin, and leaned back. 'That was good – and oysters, crab and langoustine to follow – wonderful. I love New Year's Eve.'

'Spoken like a true Frenchman,' Jules teased. 'But you'd better not drink too much champagne – not if there's going to be a mademoiselle involved later!'

'Spoilsport!'

Nicolas who, Jules noticed, was wearing his new black leather jacket, was the first to leave, and just before midnight, after he'd cleared the remnants of their meal and relaxed with a further cigarette, Jules went for his walk. As he strolled along the Champs Elysées, dominated by the illuminated Arc de Triomphe, he thought how apt it was that Paris was called the 'city of light'. He merged and jostled his way through the throng of people on the pavements, finding his spirits lifting at the atmosphere of bonhomie. But when he eventually neared the Café Henri, its burgundy awning once again brought the memory of a laughing girl with brown hair. He paused, then shivering despite his polo-necked sweater and overcoat, decided to go in for a cognac. *'Bonne Année, Gaston,'* he called as the waiter in his long white apron approached. 'You're busy tonight.'

Gaston smiled, and indicated a small group of people at a table in a corner. 'They are *Anglais*,' he said. 'And slow to serve. Why do these people not learn to speak our language?'

Jules laughed. 'And you, Gaston? Do you speak fluent English?'

The waiter shrugged. 'Enough. But then I am French and in Paris.'

'True,' Jules agreed.

The only table vacant was close to the one in the corner, and he glanced curiously at the four men, all either balding, or with greying hair. One, with spectacles and bushy eyebrows, was talking quickly, gesticulating, and Jules guessed they were having a debate. From where he was sitting, he could hear most of their conversation, and he smiled when Gaston returned with his cognac, bent down and whispered, 'They are putting the world to rights!'

Jules said, 'I know!'

He tried not to eavesdrop, but then one voice said loudly, 'I'm telling you, Nigel. The French are not at all grateful to us, despite what we did for them in the war.'

Jules felt swift anger rise in him. That statement was untrue and he had no intention of letting it pass. He turned in his chair and said over his shoulder, 'You are wrong, sir! France is well aware that it owes a huge debt to Britain.'

Startled, all four men looked at him. 'How can you be sure?' the man who had spoken protested.

'Believe me, I am sure,' Jules said. 'I'm not denying there are a few misguided people who give the wrong impression. But most are well aware that without England's intervention, France wouldn't be the country it is today.'

'I certainly hope so.' The man took a sip of his wine and smiled in appreciation. 'The one thing the French do get right is wine.'

'Oh, I think there are a few others,' Jules commented. 'Are you all over for the New Year?'

'We are, yes.' The man turned away to join his friends, and Jules glanced at his watch, wondering whether to have another drink or make his way back to the apartment. But seconds later, he heard one of the men say, 'Go on, ask him!'

'Not straight away,' was the muttered reply, and intrigued, Jules looked round to meet the eyes of the man he'd been talking to. 'Er – we wondered if you'd like to join us,' he said. 'We all belong to a debating club, and it's refreshing to hear another point of view.'

Jules thought for moment, and then nodded and turned his chair around. For several minutes, in answer to a question, he gave his opinion on the Berlin Wall, and how it not only separated families in Germany but was also affecting the whole of Europe. When he paused, one of the men grinned at the man with the bushy eyebrows. 'Go on, then, Oliver. You must have heard enough by now.'

Oliver leaned forward and said to Jules, 'Tell me I'm right! The county in England that you come from – it's Staffordshire, isn't it?'

Jules stared at him in puzzlement. 'But I'm French. My name is Jules Giscard.'

Oliver stared at him. 'French? You can't possibly be.'

Jules smiled at him with amusement. 'I'm afraid I am.'

One of the other men began to laugh. 'Caught out at last, Oliver.'

Oliver held up a hand. 'No, that's impossible. I'm never wrong.'

'Do you mind telling me what you're all talking about?' Jules said.

'Oliver is a professor of phonetics,' one of the group, a man with rimless spectacles said. 'Or at least he was, until he retired. It's a habit of his, trying to guess where people are from. He can't help himself.'

'Phonetics?' Jules repeated. 'You mean, like Professor Higgins?'

'You've seen *Pygmalion?*' Oliver asked, gazing intently at him.

'Of course.'

'Did you know that Shaw based the character on a real person, Professor Daniel Jones? He used to be Head of Department at the University College of London.'

'No, I didn't.' Jules glanced at him with surprise. 'Was he someone you knew?'

'I still do know him. He's a brilliant man. He studied here in Paris when he was young, at the Sorbonne.'

'And are you an expert in phonetics – just as he was?'

Oliver gave a self-deprecating shrug. 'I have my moments.' He frowned. 'I still can't believe you're not English. Tell me, what do you do? As a job, I mean.'

'I'm an administrator in a shipping office. And I also give private English lessons.'

'So you live in Paris?'

Jules nodded. Oliver regarded him, his frown even deeper. 'Do you know, I would have staked my reputation on the fact that you're English? It's amazing – your pronunciation, the way you use the language. As a child, did you spend much time in England?'

For one long moment Jules didn't answer, and his indecision must have shown, because Oliver said quickly, 'Forgive me, I ask too many questions.'

'No, it's not that. It's just that I can't give you a truthful answer.' Jules hesitated, finding it difficult to divulge his past to these strangers. He glanced around the table at the others and then said slowly, 'You see, many years ago, I was in a road accident, and received such extensive head injuries that it affected my memory. I simply can't remember. I don't remember either of my parents, my childhood, or my background. In fact, my life before the accident is an absolute blank.'

There were murmurs of shock and sympathy, and Oliver stared at him, his expression serious. 'That must be a dreadful affliction.' He remained silent for a few moments, thoughtfully twirling his glass, then said with triumph. 'This explains it. I knew I was right. There has to be an English connection somewhere. For instance, as far as you know, have you always been bilingual?'

Jules nodded. 'Although I didn't discover that I could speak English until six months after the accident. I was ill for a long time, and the only

179

language I heard was French. But then I began to dream in English, and that's how I found out.'

There was a rustle of interest around the table, and Jules was conscious of all four men gazing at him. Oliver said. 'Look, it's quite obvious that you've been bilingual from birth. I'd stake my reputation on it. And so it seems logical to assume that your mother must have been English. I still claim that the connection is Staffordshire. And Jules, believe me, you must have spent some considerable time there.'

'You can tell all this – just by my speech?'

'I've never known him to be wrong,' one of the men said, and the others nodded in agreement.

'I also think,' Oliver added, 'that your background was a middle-class one. And I can see that you know exactly what I mean by that. Now would a Frenchman have known so quickly?'

Jules felt his pulse begin to race. Was it possible? Could this man really do what he claimed? He was struggling to take in the implication of Oliver's words, adrenaline already rushing through his veins. 'You can't possibly know,' his voice almost trembled with excitement, 'what this information means to me. I shall never be able to thank you enough.'

'Well, it does give you something to go on.' Oliver took out a wallet and extracted a card. 'Take this, Jules. If you ever need any more help, just get in touch. And let me have your address. This is such an interesting case, who knows, something else might occur to me – I'd like to help if I can.'

Jules scribbled his address on the back of a cigarette packet then glanced at his watch. 'Half an hour to midnight – do you have any plans?'

'We two married men are meeting our wives,' one man said. 'We knew they'd only want to talk about clothes, so we escaped for the evening!'

'Whereas we two, as confirmed bachelors,' Oliver said, 'will probably enjoy being spectators, won't we, Charles?'

'You speak for yourself,' his companion, a tall cheerful man said, 'I'm hoping for a kiss from a mademoiselle.'

'More likely one from a French matron with a moustache,' Oliver grinned and they all laughed.

Jules, putting up a hand to attract Gaston's attention, said, 'Please – you must let me pay for your drinks, it's the least I can do.' Several minutes later, when they left the café together, he turned to them and said with intensity, 'Thank you again, all of you.'

Oliver said, 'Thank *you*, my friend, for a most useful discussion and a pleasant evening.'

All four men shook Jules by the hand, wishing him well, and as they parted, Jules said, *'Bonne Année*, and I hope you enjoy the rest of your stay in Paris.'

Despite the ache in his leg, Jules was euphoric as he crossed the bridge and began to walk home. For the first time in twenty years he now had an idea, a hint of his background, his family. Of course, the person who taught him English may not have been his mother; it could have been a relative or even a nanny. I have, Jules thought, lived for so long in a frustrating, seemingly endless dark void. Could it be that at last there was a glimmer of light?

20

The following morning, when Nicolas, yawning, eventually appeared from his bedroom, Jules – who had also slept late, if fitfully – was in the salon studying an atlas. Nicolas, on his way to the kitchen, paused by the door and looked at him with curiosity. 'You were late last night?'

Jules looked up. 'I had,' he told him, 'a very interesting evening. When you're ready, I'll tell you about it.'

Half an hour later, Nicolas, showered and now fully dressed, brought in his coffee. 'So,' he said. 'I'm all attention.'

'Ears,' Jules said absently. 'In England, they would say, "I'm all ears." It's a colloquial expression.'

'What a language!' Nicolas sipped appreciatively at his drink, 'And they complain about our masculine and feminine genders!'

Jules smiled, lit a cigarette, and pointed down at the atlas. 'You see that county in the middle of England called Staffordshire?'

Nicolas peered over his shoulder. 'I do.' He jabbed a finger on the page. 'I've heard of that place, Stoke-on-Trent. Isn't it famous for its pottery?'

'Yes, it is.' Jules paused, then said quietly, 'I discovered last night that I may have connections with this area.'

Astounded, Nicolas stared at him. 'How on earth...?'

Jules told him of his encounter with Oliver Sands and the conversation that had followed. 'He gave me his card,' he indicated it on the table.

Nicolas picked it up; his eyes narrowed. 'These qualifications do seem very impressive.'

Jules leaned forward, his face intent, 'What a stroke of luck, Nicolas. At last, I have something to go on, a clue to follow up.'

'What will you do?'

'I don't know yet. We will have to put our thinking caps on.'

'Another colloquial expression, I suppose,' Nicolas grinned. 'You like to keep me on my toes, don't you?'

Jules smiled at him with affection. 'And how did your evening go?'

Nicolas shrugged. 'Okay.'

'Do I detect a slight note of boredom?'

'You know me too well!' But Nicolas had no intention of revealing what had happened the previous night. To feel jaded, even though he was with a pretty girl, was a new and disconcerting experience. Maybe, he thought, it's just because 1961 had been such a sad year. He glanced at Jules, who was searching the bookshelves, guessing that he was looking for information about Staffordshire. It was unlikely that he would find anything, whereas as a journalist, Nicolas thought, I am in the ideal position.

'Papa,' he called, 'leave it to me. I'm back at work soon, and I'll do some research.'

Jules turned. 'Of course. And soon, Nicolas?'

183

'Immediately, I promise.'

Content, Jules lit a cigarette. It would not be easy – he would have to be patient. But, he thought, with some excitement, it was definitely a beginning.

In England, now that Christmas was over, Polly and Ruth applied themselves earnestly to their studies. Both were keen to qualify and hoped for teaching posts in Staffordshire, but neither wanted to leave home. Polly couldn't bear the thought of leaving The Gables, while Ruth was determined that her salary wasn't going to get swallowed up in independent living expenses. Her parents had made too many sacrifices for that.

But it wasn't all studying. Both girls enjoyed the social life at the college, Ruth perhaps rather more restrainedly than before. Polly glanced with amusement at her friend, as she fended off an amorous and rather drunk young man. 'I've told you, I've got a boyfriend, now clear off!' Ruth snapped.

Polly laughed, and then said, 'At least you've got one, which is more than I have.'

'Well, it's not for lack of offers,' Ruth pointed out. 'You're too fussy, that's your trouble.'

'Come on, I did go the pictures with that Alan.'

'Yes, and slapped his face!'

'He deserved it. Two seats in the balcony doesn't give anyone the sort of rights he wanted.'

Ruth grinned at her. 'Par for the course, Pol – they all try it on! How about him over there?'

Polly followed her gaze. 'The one with the spectacles?'

Ruth nodded. 'He looks interesting. I've seen him around – usually with his nose in a book.'

Polly considered the lanky young man, slightly older than most, with a shock of black hair untidily flopping over his forehead. He wasn't what she'd call good-looking. But Ruth could be right. He *did* look interesting. 'I can't say I've noticed him before.'

'That's because for the first year, you hardly noticed anyone,' Ruth said, but her tone was soft.

Polly turned to smile at her. 'Thank God I met you,' she said. 'I must have seemed a right sour-puss.'

'Sort of. Still,' Ruth said, 'you're right, it *is* time you got yourself a boyfriend.' She gave Polly a nudge. 'Go on, introduce yourself. This is 1962, not the Victorian era.'

'You must be joking,' Polly said with indignation. 'I don't mind giving him a bit of encouragement if I can catch his eye, but I'm not that desperate!' And she wasn't. Her comment to Ruth about not having a boyfriend had been light-hearted. When, a few days later, Ruth told her that the dark-haired young man was not only married, but it had been a shotgun wedding, Polly just laughed, saying, 'They always say the quiet ones are the worst.' And eventually, Ruth gave up matchmaking, while Polly, who felt she should make an effort, went on another couple of dates, and then resigned herself to the fact that whatever romance awaited her, she wasn't going to find it on the college campus.

Ruth, however, knew that she had already found hers. Mrs Mark Eldon was a name she intended to make her own, and it was with a quiet smile

185

that she answered Mark's increasingly frequent letters. They had spent as much time as possible together before he went back to Oxford. On the day following the New Year's Eve party, he'd taken her for a drive in the country around Stone, ending in a passionate hour parked in a country lane. There had been dancing at Trentham Ballroom, and the Majestic in Hanley. In fact, they'd become a sort of 'official couple'. But Ruth's parents were becoming increasingly concerned.

'It might only be a few weeks, but it's time we met this Mark,' Mrs Donovan had declared the previous weekend, when Ruth had gone home for the twins' birthday. 'The girls tell me he looks like a film star. Well, young lady, I just hope you're not getting your head turned.'

'And why would I be doing that?'

Her father put down his newspaper. 'Because, Ruth, he's from a different background; at Oxford, studying law? His father's a lawyer, his grandfather a judge? Heavens above, child, you live in a council house! Use the brains God was good enough to give you.'

'He knows I live in a council house. Hasn't he brought me home many a time?' Ruth said stubbornly.

But Sean Donovan wasn't to be distracted. 'And he's not a Catholic! We're not against yer having a good time, not at all, are we, Bridie? But don't get any foolish notions in yer head about it leading anywhere. Money marries money. Always did, always will. It was just the same in the ould country.'

'You don't say anything about our Teresa and Adrian.'

'Sure, that's kids' stuff,' Sean said.

Bridie nodded in agreement. 'She's got her eye on a lad at school now, according to Maria,' she said. 'Whereas you ... well, we just don't want you to get hurt.'

'Haven't I heard you say that we all have to learn from our mistakes?' Ruth got up and, standing on the black half-moon hearthrug, bent to poke the fire, easing the coals to a different position to make the flames burn brighter. Straightening up, she turned to face her parents. 'But Mark isn't going to be a mistake, Mum. You'll see.'

Sean, gazing at his daughter's flushed and determined face had serious misgivings and he exchanged glances with Bridie. 'We just hope not,' he said, 'but it doesn't change anything. We still want to meet him.'

Sadie, true to her word, had applied herself to finding a part-time job, and by the end of January, was working three days a week in a fashion boutique in Stafford. Having spent so many years with Derry & Toms, she found herself enjoying being back among lovely clothes, and the camaraderie of the other two assistants. There was, of course, competition for sales commissions, but on the whole bitchiness was rare. Bless you, Babs, she thought. If I hadn't been stung by your criticism of my lazy lifestyle, I might never have made the effort.

But Sadie, for the first time in her life, was being diplomatic and careful about her privacy. When asked where she lived, she would answer vaguely, just mentioning Brandon, never The Gables. She just said she was widowed in the war, and had one grown-up daughter, away at college. Fortunately, nobody asked for further details. Maybe, Sadie thought ruefully, the provincial mentality is beginning to rub off on me, because she was finding to her surprise, that she *did* mind what people said about her. Or was it that she was, as Babs would say, growing up at last? Certainly, and to her dismay, her sex life seemed to be on the wane. She still went out a couple of nights a week, driving herself to different restaurants and bars, but now she often came home alone. It had to be a special sort of man who attracted her these days, and with her expertise in flirtation, it was easy for her to send signals. But she often couldn't be bothered. Now was this, she pondered one evening, as she lingered at her single table, because of morality at last pricking her conscience? She shuddered – heaven forbid! Or was it, she thought with some discomfort, that now she was beginning to actually *feel* like a mother, the thought of Polly's disapproval was affecting her?

Her musings were suddenly disturbed as a man paused by her table. She glanced up at his round, slightly perspiring face and slicked back blond hair. 'Hello, Henry,' she said, recalling a night spent with him several months ago. She'd noticed him earlier in the restaurant, obviously having a business meal with a colleague.

'Sadie. Are you well?'

'I'm fine, and you?'

'Tickety-boo, thanks. I don't suppose...'

Sadie hesitated. Henry had been an unexpectedly expert lover, and had sent her a beautiful bouquet of flowers the following day, although this was the first time she'd seen him since. And then as an image of Polly came into her mind, swiftly followed by one of Babs, Sadie was suddenly filled with rebellion. She had never lived her life to please other people, so why should she begin now? 'I think,' she said with a sweet smile, 'that would be very pleasant indeed. Shall we agree that you follow me in about fifteen minutes? And Henry – as before, I will trust you to be discreet.'

'You can rely on it.' He smiled down at her, and as she watched him return to his table and begin to pay the bill, she turned to try and catch the waiter's attention for her own. A few minutes later, with a pleasant feeling of anticipation she went out to her car and after getting into the driving seat, switched on the ignition. She had no qualms – merely thinking that at least this was one night she wouldn't be alone in that vast house.

21

The following weekend, Polly came home. She'd phoned to say she'd be driving over on Friday night, and Sadie, pleased at the thought of company spent the afternoon making a beef casserole and her daughter's favourite Bakewell tart. Instead of using Bird's custard powder, Sadie followed a recipe she'd found for real custard, made with a vanilla pod and cream. And why not? she thought. After all those years of rationing, it's time we spoiled ourselves.

'Something smells good,' Polly said when she arrived. 'I can't tell you how much I'm looking forward to your cooking.'

'Isn't the food very good at college?'

'I don't suppose we can grumble – but nothing to compare with yours.'

Gratified, Sadie led the way into the kitchen. 'Cup of tea?'

Polly nodded. 'I decided to come on the spur of the moment really. Ruth was going home because Mark's up from Oxford. And I didn't fancy the weekend there without her.' She grinned. 'Mr and Mrs Donovan have insisted on meeting him.'

'Oh?' Sadie turned. 'That's no problem, is it?'

'I'm not sure. I think they're worried about her getting hurt, that there's no future in it.'

Sadie looked at her in surprise. 'I thought they seemed ideally suited. They're certainly wrapped up in each other – from what I've seen, anyway. And Ruth's a lovely girl.'

'The best. But it's this stupid class thing. I'm not sure if I've told you, but Ruth lives in a council house.'

Sadie didn't answer immediately then she said, 'No, you didn't tell me.' She brought over the teapot, and joined Polly at the kitchen table. Slowly she took a cigarette out of her silver case, and struck the flint on her matching lighter. Seconds later, she blew out a stream of smoke, looked at her daughter and said, 'Actually, I grew up in a council flat myself.'

Astonished, Polly could only stare at the elegant woman sitting before her. 'You've never told me that. In fact, you've never told me anything!'

Sadie shrugged. 'You've never asked. You've never shown any interest in my background.'

Polly felt the colour rise in her cheeks and then said awkwardly, 'I haven't felt able to ask you. Or at least, I hadn't used to.'

There was a short silence between them, then Sadie said, 'Do you feel different now?'

Polly hesitated. 'Yes, I think I do.'

Sadie gazed at her for one long measuring moment. 'Perhaps we could open a bottle of wine sometime and talk. That's if you'd like to.' Polly, feeling slightly embarrassed, said, 'Yes, I would.'

Later, as Sadie lowered the temperature in the oven, checked on the simmering saucepans, and put the plates to warm, her mind was already running ahead. So the moment had, at last, arrived. But then she'd always known that it would. I've had years to think about this, she thought, to agonise over it, and I shall tell her the truth. Although it wouldn't be easy – either for her or for Polly. But if her daughter began to probe further, to ask dangerous questions relating to André, Sadie knew she would lie. Because how could any girl, particularly one brought up as a Roman Catholic, be able to cope with the revelation that she owed her existence to a casual drunken encounter between two strangers? I may not have done much for her in her life, Sadie thought, but at least I can spare her that.

Late the following afternoon, Polly and Sadie, laden with bags, arrived thankfully back at The Gables. They'd been shopping in Stone, where they'd both spent more than they'd intended. 'I'm exhausted,' Polly complained. 'Why is it that trailing around the shops and trying on clothes is so tiring?'

Sadie laughed. 'Tell me about it! I've got a guilty conscience as well, because if I buy my clothes at the boutique, I can get a discount!'

'Yes but you wouldn't have got that suit – it's an exclusive!'

'I know, fabulous, isn't it?' She glanced at Polly. 'And thanks for finding it. It's a real change from the sort of thing I usually wear.' She laughed. 'You should have seen your face when I tried on that red cocktail dress. You were horrified!'

'Well, it was a bit much!'

'It's been fun, hasn't it?' Sadie said, and Polly, suddenly realising how much she'd enjoyed the afternoon, nodded.

After they'd been upstairs to put away their treasured purchases, neither felt like cooking dinner, so they settled for poached eggs on toast, and a slice of home-made fruit cake. It was much later, when they were relaxing in the drawing room, that Polly said hesitantly, 'Shall I open that bottle of wine?'

Sadie became very still. 'Why not?' she said. 'There's a couple in the fridge. You choose – either is fine with me.'

A few minutes later, Polly returned with an opened bottle of white wine and two glasses. She put them down on the coffee table, poured them both a drink, then sat on the leather sofa and leaned back. Her pose was relaxed, but Sadie, acutely conscious of the tension in her own body, sensed that Polly was also on edge. For a few moments there was silence between them, then Sadie said, 'So, I take it that you'd like to know a bit more about me?'

Polly nodded. 'I hardly know anything really, only what Grandad told me.'

'And that was?'

'Just that you came from London, and worked in Derry & Toms.' Polly glanced across at her mother. 'To be honest, he didn't seem comfortable talking about you. I did ask him once about my other grandparents, but he said he knew little about them, except that they were dead.'

Sadie was quiet for a moment, and then she said, 'That's true. My father died when I was twelve, and my mother four years later.'

'I'm sorry you lost them so young. That must have been really hard,' Polly said with sympathy.

'The worst was when Dad died.' Sadie's eyes shadowed. She hesitated, then looked across at Polly. 'Remember Lonnie Donegan and "My Old Man's a Dustman"?'

'Yes, of course.'

'That could have been written about me.' She looked at Polly's astonished expression. 'You're shocked, aren't you?'

Polly shook her head. 'Not in the way you mean. I'm just surprised. After all no one would...'

'Guess I was a dustman's daughter? I hope not, or I've wasted many years of my life,' Sadie said. 'I might have been born into poverty, Polly, but I was determined to rise above it. Not that there's anything wrong in being poor, and it's certainly nothing to be ashamed of. But it does stop people from realising their potential.' Sadie leaned forward, her face intent. 'Take my dad, for instance, your grandfather. He never had much education to speak of, but do you know what he did in his spare time? He wrote poetry. It was good too. Who knows, in different circumstances he might even have got it published! You wouldn't have thought it to look at him. He was built like a wrestler, but was the kindest man I ever met.'

'What was his name?'

'Arnold, but he was always called Arnie.'

'And your mother?'

Sadie's expression hardened. 'She was called Iris. Blonde, mercenary, and always on at him; wanting money for this or that – usually for make-up or clothes. We lived hand to mouth, like a lot of people did in those days. To give her credit, she did have a part-time job as a cleaner. She worked in one of the offices in Hammersmith. But she didn't do much at home. We never had decent meals, it was always something out of a tin, or she'd send me down to the fish and chip shop. Why he married her, I'll never know. And she was always telling him she could have done better for herself.'

'Not a very happy home to grow up in,' Polly said with sympathy.

'Oh, it wasn't so bad, as long as Dad was alive. But he had a massive heart attack, and after that everything changed.' Sadie's stomach clenched into a fist with nerves as she took a long sip of her wine, wishing she'd had a couple of gin and tonics first.

Polly saw her hesitation, the anxiety in her eyes, and said, 'You don't have to tell me anything you don't want to.'

'You have a right to know about your roots, Polly. Everyone does.'

But it had taken Sadie many years to bury her troubled past, and for one panic-stricken moment she wondered whether she was going to make a terrible mistake. Then glancing across at her daughter, she saw not only curiosity but also an expression in her eyes that seemed to hold a hint of affection. Have faith in her, Sadie told herself. She took a deep breath and continued, 'Mum had always been a bit "flighty", as they used to call it, but without Dad's steadying influence, she just went off the rails. Shortly after he died, she met someone at the offices where she worked. He was there late one night – I suppose he was all sharp suit and glib tongue – and she was a looker, I'll grant her that. Anyway, the next thing I knew, I was left with five bob for chips, a few tins of beans, and she was off for a week's holiday in Brighton. After that,' Sadie shrugged, 'she realised she was "sitting on a fortune" as she called it, and I soon learned to make myself scarce when she brought a man home!'

Polly could only stare at her in profound shock. Her own grandmother was a prostitute! Because surely from what Sadie was saying, that was what she became. And my mother, Polly thought wildly – she must have slept with dozens of men. And that thought was followed by swift and terrifying panic. Suppose she took after them? After all, people always said, 'Blood will out!' And then an image flashed before her of John Merton's dignity, his strict moral code; her own schooldays under the guidance of nuns. How fortunate she was to have been under his protection all those years.

Sadie, watching the fleeting expressions on Polly's face, seeing her dilated pupils, guessed what was going through her daughter's mind. She began to wonder whether she was wrong, and she should have glossed over the truth, fabricated a story. But words, once they had been spoken, could never be recalled. As silence lay between them, Sadie shakily lit a cigarette.

Polly gazed at her mother, finding it difficult to reconcile the woman before her, tastefully dressed in a camel skirt and cream twinset, with this new knowledge. Anyone would think that she came from a comfortable middle-class background – even the way she speaks gives that impression, Polly thought. 'How on earth,' she asked, 'did you manage to become the person you are, so confident and well spoken, raised in an environment like that.'

Sadie gave a wry smile. 'Well, it certainly wasn't from what I was taught at school.' She looked across at Polly. 'You won't like hearing this, but I learned everything I know about how to behave, the correct way to dress, etcetera from the men I met. I was lucky, I suppose, in that I seemed to attract a certain class of man, one who would take me to a restaurant, or to a theatre. And I've always loved reading. I used to get books out of the public library and lose myself in them. It was my only escape from what was going on in the next room. So that helped with vocabulary, and as for losing the accent, I soon found out that people judge you on how you speak. I couldn't afford elocution lessons, so I used to listen to the wireless and practise.' She paused and when she spoke again her voice was shaky, 'Polly, before you bring yourself to ask – I want you to know that I may have my faults but I've never taken money for sex in my life. Nor have I ever slept with a man unless I found him attractive. My attitude to morality might be different from your own, but believe me; a taste for prostitution *isn't* hereditary.'

Polly was staring at her when suddenly they both turned at the shrill tone of the telephone. 'Damn!' Polly muttered, and hurriedly got up. 'I won't be a minute...'

Sadie, feeling emotionally drained, stubbed out her cigarette, and leaning back in the armchair rested her head against the cool leather. Talking about her childhood had brought so many images into her mind. Her father, with his heavy features and bulging muscles, might have seemed intimidating to a stranger, but he'd been her security blanket. Left alone, her mother, always selfish, had not only neglected the flat but also her only child. And as she recalled the careless unpalatable food, Sadie thought that perhaps that was the reason she took such pride in her own cooking. But she was quite aware that she had inherited her mother's selfishness; Sadie had never been one to deny her shortcomings.

On returning, Polly paused in the doorway as she saw the strain on her mother's unguarded face and suddenly realised how much courage it must have taken for such painful honesty. There were questions she was longing to ask, even if she half-dreaded the answers, but she sensed immediately that the phone call – coming as it had at such a crucial time – had pierced the emotionally charged atmosphere, had broken the mood. 'Sorry,' she said, feeling both furious and disappointed. 'It was Anita, telling me they've set a date for the wedding. She was so excited; I hadn't the heart to cut her short.'

Sadie forced herself to smile. 'She'll make a lovely bride.'

'You look tired,' Polly said.

Sadie nodded. 'I am. I think I'll go to bed if you don't mind, I'm beginning to get a headache.'

'No, you go. There's always another time.' The two women gazed at each other for a moment, then Polly said quietly, 'Thank you for being so truthful.'

'You deserved nothing less.'

After bidding her mother goodnight, Polly remained on the sofa, struggling with conflicting emotions as she tried to come to terms with Sadie's revelations. The image of a young girl bereaved of the one person she loved, neglected and exposed to vice in her own home, was a heartrending one. We have no control over the family we're born into, Polly thought sadly. Not parents, class, religion or race. At least Sadie had loved her father, but her mother sounded an awful woman! Polly tried to console herself with the knowledge that her other grandmother, Emilie, had been beautiful and caring, adored by both her husband and son. And I must keep telling myself that, Polly thought with despair. Because she was painfully aware that the shame of what she'd just learned would stay with her for the rest of her life.

22

The following morning when Polly came downstairs to the kitchen, Sadie was already spooning
the fat over a couple of eggs in the frying pan. She
withdrew four oatcakes from beneath the grill, put
them at the side of the bacon, and carried the
warm plates into the breakfast room. 'Good
timing,' she smiled, 'but I did hear you moving
about.'

'How's your headache?' Polly felt a bit
awkward, wondering how Sadie was feeling after
her revelations last night.

'Gone, thanks.' As Polly tipped tomato ketchup
on to her plate, Sadie glanced swiftly at her,
trying to sense if there was any change, any
coolness in her attitude.

Polly simply tucked into her food with enthusiasm. 'Nothing like it is there?' she said, 'a proper
Staffordshire breakfast!'

And so afterwards when they'd washed the
dishes, instead of following Polly into the drawing room to relax before the log fire, Sadie went
upstairs to her bedroom. She hesitated, then
opened the bottom drawer of the oak tallboy that
stood in one corner. Bending down, she lifted
some jumpers and took out a creased brown
envelope, stared at it for a moment, then taking
the envelope with her went down to join Polly.

'I thought you might like to see these,' she said,

and Polly looked up from where she was lounging on the sofa propped against a cushion. As her mother hovered, envelope in hand, Polly swung her legs to the floor so that Sadie could sit by her side.

'What are they?'

'Photographs – and something else, but I'll show you the photographs first.' Sadie withdrew a black and white snapshot, slightly curling at the edges. 'This is your grandfather.' Polly took the photo from her and studied it with avid interest. It showed a massively built man, wearing a shirt with the sleeves rolled up, which revealed a tattoo on his right forearm. 'He got that,' Sadie said, pointing to it, 'in the Merchant Navy. He joined when he was seventeen.' As Polly remained silent, Sadie took out another photo. 'And this is your grandmother.' Polly stared down at the provocative pose. Iris was pouting at the camera, and was exactly as Sadie had described her, but there was a challenge in her attitude, and Polly guessed that, like her daughter, Iris would not have found it easy to conform.

'They look a mismatched couple,' she said eventually.

'That's putting it mildly. But as I told you last night, don't be misled by Dad's appearance.' Sadie took out a lined sheet of paper, obviously torn from an exercise book. 'This is one of his poems. He wrote it for my tenth birthday.'

Polly took the page from her and glanced down at the lines, thinking just to scan through them. But then she began to read more slowly, and once she reached the end, read through the poem again. 'That's beautiful,' she said in wonderment. 'You'd never think...'

'That's what I told you. It's a mistake to judge people by their physical appearance,' Sadie told her. 'Their attitude, the way they dress, yes. But we all inherit our looks – we have no control over that.'

Polly was thinking how fascinating it was to have such a link between her and this unknown man; to actually see his handwriting, to read the words he'd written, such sensitive words. Then she picked up the photo of Iris again and stared down at it. This was the woman who despite having a young daughter there had brought a succession of strange men into her home. No wonder Sadie was...

'I know what you're thinking,' Sadie said quietly. 'You're thinking – this explains a lot – about me, I mean.'

Startled, Polly looked at her and then nodded.

'I don't agree with blaming everything on one's childhood,' Sadie said. 'Oh, I'm sure it affected me in some ways, but I've never been a victim, Polly – it's not in my nature. I chose my lifestyle – I didn't drift into it.'

'I still think it must have had some effect on you,' Polly said. 'After all, you were at a very impressionable age.'

Sadie gazed at her, 'Maybe.' Suddenly feeling that she wasn't ready to deal with the thread the discussion was taking, she got up from the sofa. 'Enough reminiscing for one weekend, I think.' Picking up one of the newspapers, she sat in one of the armchairs and said in a lighter tone, 'I wonder if we'll see George at the Crown at lunchtime?'

Sensing the finality in her tone, Polly tried to hide her dismay. She glanced across at the sideboard, at the photograph of her father smiling in his RAF uniform. Although it was possible that he'd known about Sadie's background – after all she could hardly be blamed for that – surely he'd had no knowledge of her way of life? Or had that begun only after he'd died? There was so much she wanted to ask, wanted to try and understand. But the subject was too sensitive for her to pursue it at the wrong time. So taking her lead from Sadie, she merely said, 'Does he usually go?'

'Sometimes,' Sadie glanced at her daughter. 'But we're only friends, Polly. There's been nothing else, not since Felicity died.'

Over in Abbey Hulton, anticipation of Sunday lunch was not so relaxed.

Michael was in a mutinous mood, having had his hair washed, his knees scrubbed, and been told not to get his best clothes dirty. He was sitting on the sofa waiting for the twins to come down. Mrs Donovan was organising her household as though they were on the parade ground. 'You're going to eleven o'clock Mass with your sisters,' she told him, 'because I want you out from under me feet while Ruth and I get the dinner.'

'Just because this Mark's coming,' Michael grumbled. 'I wanted to come to the eight o'clock with you and Ruth. It's quicker. Now I'll have to sit through a long sermon.'

'And that won't do you any harm, you little heathen. Anyway, it'll be nice for you all to go

202

together with yer dad. And glory be to God,' she said, as Teresa and Maria came in. 'Will yer look at the pair of you!'

Ruth came in from the kitchen, 'I think they look great.'

'They do, don't they?' Mrs Donovan looked with pride at her two younger daughters, smartly dressed in similar, but not matching, blouses and skirts. Both had taken care with their hair and were wearing very discreet make-up. 'You'd better look out, Ruth, or you'll be having competition!'

Ruth laughed. 'I'm not holding my breath.'

'What time did you say he was coming?' Maria said.

'About twelve, so he should be here when you get back.' Ruth looked up as her father came into the room.

Sean Donovan's only concession to the occasion was to wear a new tie. He always wore his best suit to go to church, although normally he would change when he got home and hang it carefully in the wardrobe. But today, he'd had strict instructions from Bridie to keep it on. 'Come along then,' he said, 'we don't want to be late.'

When the door closed behind them all, both Ruth and her mother breathed a sigh of relief. 'Right,' said Ruth. 'I'll check the downstairs lav, and tidy up the bathroom.'

'He'll not be wanting to go up there?' Bridie said with alarm.

'He might have to. We can't expect him to wash his hands in the kitchen! Don't worry; I'll shut all the bedroom doors.'

'I wish he wasn't an only child,' Bridie fretted.

'I bet his house is neat as a pin.'

'I wouldn't know, I've never been,' Ruth said. She was curious to see the house where Mark had grown up. One could, she knew, learn a lot about a person by seeing them in their own environment. Not that Ruth had any doubts about him; the more time they spent together, the more sure she was of her feelings.

Once the sitting room was spick and span, with all clutter cleared away, Bridie went into the kitchen while Ruth released the centre of the dining table to extend it. She spread the best white tablecloth, polished the chrome cutlery, and wiped the glass cruet. Rubbing in vain at a few marks on the place mats, she folded white paper napkins into triangles next to them, and fetched an old dining chair from her parents' bedroom. It didn't match the other six, and the brown leatherette seat was worn and hollow, so Ruth put it in Michael's place and then stood back to survey her handiwork. She'd wanted to have wine, but her father had refused. 'Let him see us as we are,' he said, 'not as you'd like us to be!' So now, she merely filled a jug with water, and put glasses on the table. She'd already, in collaboration with Bridie, hidden the bottles of Tizer they usually drank, announcing that the 'pop man' hadn't delivered them.

'At least *you* understand,' she said to her mother. 'It's just that...'

'Ah, men have no idea,' Bridle reassured her. 'But,' she looked sharply at her daughter, 'yer father's right – there's no need to put on airs and graces.'

Mark was thoughtful as he made his way along the now familiar route to Abbey Hulton. His father had expressed disapproval of him coming away from Oxford so soon after the beginning of term. 'It's your final year,' he said with a frown. 'You shouldn't let yourself get distracted. There'll be plenty of time for that, later.'

Mark knew he was right. When Ruth had written that her parents wished to meet him, he'd merely thought that she'd meant sometime in the future. But on the phone – and that wasn't easy when he only had access to a communal one and she was in a callbox, she'd mentioned it again. Her voice had sounded anxious and on the spur of the moment he'd offered to come over the following weekend. Now, like Polly before him, Mark was curious to see inside a council house. People often spoke disparagingly of them, but in Mark's opinion, an environment that could produce an intelligent girl like Ruth – not to mention her two precocious sisters – was one likely to prove interesting.

As he turned into the road, he drove very slowly, wary of two little girls playing 'catch' with a ball on the pavement. Sure enough, the ball bounced into the road. Mark braked while one of the girls – neatly dressed in a check dress and white ankle socks – gave him a cheeky grin, and ran to pick it up. When he'd driven Ruth home before, it had been at night, and although he'd been surprised by how narrow the road was, making the identical houses facing each other seem close, it was only now that he could see the variation in how they were kept. Particularly the small front gardens;

most were neat, but others sadly neglected. The Donovans' house was one of the neat ones. He parked his maroon Ford Anglia outside the house, and opening the gate walked up the path. Standing before the green painted door with its four panels of frosted glass he knocked on the door to be welcomed by Ruth. 'Hi,' she said.

'Hi, yourself.' Mark stepped into the tiny hall, and pulled her to him. He kissed her deeply on the lips and held her close. 'Mmn,' he murmured, 'your hair smells wonderful.'

'I wish it was sleek and glamorous,' Ruth said, still despairing of its coarse texture.

'I don't,' Mark smiled. 'It's like you, prickly and full of sparks!'

Ruth laughed, and led the way into the sitting room.

'Something smells nice,' Mark said with appreciation.

'Roast lamb,' she whispered. 'Mum decided that was the easiest. No Yorkshire, no fiddly stuffing and apple sauce.'

'But what about the mint sauce?' he whispered back in mock alarm.

'No problem, we grow mint in the back garden, and I've already chopped it.'

'In that case, I'll stay,' he said, and they were both laughing when Bridie came in from the kitchen.

'I thought I heard voices!' She looked reprovingly at Ruth. 'You should have called me.'

'I've only just arrived,' Mark said quickly, and held out his hand. 'How are you, Mrs Donovan? I'm glad to meet you at last.'

'And you.' Bridie, who had discarded her apron before coming in and was dressed in a blue jersey dress that she normally wore 'for best', shook his hand. Mark saw in her features a foretaste of how Ruth might look in later years. The resemblance between mother and daughter was startling, particularly their hair, although Mrs Donovan's was now lightly streaked with grey. 'Sit yourself down, Mark,' Bridie said. 'The others will be back from Mass soon. Ruth and I went to the eight o'clock.' She waited in vain for Mark to announce that he too had been to church and compressed her lips when he didn't. A typical Protestant, she thought.

Mark glanced around at the small, tidy room, at the cheap furniture, the gaudy holy pictures on the wall, the small crucifix at the side of the beige tiled fireplace. He knew Ruth was a Catholic, of course, but it was only now that he fully realised what a large part religion played in this family's life. 'I'm looking forward to meeting everyone,' he said, and smiled at her, sensing that Ruth's mother was ill at ease. But his attempts to reassure her only made Bridie even more aware of the social gap between them. This young man, with his air of confidence, and middle-class vowels was never going to fit in with the Donovan family. She glanced sharply at her daughter, but Ruth had eyes only for Mark.

Bridie said with some trepidation, 'We're having roast lamb for dinner, Mark, and I've made a bread and butter pudding for afters, or there's an apple pie.'

'That sounds wonderful, Mrs Donovan.'

Ruth, wishing her mother had called the meal 'lunch', said, 'Would you like a glass of sherry,

Mark?' She'd never seen him drink sherry, but it was all they could offer him, unless... 'or we have some Davenport's beer?'

'A beer would be great,' he said, and Bridie breathed a sigh of relief. That might help to break the ice when Sean came home. Men always seemed to get on better with a beer glass in their hands!

And so, when Sean returned, it was to see a tall young man, not in a suit, but 'decently dressed', in grey slacks, and a shirt and tie beneath his maroon finely knit sweater. Mark stood up and looked at the stocky Irishman, noting his keen gaze, his slightly truculent expression. 'Good to meet you, Mr Donovan,' he said, holding out his hand.

Sean shook it politely and then turned to Michael, who was hovering behind him. 'And this is young Michael,' he said.

'Hello.' Mark smiled down at him and then the twins were crowding into the room.

'Hi, Mark,' they chorused. They were both looking demure, with Peter Pan collars, and each wore a medal on a chain, which Teresa told him later was called a Miraculous Medal.

'We have a special devotion to Our Lady,' she said piously, and Mark had to stifle a grin, as he recalled their sexy outfits at the New Year's Eve party.

But he was not insensitive to an undercurrent of tension around the table, as they all enjoyed an excellent roast. Occasionally, he would meet Ruth's anxious eyes and smile reassuringly. But Mark was thoughtful as later he drove back to Oxford. He'd known, of course, that their social backgrounds were very different, but hadn't realised until now just how wide the gap was. And then there was all this religious stuff...

23

The decision about how to approach their research had given Nicolas much thought. Through his work on an international magazine he had several contacts in England, but the matter was of such a sensitive nature that he knew he had to be discreet. Jules was essentially a private man, and Nicolas had no intention of revealing any of his personal details to strangers. He found out that there was a well respected, county magazine called *Staffordshire Life*. There were local newspapers too; especially a prominent one called the *Evening Sentinel*, but Nicolas was wary. Newspapers, if their journalists scented a human interest story, might decide to probe. At this initial and delicate stage, it was not a risk he was willing to take. So he sent off for a few back copies of the county magazine, and when they arrived at the office took them home so that Jules could study them.

But to their disappointment, no memories were triggered either by the coloured illustrations, the advertisements, or the many photographs.

'Perhaps,' Jules said with despair, 'we're not on the right track after all.'

'I think we should persevere,' Nicolas said. 'After all, what have we got to lose? I still want to contact the editor, and see if he'll run a short article.'

Jules frowned. 'You really think people might get in touch?'

'Trust me,' Nicolas said, 'I'll be amazed if we don't receive some replies, particularly if the tone of the article is one of appeal. Most people like to help if they can.'

'I'm glad you've retained your faith in human nature,' Jules said drily, 'particularly as a child who grew up in the war.'

'I have you and Maman to thank for that.'

Jules smiled at him, and leafed again through one of the magazines. But there was nothing, just pages of social occasions, with faces of unknown people. He didn't recognise any of the place names and surely, if he'd spent his childhood in Staffordshire, at least one of them would have struck a chord. But then nothing had before, not in twenty years, so why should he be surprised? He'd desperately hoped for more after the strange happenings during the last six months. First there had been his traumatic reaction near the café on hearing the brown-haired girl laughing. And then the emotional dream about the beautiful older woman, with that wonderful feeling of warmth and tenderness. But the dream that had affected him most deeply was that of the accident, the horror of the large grey car bearing down on him, of the violence to his body, the sickening crash of his head against the rock. He'd never been able to erase it from his mind, and Jules was positive that he'd relived the accident that had robbed him of his memory. After so many years, the recent scene in the café and Oliver's insight had made Jules impatient, and he was finding it difficult to control his frustration. Now he looked up at Nicolas and shook his head. 'There is nothing here, I'm afraid.'

'No matter; I still think that we should go ahead,' Nicolas said. 'All will depend on what the editor says, although I have an idea how to arouse his interest. They'll already have put February's issue to bed. But there's a good chance he might include it in the March one, which will go on sale in February.'

Ruth, when Polly collected her from Abbey Hulton, was full of Mark's visit. 'It went brilliantly,' she said. 'Mark even won our Michael over by asking him about Stoke City!'

'So your parents won't worry any more?'

'I wouldn't say that. Oh, they seemed to like him all right, but I can just imagine the conversation now I've left. You know – different class, different religion – all that sort of thing.'

'Different religion?' Polly glanced at her friend. 'What does that matter? You're not saying it's serious? Not marriage and all that?'

'It is on my part,' Ruth grinned, 'but you must promise not to breathe a word to Mark – I don't want to frighten him off!'

'Of course I won't.' After negotiating a difficult junction, Polly tried to examine her feelings. Ruth married to Mark? It was a startling concept. She'd known, of course, that Ruth was mad about him, but marriage? They'd only been going out together a couple of months. Polly cast another glance at Ruth, and seeing the determined set of her chin, thought with some unease, I hope Mark feels the same; otherwise she's going to be devastated. And suddenly feelings of envy swept over her. To be so in love, so sure of how you felt, to have met the one person you wanted to spend your life with – that must be wonderful! Polly sometimes agonised over whether there was anything wrong with her, because apart from her youthful crush on Mark, she hadn't felt attracted – not really attracted – to anyone for ages. But she'd found the past couple of years so difficult. There had been the shock of losing her grandfather, then the traumatic adjustment to sharing her home with Sadie – with all that entailed! Polly had been too immersed in her personal problems to be much interested in romance. Yet she'd be twenty-one this year. Look at Anita, planning her wedding already!

Polly grinned as she recalled Mrs Booth, when Anita had become engaged, scoffing, 'I told you there was no point in a girl going to university, only to get married and 'ave kids. You don't need a fancy education for that!'

But, Polly thought, as she drew up on the college campus, you are so wrong, Mrs Booth. The way children are brought up affects them for the rest of their lives. Surely having a mother with an intelligent, enquiring mind is an advantage? 'What do you think, Ruth?' she said, as they unloaded their weekend cases from the boot. '*Is* it a waste of time for a girl to have a decent education – if she's only going to stay at home and raise a family?'

'Whatever's been going through your head?' Ruth said in surprise. 'How can you even ask me such a thing?' She'd been so lost in her own thoughts, that she hadn't noticed Polly's silence.

'I don't think education is ever wasted. If the time ever comes when it's seen only as a means to get a better job, we'll all be the worse for it.'

Polly nodded in agreement, and the two girls parted to go to their respective rooms. Ruth to fling herself on the narrow bed to go over all that had happened that weekend, Polly to unpack, storing her things as neatly as she could in the confined space. But her heart and mind were back at The Gables. She was trying to analyse her feelings, her reaction to discovering the truth about Sadie's parents and background. She did feel that now she understood her mother better. And there had, even if it was hesitant, been actual warmth between them when parting. How strange, Polly thought, that it had taken such a shameful revelation to achieve it.

It was one evening, a few days later, that Polly picked up the copy of *Staffordshire Life* she'd brought from The Gables. Her grandfather had always subscribed to it and she had continued, liking to flick through the magazine to see if she recognised anyone in the photographs. The articles, usually locally based, were interesting too. Sadie, however, rarely read it, preferring *Vogue*.

Lying on her bed with a box of chocolates by her side, Polly began to leaf through the pages, and pulled a face when she saw Hilary smiling out from a photo of a dinner dance. It was only after she'd finished examining the society pages, that she saw the article. It was the heading that caught her attention: FRENCH JOURNALIST IS SEEKING INFORMATION. Intrigued, Polly glanced down and began to read. Five minutes

213

later, she went along the corridor and knocked on Ruth's door, taking both the magazine and her box of chocolates. 'What do you think about this?' she said, going in and sitting on the bed. 'Go on, read it aloud.'

Ruth popped a coffee cream into her mouth, and a few seconds later began to read.

Nicolas Giscard, a journalist in Paris, is research-ing the subject of English/French bilingual speakers. Is there a difference, he wonders, be-tween people who have been bilingual from birth, and those who have been taught at a later age? He has chosen several counties in England, Staf-fordshire being one of them, as his representative areas, and would be extremely grateful for inform-ation to help him in his research. He would like to hear from anyone who taught a child French from birth, or who learned French from birth.

Please contact: Nicolas Giscard, P.O. Box 51, at *Staffordshire Life,* etc.

Ruth looked up. 'You think this applies to you?'

Polly nodded. 'I had a French nanny right from when I was a baby. She was called Hortense. She was quite strict, but I really liked her.'

'How long did she stay?'

'Quite a while – she got married and moved to Canada when I was about nine. But by then I had the language skills, and of course we did French at the convent. That's when I began boarding. Gran-dad was always keen for me to be bilingual; he used to say that's what my father would have wanted.'

'Did he speak French? Your grandfather, I mean?'

'Yes, that's how he met Emilie. He was in Paris for an exhibition. But he always said that my French was better than his, just as my father's had been. Something to do with speaking it from birth, I suppose.' She took the magazine back from Ruth's outstretched hand. 'Do you think I should get in touch?'

'Well, you do seem to fit the bill. And you never know,' Ruth grinned, 'he might be tall, dark and handsome!'

'He's not asking to meet me, idiot. In any case, he'll probably get lots of replies.'

'Not that many,' Ruth said thoughtfully. Then, changing the subject, said, 'Have you written your essay yet? It's due in on Tuesday.'

'Crumbs, no.' Polly scrambled off the bed. 'I'd better do that, never mind thinking about strange men.'

'It's more fun, though,' Ruth called after her, and Polly laughed.

Once back in her room, Polly opened the magazine again, and looked down at the name Nicolas Giscard. I'll sleep on it, she thought, and with some reluctance tried to focus her mind on her course work.

But at midnight, Polly was up and sitting at her desk. The essay was finished, but her mind was restless. The article had awakened so many memories; of Hortense, of her grandfather taking her to Montpellier, the holidays she'd spent there. I do seem to be the sort of person he's looking for, she mused. Perhaps he wanted to send her a questionnaire to fill in. She needed to take advantage of every opportunity to use her bilingual skills as she was hoping to get a post in a school where they taught French from an early age. Polly turned quickly to glance at the time displayed on her alarm clock. Then with a slight feeling of guilt, she opened the magazine yet again. A few seconds later she hesitated, then reached out for her box of headed notepaper.

24

In Paris, time seemed to pass slowly, with Jules trying to force himself to be patient until the publication of the March issue of the magazine. And then, to his surprise, there came a letter from England. It was from Oliver Sands.

I find, my new friend, that your problem has much occupied me since my return. As I am retired you will appreciate that I have time on my hands, and so it has given me both interest and pleasure to delve further into your case. I have a library of recordings of regional accents, and have been listening intently to those of the Staffordshire region. I am even more convinced of my original deduction that you are English by birth. If you intend to follow things up, then I would advise you to concentrate on the area around Stafford and possibly Stoke-on-Trent. I have also studied recent papers on phonetics, and it is my considered opinion that you actually grew up and were educated in England, rather than spending considerable time there. Life is very strange, Jules. How fortuitous it was that we should both be in that café at the same time. But then, anyone who studies history knows that all of life is chance.

In the hope that this might be helpful,

Yours sincerely,

Oliver Sands

PS: I do hope you will inform me of any discovery or outcome.

Nicolas, when Jules showed him the letter, felt a surge of excitement. 'Don't you see, Papa,' he exclaimed, 'This will make things so much easier. Schools keep records, so it shouldn't be difficult for the authorities to give us details of any pupils called Giscard! After all, there can't be too many boys in English schools with a French surname.'

But Jules was frowning. 'Do you know what this could mean? What if I *was* actually born in England?'

Nicolas began to laugh. 'That would make you English!'

'That's what I was thinking.' But then Jules shook his head and grinned back at him. 'Impossible,' he said.

'You know,' Nicolas commented the following morning, 'I may be able to get this information about the school today, over the telephone.'

Jules was doubtful as he poured their coffee. 'Are you sure? Officials can be very obstructive.'

217

'You're thinking of your own experience when you tried to trace your background. But that was here in Paris, immediately after the war. Everything was in chaos. It will be different in England – you'll see.'

Jules smiled at his youthful optimism. He must have been like that once although, of course, he had no memory of it. Nor of any friends or adventures he'd had. What had happened in his life during those earlier years? Memories of our past help to make us the people we become, he thought. Then he tried to be positive. At least now he had this search to focus on. It had brought such a new dimension to his life. And all through the day, while his mind solved problems, his administrative skills smoothed the path of commerce, his every sense was attuned to the hours passing. Tonight, he kept thinking, tonight I might learn something tangible; find a clue to follow up. If it was indeed true that a boy named Jules Giscard went to a certain school in a specific area...

But the moment Nicolas entered the apartment, Jules, coming into the hall to meet him, sensed that his news was not good.

'No luck?'

Nicolas gave a resigned shrug. 'I couldn't get through to the person I need. I have to phone again tomorrow.'

'What will you say? I mean what reason will you give?'

'I shall just say that we are tracing our ancestry, and believe there is an English connection. Don't worry; I can turn on the charm when it's needed.'

But the following evening, Nicolas could only

say, 'I'm sorry, Papa, but the man I spoke to could find no trace of a boy of that surname attending any school in Staffordshire.'

'Nothing at all?' Jules stared at him in disbelief. 'Was he helpful? Did you trust him?'

'He was very cooperative, although he warned me first that he couldn't give out any personal information – which I understood – but in the event that wasn't a problem.' By now they were in the salon, and he went to warm his hands by the stove. Rubbing them together, he glanced round. 'He did ask me whether the child might have been privately educated – sent away to boarding school, for instance. Apparently that could have been anywhere in the country.'

Jules frowned. 'Oliver did say that he thought my background was middle-class, so I suppose that might be a possibility.'

'But,' Nicolas pointed out, 'where would you begin? It would be like looking for a needle in a...' he began to search for the English word.

'Haystack,' Jules finished the sentence for him. 'If I wasn't a pupil in a primary school, then I would have been very young to be sent away from home. Surely not – it would be barbaric! Maman and I would never have done that to you.'

'I should hope not,' Nicolas grinned. 'I would have run away!' He looked at Jules and said, 'There's always the article. These magazines come out early; we might have our copy by the end of the month.'

And he was right. On the last day of February, he entered the apartment, his face alight. 'It is in,' he called, taking off his warm coat. He hurried

219

into the kitchen and Jules turned eagerly to face him.

'Let me see.' He took the glossy magazine from Nicolas's outstretched hand.

'Page eleven,' Nicolas said, 'on the right-hand side.'

Jules carried the magazine into the salon and sat in his armchair. He stared down at it for a moment then swiftly turned the pages. A couple of minutes later, he looked across at Nicolas. 'It's excellent,' he said, 'and they've given you an eye-catching caption.'

'And it's in a good position,' Nicolas said. 'Research shows that most people read the right-hand page first.'

Jules looked doubtfully at Nicolas. 'Do you really think you'll have any replies?'

'Yes I do. But whether they'll have any relevance or not...' He shrugged.

'So,' Jules said slowly, reaching out for his cigarettes. 'It is just a matter of waiting.'

In England, Sadie was reading a letter of her own. It was from Babs, bemoaning the long winter.

Do you think you could get a few days off and come down? Before the kids come home from boarding school? I'm sick of my own company, and also getting together with you again has made me realise just how much I miss the old days. We were good pals, Sadie. It just isn't the same with anyone else.

Sadie thoughtfully put the letter down on her lap. Should she? Could she? The shop would probably

220

agree, after all this was their slack time. And she too was feeling jaded. It was pouring with rain, Mrs Booth was rattling about the place – and Sadie still avoided the old battleaxe as much as possible. But her suggestion that the cleaner should change her day to fit in with Sadie's work had met with derision. 'I've always come on Mondays and Thursdays,' she declared, 'I 'ave done for twenty years. It suits me!' And that was that, because Sadie had learned very early that Polly was intractable as far as Mrs Booth was concerned. The woman had softened slightly, due to the occasional cake that Sadie would send for Ernie, but her disapproval oozed out of every pore. Save me from self-righteous women, she thought grimly, although she had to admit that Doris Booth was loyal and hardworking. Sadie read the letter again. Why not? she thought. It will do me good to get away for a bit. She heard the vacuum cease its whirring downstairs, and glanced at her watch. Ten minutes to go, then Mrs Booth would leave.

She decided to have scrambled eggs for lunch and continued sitting by the window and gazing out at the garden she loved so much, at the way it stretched into the distance, its lawns, flowerbeds and rockeries. The well-tended vegetable patch was screened by a dividing hedge. Before she'd come to live here, she'd never tasted fresh garden-grown produce. The gardener, Harry, his skin brown and weathered by outdoor work, was a man of few words. But she felt he'd eventually come to tolerate her. How I shall miss it all, she thought, because even if Polly, by some miracle, invited her to stay on after November, Sadie knew that her daughter was almost certain to meet someone soon. Possibly a man she wanted to marry. And who would want their mother-in-law living with them? I've come to love this house, Sadie suddenly realised, and that's something I didn't expect. Her earlier lightning visits to The Gables had been full of awkwardness. Unable to pierce the barrier raised by her small daughter, who stared silently at her with wide unblinking eyes, and faced with the scrupulously polite John Merton, Sadie had always returned to London with relief.

What a selfish bitch she'd been. It was only lately that she was beginning to realise how much she had given up with that fateful decision, when she'd left her twelve-month-old baby in John Merton's care. No matter that the circumstances had been traumatic – Babs was right in her condemnation. How could she have done it? Because it was only now, as she began to discover her daughter, to feel at last the buds of warmth developing between them, that Sadie's latent and long-buried guilt was beginning to emerge. This new and surprisingly emotive relationship had its share of thorns. And that, she thought, getting up from the pink velvet-covered chair, is another reason why I need to get away.

25

There were three replies. They arrived at the office where Nicolas worked, and he closely examined every envelope, noting the postmark, trying to gauge from the handwriting the age and/or the sex of the writer. There was a pink one, impregnated with cheap scent, and two blue ones imprinted with the name Basildon Bond. He contained his curiosity and took them home unopened.

'Papa?' he called as he entered the apartment, and the eagerness with which Jules came forward betrayed his anxiety. 'I have replies,' Nicolas said, brandishing the large brown envelope.

'Have you...?'

'Of course not, we'll read them together.'

'I'll bring us both some coffee.'

Nicolas took off his coat and hung it in the small hall, then went into the salon. He sat at the mahogany circular table, took the envelopes out and spread them in a line. The editor had waited two weeks before forwarding them on, which Nicolas considered sensible. Jules came in with the steaming cups of coffee, placed them on the table, then turned away to take out a silver paper knife from a drawer of the dresser. They both looked at each other.

'Which one shall we open first?' Jules said, his stomach twisting with nerves.

Nicolas smiled and pulled forward the pink

envelope. *'Cherchez la femme?'*

Jules pulled a face at the scent, and then slit the envelope. He scanned the few lines, grimaced and passed the letter to Nicolas. 'No use. Her mother was French, and she lived with her in Dieppe until she was twelve.' Nicolas glanced at it, and then waited as Jules opened one of the blue envelopes. But it was from an old lady of eighty-one whose grandfather taught her French from birth. 'So kind of her to write,' Jules said, 'but not much help.' He slit open the last envelope, took out the sheet of paper, and again shook his head, 'No good. It's from a schoolboy whose French grammar, I'm afraid, leaves a lot to be desired!'

'There could easily be others,' Nicolas told him. 'Many people will have a magazine for days or even weeks, before they read it.'

Jules knew that was true, but it didn't make the waiting any easier. And although he knew that Nicolas had wanted to protect him, Jules was also beginning to wonder if the article had been too general in its tone. But the very idea of playing on people's sympathies, of being an object of curiosity, was anathema to Jules. He shook his head after Nicolas had left the room. This whole project was, after all, based purely on the fact that Oliver Sands refused to believe that Jules was French. The professor may be an expert in his field, Jules thought, but that didn't mean he couldn't be mistaken.

There were three more letters the following week. One was from a middle-aged woman who had learned French from her grandfather, but added that she hadn't passed on the ability to her own children.

Jules picked up the second envelope and slit it open. There was one sheet of matching notepaper, ivory in colour and of good quality. It began, *'Cher Monsieur...'*

Seconds later, he looked up at Nicolas, who was waiting expectantly, and shook his head. 'I'm afraid not. It's from someone who says that her grandmother, who died before she was born, came from Montpellier. This girl had a French nanny until she was nine, who taught her well judging by the letter. The nanny then got married, went to live in Canada and had a family of her own.'

'How old is the girl?'

'She says she's twenty. So if we do the maths, it's unlikely the nanny would have been old enough to have taught me.' He put the letter to one side and, hardly daring to hope, picked up the last one. It was from a teacher who was also interested in bilingual research. His spirits plummeting, Jules handed it to Nicolas.

'He wants me to share my findings,' Nicolas said after a moment. 'I never thought of that happening.'

'What will you do?'

'I'm replying to all the other letters, of course, simply a polite thank you. With this one, I'll have to say that I will keep his letter on file. As time goes on, if he does get in touch again – well, there's always the excuse that mail goes astray. If he persists, I'll have to think of something.'

Jules frowned and ran his fingers through his hair in exasperation. 'I don't really know what I expected.'

'I don't think I did, really,' Nicolas said. 'But it was worth a try, at least.' He was bitterly disappointed, thinking it unlikely now that they would receive any more replies.

Jules began to put the three letters back inside their envelopes, and then as his glance fell on two words embossed at the top of one page, his hand stilled. 'The Gables'. He looked up with a deep frown, staring blankly ahead. 'The Gables'? He knew of that name! How could that be? He looked down at the letter again, and read the rest of the address. 'Nicolas,' he said thoughtfully, 'could you bring over the atlas.'

'What is it?'

Jules shook his head. 'I'm not sure – it's just that there's something here that seems familiar.'

Seconds later they were poring over the map, but couldn't find any mention of the place Brandon. 'It must be just a village,' Nicolas said. 'I'll have to do some research at work.'

'It's just the name of the house that startled me,' Jules said, 'the rest of the address means nothing.' He repeated the two words, 'The Gables', and suddenly an image flashed before his eyes of an imposing house, mellow in sunlight, fronted by two large bay windows. With the image in his mind's eye, he hurriedly got up and, going to the dresser, opened a drawer. Taking a pad and pencil back to the table, Jules forced his now trembling hand to draw.

'What's wrong? What are you doing?'

Jules shook his head, unwilling to be distracted, struggling to retain the memory of what he had just seen. He had never been good at sketching, but eventually he was satisfied. Silently, he slid the pad over.

Nicolas stared down at it with incredulity. 'You've just seen this in your mind?'

Jules nodded. 'It was the name of the house, "The Gables". I knew it, Nicolas, I knew it!'

'Are you sure?' Nicolas took up the letter and slowly read it again. 'The French grandmother – could there be a connection there?'

'Who knows?'

Jules was unable to control the hope, the euphoria beginning to stir within him. He stared at the drawing again. Had he missed anything, any slight detail? He closed his eyes again fearful that he wouldn't be able to recall the exact image he'd seen. But it was still there – the sunlight glinting on the windows. Now he could see a circular drive, a glimpse of a lawn. Nicolas, glancing sharply at his strained expression, went over to the sideboard and poured a large cognac. Then he left Jules in the salon and went to turn on the oven to heat the casserole that Madame Caplat had prepared. As he busied himself making a salad, his mind was racing, hardly able to believe that his article had brought such a glimmer of light. More than a glimmer, he thought, recalling the detailed sketch that Jules had made. Of one thing, Nicolas was positive. After all these blank years, something was happening, and he was convinced that the catalyst had been Maman's sudden and unexpected death. She and Jules had been so close, so happy together. I must be very careful, Nicolas thought, how I word my reply to this young woman.

Meanwhile Jules was leaning forward, nursing his brandy glass, taking an occasional sip of the golden liquid, but found he was too full of tension to be able to relax. The letter was on a small table by his side, and he picked it up, staring down at the single written page in neat, flowing hand-writing. He studied the signature yet again. Polly Merton. He said the surname aloud, wondering, hesitating. *Was* there something there at the back of his mind? Or was he so desperate that it was in his imagination? But of one thing Jules was abso-lutely certain. His startling recognition of the name of the house was real; couldn't be denied, couldn't be explained. But what did it mean? As Nicolas returned to the salon, Jules turned. 'We need to talk.'

'We do indeed.' Nicolas came to sit opposite, but as Jules offered his cigarette case, shook his head. 'Thanks, but I'm trying to cut down.'

'I shall admire you greatly if you can,' Jules said ruefully.

'It's different for you,' Nicolas said. 'Maman told me how much smoking helped, you know, in the early days.'

Jules nodded. 'My nerves were shot to pieces. I don't know what I would have done without her.'

Jules lit a cigarette and then glanced down at the letter again, at the neat crease across the middle. It was good-quality paper, with a private address at the top. 'It fits in,' he said suddenly, 'with what Oliver said about my being from a middle-class background. Stationery like this isn't cheap.'

'And the house you saw,' Nicolas pointed out, 'from the sketch it looks quite a substantial one.'

228

Jules nodded. 'That's how I saw it.'

There was a moment's silence then Nicolas said, 'We will never be able to solve the mystery by staying in Paris.'

'I agree,' Jules said slowly, 'but I can't possibly take a vacation at this time of the year.'

'Maybe not,' Nicolas said, 'but I have more flexibility than you.' He hesitated. 'How would you feel about *my* going to England, to Staffordshire? But please say if you would prefer to wait until you can go yourself.'

Jules gazed at him thoughtfully. 'You think you would be able to go in the near future?'

'I don't see why not.' Nicolas paused. He was thinking that it would be preferable if he went. Who knew what reaction, if any, there would be to his questions, his probing. 'If I try hard,' he said persuasively, 'I can probably find a legitimate reason for going. I could offer to write an article on the monarchies of Europe, or something. Then all expenses would be paid and,' he added with a grin, 'I wouldn't use up any of my holiday allowance.'

Despite himself, Jules had to laugh. 'That's just typical of you!'

'A good idea, though?'

After a moment, Jules nodded. 'Yes, a very good idea. In the meantime, you'll write to this Polly?'

'I'll do it straight away, and show you the letter before I send it.'

'Thank you, Nicolas.' They sat in silence for a few minutes, then Jules got up. 'I shall set the table, ready to sample Madame Caplat's excellent cuisine.'

Nicolas grinned. 'Yes, I do like the nights when she cooks. Much better than when you do.'

'Ungrateful pup!'

Smiling, Nicolas watched Jules leave. Then, taking out his diary, he began to turn the pages. I'll try and go immediately after Easter, he decided. He would be able to do any interviews in London, and he could always source some photographs from the archives. Nicolas couldn't foresee any problems with his editor. Now that they had no monarchy of their own, people in France were always fascinated by the royal families of other countries. And once business was out of the way, he could travel up to Staffordshire and see what he could discover.

It was only later, when he was enjoying his Camembert, that Nicolas began to wonder about the young woman who had replied to his article. Polly Merton. Although, he recalled, as he sliced another flavoursome wedge of cheese, English people did have a reputation for being cold and reserved. But if he found her attractive – well, any red-blooded Frenchman would merely regard that as a challenge.

26

Sadie had thoroughly enjoyed her stay with Babs. It had been interesting to see her home, a large Edwardian semi-detached with ivy climbing the walls and comfortably, if slightly shabbily furnished. Sadie felt that she now had a better understanding of how traumatic Jimmy's betrayal must have been. After so many years in a marriage that had produced two children – to be replaced by a younger woman must, Sadie thought with sadness, be the most hurtful rejection a woman could experience.

But it was good to be home. She unpacked her suitcase, and then wandered to the window to gaze out at the back garden, delighted to see that the daffodils were out. She yawned, feeling tired after the long car journey, and was looking forward to a lie-in the following morning but then thought – damn, it's one of Mrs Booth's days. Why on earth wouldn't the woman agree to change her routine? Dismayed by the thought of the disturbance, the uncomfortable atmosphere and the noise of the vacuum cleaner, Sadie decided instead to stock up on groceries.

But when she arrived back at The Gables late the following morning, Mrs Booth was still there. She was sitting at the kitchen table and was, to Sadie's surprise, visibly upset. 'Is something wrong?' Sadie said, putting down her shopping bags. 'Are you all right?'

'I don't know what's come over me,' Doris sniffed, 'letting it upset me like this.'

Sadie stared at her with concern. She was usually such a tough old boot. 'But what...?'

'I've 'ad an accident,' Doris told her, 'in the drawing room. You'd better go and look.'

Giving her a sharp glance, Sadie hurried into the room and then stopped, appalled by the scene before her. On the carpet near the sideboard lay

231

the shattered remains of the silver-framed photograph of André. The glass was broken, the frame dented, and as Sadie bent down, she saw with horror that the photograph was damaged. She straightened up, turning as she heard Doris approach.

'How on earth...?'

'It was the Hoover,' Doris told her in a tight voice. 'That and me stumbling – I knocked it over with my elbow. Such a heavy knock it was, and before I could stop it, down it crashed on to the vacuum. I'm ever so sorry. It would,' she sniffed, her eyes full of anxiety, 'be that one. It meant such a lot to Mr Merton, and I daren't think what Polly will say.'

Seriously dismayed, Sadie forced herself to say, 'Accidents happen, I'm sure she'll understand.'

'I'm usually so careful.' Doris, still distressed, began to bend down to pick up the broken glass.

'Don't worry, Mrs Booth.' Sadie tried to reassure her, 'I'm sure something can be done. I'll take it into a good photographer's in Stafford. No, wait a minute – I'll fetch some rubber gloves and a dustpan.' Returning, she watched as Doris picked up the main fragments, and then Sadie opened the back of the frame and carefully rescued the photo, examining it closely. There were scratches, yes, but as she'd initially thought, André's eyes still gazed at her from an unmarked face.

'You must stop blaming yourself,' Sadie said. 'It's not impossible to repair, thank goodness. I'll take these big pieces of glass out, and then you vacuum up the rest.' Pausing in the doorway, she added, 'Then we'll have a cup of tea and I'll show you the Easter egg I've bought for Polly.'

Doris, still on her knees, turned with amazement to watch Sadie walk out of the room, finding it difficult to reconcile her with the brittle, superficial woman who had arrived at The Gables nearly three years ago – an Easter egg for Polly? That was almost like a normal mother. Doris had to admit that 'Lady Muck', as she always thought of her, had definitely changed. 'I just wish,' she muttered under her breath, 'that she'd alter some of her other ways!'

At college, Polly waited until break before she opened the thin blue airmail. As she waited for Ruth to bring their coffees over, she eagerly scanned the lines. 'He's coming to England,' she announced as Ruth sat down. 'That French journalist I told you about. He says he's received several interesting replies, wants to follow them up, and wonders if it would be an imposition for him to call and see me.'

'Let's see.' Ruth looked at the letter and the signature. 'Definitely young – I can't say whether he's handsome, though.'

Polly laughed. 'A lot of French men aren't. They're no different from anyone else. But what makes you think he's young?'

'I can tell by the handwriting.'

'Oh, you're an expert, are you?'

Ruth grinned. 'No, it's just wishful thinking. This, Polly Merton, could be the beginning of a great romance.'

'You've been reading too many novels!' But

inside, Polly knew that she was already intrigued. She liked his name too – Nicolas Giscard. But it was more than likely, she told herself, that he was middle-aged with a family. Still, whatever he was like, it would be an interesting meeting, and she'd be able to enjoy an in-depth conversation in French. I'll write back and invite him for an English tea, Polly decided. She could easily ask Sadie to make some scones and a Victoria sponge.

Her decision made, Polly cradled her warm mug in her hands. 'Have you heard from Mark?' she said.

'Not recently,' Ruth added, 'he's got his finals coming up, though, so I don't expect it leaves him much time for writing letters.' She'd only heard from him once since his visit to Abbey Hulton. He'd also written a short note to her parents, thanking them for their hospitality; another sign, Ruth thought, of his upbringing – she knew that the middle-classes set great store on etiquette. Even though his letter had been affectionate, Ruth still felt anxious.

'Only I wondered if you'd like to come and stay for a couple of days over Easter,' Polly said. 'We could all have lunch together at the Crown on Sunday, his father as well. What do you think?'

'That would be fabulous,' Ruth said with pleasure and relief.

Polly said hesitantly, 'Ruth, you don't think you could be taking it all a bit too seriously – about Mark? I don't mean he isn't crazy about you, but it is early days.'

Ruth felt the colour rise in her cheeks. 'I know what you're trying to say, Pol. And you're right. I am taking it too seriously. My logical side tells me that all the time.'

'You really love him, don't you?'

Ruth nodded. 'Right from the first time I saw him at the tennis club. Daft, isn't it?'

Polly smiled at her. 'There is such a thing as love at first sight.'

'I know. But it's supposed to happen to both people, not just one.'

'And you don't think it's happened to Mark?'

Ruth shrugged in bewilderment. 'Oh, I don't know. When I'm with him, I'm sure he feels the same as I do. But he's never actually put it into words.'

'Have you?'

'Of course I haven't! What do you take me for?' Ruth's tone was outraged. 'It's up to the man to speak first.'

Polly gazed at her for a moment. Mark had always had a light-hearted view of life – and why not? He was only young, they all were. It was doubtful if the word 'marriage' had even entered his mind. And she was astounded that Ruth was already thinking along those lines. 'I thought you were the ambitious one. You know, going to be a headmistress some day.'

'That hasn't changed,' Ruth said with indignation. 'But there's nothing to say I've got to be an old maid to do it.'

'Maybe not,' Polly pointed out. 'But if you get married too young and the babies come along, it won't exactly increase your chances!'

'Sure, but even if we got engaged, it'd probably take a couple of years to save up to get married.'

Not if you married Mark – he wouldn't need to save up, Polly thought. After all, apart from his income when he joins the law practice, he's probably inherited money from his mother.

'And,' Ruth said blithely, 'I'm sure we're both intelligent enough to practise natural birth control – the Church does allow that.'

Polly was about to say that it was also notoriously unreliable, but decided to remain silent.

It was Sadie who invited George and Mark to join them for lunch in the Crown. 'I can't promise Easter eggs and bunnies,' she said, 'just three charming companions.'

'Done!' George said promptly on the other end of the phone. 'I'll look forward to it.'

'You don't need to check with Mark?'

'Shouldn't think so, not from the way he came dashing up here the other weekend.'

'It will be nice for you to have him home.'

'Yes. You must be looking forward to seeing Polly too.'

And she was, Sadie realised, as she replaced the receiver. Humming to herself, she went into the kitchen and, opening the door to the larder, stood surveying the shelves. They were well stocked – she usually tended to buy too much. A relic, she thought, of all the times as a child she'd not exactly gone hungry, but had to 'make do', with perhaps baked beans and the remnants of a stale loaf. Now, she gloried in shopping for food, knowing that she could buy whatever she fancied and liked to plan ahead. Some plaice, she thought, for Good Friday, as Polly and Ruth certainly wouldn't eat meat. And I'll roast a chicken to use cold over the weekend with salad or on sandwiches. And on Saturday, I'll make a curry – both girls will probably like that. Her thoughts ran on, and then she halted in disbelief. What was she turning into – a housewife?

Sadie went to sit at the kitchen table, lit a cigarette and stared blankly ahead. What's happening to me, she thought? I'm changing, I can sense it. And suddenly she realised how happy she'd been these last few months. More sex would have been good, of course – she hadn't changed that much! She got up and wandered restlessly through the large hall, and into the drawing room. The still-empty space on the sideboard where André's photograph was missing seemed glaring, and she made a mental note to buy flowers to disguise the gap. I love this room, she thought. In fact, The Gables has become more of a home to me than anywhere I've lived in the past. And yet again, as she wandered over to stare out of the bay window, she wondered just how long she'd be allowed to stay there.

The lunch was a great success, with Ruth's new green sweater and chunky gilt earrings giving her a dramatic look. Mark was obviously delighted to be with her, and George and Sadie seemed so normal, so comfortable with each other, that Polly had difficulty in imagining them as two people who'd indulged in an illicit affair. Although probably not even that, she thought, as she sipped her glass of wine. It might only have been on one occasion. Her mother did seem to avoid any involvement with her lovers. How was that, Polly wondered, because she's never found anyone to measure up to my father?

Sadie's next words disturbed Polly's musing. 'Mark's just been telling us about this mysterious Frenchman who might be coming.' She raised her eyebrows at her daughter. 'You never said anything?'

Polly flashed a glance at Ruth, who looked a bit guilty. 'You didn't say not to mention it.'

'No reason why not,' Polly said, feeling embarrassed. She didn't really know why she'd felt reluctant to talk about it. She turned to Sadie, 'I was going to tell you, and then I forgot. Anyway, it's a couple of weeks yet.'

'Do I scent a mystery?' Mark teased. His gaze was warm and friendly across the table.

'Only in Ruth's mind,' Polly retorted. 'She seems to think he's going to look like Sacha Distel.'

George put down his knife and fork. 'That was a really good piece of beef. Sorry, who's Sacha Distel?'

'You must keep up, George,' Sadie said. 'He's a singer, a real heart-throb and hugely popular in France. But I'd be interested to see the article, Polly.'

'Of course, I'll show it to you when we get back. But he's much more likely to be ink-stained and grey-haired.'

'Hey, there's nothing wrong with having grey hair!' George protested.

'Sorry, I didn't mean there was,' Polly said. 'Anyway yours is silver, and makes you look very distinguished, if I may say so.'

'Stop buttering him up, he's vain enough,' Mark laughed.

'But she's right, George,' Sadie commented. 'It suits you. I think it's so unfair that going grey can improve a man's looks, whereas with women, it's the kiss of death.' She shuddered, 'I shall have my hair tinted right until I'm put in my coffin.'

'I think,' George said, 'that you could never be anything but what you are; very feminine and extremely attractive.'

Polly glanced at Mark, surprising an expression of what she interpreted as dismay, and said quickly, 'Isn't this a mutual admiration society? Come on, Mark, you have two young ladies here wanting compliments.'

He turned to her and grinned. 'Are you fishing again, Pol? Now Ruth here,' his voice became softer as he turned to her, 'doesn't need to. She knows I think she's the most perfect girl I've ever met.'

There was silence around the table as Ruth gazed at him with shining eyes. Polly saw George watching them with a slight frown. His expression, however, was carefully controlled, while Sadie said brightly, 'And who said romance was a thing of the past.' She turned as a waiter approached. 'Shall we have coffee in the lounge? Would anyone like a liqueur?' The three younger people shook their heads, but George opted for a brandy, and Sadie for a Tia Maria. It was in a mellow mood that later she drove Polly back to The Gables. Mark had taken Ruth out for a drive, although Polly thought they probably would only get as far as the nearest secluded spot.

'That was rather lovely,' Sadie said, as they drove along the quiet country roads, 'what Mark said, I mean.'

'Yes, it was.' Polly stared out of the window. She was so very fond of him, almost enough to... But then she firmly dismissed the thought. Mark had never had the depth of feeling for her that he obviously had for Ruth. I wonder, Polly thought, as they went into the house, whether those two *will* eventually get married. Neither would find their path to happiness without its problems. Ruth had already mentioned her parents' worries, and Polly suspected that Mark too had reservations.

And as if she knew what was in her daughter's mind, Sadie, before she went upstairs for a nap, said, 'You know they make a lovely couple, but as for long-term – I do wonder whether they'll be able to bridge the gap. George is a sweetie, but very much a product of his background.'

'As is Ruth,' Polly said. 'What's more, she's a strong Catholic. And you know what we're like about mixed marriages. We want it all our own way. You know, children brought up in the faith – all that stuff. How do you think George and Mark will react to that?'

'God knows,' Sadie said. 'If you believe in him, that is. I'm not sure that I do.'

'Yet Babs told me that you got married in church, and a Catholic one at that.'

Sadie paused at the foot of the stairs, her hand on the oak banister. 'I'd have married André in a tent, if that was what he wanted,' she said quietly, and stunned, Polly stood watching her as she went up the wide staircase.

27

Sadie was quite aware of the reason why Polly had decided that Friday was a good day to invite the French journalist.

'He might want me to fill in long questionnaires, etcetera,' Polly began to explain, 'so it could be quite a long session. He may as well come when you're at work, then we won't get in your way.' She was finishing her breakfast and Sadie watched her eat the last morsel of toast and marmalade.

'Don't you think,' Sadie pointed out, 'that it might be wise to have someone else in the house? After all, we know nothing about this man.'

Polly stared at her with astonishment. 'You're not telling me I need a chaperone? Honestly, you of all people.'

Sadie's eyes narrowed. 'That's different. I can judge a man's character while we're in a public place. It's not the same?'

'And you never make a mistake, I suppose?' The moment Polly had uttered the words she regretted them. The colour rising in her cheeks, she said, 'Sorry – that was a bit below the belt.'

'Yes it was,' Sadie's lips tightened. 'But it doesn't change the fact that this Nicolas Giscard is a complete stranger.'

'You read his letter,' Polly protested. 'Does he sound like an axe-murderer?'

Despite herself, Sadie had to smile. And hadn't

she taken much greater risks when she was young; particularly during the war, and at a much earlier age? The rush of protectiveness that had swept over Sadie had surprised her as much as it had her daughter. I'm not used to this, she thought, this feeling of responsibility for another human being. She decided to be direct. 'Are you worried that if I'm here I'll "vamp" him, as Mrs Booth would say?'

Polly burst into laughter. 'What an old-fashioned expression!' Then she glanced warily at Sadie. 'Would you be able to resist it if he turned out to be tall, dark and handsome?'

'What a delicious thought! Polly, I would be conspicuous by my absence – at least, unless you came upstairs and invited me to meet him.'

'You mean you'd stay up in your room?' Polly frowned. 'That doesn't seem fair.'

'But I'm right, aren't I? You'd prefer to see him on your own? Truth now, Polly.'

Feeling slightly embarrassed, Polly said, 'Yes, I would.'

Sadie got up and went over to the sink, waiting for the water to run hot before squirting in Fairy Liquid. She would have felt the same herself, particularly in her youth. 'Don't worry about me,' she said over her shoulder. 'I'll make sure I have a novel to read and a box of chocolates. The relaxation will do me good. But I do think it's better if I'm here.' Then she turned and said, half smiling, 'And if I am, I could make the scones. Unlike the Victoria sponge, they need to be made the same day and mine *are* better than yours.'

'That's true.' Polly gazed at her, realising that

she really was concerned. It was a novel thought, yet somehow reassuring. 'Okay,' she capitulated, 'you win – I'll make it Saturday instead.'

Nicolas showed the letter to Jules, who smiled as he read it. 'Very proper,' he said. 'Obviously a well-brought-up young lady.'

'English tea,' Nicolas said thoughtfully. 'Does that mean cucumber sandwiches – I saw that in a film once.'

Jules laughed, and then said, 'Possibly.'

Nicolas pulled a face, 'Sounds awful. When I went to England with my school, we ate disgustingly. I can still remember the soggy cabbage, and something called cottage pie covered in thin brown stuff. It was absolutely tasteless.'

'I'm sure you'll survive.' Jules looked down at the letter, which was still in his hand. He traced the embossed heading with his finger and said, 'You will telephone? If the house at all resembles the one I drew?'

'I promise.'

Jules watched Nicolas settle down in his armchair to read, but found himself unable to settle to his own book. His mind was too active. The possibility of discovering his previous life, perhaps even a family, had come to dominate his every waking thought. Recently he'd dreamed again of the brown-haired woman – he could still remember that lingering feeling of love and tenderness. The sense of her had been so vivid, so real – it must mean *something*. He told himself this several times a day and even had the fervent hope – as yet unrealised – that the dream of the accident would

243

also return. It might bring with it more clues, more revelations. Jules leaned his head back against the chair. He must try to stop all this agonising; it didn't achieve anything. And after all, Nicolas would soon be going not only to England, but to Staffordshire. If there *was* an answer to be found in this village called Brandon, Jules thought, then I know I can trust him to find it.

Nicolas flew from Orly to Heathrow. He spent time in London doing research in the British Library, visiting Buckingham Palace and having dinner with an English journalist who wrote a gossip column for one of the national papers. Nicolas had often given him titbits about French celebrities, and it was now – as he told him with a grin – payback time about the current royal family. Then, feeling that he'd fulfilled his obligation to his editor, on Saturday morning, Nicolas took the tube to Euston station and, going to the ticket office, found that the train he needed was the one to Glasgow Central. Booking an open return to Stafford, he asked the clerk which was the station before. 'That'll be Wolverhampton, sir. Stafford's about fifteen minutes after that.'

Once on the train, he stared out of the window, intrigued by the way the hedge-enclosed fields looked like a patchwork quilt. He liked the country stations the train passed through, with their swept platforms, some even with narrow borders planted with spring flowers. All so very typical of the England he'd read about. And the seats on the train were upholstered and much more comfortable than the wooden slats he was used to. Nicolas looked curiously at the other passengers in the carriage. A large, florid-faced woman was balancing a basket on her lap, which he suspected might contain her lunch. Next to her was a small boy with scabby knees who, from his furtive looks at the others, Nicolas suspected of having a mouse in his pocket; something was certainly moving in there. There were two business men, one reading the *Telegraph*, the other immersed in the *Financial Times*. And directly opposite were two nuns, their pale faces impassive, their hands busy with rosary beads. It will not, he thought, be the most exciting journey I've ever taken – unless the mouse escapes, of course. He felt laughter rise within him at a vision of the tiny creature scrabbling beneath the nuns' habits. But nothing so stimulating happened, and he settled to the rhythm of the wheels. He wondered whether this Polly Merton was going to be an English rose with one of those delicate complexions. Or one of the other well-known types, bookish or hearty and horsey. Well, it wouldn't be long now before he found out.

Eventually, as the train drew into the station, he reached up to the overhead rack and took down his luggage. 'Stafford, this is Stafford,' an official shouted as he walked along the platform. Nicolas lowered the window and reached out to open the heavy door. Several minutes later, hungry despite having indulged in a surprisingly good English cooked breakfast at his hotel, he went into the station buffet and bought a sticky bun and a cup of tea, the first few sips of which made him feel even more mystified as to why it was England's national beverage. Then he strode out into the early spring sunshine. There was a slight chill in the air despite the blue skies, and turning up the collar of his black leather jacket, he glanced over at the nearby Station Hotel. Remembering to look right first, he crossed the road and booked in for one night. His single room was reasonably comfortable with a bathroom and toilet along the corridor, and eventually after freshening up he decided it was time to leave. There were three cars in the taxi rank outside the station, and as he went to the first in the queue, the driver wound down his window.

'Good afternoon. I need to go to somewhere called Brandon.'

'Okay, mate.'

Nicolas climbed into the back, and as the taxi drew away and picked up speed, he gazed out of the window. He'd imagined the Midlands to be purely industrial, but as they drove along the roads he was surprised to find how rural the area was. He was glancing over to the right at an impressive-looking preparatory school, when the taxi driver, a thickset man with greying hair, said over his shoulder, 'You're French, aren't you?'

'I am,' Nicolas said. 'It's that obvious, is it?'

'Yer English is good, no doubt about it. But I served over there during the war, so I can spot a Froggy a mile off.'

'Where were you?'

'Normandy.' The taxi driver began a spiel of his wartime experiences, which Nicolas listened to with increasing interest.

'Have you been back since?' he asked. 'To France, I mean?'

The taxi driver shook his head. 'Not that there's anything wrong with your country, but too many bad memories, if you know what I mean.'

'Yes, of course.' Nicolas leaned forward as they passed a small roadside sign proclaiming 'Brandon'.

The taxi driver turned his head. 'Where was it yer wanted?'

'Shady Lane.'

'I know it.' A minute later the taxi turned into a quiet side road lined with trees. 'Only a few houses along here,' he slowed down to peer at the gateway of the first one. 'Which one is it?'

'The Gables.' Suddenly Nicolas saw the name ahead. He leaned forward and said quickly, 'No, please – stop here!'

Obediently, the taxi drew up a short distance before the house. Nicolas paid the driver and, almost guiltily, recalling the man's service in France, included a generous tip. Then he turned and watched the car disappear before, with his heart beating rapidly, he walked tentatively, almost fearfully along to the entrance to The Gables.

It was an imposing house, standing alone, with two large bay windows before a circular drive. Transfixed, Nicolas could only stare in disbelief, remembering the crude sketch by Jules – there was even the lawn he'd later described. He'd hoped, of course he had, but he was stunned to see the accurate and indisputable proof before him. Shaken, he drew swiftly back behind the high hedge, which screened the front garden. Then once he felt steadier, he took his camera from its case and almost furtively approached the entrance again.

247

Not until he had clicked the shutter several times and turned away, did Nicolas finally give in to the excitement surging through him, to the euphoria, the overwhelming sense of relief. It had worked – their strategy had worked! This English house held the key to all those lost years. And whatever that was, whatever it revealed, he was determined to discover the truth. He glanced with anxiety at his watch – but he was still twenty minutes early. I shall walk for a while, he decided, along this quiet road and try to calm down, to compose myself. Because it was vital that he made a good impression, that he gained this unknown young woman's confidence. Nicolas didn't care if she looked like a female Boris Karloff, he was going to use every ounce of charm he possessed.

28

Polly, sitting before her dressing table, was yet again brushing her hair. The weather although cold was fine, with a blue sky and even a hint of sunshine, and she'd decided after much deliberation to wear a pale blue cashmere sweater over a grey pencil skirt. She glanced at her watch again – it was half past two. Restless, she was determined to resist the temptation to go down to the drawing room and hover at the side of the bay window. Instead, she went along the landing and after a light tap on Sadie's door, went in. Polly rarely went into her mother's bedroom because she'd always hated the way Sadie had refurbished it. But now, looking at the garish pink décor, and remembering that neglected young girl in a council flat, dreaming of a more glamorous life, Polly found herself softening. What did it matter that her grandfather would have been appalled, that Mrs Booth felt scandalised? This room had fulfilled one of Sadie's dreams. She was lying on the bed, propped against a large satin pillow, a box of Cadbury's Milk Tray at her side, reading the latest Barbara Cartland.

'How do I look?' Polly said.

Sadie gazed at her daughter – at her soft, shining hair, lissom yet rounded figure and at her slim legs and ankles. She felt a surge of wistful pride. If only André could be here to see her... 'You look terrific,' she said. 'But, Polly, don't be disappointed...'

'I know,' Polly said. 'I realise I'm being completely stupid about this whole thing, the way I'm building it up. I can't even explain why.'

'It's because you're young.' Sadie put down her book. 'It's one of the gifts of youth to see the possibilities in everything. Hang on to it; believe me, it doesn't last. In any case,' she smiled, 'who wouldn't be intrigued to meet a mysterious Frenchman?'

'Well,' Polly warned with a grin, 'you keep your promise. I don't want any competition!'

Sadie laughed. 'I feel flattered that you think I could be.'

It's your experience I'm worried about, Polly thought, and glanced yet again at her watch. 'Well, I'll go down,' she said.

'Good luck!'

At precisely three o'clock, with the strap of his camera slung over his shoulder, Nicolas went up the drive to The Gables. To his relief the walk had refreshed and calmed him. It was vital that his brain remained clear and focused. This visit would be his only chance; he couldn't risk missing any detail, however abstract it might seem, that could help to solve the mystery that had haunted Jules for over twenty years.

A few seconds later Nicolas pressed the gleaming brass doorbell.

The oak door opened almost immediately. Before him stood – *a girl with brown hair!* No, it couldn't be ... and then she was speaking, holding out her hand, and saying in perfect French, 'Monsieur Giscard?'

'Please – Nicolas.'

She smiled, and stood aside. 'And I'm Polly. Do come in.'

Nicolas followed her into the spacious hall and then the girl turned left and led him through a wide door into a large, well-proportioned room. The early spring sunlight was streaming in through the large bay window, and as Polly stood before a beautiful mahogany fireplace fronted by a brass fender, she said, 'Please, do sit down. Did you have any problem finding the house?'

Nicolas was trying not to stare at her as he took a seat in one of the comfortable leather armchairs. 'Not at all. Thank you for agreeing to let me come and see you.'

'It's a pleasure,' Polly said. 'I'm looking forward to having a conversation in French. I don't often get the opportunity.'

He smiled at her. 'And I've been able to use my English. I had a chat with the taxi driver on the way here.'

'Would you like a cup of tea?'

'Thank you.' Nicolas watched her leave, his thoughts racing. *Surely she couldn't be the same one...?*

Polly, going to the kitchen, was almost breathless with excitement. The young – and he *was* young – Frenchman surpassed her wildest imagination. I bet he's married, she thought with sudden despondency as she made the tea, or at least has a girlfriend he's madly in love with. So far they'd spoken only in French, and she wondered how fluent he was in English, whether he was bilingual. Well, she would soon find out – and it was with keen anticipation that a few minutes later she carried in the tea tray.

Nicolas, who had been scribbling in his notebook every detail of the room, put it quickly aside when he heard Polly returning. As she placed the tray on the coffee table, and he saw the china teapot, milk jug, sugar bowl and cups and saucers, all in a delicate rose pattern, he said, 'What lovely china. Is it made locally – in the Potteries?'

'You're very well informed,' Polly said. 'And yes, of course. It would be sacrilege to buy china from anywhere else. Although,' she leaned forward and confided, 'don't tell anyone, but we do have some Limoges.'

Nicolas laughed. 'I'm pleased to hear it.'

'Do you take milk and sugar?'

'Both, please.' Nicolas watched as Polly poured

251

out the tea. Again he thought – was it possible? *Could* this graceful girl be the one from the café, the one Jules had seen all those months ago? But lots of girls had brown hair, and yet...

'Did you get many replies to your article – from here in Staffordshire, I mean?' Polly said.

'There were several. But yours was the most relevant one.'

'You mean you've come all this way just to talk to me?' Polly was incredulous.

'Yes,' he smiled, 'at least to Staffordshire. I spent some time in London and came up from there.' Nicolas avoided any elaboration, hoping she would think he'd been interviewing others in the capital.

'Well, I hope I can help,' Polly said. She glanced at him from beneath her lashes, and then noticed the notebook lying beside him. 'Please, feel free to ask me any questions you like.'

Nicolas replaced his cup on the low table. 'Maybe if you told me about yourself?' he said. 'Exactly how you learned to speak French, the extent of your vocabulary, the opportunities you've had to converse in the language – that sort of thing?'

'Yes, of course.' Polly thought for a moment, and then as Nicolas picked up his notebook, began to tell him that her grandfather had met and married a Frenchwoman, who had taught her only son to speak French from birth.

'But your father didn't teach you? I say that because you wrote in your letter that you had a French nanny.'

'That's right. No, my father was killed during the war, just before I was born.'

Nicolas looked at her with sympathy. 'I'm so sorry. And your mother didn't speak French?'

Polly shook her head. She had no intention of revealing the details of what she saw as Sadie's abandonment. Instead, she said, 'No, she didn't. And as my grandfather's French wasn't brilliant and he wanted me to be bilingual, he employed a French nanny. I grew up here, you see, in his house.'

'It's a very beautiful house.' Nicolas glanced round appreciatively.

'Yes, it was built especially for him. And you, Nicolas – what part of France are you from?'

'I live in Paris,' he said.

Polly, who was sitting opposite, had been watching his hands as he wrote his notes; long fingered with just a slight dusting of dark hairs. And then he added the words that made her catch her breath. 'But, of course, Papa and I don't live in a large house like this.' He smiled, 'One would have to be extremely rich to do so in Paris. We have an apartment.'

He lived with his father? Polly's pulse began to race. That meant he definitely wasn't married. Surely otherwise he would have mentioned his wife? 'I live with my mother,' she said. She didn't mention that she was actually in the house.

'Mine died last year, I'm afraid. Very suddenly – it was a big shock to both of us.'

'I'm very sorry,' Polly said, 'that must have been awful for you.'

Nicolas shrugged. 'It is life.'

What was it about the Gallic shrug, Polly thought, that made it so different, so attractive? But then so was he. She even liked his clothes, the

253

slim-fitting black leather jacket, his black trousers, the white polo-neck sweater. In fact she could hardly stop gazing at him with utter fascination.

Nicolas, who had noted down all that Polly had told him, thought he'd better do his research act. 'I wonder,' he said, 'if you would mind reading to me, perhaps from an English book – only translating it into French?'

'Of course I will.' Polly got up and went to the tall, glass-fronted bookcase at one end of the room. 'How about *A Tale of Two Cities?*' she called over her shoulder.

'Perfect.'

Polly brought the book over, sat opposite, and as she began, 'It was the best of times, it was the worst of times,' Nicolas leaned back in his armchair, closing his eyes as Polly's perfectly modulated voice flowed over him. Her French was excellent. In fact, one could almost mistake her for a Parisienne.

When she came to the end of her reading he said, 'I am very impressed.'

'Thank you.' Polly watched him write once again in his notebook, and said, 'Have you found many variations – in the people you've interviewed so far?'

He smiled at her. 'I can honestly say that your linguistic ability is the most accomplished.' And that sentence, he thought with some surprise, sounded as if I actually knew what I was talking about.

'And are there marked differences between those who learned French from birth and others who were taught later?'

254

Remembering Oliver's letter, Nicolas answered, 'Absolutely. There's no doubt about it.'

'Have you always been interested in phonetics?'

Nicolas hesitated. He was so enchanted by this English girl that he was finding it increasingly difficult to lie. 'Not always,' he said carefully, 'but over the last few months, increasingly so. Tell me about this nanny of yours. Exactly where was she brought up in France?'

'Paris,' Polly told him. 'I was there actually, last summer.'

Nicolas's hand stilled. 'You were there last summer?'

'Yes, in July.' Polly glanced at her watch and smiled at him. 'Now I must bring in the afternoon tea I invited you for. I won't be long.' She got up and left the room, leaving Nicolas stunned. But he had no time to dwell on the implication of her words. Hurriedly he took his camera out of its case. He needed to be quick, and thankful that he didn't need to fiddle with a flash bulb, went swiftly to the sideboard where he'd noticed a couple of photographs and clicked the shutter several times. He took images of the fireplace, the furniture, the chandelier; then returned to his previous position as he thought he heard a sound in the hall. Polly had been in Paris last summer! It was in July, just weeks after Maman's death, that Jules had heard a girl with brown hair laughing. Slim, he'd said, a girl who was chic, who could have been French, and Polly fitted the description. Then Nicolas remembered that the young woman Jules had first heard, and then seen, had been with a young man.

He turned as Polly came in wheeling a two-tiered wooden trolley, prettily laid out with delectable-looking food, and he smiled with appreciation as he saw sultana scones spread thickly with butter, and a tempting sponge cake. There were sandwiches too, and he couldn't help an inward smile as he recognised cucumber ones, but there were also ham and what looked like chicken.

'I hope you're hungry,' she said.

'Ravenous!'

She laughed. 'Good.' She handed him a plate, and offered in turn the selection of sandwiches.

Nicolas took one of each, and found to his surprise that the cucumber ones were not boring at all, but very refreshing. 'Would you like to talk for a while in English?' he said.

'Okay.'

For the next fifteen minutes, they chatted as they ate, each telling the other snippets of their life; that Nicolas wrote for an international magazine, that he enjoyed books and the theatre; that Polly would soon be a qualified teacher, and that she played tennis.

'I do too,' he said, as he accepted a piece of the cake which she'd told him was called a Victoria sponge.

'It's a pity you're not here longer, then,' she smiled. 'I belong to a very good tennis club.'

Nicolas thought fast. Jules *had* to come to England; it was imperative that he saw this house. He glanced down at the china plate in his hand, a plan beginning, to evolve. 'As it happens,' he said, 'we were thinking of taking a holiday in England, and Papa was saying that he'd like to see inside a pottery factory. He particularly likes that blue and white design – I think it's made by Wedgwood. Do you think that would be possible?'

Polly felt euphoria sweep over her. He was coming back! All the time she'd been in the kitchen, she'd been feeling desperate, thinking that when he walked out of the front door she would never see him again. And for the past fifteen minutes as he spoke in English, she'd been in heaven. His husky voice with its slight accent was so attractive that she got goosebumps just listening to him. 'Yes, I'm sure it would,' she said eagerly. 'You must mean Jasper ware. Actually we have some of that in the dining room; my grandfather was fond of it.'

Her transparent delight made the decision he'd made when walking in the lane nearby to use deliberate charm, seem faintly ridiculous.

'Then shall I bring my tennis racquet?'

'I shall be disappointed if you don't.'

For one long moment they gazed at each other, and Polly felt the colour rise in her cheeks. Nicolas could only think how charming her blush was, and it was with an effort that he brought his mind back to concentrate on the reason for his visit. 'So,' he said, putting his white napkin to his lips and replacing it on his plate, 'did you enjoy your trip last year to Paris?'

'It was marvellous, as always. I just love everything about it.'

'It wasn't your first visit, then?'

Polly shook her head. 'No, my grandfather took me several times as a child.' She got up and went over to the sideboard, returning with two silver-framed photographs. 'This is my grandfather,' she said. Nicolas looked down at a distinguished silver-haired man. 'He died three years ago. And this,' she said, holding out the other, 'is one of my French grandmother taken when she was quite young. I never knew her as she died before I was born, but can you see the resemblance?'

He took the photograph from her and stared down at a face full of vitality and warmth. 'You have her eyes. Her hair is also like yours, only longer.'

Polly laughed. 'Yes, I've often thought I should grow mine too.'

Nicolas looked at the way her shining hair swung in a bouffant bob. 'I like the way you wear it now,' he said. Once again their eyes briefly met and Polly in slight confusion went and replaced the photographs.

'May we,' Nicolas said, 'speak French again?'

'Yes, of course.'

'Tell me – what did you do in Paris? In July, I mean.'

'The usual things,' she told him. 'Oh, but we did go to see the Folies Bergère – my very first time. It was brilliant.'

Nicolas became very still. Then he said quietly, 'You were with a friend?'

Polly nodded. 'Yes, Mark – he's at Oxford studying law. He's not my boyfriend or anything,' she explained hastily, 'it's just that he didn't want to go on his own, and well – I'll grab any opportunity to go to France.'

Nicolas struggled against an impulse to ask her about the café with the burgundy awning. Part of him thought it was crazy to think that girl with brown hair could have been Polly – and yet why not? Everything fitted. She was in Paris in July, she looked French; she was even with a young man. But he mustn't probe any further, give any hint that his purpose for being there was anything other than it seemed. And what could he say that wouldn't involve talking about Jules?

'You know,' Polly was saying, 'this afternoon has been so different from how I expected it to be. I thought I'd have to fill in a long, complicated questionnaire, or something.'

'Oh, that isn't always necessary,' Nicolas tried to sound professional. 'It depends on the individual.' He hesitated, 'Before I leave, I wonder, Polly – would you have any objection to my taking a photo of you? I like to keep a record of the people I've interviewed; I find it useful when referring back.'

The lie didn't sit easy with him, but Polly said immediately, 'Of course not.' She went to stand before the fireplace, saying, 'Here's a good place, in the daylight.'

Nicolas took three shots from different angles then, glancing at his watch, decided it would be impolite to stay any longer. He went to replace the camera in its case and turned to her. 'Thank you for a wonderful tea and also for all your help. I need to ring for a taxi – is there a local firm I could use?'

'Yes, of course.' With some reluctance Polly found the number, showed him where the telephone was, and then went back into the drawing room while he made his call.

When Nicolas joined her he said, 'They're sending one straight away.'

'Please keep in touch,' Polly said, 'and let me know when you come in the summer.'

'That is something I can definitely promise.' They gazed at each other for what was, for Polly, a heart-stopping moment. Then when they went to watch for the taxi from the bay window Nicolas said, looking at the bright clusters in the front garden, 'I always think of Wordsworth when I see daffodils.'

'So do I, and the Lake District.' A silence fell between them, Polly feeling that she wanted to prolong every second, Nicolas knowing that under different circumstances he would by now have asked this lovely girl by his side out to dinner. Five minutes later Polly waved goodbye as he climbed into the taxi and then once it had turned into the lane and out of sight, began to wheel out the tea trolley. All at once the summer seemed a long time away.

29

In Paris, Jules was tense and restless as he waited for the promised crucial telephone call. In the office that afternoon, too distracted to work efficiently, he must have checked his watch a dozen times trying to imagine what Nicolas was doing, whether he was still at The Gables, and what, if anything, he had found out. Then just as his frustration was at fever pitch, the telephone rang; shrill and loud. Jules picked it up with a suddenly trembling hand.

'Papa?'

'Nicolas? I've been waiting...'

'I'm sorry. There is only one telephone here...'

'Do you have news?'

'I have so much to tell you. I'll be home to-morrow evening. And Papa ... the house ... it was exactly as you drew it.'

Jules felt his heart begin to thud. His mouth suddenly dry, he said in a hoarse whisper, 'Exactly?'

'I've taken photographs. Look, I don't want to tell you any more over the phone. I'll see you tomorrow.'

'Have a safe journey, Nicolas. *Au revoir.*' Jules replaced the receiver, adrenaline beginning to rush through his veins as he realised the implications of what Nicolas had told him. This house called The Gables *had* to have played a significant part in his early life. Surely it must hold the key to his past. It felt as though he was beginning to see pieces of a jigsaw puzzle. Was it possible that they might eventually all fit together? If only Gabrielle was still alive, he thought with sadness. It was so unfair that the breakthrough in his memory had come only after her death. He wandered into the kitchen, thinking that he should make something to eat, but suddenly couldn't face the prospect of spending the evening alone in the flat. I wonder if Armand is free, he thought. Jules and the grizzled ex-soldier, who lived on the floor below, often played chess together, and to Jules there was no better way of freeing his mind of racing thoughts. Because, he thought, although it will only be twenty-four hours before Nicolas arrives, it's

261

going to seem like an eternity.

Sadie, now thankfully downstairs again, was listening with amusement to Polly's glowing description of the young French journalist. 'So,' she said as she picked up a tea towel to dry the used china tea service, 'he was even more gorgeous than you'd hoped for?'

Polly began to feel embarrassed. 'I suppose I am going on a bit.'

Sadie, looking at her glowing face, said, 'It's good to see you looking so happy,' she said, 'it's about time you had some romance in your life.'

'Of course,' Polly said wistfully, 'he could have a girlfriend over in Paris.'

'That's quite possible.'

Polly swung round to face her. 'What makes you say that?'

Sadie laughed at the alarm on her face. 'Just that if he really is so attractive...'

'I know,' Polly said, feeling sudden despair. 'And yet...'

Sadie waited a moment and then said, 'And yet what?'

'I just had this feeling...' Polly tipped out the soapy water from the yellow plastic bowl.

'I'm a great believer in female intuition,' Sadie mused, seeing the uncertainty in her daughter's face. 'If you felt something between you, there probably was.'

'Until he gets back to Paris and sees *her* again!'

'But in the summer, he'll be back here and then he'll see *you* again.'

'That's true! Although,' Polly added, 'there may

be no girlfriend at all. He only mentioned his father coming with him, no one else.'

Sadie smiled. 'I'd hang on to that, if I were you, otherwise you'll drive yourself crazy. I wonder,' she said, as she put the teaspoons away, 'what the older Frenchman will be like – Louis Jourdan with a touch of the Charles Boyer?'

They both burst out laughing, and then Sadie said, 'Don't worry – I'll try and behave myself.' She glanced at her daughter. 'Did you say you were going to the pictures tomorrow night?'

'Yes, with Hazel. We thought we'd go to see *A Taste of Honey*.'

'Only,' Sadie spoke very calmly, 'I thought I'd invite George to dinner.'

'George?' Polly stared at her with astonishment.

'Yes, George! Don't say it as if he has two heads.'

Polly looked away, not knowing quite how she felt. 'So you're still seeing him?'

'We meet up now and then, yes. He seems to find it helps. He's a lonely man, Polly.'

'Mark's home at the moment,' Polly pointed out.

'Mark,' Sadie said drily, 'spends most of his time with Ruth.'

Polly turned to look at her mother and Sadie read the question in her eyes. She sighed inwardly, and then shook her head. 'I'm afraid some things, Polly, are private.'

So that means they are, Polly thought, feeling the heat rise in her cheeks. Well I hope Mark doesn't find out, because I don't think I could bear it; nor the thought of other people knowing. At least, she thought, the house is in a secluded position, because George even had a personalised number plate on his Jaguar.

There was an uneasy silence between them, and then Sadie moved away. 'I'll go and look at the *Radio Times*,' she said, 'and see if there's anything worth watching tonight.'

It was early the following evening when Jules, having seen on the noticeboard that Nicolas's flight had landed, waited just beyond the barrier for him to retrieve his luggage and to come through passport control. The two men greeted each other with a hug. 'Good flight?'

'It was fine.' Nicolas followed Jules out to the car park and put the suitcase he was carrying into the boot of their small Citroën. 'I've much to tell you, but do you mind if we wait until we get back to the apartment? I could do with a shower and a glass of wine.'

'Of course,' Jules struggled to control his impatience. But he recognised that Nicolas wanted to give the situation the seriousness it deserved – which would be impossible during a distracting car journey.

When later they eventually settled in the salon, Jules, a cigarette in his unsteady hand, waited with both anxiety and impatience.

'I'll take the photographs to be developed tomorrow,' Nicolas said, 'but in the meantime...' He went on to recount all that had happened, from his very first glimpse of The Gables, to the typically English afternoon tea with Polly, and his promise to return in the summer.

For several long moments Jules remained

silent. 'You are sure that the house was exactly as I drew it?'

'Do you have the sketch?'

Jules got up and, taking it from a drawer in the dresser, placed it before Nicolas.

'This is it!' With his index finger Nicolas indicated the borders around the lawn, 'And here, and here, there were clusters of daffodils and tulips. It was a beautiful house. Papa, it's uncanny how accurate this is. How on earth could you've known?'

Jules went to sit opposite him again. 'Tell me again about Polly. Describe her – I want to know every detail.'

Nicolas obliged and as he spoke, from the light in his eyes and warmth in his voice, Jules guessed that the fact that this English girl had brown hair – and had even been in Paris the previous summer – wasn't the only thing of interest to him. 'She seems to have made quite an impression.'

'She was lovely.'

The words hung between them for a moment, and Jules glanced sharply at him. 'Well, I shall see for myself,' he said, 'once the photographs are developed.'

'I'll take them in tomorrow and ask for Express Service.'

Once again, Jules knew he had no choice but to contain his impatience. To see actual photographs of the house, to discover whether Polly was the girl he'd seen at the café, was a prospect that intrigued and excited him so much that later he found it impossible to sleep. Over and over again, his mind went through all that Nicolas had told him, trying to analyse, to make sense of it all.

How could he have known of that house? What did it all mean? Even the fact that this Polly bore a close resemblance to her French grandmother, seemed almost too much of a coincidence not to be significant. And Nicolas had said that in the photograph she had long hair. Could the grandmother have worn it in a chignon like the woman in his dream? He could still remember her face so clearly, recall her low musical voice singing to him. Lying in the lonely double bed, it was not until dawn that eventually Jules managed to slip into a restless and uneasy sleep.

Yet when Nicolas was able to place the longed-for photographs on the dining table in the salon, Jules suddenly felt a strange reluctance to take them out of the brightly coloured folder.

'They've turned out really well,' Nicolas said, then realising how tense Jules was suggested, 'Shall I pour us both a glass of wine?'

Jules nodded as he stared down at the folder; much depended on its contents. Just a few photographs, and yet they could be the means of his discovering the life he had lost all those years ago. Would seeing an actual image of the house trigger any more memories? And Jules knew that despite all his efforts to the contrary, he was desperately hoping that this English girl *was* the one that he had seen the previous July. Her face, her hair were indelibly printed on his mind; there was no possibility of him being mistaken. He turned as Nicolas came back and, taking the glass of red wine from him, sat at the table.

Slowly, Jules extracted the photographs. The top one was of the house, and he looked down at it with utter fascination. It was just as he had seen it in his mind. There they were – the two large bay windows and the circular drive. He stared at it for one long moment, then with an almost shaking hand he put it aside. The girl, he must see an image of the girl. The next moment he was gazing down at Polly. She was standing before a handsome fireplace, smiling directly at him. *It was the same girl.* Jules put out a hand to Nicolas and clutched at his arm. 'It's her,' he said hoarsely. 'It is definitely her.'

'Are you absolutely sure?'

Jules nodded. He took a sip of his wine and tried to steady his nerves.

'She is exactly as I remember her. Nicolas, what does this all mean?'

'I don't know, Papa. But there are other photos for you to see.'

Slowly, Jules began to look through the rest of the photos, pausing to study the interior of the drawing room, and then he came to the ones taken before the sideboard. 'Nicolas,' he said quietly, 'please would you pass me the magnifying glass – I think it's in the right-hand drawer.'

Nicolas went over to the dresser and a few seconds later, Jules was examining closely the silver-framed photograph of Polly's grandmother. Tensely, Nicolas waited.

'She has a different hairstyle, but I'm almost sure this is the woman in my dream.' Jules took another sip of his wine, and leaned back in his chair, closing his eyes. He felt weak, almost dizzy. Because when her features had first been magnified, there had for one fleeting moment, been a strong sense of familiarity. Yet he hadn't felt that when dreaming of her; there had just been an overwhelming sensation of warmth, of protecting love. 'I don't understand,' he said shakily. 'I felt as if I knew her, Nicolas, had seen her before.'

'What about this one, Papa?' Nicolas handed him the photograph of Polly's grandfather.

Again Jules examined it through the magnifying glass, seeing the intelligent face, the keen gaze. Slowly he shook his head. 'I'm not sure.' He began to look through the rest of the photos, studying the shots of the interior.

'I'll leave you with them,' Nicolas said, 'I need to have something to eat, I'm absolutely starving.' He got up to go into the kitchen, but Jules said, 'Of course – you will be. I'm sorry, Nicolas, I should have thought. I'll do it, it won't take long. I've already prepared the salad, and I thought maybe an omelette? And there's some cheese, then a tarte Tatin from the delicatessen.'

'Sounds wonderful,' Nicolas said. He went into his small single room, which was furnished so plainly it was almost monastic. He reflected with affection how Maman had wanted to soften it with cushions and pastel colours. But he didn't like fussy things. His task done, he wandered back into the salon. The apartment somehow seemed small, even cramped, after the large and dignified rooms of The Gables, such a distinct contrast to the small, rented farm where Gabrielle and her parents had lived. Nicolas had looked up to his grandfather, a hardworking, decent man of few words, to the end of his life full of anger and bitter resentment about the indignities that France had suffered during the war. During the food shortages of the Occupation his grandmother had, Nicolas now suspected, deprived herself in her efforts to feed her family. And they'd fared better than many in the cities, who had suffered greatly. But one could never describe his grandparents' life as luxurious, or even comfortable. Nicolas knew that Jules, so conscious of all they had done for him, blamed the hard and often difficult life they'd had for the fact that both had died before they were sixty. First his grandmother of a heart attack, and then his grandfather, a strong man bewildered and weakened by grief, six months later.

Nicolas went to the table and picked up the photographs, sorting through until he came to the ones of Polly. He tried to decide which was his favourite and looked again at one where she was smiling into the camera and he'd caught the freshness of her, an essence of her personality. He heard Jules call, and before joining him, Nicolas swiftly extracted the negative and slipped it into his wallet.

30

On the following Saturday evening, Mark once again drove over to Abbey Hulton. He was constantly driving back and forth, particularly over the Easter vacation, and this was why he was now suggesting that Ruth should come over to stay with Polly for a weekend. 'It'll be great having you so close,' he said, 'we'll be able to spend more time together.'

They were at Trentham Ballroom, and, after spending the last half an hour 'smooching' in the middle of the floor, were enjoying a drink at a side table. 'And save on petrol,' Ruth said. Then she remembered that budgeting was not exactly high on Mark's list of priorities. She looked across at him. 'Okay, I'll give her a ring. You're so lucky,' she said, 'not having to worry about money all the time.'

'I know.' Then Mark's eyes shadowed, 'But you've got something far more important. You've still got your mum. I'd do anything to have my mother back. But only if she was well; I wouldn't want her to suffer again.'

'It must have been awful for you, seeing her like that.'

'It was, and for Dad too; but much worse for her. She knew she was dying, you see. She had to cope with the fear of that, as well as the pain.'

Ruth put out a hand and covered his. 'You're a very sensitive person, Mark, do you know that?'

'That's why you love me,' he said, smiling at her. Ruth felt a pulse leap in her throat. But his tone had been casual, almost flippant. Then he made a suggestion that made her spirits soar. 'While you're at Polly's, you'll have to come over to our place. It's about time you saw where I grew up.'

Ruth had begun to despair of Mark inviting her home. She knew that her own parents felt it a snub that although he was now a frequent visitor, there had never been a return invitation to his home for Ruth. They were suspicious of his motives, and Sean Donovan still thought that the social divide between them was too wide. 'You're going to get hurt, my girl,' was a statement she was sick of hearing. Well at least this will please him, she thought. In fact I think they will both be nearly as relieved as I am.

'How did young Michael get on at football?' Mark suddenly asked.

Ruth laughed. 'He was abject when he got home. Apparently they lost 5–1. And he was in goal...'

'Poor kid – that's rotten. Look, do you think he'd like me to give him a spot of coaching?'

Ruth stared at him. 'I didn't know you played football!'

'Well, I'm not that good, but I probably know more than he does. I played at school.'

'I'd have thought they were too posh there; that it would have been all rugby.'

'Nope, we played soccer too. Anyway ask him, Ruth. I'd be happy to, any time.' He glanced over his shoulder at the band on the stage as they began to play 'In the Mood', and got up saying, 'Come on, lazybones, let's do a fancy quickstep.'

'I wonder,' Ruth said, as they went on to the floor, 'how Polly got on with that French chap?'

Mark slipped an arm around her waist, and murmured, 'We'll soon find out.'

The following week, when she arrived to stay at The Gables, Ruth stared in disbelief at Polly. 'You're joking! He was tall, dark, handsome *and* with a sexy French accent?'

'Honestly.' Polly laughed at her friend's expression.

'How old was he?'

271

'Mid-twenties, I think. Anyway, you might meet him.' Polly told her about Nicolas's plans to come over again in the summer.

'Oh, please, Pol. Maybe we could go out as a foursome.'

'Oh yes, who with?' Mark said, as he came into the kitchen to join them after checking his tyre pressures.

'Polly's French chap, this Nicolas.'

'He's not my French chap,' Polly retorted. 'I've only met him once.'

'Maybe, but he's made quite an impression.'

Mark looked at Polly, and grinned. 'Well, well,' he said, 'I've got a rival at last!'

With sudden alarm Ruth thought, what does he mean? To have a rival means that he...

But Polly was laughing. 'I've had a rival for a long time, Mark. It just so happens that she's my best friend.'

Ruth looked from one to another. She still felt troubled at times by the easy camaraderie between them, unsure whether she had anything to worry about. Sometimes their affectionate banter had the ability to make her feel not exactly jealous, but a newcomer, and even at times an outsider. Then she felt reassured as Mark put out a hand to squeeze her own across the table. 'And sorry, Pol, she wins hands down.'

'For that,' Polly said huffily, 'I might not offer you a chocolate biscuit.'

'Oh go on ... anyway, I need at least two!' They were all laughing as Sadie came into the room.

'Would you like some coffee?' Polly said.

'I'd love some – although I'm off into Stafford

in a minute. The photographer rang earlier,' she told Polly. 'Apparently all the delay has not only been because of Easter, but because he was ill with bronchitis and wouldn't trust the repair to anyone else.'

'It's my father's photo,' Polly explained to Mark and Ruth. 'Mrs Booth had an accident with it.'

Sadie sat at the circular table. 'Good to see you again, Ruth. And how are you, Mark?'

'Fine, Sadie. And you?' Mark thought yet again what an attractive woman Polly's mother was, wondering why she'd never remarried.

'Perfectly well, thanks. How are the finals coming on?'

Sadie was recalling George's complaints the other evening. 'He should have his nose in his books,' he'd said, as they'd enjoyed their chicken supreme. 'Not be dashing over to see Ruth at every opportunity.'

'I'll be glad when they're over,' Mark said. 'Not that I haven't enjoyed Oxford, but I'm ready to go forth into the world, as they say.'

'We are too, aren't we, Pol,' Ruth bit into a chocolate finger biscuit. 'Once we've got through the dreaded exams when we get back. And then we can begin applying for posts.'

'Are you hoping to be at the same school?' Sadie asked.

Polly shook her head. 'Not really. It's not practical as we live at different ends of the county. We both want to be fairly near our homes. Of course, that doesn't mean that I wouldn't travel if necessary.'

'I couldn't afford it,' Ruth said. 'I need to help

273

my parents out. They've made a lot of sacrifices for me to stay on at training college.'

'Ruth,' Mark informed them with pride, 'is a young woman of conscience.'

'Does your dad know anyone at Wedgwood's?' Polly asked, turning to Mark. 'Only Nicolas's father would like to see inside the factory. Apparently he's a fan of Jasper ware.'

Mark considered. 'I'll ask him. Maybe there'd be someone at the golf club.'

'More than likely,' Sadie said drily. It never ceased to amaze her how middle-class people always seemed to have influential contacts.

'I don't think factory tours are that difficult to arrange,' Ruth said. 'From what my father says, someone knowledgeable just dons a white coat and shows visitors around. They have to be brought down by someone in the management, though, probably a director. You certainly can't walk in off the streets.'

'Health and Safety,' Mark informed them. 'Regulations are very strict about that sort of thing. Don't worry, Pol. I'm sure Dad can sort something out. I'll ask him to let you know.'

And then, Polly thought with satisfaction, I'll have an excuse to write to Nicolas.

But it was to Sadie that George reported back. They were having lunch at a small country restaurant; she found it a source of wry amusement that he was still choosing some 'out of the way' venue. After all, Felicity had been dead for six months now. The formal long mourning period so beloved of the Victorians no longer existed. Sensitivity, yes, she thought, but surely by now he should be able to lunch with a woman friend without causing tongues to wag. Or was it, she wondered, that it was being seen in *her* company that was the problem?

'Have you decided?' George smiled at her over the menu.

'Yes. A prawn cocktail, followed by lamb chops.'

'I'll go for the soup, and a steak.' He turned as the waiter approached, and while they were discussing wine, Sadie glanced around the oak-beamed room. It wasn't busy, there were only three other tables occupied. One by an elderly man and his wife, a sweet-faced, white-haired woman, another by two young men, thrusting executive types she decided, and the third by... Sadie stared into the sardonic eyes of a man she'd met the previous year. Someone she'd invited back to The Gables. She tried to recall what his job was and remembered that he was an estate agent. He must know George, she thought with sudden panic, and at that precise moment as the waiter left, George turned and she saw him tense, then raise a hand in greeting. She gazed down at her place setting, trying to remain calm as she shook out her pink napkin and spread it on her lap.

'Someone you know?' she said quietly.

'Yes, Antony Hollister – he's an estate agent in Stafford. I don't know him well, but he's in Rotary.'

Of course, she thought, he absolutely would, wouldn't he – the ubiquitous Rotary. You can't 'fart in a paper bag' up here, she thought, without someone knowing. The coarse expression was one of her mother's favourites and it was only on very rare occasions that Sadie allowed herself to copy her. She glanced swiftly at George, trying to read his expression, but his eyes were guarded. He might be even more disconcerted, she thought, if he actually knew the truth ... Antony Hollister had been to The Gables not just once, but several times. They'd shared many hours of lovemaking and laughter. He'd been one of her better choices, and their liaison had come to an end only when he'd met an elegant boutique owner. Later, Sadie had seen their engagement announced in the local paper.

'Oh, will you tell Polly,' George was saying, 'that once she knows the date involved – when this Frenchman is coming – to let me know, and I'll put her in touch with someone at Wedgwood's factory in Barlaston.'

'Of course I will. And thank you, George, she'll be delighted about that.'

'It's quite an unusual situation, isn't it?' George commented. 'Sort of "hands across the Channel", so to speak. You know, Europe is going to get closer and closer in the future.'

'You mean because of all these package holidays?'

'Not only that, I think there will be closer political and business ties too.'

Sadie gazed thoughtfully at him. She had great respect for George; even though his politics were so different to her own. He was a staunch Conservative whereas Sadie always voted Labour, feeling that to do otherwise would be a betrayal of her working-class background. Even though, she thought self-mockingly, I've done everything

276

I can to remove myself from it. But she didn't feel inclined to have a serious discussion, and instead applied herself to spooning up the prawns from her first course.

'Mark brought Ruth to the house,' George said, suddenly.

'Yes, I know. I think she was pleased to be invited.'

'Mmn.' George broke off a piece of bread roll and began to butter it. 'Tell me, do you think those two are serious?'

Sadie considered. 'Ruth certainly is. But you'd know better about Mark. Why, do you have reservations? She's a very intelligent girl, George. I like her very much.'

'I'm not saying she isn't. But I'm a great believer in people keeping to their own class, Sadie, and to their own religion. It just makes things easier all round.'

'It makes things easier for whom, exactly?' Although her voice was quiet, there was an edge to it, and George glanced sharply at her. He suddenly realised that he knew hardly anything about Sadie's earlier life. She was a fantastic listener; it was one of the things he valued about her, but she rarely talked about herself.

'For everyone, surely you agree?'

'I can see your point, George. But actually I'm not in favour of tight social circles; they just lead to narrow-mindedness and prejudice. A bit of strong peasant blood has strengthened many a bloodline.'

He put down his spoon, dabbed his mouth with his napkin, and began to laugh. 'We're not talking

277

here about inbred aristocracy. I'm just saying that if a couple have had a similar upbringing and education, then surely they'll have fewer problems. And as for the religion thing, well we all know how autocratic the Catholic Church is. Everything has to be on its own terms.'

He glanced up and smiled, and Sadie heard Antony's voice. 'Hello, George. I didn't know this was one of your watering holes.'

George laughed. 'Oh, I get about. Sadie, may I introduce Antony Hollister? And Antony, this is Sadie Merton.'

She looked up, saw the wariness in his eyes, and said softly, 'Hello.' Antony gave a slight nod and a social smile in return. 'Enjoy your meal,' he said, and then was gone.

So that was that, Sadie thought with relief. Antony obviously didn't want their affair to be public knowledge any more than she did. But the encounter had made her feel uncomfortable. She hated lies and deception. Discretion, yes, but deliberately concealing something like this was different. She looked across at George, who was now cutting into his steak. He was a decent man, but not the most liberal-minded. And although he must know that she'd had other lovers, to discover that one of them was a business colleague would deeply embarrass him. But I have my own rules, she thought, as she forked up a tiny Jersey Royal. While I'm a free spirit, I shall behave exactly as I please. She glanced across at him. But she had to admit that she was becoming very fond of George. Maybe, she thought, that's why – at least so far – I'm managing to be faithful to him.

31

The next few months were, for Jules, some of the longest of his life. After his accident, when he'd been in so much confusion and pain, the hours, days and even weeks had passed in an agonising blur. Then when his wounds had gradually begun to heal, his recovery had been tempered by his shock and frustration on finding that he was unable to remember what had happened, to recall anything of his previous life. In his distress and bewilderment, it had been Gabrielle, the dark-haired daughter of the farmer who had originally found him, who had coaxed him out of his depression. And eventually, the love that flowered between them gave him the strength to at least try to return to normal life. If, he thought bitterly, it was possible for anyone in France to do so during those war years. But not even then, had he experienced this agony of impatience.

'Papa,' Nicolas said, 'we've talked about this before. There would be no point in going to England before July. Polly will be away at college – she's in her final term.'

'I know. And, of course, you're right, but it doesn't make it any easier.' At least it was now the end of May, Jules thought, so that meant only one more month to get through.

'Why don't you go out for a walk and get some fresh air,' Nicolas suggested, who was trying to read and finding Jules's restlessness distracting.

'Yes, I think I will. I need some exercise too.' It was only by regularly using the muscles in his leg that Jules was able to be reasonably free from pain. And during the summer months his old injury didn't trouble him quite so much. He regarded the discomfort as trivial compared to the injuries sustained by many others of his age. Whichever side their country had been on during the Second World War, people who had no choice but to fight had been maimed or tortured, often leaving deep psychological scars. For many years Jules had carried a sense of guilt that he hadn't been able to play a more active part in the conflict. His health problems during those first few years meant that he would have been a liability to his compatriots. But he often wondered what had been his role before the accident. Perhaps soon, he thought, as he walked along the sunny, tree-lined pavements, I'll discover more about my past, and then I may find out.

After Jules had gone, Nicolas, instead of returning to his book, went into his room. Going to the wardrobe, he reached inside his jacket and took his leather wallet from the inside pocket. Extracting the photo of Polly that he now always carried with him, he gazed down at her smiling face. 'I too am impatient,' he murmured. The thought of the elegant Eloise who, as the fulfilment of a long-standing promise, he was taking to the theatre the following evening, was not the tempting prospect it might once have been. Since his return from England, Nicolas hadn't felt inclined to become involved with anyone. Yet while the attraction between him and Polly had been tangible, undeniable even, since then she could easily have met someone else. In fact, although she'd been swift to assure him that the Oxford student she'd travelled to Paris with was not her boyfriend, that didn't mean someone else wasn't in her life. Jules isn't the only one, Nicolas thought, who is hoping that this holiday in England will be one of discovery.

In England, June meant for Polly and Ruth the relief of having passed their exams and the prospect of long-awaited freedom from studying. Both had applied for teaching posts, and the last few weeks at college were tense as they awaited the results of interviews. Polly was particularly keen on a preparatory school in Stafford, although Ruth didn't really approve.

'You should get out into the state system,' she complained. 'Honestly, Polly, if you always lead such a rarefied life, you're missing out on so much. It's a different world out there, you know.'

Stung, Polly said, 'I don't think you could ever accuse me of being a snob, Ruth.'

'Did I say that? What I mean is that it would be good for you, teaching ordinary kids, it would widen your experience of life.' Ruth was becoming very interested in socialism; she didn't believe in narrow social circles.

'Maybe it would,' Polly retorted. 'And actually I agree with you. But you know I want to teach French. What other opening is there?'

'I suppose you're right. As for me,' Ruth said gloomily. 'There were four of us short-listed for the one I'd really like – that Catholic school in

Hanley. With living so close, it would only mean a short bus ride.'

'Well, fingers crossed for both of us.'

It must have worked because both girls were appointed, and so it was with a sense of high spirits that Polly, with Ruth in the passenger seat and the boot packed with their belongings, drove for the last time away from the college campus.

'Mark's coming over tomorrow,' Ruth told her. 'He got a 2.1, to his Dad's relief. I think he was worried that I was becoming too much of a distraction.'

'Which, of course, you were.'

Ruth grinned. 'Hope so, but obviously not enough to make him fail his finals. I think I was actually a good influence – it stopped the pressure getting to him.'

Polly laughed. 'When do you start working in Woolworths?'

'Next week. I don't really mind. Apart from the money, it'll be good to see the girls again.' She glanced at Polly. 'You should try it, you know, you can learn about people by serving the general public.'

Polly drew up at a set of traffic lights. 'I'm sure you're right. And in a way I'd rather like to – just for the experience. But then I'd be depriving someone else of a job they really need.'

'That's a point,' Ruth said. 'Anyway, what I wanted to say is that I won't always be working there full-time – that's just over the Wakes fortnight. The rest of the time it will only be three days, so if there's any chance of coming over for some tennis…'

Polly lifted a hand to acknowledge a passing AA patrolman's salute, and grinned. 'Brilliant, you'll be able to put Hilary's nose out of joint.'

It was Michael who opened the door to Mark. He winked and slipped the boy a florin before going into the now familiar sitting room. The Donovans no longer 'stood on ceremony', as Ruth called it, when Mark came. As Sean said, 'He can take us as he finds us and if it doesn't suit...' He looked up from the armchair where he was studying the racing and stared in astonishment as Mark held up two bottles of champagne in triumph.

'Please could you put them in cold water for a bit,' Mark said, 'They've been in the fridge at home, but the car was a bit hot...'

And that remark, Ruth thought, coming in to hear his words, has shown how far he's come since that first time. Then he would have assumed that they had a refrigerator. She went to kiss him. 'What's all this, then? Have you won the Pools or something?'

He laughed. 'If only. No, I shall leave that to your father.' Sean regularly filled in both Little-woods and Vernons coupons, and all his family had learned to stay quiet at five o'clock on Satur-day afternoons, when the football results were read out. Bridie's only gambling flutter was to try and 'Spot the Ball', in the *People*. Neither so far had ever won anything, but Ruth had told Mark that each was convinced it was only a matter of time.

'I thought,' Mark said, 'that having a qualified teacher in the family, not to mention her boyfriend becoming a graduate, was definitely worth celebrating.'

'Can I have some, Dad?' Michael said. 'I've never tasted champagne.'

Neither had Bridie, but she wasn't about to admit it. 'No, you can't,' she scolded. 'It's not for children.'

'Aw, it's not fair.'

'You can have a sip of mine,' promised Ruth. 'Go and call the twins. They can have some, can't they, Mum?'

'What do you think, Sean?'

Sean looked at their expectant faces and decided to enter into the spirit of the occasion. 'Sure and why not? And you're right, Mark, we do have something to celebrate. Get some glasses, Bridie.'

'I'll get them.' Flashing a grateful smile at Mark, Ruth went to the sideboard and took out some rather small wine glasses. Mark looked at them with some dismay, but then felt ashamed. Why on earth should this family possess champagne flutes? He laughed as he heard Michael's excited treble as he raced noisily up the stairs.

'Come on down, you're missing it all!'

Maria put her head around the bedroom doom. 'Missing what, monkey face?'

'Champagne! Mark's brought champagne.'

'Champagne?' Teresa pushed her twin sister out on to the landing.

'You're not kidding us, are yer?'

'Cut my throat and hope to die!'

The girls both scrambled back into their bedrooms to comb their hair and hurriedly apply a dash of lipstick, before clattering down the stairs.

284

That carpet, Ruth thought, gets more threadbare every day.

'Why have we got champagne?' Teresa demanded, her eyes glancing suspiciously from Mark to Ruth. Her inference was unmistakable, and Ruth felt her colour rise.

'Because,' Mark said, 'you've got a clever sister and she has an absolutely brilliant boyfriend.'

'Modest, isn't he?' Maria nudged her sister and they both turned as Sean, who had been running cold water over the bottles resting in the sink, called out from the kitchen.

'What do you think, Mark? Are these cold enough yet?'

Mark went through to the untidy, if clean kitchen to check, while Ruth turned to the twins. 'Will you stop embarrassing me,' she hissed.

'What do you mean?'

'You know very well, Teresa – looking at the pair of us like that!'

'You can't blame her,' Maria defended, 'we've seen you looking in jewellers' windows!'

'It's far too soon for that,' Bridie said sharply, and then Mark was coming through, opening the bottles with a flourish, the explosive pop of the cork startling them all and making them laugh as the champagne brimmed over. He went to the table where Ruth had put the glasses, and began to pour. 'Just a little for the twins,' Bridie began to say, as she took her own, but it was too late, as Mark was already handing them full glasses.

Michael stood watching them all with a glum expression, and Mark turned to Sean. 'What do you think – maybe just a drop?'

Sean glanced at his son. 'Okay, but not too much, now.'

Michael's face lit up. 'Only a tiny sip,' Ruth warned, 'but not yet – after the toast.'

'Will you do the honours, Mr Donovan?' Mark said.

They all turned expectantly to Sean, who cleared his throat and then said, 'To Ruth, the first member of the Donovan family to qualify as a teacher.'

'And I give you a future headmistress!' Mark added.

'Hear, hear,' everyone chorused, and took sips of their champagne, in Michael's case with a splutter as he grimaced and screwed up his face.

'Don't you like it?' Mark laughed.

'I'd rather have pop.'

'And another toast,' announced Ruth. 'I give you Mark Eldon, a future brilliant lawyer.'

'Hear, hear!' This time it was Michael who led the choruses and they all laughed.

'We could do with some crisps, Bridie,' Sean grinned, making Mark wince at the thought of them with his Bollinger.

'I can do better than that,' Ruth interspersed quickly. 'Didn't you pick some strawberries from the garden this morning, Dad? I'll just rinse them through. I read somewhere they're wonderful with champagne.'

'Nectar of the gods,' Mark said, gazing admiringly at her as she disappeared into the kitchen. Trust Ruth to save the situation! He picked up the other bottle, preparing to open it.

'Steady on,' Sean said. 'Surely, lad, one bottle's enough.'

But Mark had brought two, and he certainly wasn't going to take one back. 'One glass of champagne is never enough.'

'Absolutely,' Maria giggled.

'The bubbles keep going up my nose,' Teresa wailed.

'Here you are, Michael. You can have the corks if you like,' Mark offered.

'Thanks. But I'd rather have a puppy.'

'Now don't start all that again,' Sean said. 'Yer know what your mother's told you. They're too expensive, both to buy and to feed.'

'Aw, Mum. I bet you had a dog when you were young, Mark.'

They all looked at him, and he admitted, 'Yes, I did actually. A golden retriever called Sandy.'

'There you are. Everyone knows that boys and dogs go together.'

Bridie looked despairingly at him. It wasn't the buying and feeding that bothered her – there was usually someone who had a litter of puppies they were selling cheap. It was the thought of the dog hairs and muddy paw prints. Haven't I enough to do, she thought, without cleaning up after a blessed animal! But Michael was looking so pleadingly at her, that the effect of the unaccustomed champagne, as she complained later, overrode her common sense. 'Oh all right, then. But it will have to be your responsibility,' she warned, 'don't expect the rest of us to take it for walks.'

'Oh, Mum, can I?' Michael's expression was enough to light up a Christmas tree, as Ruth told Polly later.

Mark, who was busy replenishing everyone's

glasses, said, 'What sort of dog do you fancy, Michael?'

'He's not having a big one!' Bridie said quickly.

'It's just that someone I know has a West Highland terrier, and she's just had pups.'

'Oh, I like those, they're right little characters,' Ruth said, who had returned and was handing round a glass dish full of strawberries. 'I don't think they moult much either, Mum.'

'Hang on a minute,' Sean said. 'That's a pedigree, isn't it? We can't afford one of those. Yer'll have to have a Heinz 57, lad.'

Michael looked bewildered. 'I've never heard of them. What do they look like?'

'Dad means a mongrel, silly!' Maria said. 'What sort of dog *do* you want?'

'I don't want one of those squashed-face ones. Yer know, Mum, like the one along the street that growls at everybody.'

'It all depends on how you bring them up,' Mark said. 'There are more bad owners than bad dogs. Look, do you like Westies, Michael?'

'Are they those little white ones who wear a tartan collar?'

'That's right.'

Michael nodded.

'Well, leave it with me,' Mark said. 'The owners aren't short of money, and if they knew one of their pups was going to a good home...' He began to replenish their glasses, 'I can't promise anything, mind, but I'll do my best.'

Ruth looked at the happiness shining on her small brother's face, at the sparkling eyes of the twins, the pride of her parents, and knew that no matter what happened in the future, she would always remember this scene. But would it be a nostalgic memory of something that never happened? Or was it a precursor to Mark becoming not just her boyfriend, but part of her family.

32

When the thin blue airmail arrived at the office, Nicolas at first assumed it to be a late reply forwarded by *Staffordshire Life*. Possibly from the person who was interested in his supposed research into phonetics. But then he saw the slanted handwriting. It was from Polly! Swiftly he slipped it into his pocket, only taking it out later when he was alone. The tone was warm, friendly, and he blessed her for being so helpful. Then laying it aside, he leaned thoughtfully back in his swivel chair. Plans needed to be made, careful plans.

And that was what he explained to Jules later that evening. They were eating at a bistro on the Rue de Rivoli, and as Jules finished his oeuf mimosa, Nicolas said, 'First of all, I'll write and let Polly have our dates. Then we must decide where to stay, hopefully somewhere not too far from Brandon.'

'It really is kind of her to try and arrange the factory visit for me,' Jules said, replacing his cutlery, 'and I shall look forward to it. But, of course, the whole purpose of this visit is to find a link to my past, however tenuous it may be.

Nicolas, I don't know how we can manipulate this, but what I need is to be completely alone when I first see the house. In fact, I think it's essential.' He leaned forward and said intensely, 'Can you understand what I mean? To be among other people coming forward with greetings and introductions would be far too distracting. It could block those vital first impressions.'

Nicolas frowned thoughtfully. 'Yes, I do see what you mean. But the problem is that with those two bay windows overlooking the drive, it would be difficult for you. I had to be very furtive when I took those photographs.'

'Exactly,' Jules said, 'and to have that anxiety would cloud my mind, might even prevent a memory from resurfacing.'

Nicolas, seeing the desperation in his eyes, gazed at him with sympathy. 'I can make sure Polly isn't there,' he said slowly, 'but she lives with her mother.'

'Maybe she has a regular time that she's not at home,' Jules suggested.

'Possibly, yes. But we can't know that, neither can we plan for it in advance. I think that we're going to have to ... what is that saying ... oh yes, play it by ear.'

Jules nodded. 'Also I did notice on the photo that there's a side gate. Now if that wasn't locked, I could walk through to the back of the house. Perhaps spend some time quietly in the garden.'

'You'd better be careful, or you'll be suspected of being a burglar!'

As Jules looked alarmed, Nicolas grinned. 'Not really,' he reassured him. 'The nearest neighbours are some distance away. The chance of that is very slight.'

'That's a relief,' Jules said, then after pausing when the waiter brought their steak frites, continued, 'of course when I go into the house there's no alternative than to be with other people. Although,' he murmured with a glint of amusement in his voice, 'you have given me an idea. I could always wait until I know The Gables is empty, and then break a window or something.'

'Papa!' Nicolas was obviously horrified, and Jules laughed, 'I'm only joking.'

'I should hope so!'

But although originally it had only been a flippant suggestion, Jules began to brood. The prospect of being able to wander around in the large house, to absorb the atmosphere, to explore undisturbed, had now become not only alluring, but perhaps even a possibility. Breaking a window was obviously out of the question, but could there be another way? He glanced across the table. What if Nicolas invited Polly out on a day when they knew that her mother would be absent? Could he find a way of unlocking the back door before they left? And then, on their return, discreetly lock it again? It wouldn't be easy, but Jules had great faith in the young journalist's ingenuity. All would, of course, depend on Jules being able to enter the side gate. But even if he did – could he do such an unforgiveable thing? Be guilty of an intrusion, an invasion of some unknown people's privacy?

'Are you not eating?' Nicolas said, glancing at Jules's as yet untouched food.

'I've been deep in thought.' Jules gazed across

291

the table and said, not without some misgiving, 'I don't suppose you'd agree to be my accomplice in a criminal act?'

A week later Polly, after hearing the clatter of the letter box, hurried into the hall to collect the morning post. There were two letters, and to her joy one was an airmail. She didn't need to check the postmark to know it would be the reply from Nicolas. And it was. Sadie was still in the breakfast room so, wanting to be alone, Polly went into the drawing room and carefully opened out the thin blue paper. They were coming at the beginning of July, and planned to stay in England for two weeks. Two whole weeks! Polly's pulse was racing as she read the rest of the letter.

Papa wishes me to thank you, and to say that he would very much like to visit the Wedgwood factory perhaps on the day after we arrive, if that would be convenient.

Nicolas went on to ask whether Polly knew of a small hotel in the area, and also a reliable car hire firm.

I am looking forward very much to seeing you again, Polly, and also to that promised game of tennis.

He signed the letter simply, *Nicolas*.
Polly took the letters into the breakfast room. 'There's one for you, from Hereford, so I suppose that will be from Babs,' she said, 'and this is from Nicolas. It's in French so I'll translate and

read it to you.'

Sadie, who was enjoying a cigarette with her coffee, seeing her daughter's shining eyes, looked quizzically at her. It will be interesting, she thought, to meet this young man.

A couple of minutes later, Polly's forehead creased in a frown. 'Where do you think I should suggest they stay?'

'Well, a fortnight at the Crown might be too expensive,' Sadie mused. 'I tell you what, I'll ask around at the boutique, and see if anyone can recommend somewhere. I'll also ask George if he knows of a good car hire firm.'

Polly gazed at her, feeling slightly uneasy. So that relationship was still going on. She wondered whether Mark was aware of it yet. Then she said thoughtfully, 'You know, two weeks is a long time to come for a holiday around here. I'd have thought they would have wanted to spend some time in London, or perhaps the Lake District.'

'Well, we are pretty central,' Sadie said, 'and he does say they're hiring a car. Maybe they both know London quite well already.'

'That's true. And the North Wales coast isn't too far. And wouldn't Blackpool be a culture experience for them!'

'You know I've never been to Blackpool,' mused Sadie.

'I can just see you in a "Kiss Me Quick" hat,' Polly grinned. 'The problem is...'

'I'd mean it!'

Polly laughed. 'You're not joking, either!'

Sadie smiled back, thinking what a long way they had come from those early days. Polly yawned and then got up from the table. 'Well, this won't 'get the baby a new bonnet', as Mrs Booth would say. I'd better be off – I'm supposed to be meeting Anita in Stone. She wants to look at bridesmaids' dresses.'

'How many is she having?'

'Four. Hazel and myself and two little girls. One's Andy's niece and the other one is Anita's. Apparently she looks like a little angel – you know, blonde hair and blue eyes – but I've been told she's a handful. They're both five.'

Sadie smiled. 'Keeping them in order will be good practice for you.'

'Actually, I shall be teaching seven- and eight-year-olds,' Polly said, 'but I know what you mean.'

After Polly had left Sadie went into the drawing room and settled down to read her own letter. She and Babs now wrote fairly frequently, and Sadie's gaze skimmed over the usual chatty lines about Babs's offspring; her pride in their achievements, her worries about their sometimes unsuitable friends. And then right at the end of the letter, there was a short paragraph that Sadie read over again.

I've met someone, and although it's early days I feel so happy, Sadie. It was at a friend's wedding. He was on his own, just as I was, and we sat next to each other at the reception. He's a widower with two children – his wife died four years ago. I'll let you know how things develop.

Sadie put the letter on her lap, and stared unseeingly before her. It was, of course, wonderful that

Babs might have a new future. She deserved to be happy again. So why, Sadie thought, do I feel suddenly flat, perhaps even envious? Restless, she got up and wandered over to the bay window, looking out at the neatly mown lawn, at the roses already in bud, the borders edged with alyssum and aubretia. She was thinking as she often did, of November, when Polly would reach her twenty-first birthday. The subject had never been discussed between them, but Sadie knew that a decision would then need to be made as to her future. She had too much pride simply to linger on at The Gables, to feel in any way that she was there on sufferance. Of course, under the terms of John Merton's will, the substantially increased allowance that she'd come to enjoy would cease as soon as Polly became of age. But Sadie knew that she had much to thank him for. Even though she'd returned to London, leaving her twelve-month-old baby with him, her father-in-law had written monthly with news of Polly and always enclosing a generous cheque. He'd been a man of strong principle, taking his responsibilities seriously, she thought with sadness, as had his son. She went over to the sideboard and picked up the photograph of André, gazing down at it. She'd been so relieved to find that due to the photographer's expertise the damage could hardly be detected. And the antique silver frame, although it had taken time to find, was almost an exact replica of the original. But then she replaced it and turned away. What was the point in dwelling on what might have been; nothing could change the past.

33

Jules and Nicolas arrived in England on the first Sunday in July. Jules, who had done little travelling during the past twenty years, was a quiet companion and Nicolas, reluctant to disturb his thoughts, occupied himself reading. He guessed that Jules, who was staring intensely at every landmark, was trying to retrieve some knowledge, some sense of familiarity with the country, particularly as they passed through London. As he eventually said, it was inconceivable that from his supposed background, he wouldn't have known the capital city. Nicolas had initially suggested that they spend a couple of days there, but Jules had waited too long, was too impatient, to delay his crucial visit to The Gables. 'No,' he'd said. 'I'd prefer to go directly to our hotel in Staffordshire. If we think it might help, we could always go to London later.'

At Euston, they followed the crowd of passengers along the platform and after managing to find an empty carriage, lifted their luggage on to the overhead rack and made themselves comfortable in window seats. 'A bit different, aren't they,' Nicolas said, 'the upholstered seats, I mean. Not like our hard wooden ones on the Metro.'

Jules glanced at him in surprise. 'I hadn't noticed,' he said slowly. 'It all seems...' He put a hand down and stroked the seat cover, then touched the leather strap of the sash window. His gaze travelled upwards, lingering on the prints hanging on the carriage wall behind Nicolas. They were of country scenes and he got up and leaned forward to read the inscriptions. 'Lake Windermere', one said, and another, 'Loch Lomond'. Jules studied them for a moment then frowned. Nothing seemed strange or even foreign. He spread his hands in a gesture of helplessness, 'This all feels sort of normal to me.'

'But that's wonderful,' Nicolas said, his face lighting up. 'A good sign, surely.'

'But I don't feel English, Nicolas. I feel so attuned to France.'

'But you would,' Nicolas pointed out. 'After all, it's what you've believed for over twenty years. All your experience of life is condensed into that particular period. There is such a thing as learned behaviour.'

'That's true,' Jules conceded. And then the train began to move slowly out of the railway station, and to their relief they still had the carriage to themselves. 'We must, of course,' Jules said, 'be prepared for the fact that Oliver could be completely mistaken.'

'Then how do you account for your sketch of The Gables?'

'I can't.' Jules relapsed again into silence, watching the scenery flow by, and then they were stopping at small stations and their carriage began to fill up.

Like Nicolas before him, Jules looked with curiosity at the other occupants. There was a prim woman sitting opposite, her thin brown hair scraped back into a bun, her pale face devoid of make-up. A spinster, he decided, even before glancing at the folded hands in her lap. Yes, they were devoid of rings. Finding such musings eased his growing tension, he tried to sum up the other passengers. Now what could be the profession of the man with a shiny pink scalp surrounded by a tonsure of white hair? He might be a solicitor or a doctor. The motherly woman next to him was obviously a housewife, Jules decided. She was knitting a complicated garment of many colours, its shape indeterminate. He watched her mouth moving silently as she counted the stitches. Gabrielle too had been a knitter, but mainly of baby clothes. She'd always been delighted when any acquaintance announced that she was *enceinte*, but underlying that genuine pleasure was her own sadness that she was unable to have another child. Gabrielle's mother had told him that when Nicolas had been born the delivery had been botched; not through deliberate neglect, but because of ignorance and inexperience.

Jules turned his attention back to the unfolding landscape, and when one of the passengers asked if the window could be lowered, he lifted the strap with what was almost an automatic gesture, and let fresh clean air inside.

'Do remember to close it if we approach a tunnel,' the spinster said sharply. 'I don't want smuts all over me, thank you!'

'I'm sorry, you will have to remind me,' Jules said politely. 'I'm afraid I haven't travelled on this line before.'

She looked at him with suspicion, while Nicolas

tried to suppress a grin. The man with the white hair glanced up. 'We go through Kilsby Tunnel, near Rugby. I'll let you know.'

'Thank you,' Jules said, and relapsed into silence.

Nicolas checked his watch. There was still quite a distance to travel, and it would be early evening by the time they arrived. The hotel brochure specified that dinner was served at seven thirty, which had seemed early at the time, but would, he thought as he felt the first pangs of hunger, now be extremely welcome.

Food, however, was the last thing on Jules's mind as their journey began to near its end. Nervousness, anticipation, excitement and the fear of disappointment all warred within him as he realised it was only a matter of minutes now before he actually set foot in Staffordshire; the county with which, according to Oliver, he had close ties. His fingers went up to pluck at his short dark beard, a habit he had when under stress. Nicolas, in the seat opposite, guessed the thoughts that were going through the older man's mind; knowing that he would be in an agony of impatience. It was then that Nicolas made a sudden decision. Instead of waiting until tomorrow as he'd planned, he would phone Polly tonight. This mystery that had dominated their lives over the past few months needed to be solved. Why waste time?

It was Sadie who answered the telephone. She hurried into the drawing room where Polly was watching TV. 'It's him,' she hissed. 'Nicolas.'

Polly jumped up. 'What? Are you sure?'

'Well unless it's Sacha Distel!'

Her pulse racing, Polly went into the hall and picked up the receiver. She spoke in English. 'Hello, Nicolas. Are you in England?'

'Yes, we arrived earlier this evening. How are you?'

Her heart did a flip at the sound of that distinctive voice. 'I'm fine, thank you. Is the hotel all right?'

'It's very comfortable, thank you. Polly, as you know, we're going to the Wedgwood factory tomorrow morning, but I wondered if I could repay your hospitality and take you for afternoon tea somewhere – unless you have other arrangements, of course.'

She said quickly, 'No, that would be fine. I'd love to, Nicolas.'

'Good. I'll call for you at about three o'clock, and will try to remember to drive on the left!'

She laughed. 'I shall look forward to it.' She almost danced into the drawing room. 'He's taking me out for afternoon tea tomorrow!'

Sadie smiled at her daughter's high spirits. 'He hasn't wasted much time.'

'He hasn't, has he? I think that's a good sign, don't you?'

'It could be. Of course, he could merely be returning your hospitality.' Sadie smiled reflectively. 'I must say that he's got a very sexy voice.'

'Hasn't he just.' Even the sound of it had set Polly's nerves tingling.

'We can go into Stone,' she said, her mind running ahead, planning. 'To that nice teashop – you know, the one we went to the other week?'

'Yes, that's the best choice. But don't forget about his father. Have you thought he might be bringing him along?'

Suddenly deflated, Polly slumped into the armchair. 'Oh, I never thought of that.'

'He can hardly just leave him alone in that small hotel. Not if Nicolas has the car.'

'I suppose not.' Damn, Polly thought; that puts a different slant on the whole thing. Meanwhile Sadie thought quietly that this time, when the young Frenchman arrived, she intended to be very much in evidence.

But when Nicolas turned into the drive the following afternoon, Polly was ready and waiting; strolling around the front lawn in the sunshine, hoping to give the impression of casually enjoying the roses. In reality, she'd been too restless, too full of fluttering nerves to remain indoors. She was unaware of Sadie hovering at a bedroom window.

Polly turned as she heard the car engine, delighted to see that Nicolas was alone. He was even more attractive than she remembered; his throat tanned and bare beneath his open-necked white linen shirt.

'Nicolas,' she went forward to greet him, and he smiled at her, a warm, happy smile.

'Polly. It's good to see you again.' She was looking vibrant, beautiful, in a white dress with a scarlet belt.

Polly glanced again at the back seat of the car, just in case she'd been mistaken. But no, it was empty. Was his father already in Stone, planning to meet them at the teashop?

Nicolas said softly, 'You look marvellous.'

301

'Thank you.' Seconds later Polly was in the passenger seat of the blue Cortina. Driving very carefully, Nicolas turned into the lane and out into the road to Stone. 'How's the car?' Polly asked.

'It runs well.'

'And the tour – was it good?'

'Polly, I can't tell you how much we enjoyed it, although Papa needs to rest this afternoon. He has a problem with his leg after an old injury. Have you been there?'

Her spirits lifting even more at the news that they would be alone, Polly said, 'No, I'm afraid not. It's one of those things I've always intended to do. But you know what it's like when you live locally, you just never get around to these things.'

'You should go. The artistry – the skill involved in pottery production – was fascinating. And we learned so much about the history of the industry too, and about Josiah Wedgwood himself, particularly when we went to the museum in the Long Gallery.'

'You found your way all right?'

Nicolas nodded. 'Yes, the young lady in reception at the hotel was very helpful.'

I bet she was, Polly thought, glancing sideways at him. As he concentrated on the road ahead she was able to indulge herself, to linger on his profile, his slightly aquiline nose and those dark eyebrows that gave him such an intense look. Then, 'You need to turn right here,' she said and, concentrating on the road ahead, Nicolas obeyed. Minutes later, the car safely parked, they were walking along the sunlit pavements towards the teashop that Polly liked.

34

Nicolas had not been untruthful when he'd said that Jules was resting at the hotel. That morning at the factory, there had not only been a certain amount of walking, but also much standing behind operatives, watching their skilled hands throwing clay, turning a wheel, painting china, gilding and applying transfers. A white-coated supervisor had been constantly with them, explaining the technicalities of the different processes. It had been an educational and interesting morning, but Jules was thankful for the chance to rest his tired leg. He spent the latter part of the afternoon propped against the pillows on his bed, alternately dozing and reading. But always there was the anxiety, the desire to know whether Nicolas was managing to discover the details they needed. And yet Jules broke out in a sweat when he thought of what he planned to do. As someone who was fiercely protective of his own privacy, the fact that he intended to abuse that of two defenceless women both appalled and shamed him. But his inner core of steel, the one that had helped him to forge a new life at the end of the war, held firm. Unless he was willing to go to his grave without knowing who he was or where he came from, he had no alternative.

So when Nicolas came back, smiling and with a bounce in his step, Jules said immediately, 'I take it all went well?'

'Yes, it did.' Nicolas perched on the end of the other twin bed. 'We had scones with cream and jam, two pots of tea – and,' he laughed, as he saw Jules's impatience, 'don't worry – lots of conversation.' He frowned, 'But it wasn't easy to play the spy, to be so calculating. She's such a lovely girl that I felt quite badly about it.'

Jules gazed at him with sudden guilt. 'I'm sorry, Nicolas. Perhaps it was too much to ask of you.'

'But necessary.' Nicolas leaned forward. 'What I do have to tell you is that tomorrow is D-Day.'

'Tomorrow?' Jules stared at him, every pulse racing. 'Are you sure?'

'Apparently her mother works on Tuesdays, so as long as Polly is out of the way, the house will be empty.'

Jules frowned. 'But do they have a cleaner?'

Nicolas smiled. 'I'm not a journalist for nothing, Papa. I'm quite good at drawing people out, in getting them to talk about themselves. Yes, they do have a cleaner, quite a character from the sound of her, but she "does for them", as Polly put it, on Mondays and Thursdays.'

'So,' Jules said slowly, 'what exactly is our plan?'

Nicolas said, 'I have to get myself inside the house in order to unlock the back door. But that's no problem. We've arranged to play tennis tomorrow afternoon. I intend to arrive so early that she'll have no alternative but to invite me in. After that I'll do my best, but you'll have to forgive me if...'

'Of course,' Jules said quickly. 'I'll still be able to see the house from the outside. I don't suppose you know if the side gate's kept unlocked?'

Nicolas shook his head. 'I had no way of finding that out. But it's a quiet lane, Papa, in an English village. I wouldn't think there's much crime.'

'I might be lucky,' Jules mused, 'but what about a gardener? With a house like that, they're bound to have one.'

Nicolas grinned. 'I talked about how well tended the garden was, and Polly said that someone came three mornings a week. So as long as you go in the afternoon, there should be no problem.' He got up and stretched. 'I think I'll go and have a bath before dinner. How is your leg?'

'It's easing after the rest, thank you.' Jules smiled as the younger man took off his shirt, revealing taut muscles. Was I ever as fit and healthy as that, he wondered? Did I also play tennis? And then he said, 'You did well, Nicolas.'

'You think I would have been a good spy, a useful member of the Resistance, then?' Nicolas had never forgotten the day a school friend, his eyes full of unshed tears, had told him that his father had been betrayed and shot.

'And all,' the boy had said with burning pride, 'for being a true patriot.'

Jules said quietly, 'With a grandfather as brave as yours, I have no doubt. He risked much to drag me from that wayside ditch and take me to the hospital.'

'Yes, I know.' Nicolas took his cotton robe from the hook behind the door. 'Stone is a lovely little town. I thought maybe we could go in tomorrow morning and walk along by the canal there. It looked very pleasant. Not far, just to relax.'

'A good idea,' Jules agreed, and after Nicolas

305

closed the door behind him allowed his thoughts to run ahead. He refused to believe that all the significant happenings of the past year meant nothing. If it had just been the sound of a young woman laughing, a dream, a nightmare, the opinion of a complete stranger, then he might have been prepared to believe the chain of events was simply a bizarre coincidence. But his mental image, his accurate sketch of the house – these were facts, not to be disputed. The house had to hold the answer, or at least provide a clue to the next link in the chain. Tomorrow afternoon must, Jules thought, be planned with military precision.

The following day, relieved to find the weather fine and sunny, Polly was ready an hour before Nicolas was due to arrive. In the hall lay her sports bag with her tennis racquet, balls, towel, and plastic bottle filled with diluted Robinson's orange barley water. And now she added an extra paper cup, and a small pouch containing a comb, mirror and lipstick. The thought of Nicolas in white shorts was one to be deliciously anticipated, and she just hoped that her own standard of tennis was equal to his. But when the doorbell rang it was much earlier than she expected, and then she stared in astonishment. Mark stood there, a huge grin on his face and a tiny white puppy in his arms. 'He's for young Michael. I thought I'd show him to you. What do you think?' Mark came in as she stood aside and Polly held out her arms. 'Watch it,' he said, 'he's just been sick.'

'Oh, hang on a minute. That's all I need, to meet Nicolas with a smelly stain down my front.'

'So that's why you're being so fussy,' he called after her, and then when she returned seconds later wearing an old cardigan, carefully handed the Westie pup to her.

'He's trembling,' she said, as she held him close.

'It's because he's been taken away from his mother, and I don't suppose the car journey helped.'

Polly gazed down into black button eyes, loving the feel of the warm little body. 'He smells wonderful,' she said, her fingers gently caressing him, 'even if he has been sick. What have you got him in, a cage or something?'

'Nothing so scary,' Mark told her. 'The owner gave me a cardboard box, and I've got one of Michael's old unwashed jumpers in the bottom. Apparently the smell will help the dog to bond with him.'

'He's absolutely gorgeous,' Polly said. 'They'll be thrilled to bits, Mark.'

'I hope so. Just between the two of us, he's cost me a bit, but I'll cook up some story.'

Polly glanced at him and then thought better of the question she was going to ask. If Mark wanted to discuss how serious his relationship was with Ruth, then he would. But buying her young brother an expensive puppy certainly wasn't a casual gesture.

'Do you think you could put him on the back lawn for a few minutes, you know – in case he wants to...'

'Oh yes, good idea.'

That afternoon Nicolas bid goodbye to a pale and

307

tense Jules. He too was full of tension as he set out to drive to Brandon knowing how much Jules was relying on him. But when, in keeping with the first stage of their plan, he turned into the drive of The Gables half an hour before he was expected, he was alarmed to see a strange car parked before the front door. Nicolas drew in a sharp intake of breath. That wasn't the car Polly told him she drove! Could her mother be at home? Or was it simply a visitor? Either way, this could wreck their whole carefully structured plan. Swiftly he parked the hired Cortina and went to ring the brass doorbell, his mind already trying to plan how he could warn Jules. There was no immediate reply, and with increasing unease he rang the bell again. This time Polly, who had hurriedly been taking off the old cardigan, opened the door. 'Sorry,' she said, 'I was in the garden.'

'I hope I'm not too early.'

'No, of course not,' Polly smiled back. 'Come on in – there's someone I'd like you to meet.'

His tennis shoes soundless on the tiled floor, Nicolas followed her anxiously into a large, sunny kitchen, through a small utility room and out of the open back door. A tall young man with dark hair was standing on the back lawn and she called, 'Mark, come and meet Nicolas.' She turned and said, 'This is Mark –the friend I went to Paris with last year. Do you remember?'

'Yes, of course.' The two young men shook hands, Nicolas with a smile that hid his alarm. Polly's mother might not be here but would Mark's presence make Polly late in leaving for the tennis club? Nicolas felt sweat break out on his brow. It would ruin everything for Jules to arrive before then. His taxi was booked for two fifteen and the journey only took ten minutes.

But now Polly was darting across the grass and picking up a tiny puppy. 'Isn't he cute? Do you like dogs, Nicolas?'

'I most certainly do.' He reached out a finger and stroked the small head, causing its tail to wag furiously. 'Is he yours?'

Polly shook her head. 'No, Mark's bought him for his girlfriend's young brother. Ruth's my closest friend and a smashing tennis player. We're hoping to have a doubles while you're over here, aren't we, Mark?' Then she turned anxiously to Nicolas, hoping she wasn't taking too much for granted. 'That's if you'd like to, of course.'

'You'd better see my standard of play first,' he teased.

Mark grinned, as he looked curiously at the young Frenchman. There was no denying that Polly was smitten – one had only to see the glow in her eyes, and suddenly Mark felt a fleeting regret. Maybe if he hadn't let himself be influenced by the charisma of Oxford, things might have developed differently for the two of them. Then an image of Ruth with her thin, clever face and amazing green eyes flashed into his mind. The intensity of his feelings for her had never been there with Polly, however fond he was of her.

'I'd better go,' he said, 'and let you two get off to tennis. Here, give him to me, Pol.' She obeyed and then as they all began to walk back across the lawn, Mark said, 'Do you and Nicolas fancy a meal out tomorrow night? I can easily go and fetch Ruth.'

Polly felt slightly embarrassed. 'I'm not sure what plans Nicolas has, Mark. They only arrived a couple of days ago.'

'Oh, right. Anyway, ring and let me know.'

'Okay.' Polly led the way into the utility room and stood aside to let Mark, followed by Nicolas, pass by her into the kitchen.

His ears keenly attuned, Nicolas heard the click of the key being turned in the lock of the back door, and then Polly said, trying to control the wriggling puppy, 'I'll bring him out to the car for you. I won't be a minute, Nicolas.'

He watched them go, and then seizing his opportunity hurried to the back door. A moment later, secure in the knowledge that the first stage of their plan was successful, he glanced at his watch with profound relief. It was exactly two o'clock. He went into the hall and, as he stood in the doorway, saw Polly reach up and hug Mark before he got into the car. A stab of jealousy shot through him and he wondered exactly what, if anything, there was between them. But hadn't Polly mentioned that Mark was with this other girl, Ruth? And then as Polly came towards him, the light in her eyes told Nicolas all he needed to know. This girl was full of honesty, and he knew he was right; their attraction was mutual. He smiled at her as she collected her tennis bag and closed the heavy oak door behind them. 'I hope I play well,' he said. 'After all, I have the honour of France to uphold.'

But as he drew slowly down the drive Nicolas couldn't help glancing over his shoulder towards the side gate leading to the back garden. That was one aspect of their strategy that would have to remain in God's hands.

35

It was exactly half past two when Jules paid the taxi driver. He'd asked him to pull up just before Shady Lane and once the car had driven away, he stood for a moment looking curiously in each direction along the winding road; but there was little to see. His pulse racing now that the long-awaited moment had actually arrived, he turned the corner into the lane and tried to stroll along in a casual way. But no cars passed; the area was quiet, sleepy even, in the sunlight that lay dappled on the pavements beneath the mature overhanging trees. Then suddenly he saw the sign. It was displayed on a curved wall leading into an entrance, and those two words that had haunted him for months were painted in black on a white wooden board: *The Gables*. Jules turned into the drive.

It was the house he had sketched. There were the large bay windows with the sunlight glinting on them, the circular drive and the lawn. And now a fine display of flowers in the borders. Jules gazed up at the gabled roof and imposing oak front door; did he ... was he feeling anything? He did feel a sense of awareness. But this scene was already imprinted on his mind; after all, hadn't he been obsessed with it over the past few months? He turned and retreated to stand on the lawn before the high front hedge, where he would be out of sight. His gaze went upwards, lingering on the windows of two front bedrooms, on the smaller one of another room over the front door. A substantial house, he thought, a house that would fit in with Oliver's description of a middle-class background. The truth was here, he was sure of it.

Jules walked hesitantly towards the black wrought-iron side gate. It was tall with a rounded top, and possessed a strong-looking latch. There was a small padlock, but to his profound relief it was hanging slightly open. Jules put out a hand and the latch easily lifted. His heart hammering in his chest, he closed the gate behind him and seconds later was at the back of the house and facing the garden, which seemed to stretch for ever into the distance. Breathing more easily now that he felt secure from any watching eyes, Jules walked along the stone terrace to sit on a polished teak bench. The sun was directly upon him and he squinted, taking out sunglasses from his pocket. His need for his first sight of The Gables to be absolutely clear had overcome his usual caution, but now he needed to be careful as bright light could bring on one of his frequent headaches.

He gazed slowly, intently, around the garden; at the trees, the sweeping lawn, the colourful herbaceous border and rose beds. And as he sat in the peace of the garden among the fragrance of the flowers and the sound of birdsong, Jules tried to calm his frayed nerves, to ease the tension inside him, the guilt he was feeling by trespassing. He looked at the vista before him, at the graceful willow tree, and knew with absolute certainty that he had sat here before. Possibly not on this particular bench; it looked quite new. But surely there used to be a swing – hanging from that old apple tree? And next to it a large plum tree, not a silver birch? He got up and limped across the grass to the old apple tree and then, as he peered upwards through its spreading foliage, he saw them. Two rusting metal rings attached to one of the thick branches – and the width between them would have been exactly right to hold a child's swing. Jules turned to examine the silver birch – resting his hand against its slender young trunk.

He went further, to a hedge beyond which was a vegetable garden, to walk between ordered rows of carrots and lettuce, sticks of runner beans, strawberry canes and bushes laden with soft fruit. Through the glass of a greenhouse he could see ripening tomatoes, and plants being nurtured. Jules could almost feel the moist soil, the joy of discovering small green shoots, the hard work involved in weeding, and his gaze was drawn to a small bed, filled with flourishing herbs. He bent to inhale their pungent scent, and then straightened up and began to walk back to the house. He couldn't delay any longer, and yet he dreaded to try. He was desperate to enter this evocative house, to wander through the rooms, to submit, to open his mind to impressions, to memories. And the disappointment if Nicolas had failed would now be so acute, so bitter.

Jules approached the kitchen door. It was solid, painted green, with small panes of frosted glass in the upper half. He put out his hand, tried to remain calm and tentatively turned the handle. The door was opening. Jules hesitated and then stepped inside and closed it carefully behind him. He stood for a moment, hardly able to believe he was actually inside, then went through a small room containing a washing machine and sink, and into a large, square kitchen. He stood for a moment looking around, at the circular pine table and raffia-backed chairs, the striped tea towel draped over the front of the cream Aga. The floor was of polished red quarry tiles, and there were three doors. One was slightly ajar and led to a small, comfortable room with another table; probably a breakfast room. There was a decorative tiled fireplace with a shelf above, and a comfortable-looking armchair. He went to sit in it, closing his eyes, hearing the steady tick of a mahogany clock on the wall, his feet resting on the faded Axminster carpet.

Jules didn't feel strange, didn't have that sensation of being in someone else's house. This familiarity – was he imagining it? He got up and began to look at the photographs on the shelf. They were all of a child; as a baby, a toddler, a small girl with her dog. And there was one of her as a young woman – it was Polly, who he had seen at the café in Paris. For one long moment he gazed down at her smiling face, and then turned to go back into the kitchen.

Jules peered through a narrow door into a neat, well-stocked larder, and then went into a wide hall with a black and white tiled floor. There was a small cloakroom on the left, and a dining room with Wedgwood pieces displayed on the deep window sill and decorative plaques in Jasper ware adorning one wall; the same design that he collected himself. And then he crossed to a matching door on the other side of the hall and into the room that Nicolas had photographed.

For one long moment Jules stood in the doorway. A heavy oval gilt mirror hung over the handsome fireplace; sunlight streamed through the large bay window. Slowly he entered the room, and stood in the silence looking at the high ceiling with its decorative rose and plaster cornicing, at the leather furniture, the television in its mahogany cabinet, the long, low coffee table. He went over to an impressive double-fronted bookcase, opened the leaded glass doors and began to study its contents; Shakespeare, Dickens, Thackeray, a set of encyclopaedias, a heavy-looking dictionary, several books on the shoe industry, and a row of poetry books. He suddenly felt himself drawn to one. It was small, almost insignificant against some of the others, which had handsome leather bindings. The title, *A Book of Narrative Verse*, was in faded gold lettering. Slowly Jules began to skim through the pages, and as the book fell open at what he assumed to be favourite passages, he suddenly saw 'The Highwayman' by Alfred Noyes. Even before his glance fell on the first line, Jules's lips began to move, saying the words, the rhythm of the poem gaining momentum. When he reached 'ribbon of moonlight', his voice faltered in confusion. His gaze went down to the next verse and the next. And then, turning to the flyleaf, he saw the handwritten inscription: *'To André, with much love from Maman, Christmas 1924.'*

315

Jules suddenly felt his hand begin to tremble as he stared down at the name: *André*. Carefully replacing the book, he closed the glass doors and on suddenly weak legs went to sit in one of the winged leather armchairs. His brain was struggling desperately to find the meaning of what was happening to him: this house that was strange and yet familiar; the garden where he knew there used to be a swing, a different tree; that so-familiar poem. *André*. The name echoed in his mind, and he closed his eyes and leaned his head back against the firm support of the chair. Think, he told himself, try to remember. But it was hopeless; there was no flash of insight, no widening of the chink in his elusive memory. He only knew that the name had enormous significance. In sudden frustration he rose and went over to the sideboard – perhaps if he studied more closely the photograph of the French grandmother...

And then his whole body stilled. There was another silver-framed photograph – one that he hadn't seen before. It was the image of a young officer in an RAF uniform; tall and thin with a narrow, dark face. Stunned, Jules slowly picked it up to stare into intense, intelligent eyes beneath a peaked cap; the same eyes that he saw every morning in his shaving mirror.

36

During the drive along the country roads to the tennis club, Nicolas made a determined effort to put all thoughts of what was happening at The Gables out of his mind. It was a lovely afternoon; he had Polly at his side, and the prospect of a game of tennis. He believed in enjoying life; there was nothing more he could do for Jules now. But that didn't prevent Nicolas from saying a silent prayer as he followed Polly into the pavilion.

Damn, Polly thought, as they went through the door – just my luck for *her* to be here! Hilary was lounging languidly on one of the chairs, talking to Adrian, her expression one of total boredom. She glanced up at the new arrivals. As her gaze slid swiftly past Polly to the tall stranger behind her and to his undeniable good looks, the tanned legs beneath his white shorts with their dusting of dark hairs, and his muscular forearms, her face underwent a metamorphosis. Polly watched with irony Hilary's pale blue eyes, normally hard and calculating, light up. She smiled, showing the perfect teeth of which she was so proud, and said brightly, 'Hello, Polly.'

'Hello, Hilary,' Polly said shortly. 'Hi, Adrian,' she added in a warmer tone. 'I've brought a visitor – Nicolas Giscard.'

Nicolas looked at the blonde girl, who reminded him of someone, and he suddenly realised who it was – the American film star, Grace Kelly. The young man seated by her side got up and held out his hand. 'You're very welcome,' he said.

'I don't think we've had a French player before,' Hilary said with a brilliant smile. 'Are you over here on holiday?'

'Yes, I am – and hoping to get in some tennis.'

'Well, you've come to the right place. We could have a doubles, Polly. What do you think?'

I can't think of a worse scenario, Polly thought glumly, but said with a forced smile, 'Great. But when a court becomes free, give Nicolas and me some time for a knock-up first. We haven't played together before.'

'Of course,' Adrian said.

Hilary gazed up at Nicolas with undisguised admiration, 'How do you know Polly? Are you one of her French relatives?'

Before he could reply, Polly said abruptly, 'No, we're not related.' She was saved from having to elaborate because four other perspiring members came in noisily to flop on vacant chairs around the table.

After several minutes, during which Polly introduced Nicolas, the two of them went out to the now vacant court. She soon realised that he would be a challenging opponent; even taking into account his male strength, he far outclassed her as a player, and laughed as she yet again failed to return one of his powerful serves. 'Okay, enough,' she called, and as she left to fetch the others, added, 'I'd better warn you. Hilary is a cracking player – much better than me.'

The match was hard fought. Adrian was competent, Polly determined, Hilary fiercely competitive and Nicolas ruthless. Hilary, to Polly's amazement, managed to conceal her usual ill temper on losing, when she and Adrian were beaten 6–3, 5–7, 6–4, and instead insinuated herself at the side of Nicolas as they began to walk back to the club.

Adrian glanced down at Polly. 'Nice chap,' he said.

'Yes he is.' She looked up at him, 'Sorry things didn't work out with you and Teresa.'

'I still have hopes,' he said, 'although I met a smashing girl at Trentham last week.'

'Good for you!' No longer embarrassed by his complexion – which had now almost cleared – Adrian was rapidly growing in confidence.

'You'll be fighting them off soon, you'll see,' she told him.

He grinned. 'Thanks, Pol. Pity I'm too young for you!'

She laughed aloud and Nicolas, ahead, realised how the deep, throaty sound carried in the air, that same distinctive sound that had so startled Jules last July.

'What part of France are you from?' Hilary was saying.

He turned politely to her. 'Paris.'

'Oh – Polly went off to Paris last year with Mark Eldon, one of our members,' Hilary murmured, glancing sideways at him. Her tone was light, casual. 'We were all a bit shocked; after all, they used to be quite an item. Still, I'm sure they enjoyed themselves; it's such a romantic city.'

There was no mistaking her underlying meaning, and Nicolas's eyes narrowed. Polly had told

319

him that Mark *wasn't* her boyfriend. And then he realised that she'd been speaking in the present tense. But had there, Nicolas wondered with growing disquiet, still been something between them when they were in Paris? If so, then two young people together in what was, as Hilary said, such a romantic city...

Polly, turning towards Nicolas after they entered the pavilion, felt slightly disconcerted as she saw his tense expression. Now what, she thought, has that she-cat been saying? For God's sake, she's only had a few minutes with him. And then Hilary really 'turned on the charm', as Polly later told Hazel on the phone. 'It was all, "Oh, what a terrific player you are," and then she actually said – I tell you no lie,' Polly did a fair imitation of Hilary's clear voice, '"Is it true what they say about the French – that they're great lovers?"'

Hazel went into peals of giggles, 'She never did! What on earth did he say?'

'He deliberately accentuated his French accent, leaned towards her and said in a loud whisper, "I've never had any complaints so far."'

Polly heard Hazel gasp before saying, 'Blimey! How did you feel about that?'

'I'm not sure,' Polly said. At the time she'd simply laughed like everyone else. And then Nicolas had kept looking at his watch, and she began to be anxious that he was bored and wanted to leave. So after they'd both finished their drinks, she said, 'Would you like another match, Nicolas, or prefer to play another time? We might have quite a wait for a free court.'

Nicolas, who had decided that Jules would by

320

now have left The Gables, judged it should be safe to return and said, 'Another time would perhaps be better. Unless you...'

Polly shook her head. She'd had enough of Hilary's simpering for one day. 'No, that's fine with me.'

She got up and, rising as well, Nicolas turned to the group of members. 'It has been a pleasure, thank you.'

'I wouldn't mind a singles next time,' Peter, their best player, said with a grin. 'How about England versus France?'

Nicolas laughed. 'That's a promise.'

It was five o'clock when they arrived back at The Gables, and Nicolas was relieved to see that the house looked peaceful and undisturbed. If Jules had been, and only a catastrophe would have prevented him, then there was no sign of anything untoward. He drew up, put on the handbrake, and as he'd hoped, Polly said, 'Would you like to come in for a cup of tea? I've got some chocolate biscuits...' she was smiling, and he grinned.

'Now that's an offer I can't refuse.'

With Nicolas behind her, she unlocked the front door and led the way into the sunny kitchen. 'Take a seat, while I put the kettle on,' she said, and Nicolas watched her graceful movements as she moved around, fetching milk from the fridge, and putting biscuits on a plate. 'Sorry, I won't be a minute.'

She went into the hall. As soon as he heard her close the door to the cloakroom, Nicolas jumped up and, hurrying into the utility room, reached

321

out to the brass key and swiftly turned it. When Polly came back, he was sitting with a slightly guilty look on his face and a chocolate biscuit in his hand. 'I couldn't wait,' he confessed.

She laughed, 'Neither can I,' and reaching out bit into one as she made the tea. It amazed Polly how comfortable she felt with him, despite the tingling inside her every time her eyes met his. Happily, she went to join him, and several minutes later said, 'I was thinking of Mark's suggestion about dinner tomorrow. You'd like Ruth – we met at training college and have become firm friends.'

'Is that how Mark met her – through you?' Nicolas was trying very hard to remain relaxed, to enjoy sitting here with Polly. But he was desperate to learn whether the house had triggered any memories for Jules. What, if anything, he had discovered.

But Polly was nodding, and saying, 'Ruth sometimes comes over to stay. She lives at the other end of the county.'

'And has a small brother who likes dogs,' Nicolas smiled, finishing his tea.

Polly laughed. 'Plus younger twin sisters who are an absolute scream.'

'Scream?' Nicolas frowned, and Polly quickly explained in French.

Then he said, 'I'd like very much to meet your friend, but I'd have to find out if Papa has any plans. And maybe,' he said, beginning to get up from the table, 'I should get back to the hotel and see if he's had an enjoyable afternoon.'

Polly followed him into the hall, and opening the front door stood aside, smiling up at him. 'Maybe another game while you're here?' She hoped she didn't sound pushy, but she was acutely, painfully aware that he was in England for only two weeks.

Nicolas paused and for one heart-stopping moment Polly thought he was about to kiss her, but instead he touched her cheek gently with one finger and said, 'Of course. And I'll ring you later about tomorrow.'

Seconds later he was gone, and Polly wandered dreamily back to the kitchen. It would be terrific if he *could* make it the following evening, and then as she began to collect the teacups, she had what she thought was a brilliant idea; one that might just prove to be the ideal solution.

37

Nicolas drove swiftly back to the hotel and as soon as he entered the bedroom, knew immediately that something momentous had happened. 'I got back as quickly as I could,' he said, putting down his tennis kit. 'There were no problems, I hope – I mean, about seeing the house?'

Jules shook his head. The ashtray by his side was filled with stubs. The room was stifling, and Nicolas went to open a window before going to sit on the edge of the other bed. He saw the suppressed excitement in the other man's face, but there was also pallor there and strain, and Nicolas said quietly, 'Begin at the beginning, Papa.'

Jules nodded. When he began to recount how

he'd gone to the apple tree to see the rusty rings where a swing would have hung, Nicolas drew a sharp intake of breath.

'But that's not all.' Jules paused, and then went on to describe his vague sense of familiarity when he'd entered the house and how he'd been drawn to the small book of poetry, how it had fallen open at 'The Highwayman'.

As Nicolas listened, Jules, his voice strong and resonant, began to quote:

The wind was a torrent of darkness among the
   gusty trees,
The moon was a ghostly galleon tossed upon
   cloudy seas,
The road was a ribbon of moonlight across the
   purple moor,
And the highwayman came riding—
Riding – riding–
The highwayman came riding, up to the old inn-door.

'I don't know how I know that!' Jules spread his hands helplessly. He related the inscription he'd read on the flyleaf; his voice hoarse with tension as he said, 'The name, *André* – it means something to me, I know it does.' And then he closed his eyes for a moment, before saying quietly, 'It has, Nicolas, been a very odd afternoon.'

Nicolas, although bewildered by all that he'd heard, waited in silence, sensing that there was more to come.

Jules said slowly, 'Do you remember the sideboard with the silver-framed photographs?'

'Yes, of course.'

'There were just the two photographs – the ones you showed me?'

Nicolas nodded.

'There was another one there today – one of a young officer in the RAF.' Jules paused. 'That photograph was of me, Nicolas.'

The words hung in the air as Nicolas stared at him in astonishment. 'You...? Are you sure?'

Jules nodded. 'I'm positive. I have a beard now and I'm older, but I recognised my own eyes. It was definitely me, Nicolas.'

'But how on earth...?' Nicolas ran a hand through his hair in perplexity. 'You say he was in the RAF?'

Jules nodded.

Nicolas thought for a moment. 'Polly did say that her father was killed in the war. Could the photograph have been of him? Could he have had an identical twin?'

'It's a possibility.' The same thought had occurred to Jules. Could the twins have been separated, with one being brought up in France? But the expression in those eyes had been...

'Well,' Nicolas said briskly, 'we'll have to find out.'

'When are you next seeing Polly?'

Nicolas told him about the dinner invitation. 'I said I'd have to check what your plans are.'

'You must go. We can make up some story about my plans. You know seeing that photo really shook me. I never even went upstairs, I just wanted to get away, to come back here and try to make sense of it all.'

Nicolas gazed at him in concern. 'Papa, don't

you think the time has come to drop any pretence. To go to The Gables and simply ask all these questions?'

'But I would have to confess what I did this afternoon!' Jules shook his head. 'No, Nicolas. I think it's safe to assume that I'll eventually be invited to tea. The English pride themselves on their good manners.'

'But how will you bear it – the waiting, I mean? And we don't have too much time.'

Jules gave a helpless shrug. 'I know – but what choice do I have?'

That evening Sadie arrived home from work and was relieved to find that Polly had already prepared a crisp ham salad, and was cutting into a crusty loaf.

'It's been a pig of a day,' Sadie said. 'We had two awful women in this afternoon. Talk about patronising! Why do some people think they're superior to everyone else?'

Polly laughed. 'I can't imagine they got away with it for very long – not where you're concerned.'

'Not so easy, when you're an employee, I'm afraid – you'll find that out. Well, I need a gin and tonic! Anyway,' Sadie added, as she paused in the doorway, 'one of them went off with a dress that made her look like a fat sausage squeezed in the middle, and I took great delight in cooing over it.'

Fifteen minutes later, their meal was ready in the dining room, with a bowl of buttered new potatoes, an apple pie and a jug of fresh cream to follow.

'That looks lovely,' Sadie said as she came in, and then glanced over at Polly. 'How did the tennis go?'

'Great. Except that we had to play against horrible Hilary! We won though, thanks mainly to Nicolas.'

'I bet he looks good in shorts,' Sadie said, who had confessed to spying on him from the bed-room window.

'Not half – mind you, he has got quite hairy legs.'

'Personally, I've always found that sexy. It's hairy backs that turn me off.'

Polly spluttered with laughter, although she couldn't help thinking that this wasn't exactly a normal mother–daughter conversation, but then how would she know? She'd never had a normal mother. She gazed across the table. 'Can you do me a favour?'

Sadie glanced up from her plate. 'Yes, of course, if I can.'

'It's just that...' Polly told her about Mark's invitation. 'Nicolas said he had to check what his father's plans were and, well...' She hesitated. 'I was rather hoping you might invite him to din-ner. You could always invite George too.'

'Why?' Sadie raised her eyebrows and said teas-ingly, 'Surely you don't think that I, of all people, need protection from entertaining a strange man – even if he is French! In any case, George is away visiting his mother.'

Polly laughed and then said anxiously, 'You will, then?'

Sadie nodded. 'But I shall expect a box of

327

chocolates from you if this Jules turns out to be totally boring!' Then she frowned, 'You'd better check that he can speak English, though, because my French is limited to "yes" and "no". Although I can just about manage "good morning". That's *"bonjour"*, isn't it?'

Polly grinned. 'Quite the linguist, aren't you! I'll ask Nicolas when he rings.' I certainly hope Jules speaks English, she thought in panic, otherwise ... she couldn't wait to see Nicolas again; every day was precious.

Sadie, watching her, guessed her daughter's thoughts. She's fallen heavily, and who can blame her? I suppose, Sadie mused, it would be too much to ask that his father was equally devastating. She sighed. Probably the anticipation would be better than the reality...

After dinner at their hotel, a meal they both to their surprise enjoyed, Jules went to try and relax in one of the chintz-covered armchairs in the lounge while Nicolas went to make his phone call. Minutes later he returned, his face alight with excitement. 'It's all organised,' he said as he swiftly sat near Jules. 'Polly's mother has invited you to dinner – tomorrow night!'

Jules stared at him. 'You mean...?'

'Yes. It means that while I go out with Polly, you can go to The Gables and be free to ask any questions you need to.'

Jules put a hand up to his beard and absently began to pluck at the short hairs. Then he looked keenly at Nicolas. 'There will be other people there?'

Nicolas frowned. 'I'm not sure. As she hasn't met you before, I would think it likely.'

'Then I shall go early,' Jules said decisively.

'Polly asked if you spoke English, as apparently her mother has little French.' Nicolas smiled, 'I think she will have a surprise.'

Jules didn't answer, and seeing that he was deep in thought, Nicolas crossed his legs and stared across the room, looking yet again at an old photograph on the opposite wall. It was of Stafford, and he decided it might be a good idea to spend a day there. We could go tomorrow, he thought; it would prove a much-needed distraction for them both.

Jules, his imagination feverish, suddenly looked across at Nicolas and was about to speak when a waitress, neat in her black dress and white frilled apron, bustled in with their coffee. However, once she'd left he changed his mind. With a tense expression he began to spoon brown sugar crystals into his coffee. Some things, he decided, were better left unsaid.

38

The following morning after breakfast, Sadie sat at the breakfast table, finished her coffee and cigarette, and began to think about that evening's menu. She'd only been to France once and that had been a weekend in Paris with a man more interested in copious amounts of red wine than the romantic and sexy break she'd hoped for. She did remember that food had played an important part in people's lives. And Sadie was now proud of her culinary expertise. Not only that, but it irritated her that foreigners continually derided English cuisine.

I shall, she thought, cook this man the best roast beef and Yorkshire pudding he's ever likely to taste. She decided on a salmon mousse to start with, and a simple fresh fruit salad for pudding. And cheese, of course. English cheese, although there was also some Brie in the fridge, mainly because Polly liked it. And so later, she called upstairs, 'Polly, I'm off to do some shopping.'

'Okay.' Polly's voice drifted down the stairs, and Sadie smiled, knowing that her daughter was engaged in the well-known female dilemma of searching her wardrobe for 'what to wear'. And that, thought Sadie suddenly, is something that I too have to decide.

At seven o'clock, Jules left the hotel and drove carefully along the route he remembered the taxi taking. It was a lovely evening, warm and with only the hint of a gentle breeze. He wound down the car window, glad of the air, desperate for anything that might help him to become calm, cool and in control. For in reality, his insides were churning with nerves. Not even to Nicolas had he confessed his inner, secret suspicion, an inkling he felt; one so bizarre, so astounding, that he kept trying to bury it in his subconscious. Jules kept telling himself that he was wrong, that there was probably a simple, logical explanation for all this, but even so, he had been unable to face meeting

330

Polly. Not yet. Not until he knew the truth.

He'd said to Nicolas, as he was leaving to go down to reception to wait for his lift. 'I know Mark is coming with Polly and her friend, but if they express a wish to meet me, make an excuse. Say I'm out or something.' Seeing his surprise, Jules added tersely, 'I can't explain why.'

Nicolas knew that tone. He hesitated, then came over to give Jules a warm hug before drawing back and gazing deeply into the older man's eyes. 'Good luck,' he said, his voice suddenly breaking. 'I'm sorry to be so emotional. I just know how important this is.'

Jules tried, but failed, to smile. 'Don't worry,' he said. 'I think I'm strong enough to face whatever the evening brings.'

And now, as eventually he turned into the drive of The Gables, Jules stiffened his resolve even more. All these months of wondering, all the bewilderment about what was happening to him, all the years of living in a dark void of emptiness, of not knowing who he was or where he came from. And now he was certain that the answers lay through that front door. And it was with his shoulders back, and drawn up to his full height, that Jules went and for the first time pressed the brass doorbell.

Sadie was in the kitchen, checking on the roast potatoes, when half an hour before the appointed time, she heard with some irritation the peal of the bell. He was early! Hurriedly she took off her apron, touched the pearls at her neck, and went into the hall. After one swift, slightly nervous

331

glance in the mirror, she opened the heavy oak door to find a tall, thin man standing before her.

She had a fleeting impression of a dark beard and eyes obscured by a pair of sunglasses and smiled a welcome. 'You must be Jules. Please – come in.' She stood aside, 'I'm Sadie, Polly's mother. I'm so glad you could come.' She was wondering whether to shake his hand or, as he was French, to kiss him on both cheeks. But she did neither, because the next moment and for the first time in her life, Sadie became incapable of coherent thought.

Jules said, 'Thank you for inviting me.'

For one long moment time stood still, then Sadie's heart began to pound. Wildly she told herself that she was mad, hallucinating. But when she led the way into the drawing room and said, 'Please – do sit down,' it was to find her voice shaking. 'I hope you found us easily?'

'Yes, very easily, thank you.' It was not the voice of a Frenchman. And it was there again, that almost forgotten resonance. For one long moment there was silence, then Sadie managed to say, 'May I get you a glass of red wine, or would you prefer white?'

Jules, who had remained standing, seemed tense, almost distracted. 'Red would be fine, thank you.'

As soon as she reached the kitchen, Sadie closed the door behind her and leaned back against it, telling herself not to be so neurotic. She took several deep breaths before going to a cupboard and taking out two crystal-stemmed glasses. Somehow, despite an unsteady hand, she poured from an open bottle of Burgundy, then straightened her shoulders, and went back to join her visitor.

Jules was standing before the large bay window, gazing out at the garden. She walked towards him and stood by his side, silently handing him a glass of wine. Then she said, 'The garden's lovely at this time of the year.'

'Yes, it is.' Jules turned to face her. He waited until Sadie was looking up at him and then slowly removed his sunglasses.

Sadie looked into his eyes, and he saw her own widen, her pupils dilating with profound shock. In confusion she wildly searched his features, his hair, her gaze darting over him, before returning to his face and then finally resting on his mouth above the short dark beard. Jules submitted to her intensive scrutiny, trying to remain calm. From the first moment he'd seen this attractive woman with her startlingly blue eyes and blonde hair, he had known her. And since then he had frantically and without success been trying to remember when they could have met.

Sadie's hand suddenly became lifeless; the wine from her glass spilling on to her cream skirt, seeping like a pool of blood into the fabric. But she hardly noticed; her eyes were locking into ones she'd thought never to see again, her face draining of colour. 'André?' Her voice was almost a whisper, one of incredulity, 'Is it really you?'

A nerve flickered in his right temple. 'I don't know.'

And then he was taking Sadie's glass from her and putting it and his own safely on to the sideboard. Gently taking her arm, he ushered her to one of the armchairs. 'Can I get you some brandy?'

She whispered, 'There's some over there,' and a few seconds later was taking small sips of the smooth golden spirit, its warmth helping to strengthen her shattered nerves. She looked across to where Jules, now sitting opposite, was gazing at her with increasing intensity. 'You're alive? You're actually alive?' She was trying to convince herself that this was really happening...

Then Jules got up and, going over to the sideboard, again picked up the photograph of the RAF officer and turned towards her. 'Please – I have to ask you – is *this* André?'

Sadie, still numb with shock, stared at him in bewilderment, then nodded.

'May I also ask,' Jules said quietly, 'whether he had a twin brother?'

'No,' she whispered.

'Then,' Jules said slowly, 'I think I *must* be him.'

'I don't understand...' Sadie's voice was shaking.

'I don't know exactly who André is!' Jules's voice was harsh with tension. 'I know who I think he is. But I need you to tell me, I need to hear you say it. Please – just one sentence, Sadie. I promise I'll explain everything then. Who's André?'

The sound of her name on his lips brought un-shed tears to her eyes. But hearing the desperation in his voice, Sadie knew that however bizarre the question, the man before her was in turmoil. She gazed up at him, and said simply, 'My husband.'

So now he knew. Knew what he had suspected

during the long, dark hours of the previous night. This woman was telling him that she was his wife. He had already been married when he'd stood before the altar in that small church in France and made his vows to Gabrielle. But there was another answer he was desperate for, and he was praying that it might be – that it could be – the one he wanted to hear. With every nerve tense, his eyes held Sadie's, who was staring at him as if fearful he would suddenly disappear.

In a hoarse voice he asked, 'And is Polly his daughter?'

At first perplexed, Sadie stared at him, and then with horror realised what he was asking. Had her husband returned from the dead simply to imply...?

'Yes, of course she is!'

Jules became very still. And then euphoria swept through him. That lovely girl he had seen in the café in Paris had actually been his daughter – and he hadn't known. And then he suddenly saw the hurt in Sadie's eyes and realised that his words had been careless, cruel. 'No,' he said quickly, 'I didn't mean ... please, I must apologise.' He drew a ragged breath, 'Sadie, twenty years ago I was found in a ditch with a serious head injury. When I recovered, my memory was a complete blank and that's how it's been ever since. Only during the past twelve months have things begun to happen...' And now his voice was breaking as he said, 'You are absolutely sure? I *am* the man you married?'

On hearing those emotive words, compassion swept through her. Instinctively, Sadie rose and went to crouch before him. She took his hands, those hands she had loved so much, and gazed intensely into his brown eyes. 'I was shaken as soon as I heard your voice,' she told him. 'And then, when you took off your sunglasses ... the beard makes a difference, but there's no mistake. Oh, André, we were told you were missing, believed killed. I can't believe it. You're alive, you're here,' she looked down at their clasped hands, 'I'm actually touching you.' Then as the thought struck her and she said with horror, 'You do remember *me?*'

Jules gazed sadly down at her, knowing that he was going to hurt her yet again. 'When you opened the door I knew you weren't a stranger, but I'm sorry, I can't remember anything else.'

Stunned, she stared at him in disbelief. 'You mean you are looking at me, and yet you don't know who I am?'

'I'm sorry. Perhaps in the future...' he shrugged, 'I don't know, Sadie. But some things are beginning to come back to me now.' He looked down to where she was still holding his hands. 'I have so much to tell you, and so many questions to ask.'

Blindly, Sadie took her hands away and straightened up. She picked up their untouched glasses of wine from the sideboard, her own half empty from the spillage, and looking down at the ugly red stain on her skirt, said in a tight voice, 'I'd better change.' She handed André his glass and turning, walked unsteadily towards the door. Ignoring the aroma of cooking from the kitchen, she went slowly up the wide stairs to the refuge of her room where, sinking on to the satin eiderdown, she was able at last to give way to her tears. Shocked, overwhelmed with joy that André was alive, her heart was also breaking at the bitter and painful realisation that despite their short marriage and the time they had spent together, all her precious memories, she meant no more to him than a complete stranger.

39

It was some time before Sadie felt able to go to her dressing table and begin to try and conceal the ravages of her weeping fit. Even when she'd removed her stained skirt and selected another, she still didn't feel able to go down and face André; not yet, not until she was more in control. Could there ever be a more bitter rejection? Maybe she deserved it – maybe in some way she'd failed him, even as she'd failed his child. Self-pity threatened to overwhelm her, but Sadie brushed it aside. The important thing, the wonderful thing, was that André was alive and hopefully back in her life! She could never have imagined that, not in her wildest dreams. And he was downstairs, waiting for her. Then eventually, she managed to regain her self-control and went down to join him.

He was standing by the sideboard, holding the silver-framed photograph of John Merton. He turned as she came into the room. It was obvious that she'd been crying, he thought with a stab of guilt – despite her brave efforts to disguise it. Filled with sudden compassion, he said gently,

'Are you all right?'

She nodded. 'Sorry, I was just getting over the shock and everything.' Sadie looked away, blinking hard. 'This just isn't like me,' she said, 'I never cry.'

'It has been a terrible shock,' he said, 'and I really am sorry. I wish I could say I remember; about us, I mean. It doesn't mean I never will, you know.'

She smiled at him, 'Yes, I know,' she said.

André indicated the photograph. 'Is this...?'

'Yes, that's your father. I'm afraid he died three years ago.'

'Was I an only child?'

Sadie nodded; Jules continued gazing down at the photograph, slowly shaking his head. She said, 'You may not recognise him from that. I'll show you some more photos later, when he was younger. Now,' she gave a slight shrug, 'I'm afraid I really will have to attend to the dinner.'

'Yes, of course.' He watched her go and went to sit in one of the armchairs. But he was too restless to relax, and eventually made his way to the kitchen, where he hovered uncertainly in the doorway. As the light from the large kitchen window fell on her face, he realised how hurt she must be. 'I'm sorry, Sadie,' he said with guilt, 'I really do wish I could remember you, that it would all come back to me.'

She twisted round to face him. 'The main thing is that you're here, back in my life, our lives! Can you think what this will mean to Polly?' And then she stared at him in sudden panic. 'Nicolas! I've only just thought! He and Polly...'

Already she was moving towards the door, and Jules jumped up and caught at her shoulder.

'Sadie, calm down. Listen to me! They're not brother and sister! He's Gabrielle's son – not mine.' He saw the colour come back into her face.

She said shakily, 'I think that was one of the worst moments of my life! It's just that I know how attracted Polly is to him and the thought of...'

Jules said, 'I've become so used to thinking of him as my son, that I forget other people don't know the real situation.' And then, with a slight smile, he added, 'I think the attraction is mutual.'

Sadie drew a shaky breath. 'God, I feel dreadful, I don't know about you. It must be the shock. Hopefully we'll feel better after we've eaten.'

'That's what Gabrielle used to say.'

Sadie turned her head away, not wanting him to see how those words hurt her. She couldn't bear the thought of André with another woman. Not the sex thing – that would be hypocritical, and she was never that – but loving someone else, wanting to be with her. She turned back to the Aga and, opening the oven, retrieved the Yorkshire pudding tin and poured batter into the spitting fat. Then going to the fridge, she took out the salmon mousse.

He followed her through into the dining room, and once they were seated glanced around saying, 'I've several pieces of Wedgwood in the apartment. I often wondered why I was so drawn to it rather than Limoges.'

'There is some Limoges too. It's upstairs in your parents' bedroom.' Sadie poured them both a glass of wine.

'I can't wait to meet Polly,' Jules said. 'I still can't believe I have a daughter. And she's such a

339

lovely girl.'

Sadie, fork in mid-air, glanced sharply at him. 'How do you know that? I didn't think you'd met her yet.'

Jules hesitated, and then told her what had happened that previous summer in Paris. How hearing Polly's distinctive laugh as he'd passed the café that night had been a catalyst. 'It seemed to cast a shaft of light into the darkness of my mind.' Then he grinned, and she saw the old André, whose smile had lit up his normally serious face. 'Sorry, that sounded a bit precious. But it was exactly what happened. The dream was of my mother, although I didn't know it at the time.' He tasted the mousse. 'This is delicious.'

'Thank you.' Sadie gazed at him, thinking about the evening in Paris, trying to imagine the scene at the café. 'You know,' she said, 'we may think we have control over our lives, but we don't. It's all down to coincidence, to chance; the road we take and the people we meet.'

Eventually left on his own, while Sadie went to fetch their main course, Jules tried to make sense of it all. He had so many questions. How had he come to be flying over France with a false identity? The obvious answer would be that he was in Intelligence, which seemed likely considering his fluent French. Was he on a mission? Had he had contacts in the, Resistance? Had he already stayed at the 'safe house', or would this have been his first time? And what had happened to the pilot of the plane? The wings on his uniform in the photograph showed he was a navigator, so there must have been another officer with him. And then his thoughts were disturbed as Sadie came in carrying entrée dishes, and a minute later, large white china plates edged with gold on which rested generous slices of beef, flanked by crisp Yorkshire puddings.

'Slightly overcooked, I'm afraid,' she said, 'but it's been a rather unusual evening.'

'And that,' he said wryly, 'is the understatement of the year. In any case, don't worry – I like my meat well done.'

'Yes, I remember.' Their eyes held for one long moment.

The sight of the food aroused his normal healthy appetite, a fact Jules felt slightly embarrassed about when he saw that Sadie was only able to pick at her food. Eventually he said, 'I'm still trying to come to terms with the fact that you and I were man and wife. How long were we married?'

'Less than twelve months,' she said quietly. 'Polly was born three weeks after we got the telegram.'

'That must have been terribly hard. Was she born here?'

Sadie nodded.

'Did you ever marry again?'

'No, I never did.'

He glanced at her, but her eyes were lowered. 'Gabrielle,' he said, 'was the daughter of the farmer who found me and took me to a hospital. Afterwards, knowing my story – that I had no idea who I was, her father went to Paris to check on my address. He couldn't understand why no one knew me, none of us could. My identity card said I was Jules Giscard, and that's who I remained. I married Gabrielle two years later.'

'Were you happy?' Sadie had given up all pretence of eating, and almost whispered the words.

Jules gazed at her. However painful, he felt he had to tell her the truth. 'Yes, Sadie, we were. When she died so suddenly last year ... well, Nicolas thinks the shock was a contributory factor in my beginning to remember things. And Sadie,' Jules put down his knife and fork, 'discovering that I actually have a child – I can't explain how that makes me feel.'

She watched as he finished eating, her eyes drawn to his slender hands. Those hands she remembered moving so sensitively over her body that first time they had made love. André had made her feel cherished, worthy of tenderness and respect, and she had felt a love for him then that had never faded. She'd thought she'd lost him for ever, and suddenly had to fight the tears that once again threatened to overwhelm her.

And then he said in a lighter tone, 'I must look very different to you with this beard.'

'You do, rather.'

'I grew it originally to disguise the scars on my face. And then I suppose I just got used to it.'

'You mean you might shave it off some day?'

'It's not impossible. I suppose they may have faded by now.' He glanced down at his empty plate and smiled at her. 'That was good. Thank you.'

'There's a fruit salad to follow, and then some cheese.'

'Of course, you have your cheese course last, don't you? In France, we have it before dessert.'

'Oh, in that case...'

Jules shook his head. 'Actually, I'm quite happy to skip anything else. I've noticed that you're not eating much.' He looked at her with sudden concern, 'Are you all right?'

'To be honest, I think I'm more in need of another brandy. You go into the drawing room and I'll bring some coffee in.'

Fifteen minutes later, they were seated on the leather sofa, while Jules leafed through a photograph album, Sadie pointing out faces and explaining who they were. 'This is your mother and father on their wedding day and this is one of John taken about the time that I first met him.' She pointed to a group photograph taken at a business dinner. Jules gazed down at the dignified man in a dinner jacket, his hair not thinning and grey as on the photograph on the sideboard, but thick and dark. 'Yes,' he said quietly, 'I recognise him now. But I still can't make the connection that he's my father.'

'It's weird.' Sadie turned towards him. 'You were terribly close.'

'As you and I must have been,' Jules said with some embarrassment. 'I'm just hoping that...'

'From what you've told me so far, it's early days yet.' She reached out a hand and, after a slight hesitation, he took it. But it was only for a moment, and then he returned to browsing through the album, looking at photographs of himself as a young child, an adolescent, a young man. He lingered over one of his French mother where she was wearing her hair up, and told Sadie that was how he'd seen her in his dream.

She frowned. 'One thing I don't understand is how you came to make the leap – to find out about The Gables? You expected me to know you, didn't you? Once you took off the sunglasses, I mean. And the photograph on the sideboard – you seemed to go straight to it.'

Jules plucked at his beard. 'Would you mind if we waited until we were all together before I explain everything? With Nicolas and Polly present, I mean? I'm afraid it's a long and complicated story and...'

'You don't want to have to tell it twice.'

He nodded. 'At the moment I'm still finding it difficult to take it all in.' Then he looked at her and said in an uneven voice, 'And now that I am sure of my identity, I desperately need to meet my daughter, and for her to discover that her father, instead of being dead, is very much alive.'

40

Earlier, Nicolas was waiting in the evening sunshine when the maroon Anglia eventually drew up outside the hotel entrance. Polly was the first to get out of the car and then, as Mark and a dark-haired girl joined her, she smilingly introduced Ruth, whose quick glance of appraisal amused Nicolas. He smiled, 'It's good to meet you.'

Mark said, 'I thought we could go for a run first – let Nicolas see a bit more of the area – and then on to the restaurant. That okay with you, Nicolas?'

'Fine, thank you.' Seconds later he was sitting beside Polly on the back seat as Mark drove swiftly away.

'How do you like England?' Ruth called over her shoulder.

'I like it very much.'

'Isn't his English good, Ruth?' Polly said, 'A bit better than your French!'

'Don't mention it! I'm trying, Nicolas, to learn a bit of conversational French, because a certain person has promised to take me to Paris later this year.'

'If your parents will let you go!' Mark said, as he drove down the country roads.

'Well, if not, I can come along as a sort of chaperone,' Polly offered. 'I can always disappear when we get there.'

Nicolas glanced sharply at her, but there was no edge to her voice, no hint of jealousy, and he began to relax. He suddenly realised how long it had been since he'd enjoyed a convivial meal with a pretty girl by his side. The last few months had been so intense. And since he'd met Polly, he hadn't been interested in anyone else. Suddenly she turned to look at him and as their eyes met, Nicolas slowly reached out to take her hand. He curled his fingers around hers and gently squeezed. Her pulse began to race, and in a silent message, she squeezed back.

'Now along here,' Mark said, as they approached a winding road through a small village, 'is a good example of an English thatch.'

Nicolas peered through the window as the car slowed down, to see a cottage complete with thatched roof and roses flowering around the front timber-framed door. 'I have seen pictures like that,' he said.

'We call them "chocolate-box" cottages,' Ruth told him.

Nicolas looked puzzled, and Polly laughed. 'They're often portrayed on the top of boxes of chocolates, or tins of biscuits.'

'Oh, I see. In France we have the Eiffel Tower.'

'And that,' Ruth said, 'is something I can't wait to see.'

Mark drove for a while, and Nicolas gazed out of the windows, enjoying scenery so different from the French countryside. They drove along a road shaded beneath a canopy of trees in full leaf. Both our countries are so green, he thought, so beautiful.

The restaurant, when they reached it, was well patronised, and there was an atmosphere of light-hearted banter and good humour as the four of them went first into the small bar.

'Right, what are we all having?' Mark turned to Nicolas.

'What do you recommend?'

'Well, I'm having a beer.'

'Then I will have the same.'

The girls opted for gin and tonics, and leaving the two men at the bar found a small table in a corner. Once they were all seated, a smiling girl brought four menus, her blonde hair, curvaceous figure and bright red lipstick reminding Ruth of Marilyn Monroe. But when she said so, Mark wiped a rim of froth from his upper lip and said, 'I prefer brunettes myself. What about you, Nicolas?'

Nicolas turned to look at Polly, delighted to see the colour rise in her cheeks when he said, 'Definitely.'

Ruth looked first at her friend and then at the young Frenchman. The attraction between them was tangible. He could be perfect for her, she suddenly thought. Good-looking, intelligent, and above all French! This promised to be a very interesting evening because, by the end of it, Ruth was hoping that she would have some idea whether this Nicolas deserved a lovely girl like Polly. I shall, she decided, be watching and listening very closely.

Once they'd chosen their meals, Ruth began laughingly to regale them with tales of Michael and his new best friend. The Westie pup had been a great success, with even Bridie taking to him. 'Michael named him Whisky,' Ruth told Nicolas, 'because when Mark brought him, he was quivering inside a cardboard box that had contained bottles of whisky.'

'He was a little sweetheart,' Polly said.

'You wouldn't think that if you could see where he's chewed the chair legs,' Ruth told them, 'not to mention having a go at the skirting board in the kitchen.'

'But you're glad you had him?'

'Absolutely. And as for Mum – well, she was dead against having a dog at all, but now I swear he gets the best bits of meat!'

Nicolas watched her, liking her expressive and intelligent eyes. She wasn't as beautiful as Polly, at least not to him, but he liked the warm friendship between the two girls. Mark too was making every effort to be friendly. And then as the three others chatted, his thoughts were able to return to The Gables. Nicolas could only hope that by

347

arriving early, Jules had been able to ask those so vital questions. Surely the only answer could be that the RAF officer in the photograph *must* have an identical twin. Otherwise... Nicolas turned to look thoughtfully at the smiling brown-haired girl beside him...

It was when they were finishing their coffee that the phone call came. Startled, the laughing group at the table glanced up as they heard Nicolas's name being called. The blonde waitress was standing just inside the doorway. 'Mr Nicolas Giscard?' she called. Nicolas glanced with alarm at Polly, and hurriedly got up to follow her to the small vestibule.

'Who could that be?' Mark said.

'I did tell Sadie where we were coming,' Polly said, with a worried frown.

Nicolas also felt anxious as he picked up the receiver. Jules's voice was quiet, his words succinct. 'I need to see you. Can you and Polly return to The Gables as soon as it's convenient?'

'Yes, of course.'

Nicolas returned to the table. 'Nothing to worry about,' he smiled.

Mark said, 'I was thinking – seeing as Dad is away, how about you two coming back to the house for a nightcap. We could play some records.'

Polly glanced at Nicholas, who said quickly, 'Thank you, Mark. But I think I'd better get back.'

'Your father *is* all right?' Ruth said.

'He's fine, thank you.'

Ruth looked across at Polly, raising her eyebrows. Polly signalled her bewilderment, while

Mark felt relieved. It had been an impulsive invitation, swiftly regretted. After all, he and Ruth had few opportunities to be alone together.

Fifteen minutes later they left the restaurant and the two couples walked hand in hand to the car. As he drove along the quiet roads with his headlights dipped, Mark switched on the radio and, as Nat King Cole's velvety voice drifted out, Nicolas leaned forward. 'Thank you both for such a splendid evening. Mark, could you take me to The Gables with Polly, rather than back to my hotel?'

'No problem.'

Now Polly did begin to feel anxious. First there had been the mysterious phone call, and now Nicolas was saying he wanted to come to The Gables. With sudden alarm she turned towards him. Had something happened? Was there something he wasn't telling her? But before she could question him, he put a finger to his lips and gave a slight shake of his head.

'So,' Mark said, once they were on their own, 'what do you think of him?'

'I liked him,' Ruth said, 'how about you?'

'Yes, I did.' He turned and grinned at her as they drew up at a set of traffic lights. 'Polly certainly does.'

Ruth looked at him. 'Do you mind?' she said quietly.

Mark stared at her and then began to laugh. 'Of course I don't, you silly goose. Surely you didn't think...'

Ruth felt a bit sheepish. 'It's just that you two

always joke together so much. You can't deny you're still quite close.'

'I hope we always will be,' he told her, putting the car into gear and moving forward as the lights changed to green. 'We're good mates, Polly and I. But that's all it is, Ruth. It was never a big thing between us, you know. And once I met you,' his hand came over to cover hers, 'I've never had eyes for anyone else.'

'I should think not,' she said sharply, and he laughed.

'That's my girl!'

'I hope I always will be.' The words came out impulsively, and Ruth instantly regretted them. All these months she'd been so careful not to say anything that might make Mark feel that he had to make a commitment, or give her promises. It must have been that cherry brandy, she thought. I ought to know that a gin and tonic and two glasses of wine is my limit.

Mark didn't answer. He seemed to be concentrating on the road ahead and Ruth tensed, annoyed with herself. Her careless remark had spoiled the teasing atmosphere between them. She had sensed for a long time that Mark wasn't yet ready to 'get heavy', as the twins would call it. And she was prepared to wait until the right moment, was happy for their relationship to deepen, to develop at its own pace. Bridie, who knew how intense Ruth's feelings were, had warned her not to be impatient, stressing that it was far too soon for either of them to make such an important decision.

'You marry not only the man, but his way of

350

life,' she had warned. 'And remember there's the religious aspect to consider. There's still a lot of prejudice against Catholics.'

'Mark isn't like that,' Ruth had protested. They had been sitting outside on a couple of kitchen chairs, enjoying the sunshine and watching Sean mow the back lawn.

'Maybe not,' Bridie said, 'but what about his father?'

Ruth shrugged. 'I don't know him that well, but he seems to like me.'

'You can never tell with these people. It's all about good manners and hiding their real feelings. I'm just saying, Ruth, take things slowly, don't try to rush things.'

'You seem to have come round a lot,' Ruth said, 'you were dead against Mark at first.'

'I still have my reservations – not about him, he's a nice lad. Just what your dad and I have said before; he's a different religion and from a different background.'

'We can overcome that,' Ruth said.

'Yes,' Bridie said slowly, 'knowing you – I think you probably could. But if you don't want to frighten him off, just slow down a bit.'

And now, as the silence in the car grew tangible, Ruth wished – and not for the first time in her life – that she'd listened to her mother.

41

At The Gables, the scene in the drawing room was one full of expectancy. The mahogany standard lamp with its cream silken fringed shade cast a soft glow, while in one armchair sat Sadie and opposite, André – his every nerve on edge.

They had already discussed the best way to handle the situation. Sadie felt that she should be the one to tell Polly – quietly and in private – only then bringing her in to meet the father she'd always believed to be dead.

'I need to see Nicolas,' André said. 'He's been such a support, Sadie. You'll realise how much when we explain everything.' He looked across at her with concern. 'You're tired, aren't you?'

She nodded. She was emotionally exhausted, but to wait until the next day, to delay giving Polly the news ... her daughter would never forgive her.

Polly had managed to contain her impatience while they were in the car, but as soon as they reached The Gables and waved goodbye to Mark and Ruth, she turned and looked up at Nicolas. 'What was that phone call about?'

'I'm not exactly sure,' he said. 'But we will soon find out.'

As soon as they entered the hall and Sadie came out of the drawing room, closing the door behind her, Polly could sense tension in the atmosphere. She glanced quickly at her mother and realised immediately that she'd been crying. Sadie never cried. Polly moved swiftly towards her. 'What's wrong? What's happened?'

But Sadie merely shook her head, and instead of answering, turned to the young man standing by her daughter. 'It's good to meet you, Nicolas.'

'I am delighted to meet you too.' But he was glancing at the closed door of the drawing room and Polly could see impatience in his taut expression.

Sadie said quietly, 'He's waiting for you.'

Nicolas gave a slight nod, and Polly watched with stupefaction as he went straight into the drawing room. She whirled to face her mother, but she had turned and was going into the dining room. Polly followed and as soon as Sadie closed the door behind them, demanded, 'For heaven's sake, will you tell me what's going on? You've been crying, haven't you?'

'Before I do,' Sadie said, 'tell me, did you know that Jules is only Nicolas's stepfather?'

Polly gazed at her in bewilderment. 'No, I didn't, but what difference does it make?'

Sadie said in a strained voice, 'Polly, I have something to tell you.' Her mother reached out to take her hands and gripped them tightly. 'I want you to prepare yourself for a shock – a wonderful one. It's your father. He isn't dead as we all thought. He's alive.'

Polly stared at her with incredulity. What did she mean – her father was alive? She slowly shook her head in disbelief. Had her mother taken leave of her senses? But Sadie's eyes were not only

353

tearful, they were radiant, shining with truth. 'Alive?' Polly's words came out in a whisper. 'But how can he be?'

'He is, Polly. Believe me.' And as they sat together by the dining table, Sadie went on to tell Polly everything she knew. 'He looks quite different, but that's because he's older and has a beard. But you'll see for yourself – it's definitely André.'

Polly had listened with fascination to all that Sadie had told her, but it still seemed unreal. 'I just can't take it in,' she said, her voice shaking. 'Has he now got his memory back?'

Sadie shook her head, 'Only a very small part of it. I don't really know any more, not yet. But,' Polly watched her struggle for the words, saw the pain in her eyes, 'he doesn't remember me at all.'

Polly stared at her. 'Doesn't remember you?' She put a hand to her mouth in astonishment and dismay. 'No wonder you were upset.'

'He didn't even know he had a daughter until I told him.'

Polly was stunned. 'But how did he find us?'

'That, Polly, is a long story, and I only know a little of it. He's going to explain it all later.' Sadie began to rise as she heard footsteps in the hall. 'I think that will be Nicolas going into the kitchen.'

'In that case,' Polly said unsteadily, 'I'd better go and meet this father of mine.'

'Do you want me to come with you?'

Polly hesitated, then shook her head. She pushed back her chair, stood up and nervously smoothed her hair, 'Do I look all right?'

'You look fine.'

Feeling sick with nerves, Polly went into the

354

hall. She glanced for reassurance in the oval gilt mirror and then paused outside the closed drawing-room door. Then, with one last glance over her shoulder at Sadie, she slowly turned the gleaming brass knob.

He was standing before the fireplace. He was tall and thin with a short dark beard, and was, as Sadie had said, very different from the young airman in the photograph. Polly was uncertain what to do and then, limping slightly, he began to walk towards her.

'Hello, Polly.'

'Hello.' She didn't move.

They both gazed at each other for one long moment, and then he slowly stretched out one hand. Hesitantly, she took it. His skin was warm and dry, his clasp firm, as without speaking he gently led her over to the sideboard where he picked up the silver-framed tinted photograph of the smiling RAF officer. 'Look at it, Polly,' he said quietly, 'look at the eyes.'

She stared down at the brown eyes, at the face she had studied so many times with such sadness. Then she turned and gazed into those same eyes, older now with fine lines surrounding them, and suddenly she felt her throat thicken with emotion. 'You really are...?'

'Yes, Polly. I really am. I'm your father.' André carefully replaced the photograph.

'I don't know what to say,' her voice was trembling. 'I can't believe it – all these years I've thought...'

'I'm sorry, Polly. I wish I'd been able to find you sooner.' His eyes were troubled, anxious. 'Discovering that I have a daughter...' André's voice broke '...I can't tell you what it means to me.'

'Me too,' she said, struggling against threatening tears. She was finding it all difficult to take in. And then she looked up at the man before her to see uncertainty in his eyes.

'May I,' he said in a low voice, 'hold you – just for a moment?'

Her eyes still fixed on his, she gave a slight nod. Tentatively André held out his arms and held her as if she was fragile china. For one fleeting moment she rested her head against his shoulder and then he was releasing her, and bending, kissed her gently on the cheek. She breathed in the scent of his aftershave, felt the slight prickliness of his beard, and suddenly her cheeks were damp with tears.

'I seem,' he said, 'to have come back only to make the women in my life weep. Although I think your tears are ones of happiness. But your mother is very hurt, Polly.' He looked down at her with anguish in his eyes. 'You see, I don't remember her.'

'Yes, she told me. Might it come back? Your memory of her, I mean?'

'We're both hoping so.'

There was an awkward silence, then she said, 'Did Nicolas know? That you're my father, I mean?'

He shook his head. 'Not until a few minutes ago. Although I think he had his suspicions. We have much to tell you, a lot to explain.' He smiled at her. 'I'm very lucky. A son – and that is how I think of him – as exceptional as Nicolas, and now to find that I also have a beautiful daughter.'

Polly suddenly thought of her grandfather, how proud he had been of his brave son, and the depth of his grief on losing him. Seeing the sudden sadness in her eyes, André said quickly, 'What's wrong?'

'I was just wishing my grandfather could have been here.'

'You were close?'

She nodded. 'Very. He was always there for me.'

'As I should have been,' André said. He thought with bitter regret of how much he had missed of her life. 'Come,' he said, holding out a hand, 'come and tell me about yourself.' They moved away and went to sit on the sofa. And for the next thirty minutes, André tried to find out more about the girl sitting beside him, what her hopes were, her plans for the future. He watched her face as she talked, liking her openness, her expressive eyes. She was, he thought, very like her French grandmother.

Polly still couldn't believe that this quiet, sensitive man beside her was actually her father. I shall wonder if I've dreamed all this when I go to bed, she thought. She'd often envied those other girls who were part of a normal family with a mother and a father. And suddenly reminded of Sadie and Nicolas waiting in the kitchen, she said, 'I'd better go and see what the others are doing.'

André smiled, 'Of course.'

Polly got up and went towards the door, and then paused. She turned to see André watching her. Almost shyly she said, 'What would you like me to call you?'

Taken by surprise, André said, 'Call me? Oh, I see. Well, I'm Papa to Nicolas but...'

Polly said softly, 'Would you like me to call you Dad?'

André, his throat closing with emotion, could only nod.

42

Later that evening, lying silently in the single bed at the hotel, Nicolas sleeping in the other as deeply as only the young can sleep, André thought about the evening that had held so many poignant scenes, and yet he knew that the one that would be engraved on his heart would be the last one. His daughter – and how he loved that word – was even lovelier than he remembered. His leg began to ache, and absently he reached down to massage it. And his name – he must try to think of himself as André. After all, Jules Giscard was a fabrication, a man who had never existed. My name now is André Merton, he told himself, and said it aloud, concentrating, hoping without success that the words might bring with them a flash of insight. But then, as Sadie had said, it was early days yet.

He thought of her, this blonde woman who had gazed at him first with disbelief then with eyes alight with joy. A joy that later became tinged with anguish. How could he have made love to a woman, how could they have conceived a child together, and yet he couldn't remember? André realised that the return of his memory, however fragmented, was going to bring with it not only the discovery of his true identity, but also pain. How could one love someone, and then when meeting her again – apart from any man's appreciation of an attractive woman – feel nothing? Compassion and gratitude, yes, because Sadie had shown him kindness and understanding. But he had seen the hope in her eyes, had known instinctively that she still loved him, or at least the man he had been. And she had never remarried – not in all these years.

The following morning both Polly and Sadie were asleep when Mrs Booth arrived, and she'd already been at The Gables for an hour when Polly eventually made her way down to the kitchen.

'Good afternoon!' Doris said with some sarcasm. She glanced at Polly's new quilted dressing gown, which was ivory with small sprigs of pink flowers, and felt a pang of envy. She could do with a new one herself, she was sick of her old candlewick zip-up. 'Whatever was going on here last night? The drawing room stinks of fags. I've just opened the windows.'

Polly, who had been filling the kettle and switching it on while the cleaner was complaining, turned to face her. 'Mrs Booth,' she said, her eyes shining with excitement, 'you'll never believe what's happened!'

'Don't tell me yer've won the Pools?' That would be just typical, Doris thought. Talk about 'apples to orchards'!

Polly laughed. 'No, it's much better than that!'

'Come on, then,' Doris said with impatience. 'Don't leave me in suspense!'

'It's my father – he's alive!'

Doris stared at her in astonishment. 'What do yer mean – he's alive?'

'He was here, last night! Honestly, it's true. He's been living in France all this time, not knowing who he was.' Polly began to spoon tea into the pot. 'Look, just let me make this, and then I'll tell you all about it.' And when Sadie came downstairs to pause on the threshold of the kitchen, it was to see them both sitting at the table with Mrs Booth gazing with a rapt expression at Polly who, mug in hand, was relating the whole story. Silently Sadie withdrew. She didn't feel able to talk about what had happened yet, certainly not to Mrs Booth. Instead she went into the drawing room and sat on the leather sofa to relive it all again.

In the kitchen, Doris was saying, 'It's just like something off the films. I can't believe it! And the times I've dusted that photo.'

'I know,' Polly smiled across at her. 'Of course, you never knew him, did you?'

'No, I started here after her ladyship skipped off to London.' Doris sniffed and wondered yet again how any decent woman could leave her twelve-month-old baby – her first baby at that? But even so it must be terrible, she thought. Fancy having your dead husband turn up and not even know you! 'I haven't met this Nicolas you're so keen on either,' she added. 'And don't deny it, cos it shows on yer face every time you mention his name. All I can say is, thank goodness he *isn't* your brother, else that would have been a right kettle of fish!'

360

She began to haul herself out of the chair. 'Well, I'd better get on.'

'And I'd better have some breakfast and get dressed. They're both coming round later,' Polly told her, 'there's a lot we don't know yet; we were too shattered last night to go into it all.'

When Sadie saw what a beautiful morning it was, she suggested to Polly they should all go to Barlaston Downs. 'We could have a ploughman's lunch at a pub I know,' she said, 'and then go for a walk. The alternative is either to be closeted in the drawing room again, or to sit out in the garden.'

'That's a brilliant idea,' Polly said.

'You and Nicolas could go on ahead, while André and I take it easier. I know his leg still causes him problems at times.'

Polly glanced sharply at her and guessed accurately that her mother's casual tone was deceptive. The strain of the previous evening was still there in her eyes, shadowing a blazing excitement. Polly suddenly realised what was behind Sadie's suggestion; she'd never been one for exercise and the great outdoors, rarely straying beyond the garden for her fresh air. No, she had her own reason: she didn't want to share André. 'Fine,' she said. 'And that will give you a chance to talk alone with Dad.' She saw the startled look in Sadie's eyes at her use of the name, and smiled at her. 'That's what he wants me to call him.'

There came a tap on the drawing-room door, and Polly jumped up and went into the hall. 'You're off then, Mrs Booth.'

'I am that. And won't I have a tale to tell Ernie

when I get home.' Doris hesitated. 'Er, is your mother in there? Only I wouldn't mind a word.'

'Yes, of course.'

Sadie looked up in surprise as the cleaner came into the room. 'I'd just like ter say,' Doris said stiffly, 'that I'm very pleased for you. About what's 'appened, I mean.'

'Thank you, Mrs Booth. As you can imagine, it's all been a bit of a shock, but a wonderful one.' Sadie smiled at her, knowing the effort it must have cost the woman, and for one moment Doris almost smiled back, but decided just in time – as she told Ernie afterwards – that it would have gone against her principles. After all, nothing had changed, had it? And what, she thought, as carrying her shopping bag she trudged down the drive, is Polly's father going to think of his wife's 'carryings on' all these years – because he was bound to find out. The old saying that 'sins come home to roost' was well founded, at least in Doris's experience.

André and Nicolas arrived as planned, shortly after Mrs Booth had left, and they agreed with alacrity to Sadie's suggestion. 'We'll take the Cortina,' Nicolas said, 'it will be more comfortable with four of us.' And so with Polly beside him giving directions, he drove them through the leafy country roads to the pub that Sadie knew – one where she often met George. Thanking Providence that he was away, she glanced with some discomfort at their usual seat in an alcove, then led the way firmly to one on the opposite side of the room.

André looked around the bar, trying to see if it meant anything to him. Surely as a young man he would have known the local pubs? There was a display of Doulton Toby jugs on the wide window sills, arranged in order of size, a copper warming pan hung by the door, and the small round mahogany tables were surrounded by seats and stools upholstered in shabby red velvet. The sunlight, bright outside, filtered mistily in through small windows framed by tapestry curtains. But although he liked the ambience, he had no memory of it at all.

While Nicolas went to the bar to order their drinks, André remained quiet, watching Sadie and Polly as they chatted. It seemed so strange, being here, all of them sitting at this table together. He still couldn't quite believe it; that they were actually his wife and daughter.

Then as they waited for their ploughman's lunch, André began to explain what he knew of his accident. 'No connection was ever made between me and any British plane that had either been shot down or crashed,' he said, 'so I'm assuming that the plane exploded shortly after impact. I must have managed to crawl out in time. Now that I know I was on a mission, I've been able to work this out. How far away from the scene I was when I was hit by the car, I don't know. The Gestapo came to check me out in the hospital and decided I was just another victim of dangerous driving. They had far more urgent things to do than bother with a lowly French clerk.'

'Such as executing members of the Resistance,' Nicolas said with bitterness, and Polly put out a hand to touch his.

'It must have been awful,' she said, 'the Occupation, I mean. Was that how your father died?'

Nicolas shook his head. 'No, he died from a heart attack just before the Germans entered Paris. He was a lot older than my mother.'

Sadie glanced at André; no wonder Gabrielle fell in love with him, especially as she nursed him when he was ill. 'So you lived at the farm for how long?' she asked.

'Until the war ended. It took a couple of years for me to completely recover, apart from my memory. We grew as much food as we could to help with the shortages, we sheltered any refugees we were sent, and were part of an escape route. I wanted to go to Paris to join the Resistance there but...' He shrugged.

Nicolas turned as a smiling waitress came with their lunches, and looked suspiciously down at the brown pickle at the side of the slab of English cheddar. 'He's always felt guilty about not being able to do that,' he explained, as he picked up his knife and fork, 'but with his memory problem and his limp – it was much worse in the early days, or at least that's what Maman told me – he could have put others in danger.'

'I still think I should have done more,' André insisted.

Sadie said, 'You always had a strong sense of duty.' As he'd proved, she reflected, when she'd told him she was pregnant. If he'd been a different man, one without such high principles, then Polly would never have been born. She glanced with some guilt at the girl sitting opposite, finding the thought unbearable. 'I actually met some of your crew,' she told André, 'and they thought the world of you.' She paused for a moment, 'Do the names Sandy McBane or Kelly mean anything?'

Conscious of everyone looking at him expectantly, André repeated the names. 'Sandy Mc-Bane?' He slowly shook his head, and then said, 'Kelly – Kelly from the Isle of Man?'

'That's it!' Sadie said with excitement. 'That's what I said the first time I met him. He was your pilot – a stocky chap with a black moustache.'

André stared at her, his brow creasing in a frown. 'I think so,' he said slowly, 'what you say certainly rings a bell.'

'I'll ask Babs if she has any photos,' Sadie said. 'She was always snapping away with her old Brownie.'

'Babs?'

'My mother's friend from the war years,' Polly explained. 'She lives in Hereford.' She had been listening intently, her eyes fixed on her father.

'And she knew me?'

'She was our bridesmaid,' Sadie said, and then as André looked up at her in surprise added, 'I'm sorry but I can't show you any wedding photographs – they were destroyed in an air raid.'

Nicolas gazed at her with sudden sympathy. That must have been an added blow, not only to lose her young husband, but also not to have any lasting image of their wedding day. His first impression of Sadie had been one of surprise. She was so very different from his mother. Gabrielle, dark and serious, had been a homemaker, neat and subdued in her appearance. Any man could recognise

365

Sadie's overt sexuality, and it made him feel slightly uncomfortable. It seemed strange that his father would choose to marry such very different women.

'What I don't understand,' Polly said slowly, 'is why you believed yourself to be French. I know you had the forged papers, but wouldn't you have spoken English? Instinctively, I mean.'

'You'd think so, wouldn't you, now that we know the truth. But I didn't. You must remember that when I was ill in hospital I only ever heard French voices, even when I wasn't fully conscious. And if I was on a mission then I would have been trained not only to speak in French, but to think of myself as French.'

'And how did you find out that you were fluent in English?'

'That came,' André said slowly, shaking his head as a waitress offered them a dessert menu, 'several months later, after I was taken to the farm. Remember, I'd still only heard French being spoken, and in my confused state I even thought in French. And then one day I went to the home of the local priest, and while I was waiting for him, I began to browse through his bookshelves.' He smiled reflectively. 'And there they were – a set of Dickens, all English editions. He couldn't read them himself; apparently they'd belonged to the previous priest who died. When he came in, I was reading one aloud, in complete amazement I might say. I could only assume that one of my parents must have been English.'

'That must have been a useful case study for you.' Polly turned swiftly to smile at Nicolas and

366

was surprised to see a look of embarrassment on his face. He and André exchanged glances.

Polly frowned. 'What's wrong? What did I say?'

'Shall I?' Nicolas said, and André nodded.

Slowly, while they sipped their coffee, Nicolas told them the whole story. How André had met Oliver Sands, of the advertisement in *Staffordshire Life*, of Polly's letter and the headed note paper with the name 'The Gables'. And then, with some embarrassment, he confessed to the elaborate charade of his own visit to The Gables on the pretext of doing research. 'I'm actually a journalist,' he said, 'I know nothing at all about phonetics. But it was the only plan we could come up with.'

Polly stared at him. 'You absolute fraud! I believed every word!'

'There's something else you don't know, Polly,' Sadie said, one finger tapping her cigarette so that the ash fell into an ashtray, 'last night wasn't the first time your father had seen you.'

'How do you mean?'

Quietly, André told her of that evening in Paris the previous July. About the café, about hearing her laugh, how that distinctive sound had given birth to the trail that had eventually led him to The Gables.

Polly gazed at him, her eyes widening. 'So you were actually sitting there, watching me? And yet you didn't know...?'

Nicolas glanced out of the window, and suddenly he'd had enough of the dim interior of the pub, of the intense conversation. 'Come on,' he said. 'Why don't we leave any more explanations

367

for another time, and go for this walk?'

The others agreed, and several minutes later Nicolas led the way out into the car park. 'These Downs,' he murmured to Polly. 'Are there any private places?'

His eyes briefly held hers and a message flashed between them. Polly nodded. 'I know several,' she whispered.

43

Barlaston Downs was an idyllic backdrop to the village and, as the two Frenchmen had learned during their tour of the nearby Wedgwood factory, the architects and planners had been careful to preserve the beauty of the area.

'Do you remember it?' Sadie asked André. The younger couple were already forging ahead, and they had agreed to meet later at the car.

They were walking slowly past Barlaston Hall and André halted and stared at it for a moment. He shook his head, 'No, sorry. But all this' – he waved a hand at the bracken-covered hills – 'it's beautiful. I'm so pleased you suggested coming.'

'I just thought we all needed some space,' she said quietly. 'I couldn't face being closeted in the drawing room again, not after last night.'

'I know what you mean,' André said. 'Somehow, being beneath an open sky with the sun shining, and among nature – well, it has a calming effect.'

'And I think those two,' Sadie smiled, waving a hand in the direction of Polly and Nicolas, 'can't wait to be on their own.'

André laughed, 'Yes, I remember what that used to be like.' Sadie felt a stab of pain. He remembered, yes, but he was thinking of Gabrielle, not of her.

They walked slowly for a while in silence, both enjoying the sunshine and the breathtaking views, and then André turned to her. 'Sadie, I'm sorry, I've done nothing but talk about myself, and my life; but what of yours all these years? There's so much I want to know – how you managed when Polly was born; what she was like as a baby, a little girl. She told Nicolas that she'd grown up at The Gables – so did you come to live here after I was reported missing? In fact, I don't even know where we were living before then.'

Sadie managed to keep her voice steady. 'We were already living at The Gables. As soon as he knew I was pregnant, your father insisted on my leaving London for somewhere safer.' She looked away, struggling to suppress her panic. This was what she'd been dreading, that André would begin to ask questions about Polly; ones that would be natural for any father to ask. But how was she to answer them? In desperation Sadie stared straight ahead, oblivious now to her surroundings. This was all too soon. So much depended on what she told André, it was vital that she made him understand, and she wasn't ready yet. Not now, not when she was emotionally fragile.

André too was silent. Sadie's words about his father had somehow made him seem more real. I wish I could remember him, André thought fiercely. His ignorance seemed uncaring, an affront.

Meanwhile, Polly and Nicolas were already much further on; walking along the moorland with hands linked, and it was in a secluded spot near a rippling stream that at last he drew her into his arms. Polly gazed up into his eyes for one long moment and then his lips came down to hers in their first, almost unbearably sweet kiss. His mouth was warm, gentle at first, and then their lips were clinging to each other, becoming harder, more searching. When Nicolas drew back, raising one hand to stroke her hair, he said, 'It's so soft, just like silk.'

'I washed it especially this morning,' she said, and he smiled.

'That's my Polly, always so honest.'

'Am I?' she said, as with arms entwined, they began to slowly stroll by the water. 'Your Polly, I mean?'

'I hope so,' he said, and she smiled up at him, a smile so brilliant that Nicolas caught his breath. They stopped in the middle of the narrow path, once more wrapped in each other's arms. For Polly there was nothing in the world but this moment, with Nicolas's strong athletic body pressed close to hers, the delicious sensation of his hands moving urgently over her body, the feel of his mouth ... and then suddenly there came the sound of a dog barking, closely followed by voices.

Seconds later when a family came into view, Nicolas and Polly were gazing sedately down at the running water. The young father was wearing a white shirt with the sleeves rolled up, the two children were in shorts, and their mother was hot and perspiring in a turquoise dress that was too tight for her. The dog, a handsome rough collie, pranced around them, its tail waving in excitement.

'Lovely day,' the mother called. 'Kevin, come away from that edge,' she called crossly, as the small ginger-haired boy ran to kneel by the stream. 'You know what you're like for falling in.'

His sister gave him a sly push with the edge of her sandal and Polly laughed even though, still intoxicated with what had just happened with Nicolas, she was longing for the small group to leave. But the dog flopped down, panting, the children began to clamour for a drink, and Nicolas caught her eye and began to move away. Polly joined him, and hand in hand they explored the Downs; talking, teasing, laughing – and each time they found a secluded spot, turning with one accord towards each other.

The following morning, full of resolve, Sadie telephoned the boutique where she worked and said that she wouldn't be in for the next ten days.

'Are you ill?' Angela, the woman who owned the shop, and who Sadie got on well with, sounded harassed.

'No, I'm not ill,' Sadie said. 'It's because of personal reasons, Angela.'

'What sort of personal reasons?' Angela demanded.

'I can't tell you now,' Sadie said, the older woman's blunt manner irritating her, 'but I know you'll understand when I do. I wouldn't let you down if it wasn't important.'

'Well, I certainly hope so, Sadie, because it's very inconvenient. We're getting ready for our summer sale.'

'I know and I'm sorry. But I'll be back before it starts.'

'Was she all right about it?' Polly said, coming into the hall as Sadie put down the phone.

'She wasn't pleased, but she'll have to get over it.' Sadie had no intention of missing any opportunity of spending time with André while he was in England. Already the days were disappearing at an alarming rate.

Almost at the same time André, after waiting until the reception area was empty, made a trunk call to the company he worked for in Paris, explaining that he needed to extend his leave. He'd been with the firm for many years, and most of his colleagues were aware of his amnesia. André briefly explained what had happened and the reaction was one of congratulation and sympathetic understanding. 'Take as long as you need, Jules, or have we to learn to call you André, now?'

André laughed. 'I'm still trying to come to terms with it myself. But thanks, François, I appreciate it.'

'Well, good luck!'

André went to join Nicolas in the hotel lounge and sat opposite him. 'They were fine about it,' he said. 'I can't possibly go back to Paris at the end of next week,' he said slowly. 'There are so many things I need to do. I'll have to go down to the Air Ministry, for instance, and get the records put straight. I also want to find out more about the mission I was on. And,' he added, 'I'd like to know who that poor pilot was.'

'Will you phone for an appointment first?'

André nodded. 'Yes, I think I should. But I'll ring from The Gables later. Polly will soon be here – she's going to take me to see my parents' grave.' He glanced at Nicolas. 'What are your plans for today?'

'I think we're playing tennis,' Nicolas said.

André gazed thoughtfully at him. The casual 'we' was revealing. But how significant was it? He had always teased Nicolas about his 'love life', who'd laughingly assured him that the flirtations he enjoyed were light-hearted and caused no one any serious heartbreak. But this was Polly. André might only recently have discovered that she was his daughter, but already he felt protective towards her. And he'd seen the light in her eyes when she looked at Nicolas. 'I would hate,' he said slowly, 'to think of Polly getting hurt. I'm sure you know what I mean, Nicolas.'

Stiffening, Nicolas said, 'I can assure you that I have no intention of hurting her.' And then he added with some awkwardness, 'Look, Papa, we're both adults. And you can see how things are between us. I've never been interested in anyone else since I first met her. Believe it or not, during all those weeks of waiting to come to England, I lived like a monk!'

André laughed. 'I never thought I'd hear you, of all people, say that!'

'Come on,' Nicolas protested. 'I'm not that bad. And most of my girlfriends have remained exactly as they were when I met them.'

'I'm glad to hear it,' André said drily. But there was no humour in his eyes as he gazed at the younger man, and his meaning was clear. Nicolas hesitated then gave a slight nod. And that was all André needed.

When Polly and Nicolas entered the tennis pavilion it was, much to Polly's relief, devoid of Hilary's presence. The blonde girl almost seemed to be a permanent fixture there, despite the fact that she was supposed to work in her mother's china shop. The only occupants were Hazel and Anita, who were sitting at the long table engrossed in conversation.

They glanced up on hearing the door open, and Polly watched, with delight and some amusement, their eyes light up with avid curiosity when they saw Nicolas follow her in. 'These, Nicolas,' she said, 'are two of my closest friends. The one wearing an engagement ring is Anita, and the other one who can't take her eyes off you, is Hazel. Down, girl,' she added with a grin, 'he's spoken for! May I introduce Nicolas Giscard from Paris.'

'You're French?' Anita leaned forward. *'Bonjour, monsieur, comment allez-vous?'*

'That was awful!' Hazel said. 'She was always rubbish at languages at school.' Then she paused. 'Sorry, Nicolas – I take it you speak English?'

'I most certainly do,' Nicolas said, laughing. 'And it is a pleasure to meet two such charming young ladies.'

'Oh, I should watch him, Pol,' Hazel said, 'he's too good to be true.' Then she glanced from one to the other. 'When you said he was spoken for, you did mean...'

'Yes, I did.'

'Oh, in that case, I'll accept defeat. Now if it had been that cat, Hilary...'

'You mean the tennis champion?' Nicolas was finding the camaraderie between the girls highly amusing.

'Oh, you were the French chap who showed her up? I heard about that,' Hazel said. 'Hey, I bet she fluttered her eyelashes at you, though?'

'Amongst other things,' he said, his lips twitching.

Anita began to laugh. 'Don't tell me she was wearing her vamp's tennis dress?'

'She certainly was,' Polly said. 'But it didn't,' she said with some satisfaction, 'get her anywhere.' She turned to Nicolas. 'Anita is getting married soon. Hazel and I are going to be bridesmaids.'

'Nicolas, I could easily send you an invitation. I'm sure Polly would love you to be there,' Anita offered.

'That's very kind of you,' Nicolas said, 'but I'm afraid I'm going back to Paris at the end of next week.'

Both girls looked first at him and then at Polly, and she guessed what they were thinking. A holiday romance, that's all it was. But, she thought, hugging the knowledge to her, they don't know the circumstances. And she wondered just when Sadie was going to feel ready for the news to become public, although it probably already was now that Mrs Booth knew; at least in the village. Besides, surely meeting people who had known her father as a boy, as a young man, would help parts of his memory to return?

And then she turned to greet Adrian as he arrived, and for the rest of the afternoon, all problems were forgotten in the joy of exercise, fresh air, and friendly competition. Nicolas, of course, outshone them all.

44

As soon as Polly knew that André was going to remain in England for a while, she insisted that he must move into The Gables. 'Just as soon as Nicolas leaves,' she said. And then she glanced uncertainly from him to Sadie. They were sitting out in the garden, but her mother, who had been flicking through a magazine, remained silent. So did André. 'I'm afraid I have your old bedroom...' Polly floundered, suddenly feeling embarrassed.

Sadie said quietly, 'André can have your grandfather's room.'

There was an awkward silence and after a moment, Polly got up saying she was going to fetch some cold drinks.

André said quietly, 'Thank you, Sadie.'

She saw the tension in his eyes and said, 'André, we're both in a very strange situation. It's all going to take time – getting to know each other all over again. Even if you could remember me, we'll both have changed over the past twenty years.'

'Are we still...?' André turned to look at her.

Sadie nodded. 'Yes, we're still married. I never applied after seven years to have you legally declared dead. There seemed no point.'

'You never considered marrying again?'

'No.' Her answer was almost curt.

'And yet we were married less than a year.' He gazed at her reflectively. Sadie was a very attractive woman, and a blatantly sensual one. Unless he was mistaken, she wasn't someone who would have sat at home wearing widow's weeds. She must have had proposals.

Sadie was gazing out at the lawns, the shady trees, at the scene she loved so much. 'It was the happiest year of my life,' she said, 'even if there was a war on.' Again there was a silence and when André didn't comment, she decided to change the subject. 'Is it on Monday that you're going down to the Air Ministry?'

He nodded. 'Yes, on the train. And Nicolas says that he and Polly might come and do some sightseeing. Maybe you'd like to go shopping or something?'

Sadie brightened. 'Yes, I think I would.'

'I also thought,' André said, turning as Polly came out with some lemonade, 'that I'd take the opportunity to wander around a bit. See if I can spot any familiar landmarks. Thanks, Polly.' He took a glass from her outstretched hand.

Polly flopped down beside them. 'Gosh, it's hot. Poor Nicolas playing tennis with our club champion,' she grinned. 'And Peter's determined to uphold the honour of England.'

'Nicolas tells me that you have some delightful friends,' André said, smiling at her.

377

'Yes, I'm very lucky. Anita invited him to her wedding but, of course, he won't be able to come.' Suddenly Polly stared at him. 'But you'll still be here. I'd love you to be there, I really would.'

'Polly's one of the bridesmaids,' Sadie explained. André turned to face her. 'Are you going?'

A startled glance flashed between mother and daughter. Sadie shook her head. 'Well, no,' she evaded. 'I've only met Anita a couple of times.' The fact that she hadn't received an invitation had rankled, but she hadn't made an issue of it.

André hesitated. It hardly seemed appropriate for him to attend without Sadie. When he told Polly this, she bit her lip. Neither Anita nor Hazel had ever commented on the spiteful gossip that Hilary had spread, but that didn't mean they weren't aware of it. She turned to Sadie and said slowly, 'What if Anita invited you?'

Sadie knew exactly what Polly was thinking. 'Fine,' she said.

'In that case,' Polly said, getting up, 'there's no time like the present. I'll find out.' And please, Anita, she thought, crossing her fingers before picking up the phone; don't let me hear any reluctance in your voice. Respecting Sadie's wishes, she didn't mention the news about André; she simply said she had a special reason for asking. Moments later, Sadie and André looked up to see their daughter's closed expression as she came back into the garden. 'She's not sure. She thinks it might be too late. And her mother's away for a couple of weeks. But she promised to ask.' However, Polly wasn't hopeful; she'd heard the embarrassment in Anita's voice.

Sadie felt a warm glow of pleasure at the thought of appearing in public with her husband by her side. Wouldn't that be one in the eye for all the local disapproving busybodies? And that amusing thought suddenly made her realise that she was beginning to feel more like her usual self. The numbness, the shock, the emotional turmoil, were at last thankfully fading. She turned to André and when she caught his eye said, 'I hope you know that if we go, you'll have to wear a morning suit – and a top hat!' Both she and Polly broke into peals of laughter as they saw his expression change to one of alarm.

The following day, Sadie drove to the hotel to find André waiting for her outside the front entrance. 'So,' he said, 'what is it that you want to show me?'

Sadie didn't answer, she just flashed him a smile, and then once they reached Stone, parked at the Crown. 'We'll be coming here for lunch tomorrow. It's been a family tradition for years.'

'In that case I would have come as a child. Well,' he said, matching his long stride to her shorter one as they walked along the pavements, 'let's hope it triggers off some memories.'

'But Stone itself didn't? I know you came here with Nicolas.'

He shook his head. 'Yes, I did, but only briefly. We didn't come up the High Street – it's charming.'

'Yes. And this,' Sadie said quietly, 'is what I've brought you to see.'

It was a War Memorial in the centre of a small

square. André stood for one long moment before the Post Office facing it, and then crossed slowly over. He guessed what he would find. Slowly he read the inscription, before almost unwillingly his gaze dropped to the names of the dead engraved on the plaques. It was there: *Merton, André. Flight Lieutenant, RAF.*

'I feel ashamed,' he said, and his tone was bleak. 'I haven't the right to be on here. Not among all these brave men who lost their lives.'

'Although the telegram said "Missing in action", your father didn't give up hope, not for a long time,' she said.

André fell silent. How he wished he'd been able to discover his true identity a few years earlier. Then he said, 'The Air Ministry will need to debrief me, so I'm going to make a note of everything I can remember. And I'll need proof, of course. All I have are the forged documents I was issued with, naming me as Jules Giscard. But Polly's already found my birth certificate and if you could let me have our marriage lines...'

He turned to her and frantically Sadie tried to disguise her sudden panic. She hadn't anticipated that he would ask to see their marriage certificate! How stupid she'd been to try and plan for the right moment, to delay in telling him the whole truth. And now she had no choice except to say, 'Yes, of course.'

On Sunday the four young people went to the seaside for the day. 'Never mind the Eiffel Tower, Nicolas,' Ruth called from the passenger seat as Mark drove swiftly along the main roads. 'Wait until you see the one in Blackpool!'

Polly confessed, 'I've never seen it myself, apart from on postcards.'

'That's because you'd have been too posh to go to Blackpool for a holiday!'

Nicolas queried, 'Posh? What does that mean?'

'Rich and privileged,' Ruth said over her shoulder. 'It originates from when wealthy people travelling on ships to India – in order to be sheltered from the sun – would book port out, starboard home. The initials spelt out the word 'posh'.'

'Take no notice of Ruth,' Mark said. 'She fancies herself as a socialist. Loads of people go to Blackpool. It's one of our nearest seaside resorts.'

'But not as select as somewhere like Llandudno,' Ruth teased. 'I bet you've been there, Polly.'

'Well, yes. My grandfather was very fond of it.'

'I've been to Blackpool,' Mark said. 'I was taken to see the illuminations. I think I'd have been about ten.'

'Where did you go on holiday as a child, Nicolas?' Polly asked.

'Maman liked Deauville.' He turned his head and gazed out of the window and Mark suddenly remembered that Nicolas, like himself, had lost his mother the previous year.

A couple of hours later they were walking along the wide promenade, with the grey waves of the Irish Sea surging inwards. The air was bracing even though there was sunshine, and laughingly they walked along four abreast, all swinging their arms and taking deep breaths of the salty air. 'This will blow the cobwebs away,' Mark grinned, putting his arm around Ruth's shoulder. She leaned into him and they drew away, a couple again.

Nicolas glanced down at Polly, and swiftly bent and kissed her. 'Do you like it here?'

'I like anywhere when I'm with you.' She smiled up at him, thinking how happy she felt.

When later they went into a fish and chip restaurant, Nicolas made them laugh with his look of alarm when he saw his huge fillet of fish in golden batter. It was surrounded by an extravagant helping of chips and with a soggy green mess that Ruth told him was mushy peas. He wondered how he would be able to eat such a heavy meal, but fifteen minutes later, he was enjoying a strong sweet mug of tea with the rest of them, his plate empty.

'Now you can really say you've been to England,' Mark declared with a grin, 'especially once you've worn a "Kiss Me Quick" hat!'

Nicolas looked startled, 'A what?'

'You'll see,' Ruth began to laugh. 'And in one of those, and with your sexy French accent, you'll soon have the girls falling at your feet.'

'I usually do,' he grinned.

Polly pulled a face at him, and then glanced at Mark. She said in a low voice, 'When is your father back?'

'Tomorrow night. Why?'

'Oh, I just wondered.'

Nicolas glanced sharply from one to another. Used to interviewing people, he had learned to read nuances, hidden meanings behind words. And body language. Why should Polly tense when asking such a casual question? He thought of what she'd said before they left.

382

'Sadie would prefer us not to mention what's happened – about my father – not just yet.'

Nicolas now wondered whether her reluctance had any connection with the man returning to-morrow night. Could this be someone Sadie was involved with? As far as Nicolas was aware, there had been no flurry of phoning people with the news of André's reappearance, which had seemed a bit odd. However, if Sadie felt she needed to tell this man the news first, that could explain why.

But if what he suspected was true, Nicolas couldn't help wondering, as he followed the others out of the restaurant, whether André was aware of it.

45

On Monday morning they caught an early train and during the journey down to Euston, dis-cussed their plans for the day. André's appoint-ment at the Air Ministry was at twelve o'clock. They had the carriage to themselves, and were sitting opposite each other, Sadie by André, and Polly by Nicolas.

Nicolas, of course, had visited London before, but there were still several attractions he wanted to see. 'Definitely Madame Tussaud's,' he declared. 'I want to see how scared Polly is in the famous Chamber of Horrors.'

'I'm tougher than you think,' she retorted.

'And the Tower of London,' he continued.

'They have dungeons there, don't they?'

'What are you trying to do to my daughter,' André said, 'make her hair go white?'

Nicolas laughed. 'Don't you remember – girls cuddle up to you when they feel frightened.'

'I don't need an excuse,' Polly said, and slipped her arm into his, resting her head for a moment on his shoulder. Nicolas gently kissed the top of her hair.

Sadie watched them, finding it difficult to reconcile this openly affectionate girl with the one who had regarded her with such hostility so many times in the past. And when Polly glanced up and smiled warmly at her, Sadie felt a lump in her throat. For heaven's sake, she told herself, you're turning into a right waterworks. Sadie had never had any patience with what she called 'weepy women', regarding them as weak and helpless. She'd always been proud of what she saw as her strength, her independence. And yet, had she ever really been that she mused, as she gazed out of the window at the passing scenery. Hadn't she, for the past twenty years, always been cushioned by John Merton's generous allowance?

But then her thoughts returned to the cause of her underlying anxiety. Should she have talked to André yesterday? Shown him the marriage certificate? Why had she been such a coward? Was it because she was desperately hoping that he wouldn't have to produce it, that it wouldn't be needed? That he would return it to her intact inside the sealed envelope? At least then she could delay talking to him, wait until their new and sensitive relationship was stronger. At the moment

André had no inkling of the circumstances that had led to their marriage, and she wanted it to remain that way for as long as possible.

It is going to be, she thought, a very long day. But then she shrugged. She had money to spend, and it had been a long time since she'd done any serious shopping. Thank God she still had that selfish streak – it had always been her passport to survival.

They had arranged to meet at the end of the day at seven o'clock, and Polly and Nicolas were the first to arrive at Euston. Exhausted but happy, they headed for the station café where Polly ordered iced buns and tea. Nicolas looked with suspicion at the latter, and then thoughtfully stirred sugar into it. 'I wonder how Papa has got on.'

'That's exactly what I'm wondering.' Sadie sank down on one of the other chairs, and put down her shopping. Polly glanced at the expensive names on the bags, seeing one was from Liberty's, and hid a smile. She's obviously made the most of it, she thought. 'You haven't seen him?'

Sadie shook her head. 'Not a sign.'

'Do you want some tea?' Polly offered.

'Yes, please.' Sadie lit a cigarette and inhaled. 'Gosh, but I'm tired.'

Nicolas smiled at her. Somehow Polly's mother looked more at home here in the capital than she did in Staffordshire, and then he remembered that she used to live in London.

'Do you miss it?' he said. 'The city, I mean?'

Sadie blew out a stream of smoke and considered. 'I did at first,' she confessed, 'terribly. But now ... I'm not so sure.'

Nicolas glanced at his watch. There was still no sign of André.

'Maybe they've confined him to barracks! Sorry, that was a joke,' Sadie added swiftly as she saw his startled expression. 'One we used to make during the war.' And then as she saw André enter the café, her eyes met his. And her stomach knitted itself into knots.

But André seemed fairly relaxed and once they were on the train, told them about his visit to the Air Ministry. 'They were very helpful and efficient,' he said. 'Apparently the most likely airfield I would have flown from was RAF Tempsford in Bedfordshire. Although I wasn't with RAF Intelligence, as I'd thought. I was seconded to the Special Operations Executive; they were the ones who undertook covert work and had agents in occupied countries.'

'I bet they were amazed,' Polly said. 'The RAF, I mean. About what happened to you, and that you've found your way back to England.'

Sadie remained silent. She'd avoided eye contact with her husband ever since he'd arrived at Euston.

'So I'll need to be debriefed by the Foreign Office,' André continued, 'and then eventually I should receive an official letter of discharge from the RAF.'

'How long were you at the Air Ministry?' Polly asked.

'Oh, it was quite a while – about a couple of hours. Afterwards I wandered around a bit on my own, hoping that something might trigger a memory. Things come back more easily to me when I'm alone.' He turned to Sadie. 'There was one thing.' He mentioned an area that was all too familiar to her. 'I had a very strong feeling that I'd been there before.'

Sadie said quietly. 'You *had* been there before, André. There was a nightclub in one of those streets that was very popular with servicemen. It's where we met.'

Polly stared across the carriage at her. Babs had told her that Sadie met her father at a party. But she supposed it could easily have been held at a nightclub. She glanced curiously at her mother, wondering why she was so quiet. Sadie looked pale and strained but it was probably the result of too much shopping.

'I think that's very encouraging, Papa,' Nicolas said.

'Yes it is, isn't it?' André began to gaze out of the window, and Sadie watched him from beneath her lashes. Had she imagined the expression in his eyes when he'd arrived at Euston? She desperately hoped so.

The following morning, when Polly had finished her last slice of toast and marmalade, Sadie slowly stubbed out her cigarette, finished her cup of tea and glanced across the table.

'I'm going to have to see George,' she said. 'I need to tell him about your father before he hears it from anyone else. I do wish you hadn't told Mrs Booth.'

'Sorry, I never thought,' Polly said. 'I was so excited about it all. When are you going to see him?'

'As soon as possible – I'll ring him this morning. And I was wondering whether when I do – probably for lunch – could you take your father and Nicolas somewhere?'

'Safely out of the way, you mean? Yes, all right.' But Polly's voice was tense and Sadie knew very well the question she was burning to ask.

'The answer is no,' she said quietly. 'Not now, not when I know that André is alive. It changes everything.'

'And does that apply to any other men?' Polly's voice was deceptively soft, but Sadie could hear the steel behind it.

'It applies to any other men.'

Polly looked down and began to fiddle with the teaspoon in her saucer. That was all very well, but what of the past? Already she was feeling fiercely protective towards her father. He seemed such a straightforward, caring man. He could have no idea of Sadie's lack of morals, of the vast number of men she'd slept with. But what if he started to become close to her again, if it seemed that their marriage might become a real one? Could she knowingly let him share a bedroom with Sadie in ignorance of the truth? Would she be failing him as a daughter if she didn't tell him? Yet Polly was painfully aware that to do so could destroy any chance of her parents' future happiness together.

Sadie lit another cigarette and steadily regarded the girl opposite. She hadn't lived with Polly for the past three years without gaining some insight into her character. Sadie knew very well what her daughter was thinking, what she was brooding over. 'What's the matter?'

Polly looked up and shrugged. 'Nothing, I was just miles away.'

Sadie hesitated, trying to choose her words carefully. 'Polly, when a couple are married, they sort things out between them. And I think you'll agree that I may have many faults but I do believe in honesty. I have no intention of deceiving your father in any way whatsoever.'

'I believe you, but...' Polly still felt troubled.

'Let me finish. I promise you that if ever André needs to know about the way I've been living all these years, then I will tell him.' She saw uncertainty in Polly's eyes and said, 'Have you ever known me to lie to you?'

Polly slowly shook her head. 'No, never.'

'So will you trust me and stop worrying about it?'

Polly gazed at her mother for one long moment. Then, with some reluctance, she made her decision. 'Yes,' she said, 'I will. There's always the chance that he may hear rumours, though. But I won't say anything to him – not without consulting you first.'

46

It was Wednesday lunchtime when Sadie met George. Pleading a headache, she watched the others leave for Stafford – where Polly had promised Nicolas and André a guided tour of the historic county town – then drove to a small hotel where she and George often had lunch. It was quiet, discreet, and the restaurant overlooked a beautiful garden. Eventually, after Sadie had enquired about his mother's health, and they had both commented on the beauty of the roses, George said, 'What's wrong, Sadie? You seem rather distracted.'

'You're very intuitive,' Sadie smiled. 'Someone's going to be very lucky when you eventually decide to marry again.' And it was true, she thought. With his silver hair and slightly ruddy complexion, he was still an attractive man. 'And you will, George. You'll be lonely once Mark leaves – not that I've heard that he's planning to,' she was quick to reassure him. 'But it's bound to come.' She laughed lightly at the growing wariness – or was it alarm – in his eyes? 'Don't be silly, I'm not about to propose, or even expect that you ever will. And we both know why.'

'It's such a parochial area,' he said defensively.

'And you have a position to uphold. I know, George, don't look so worried.'

'You make me feel ashamed, Sadie.'

'There's no need – especially now.'

They stopped talking as the waiter arrived with their main course. When he left, they were both busy for a few moments, George adding horseradish to his beef while Sadie put mint sauce on her lamb, and they began to eat.

'What did you mean?' George said eventually, 'by "especially now"?'

Sadie, who had already finished eating, leaned forward slightly, put her elbows on the table, and told him. George listened at first with disbelief, then with growing astonishment. 'That's the most fascinating story I've ever heard.' Sadie could hear the genuine pleasure in his voice. 'I can't tell you how pleased I am for you and for Polly. It's absolutely amazing.' He put out a hand to cover hers, then drew back as the waitress came to ask if they wanted a dessert. Sadie gave into temptation and ordered Black Forest gateau, while George opted for cheese.

'So you'll understand, George,' she said quietly a few minutes later, 'that this will have to be not only our last lunch together but also...'

'Of course,' he said. 'But I want you to know, Sadie, that our...'

'Assignations...?' Sadie smiled.

'They've been more than that Sadie – you've been a good friend. Both before Felicity died and afterwards.'

'It's been good for me too.'

The following day, Nicolas and Polly went to Stoke-on-Trent. Nicolas was keen to see the famous five towns, although Polly told him there were actually six. 'We can drive through all of them,' she said. 'I just keep on the A50.' And that's what they did, beginning with Longton, then Stoke, Hanley, Burslem and Tunstall. 'Burslem is the mother town, the Bursley that Arnold Bennett wrote about.' She glanced sideways at him. 'But I don't suppose you've read any of his books.'

'No,' he sighed. 'I am very uneducated.'

'I'll lend you one of mine,' she laughed.

Nicolas had been enthralled by the forbidding-looking pottery factories lining the roads. 'They look so grim,' he said.

'Grimy, you mean. People here call them potbanks.' They had turned back from Tunstall and stopped at the George Hotel in Burslem for lunch. Nicolas grinned at her across the table. 'You're not going to teach mathematics, are you?'

'Only sums. I'm going to be a primary school teacher, not a university lecturer. Why?'

'You said there were six towns, but you've only shown me five.'

'Have faith, my darling. We'll go through Fenton on the way back.'

Nicolas gazed at her. He loved the easy camaraderie between them. Polly was unlike any other girl he'd ever met. She was so natural, so genuine. Maman had been fond of describing people she liked as 'genuine'. She would have approved of his choice. The thought startled him. When Polly excused herself to go to the powder room, Nicolas lit a cigarette. For God's sake, he told himself, you've only known the girl for almost two weeks. Admittedly there had been that first meeting, when he'd gone to The Gables for afternoon tea, and all those weeks afterwards when he'd thought of no one else. As far as Nicolas had been concerned, marriage had always been something in the distant future. Yet when he was with her... Nicolas pushed the concept out of his mind. They were having a great time together, it was best to leave it at that. And he knew himself very well. He may have resisted the temptations of attractive Parisian girls over the past few months, but would that continue? He glanced up as Polly, her lipstick refreshed, came back to the table.

'Ready?' she smiled.

Next Polly stopped in Hanley, and took him into Woolworths. And there she was; standing behind a large glass-fronted sweet counter. They stood and watched as Ruth efficiently served two elderly ladies. Then glancing up she saw them, and her expression changed to one of surprise and delight. 'Hello! What brings you two here?'

'I'm giving him a tour of the Potteries,' Polly said. 'Well, sort of.'

Ruth glanced over her shoulder. 'Pretend you're buying something. We're not supposed to chat to our friends in working time.'

'What does Michael like?' Polly said.

'Well, lemon sherbets – but you don't have to...'

'A quarter please,' Polly said briskly. 'And what else?'

'He's a devil for chocolate caramels.'

'I'll take a half a pound of those as well.'

Nicolas was gazing with fascination at all the confectionery displayed. 'What are those?' he asked, looking at a mixture of small squares in different colours.

'Dolly mixtures, but you're far too old for them,' Ruth laughed.

'I brought Nicolas to say goodbye,' Polly said. 'He leaves on Sunday.'

Ruth glanced from one to the other. Gosh, she thought, that's gone quickly. Polly won't half miss him. She weighed out the sweets into two white paper bags, expertly twisted the ends and passed them over the counter, saying, 'I'm determined to see Paris before term begins. Mark's keen too

– how about you, Pol?'

She glanced mischievously at Nicolas. 'I think I might consider it.'

He grinned at Ruth and said, 'How could she resist, when I'm there?'

But later, as they made their way home, Nicolas said, 'Is it serious between those two? Ruth and Mark, I mean.'

'It is on Ruth's part,' Polly told him. 'With Mark – well there are complications.'

'What sort of complications?'

Polly hesitated, unsure of whether Nicolas would understand about the class system in England. It was less prevalent than it used to be – two world wars had seen to that. But the old snobbery was ingrained. It would take decades to erase it, she thought. And she supposed some remnants would always remain. 'Mark comes from an old county family,' she explained. 'His father is a professional man, his grandfather was a judge. Whereas Ruth's family is working class; her father works on a potbank. They're really nice people. I'm very fond of them.'

'But that doesn't count?' Nicolas frowned. There was, of course, snobbery in France too. It was something he'd always despised.

'Maybe a bit – but the fact that Ruth is a Catholic doesn't help either.'

'And Mark isn't?'

Polly shook her head. 'No, he's Church of England.'

'But surely if he loves her...'

'I'm hoping so.'

'How long have they been together?'

'Only seven months.' She began to pick up speed as they drew away from the city. 'So it's early days yet. But Ruth knew from the first.'

Nicolas fell silent. He glanced at Polly, at her lovely but intent profile as she concentrated on driving. He understood how Ruth felt. But he still believed that as far as he and Polly were concerned, it would be the next few months that would be the deciding factor.

47

Once Nicolas had returned to Paris, André left the hotel and moved into The Gables. As he unpacked his belongings in the spacious bedroom that had belonged to his parents he kept pausing, gazing around at the heavy oak furniture, going to look out of the window at the circular drive and front garden. He felt almost an intruder in this intimate room where his mother and father had slept, where it was almost certain that he'd been conceived. He wondered briefly why he'd been an only child. Perhaps, as with Gabrielle, there had been a gynaecological reason. He crossed over to a bookshelf and picked up a large framed wedding photograph. Emilie gazed out at him, her brown eyes full of vitality and happiness. Polly was so like her, it was uncanny. He looked down at the image of John Merton, smiling and proud. Why couldn't he remember them? It felt almost like a betrayal.

Downstairs, Polly walked slowly around the

quiet back garden, deep in thought. She had no idea how long her father was going to stay, but it didn't make any difference. There were serious issues that had to be faced. But first there was someone she needed to see, to discuss things with; to ask for advice. And she needed to see him alone. And so, while André was closeted in what was now to be his bedroom, and Sadie was in her own preparing to go to the Crown for lunch, Polly went into the hall, ran her finger down the telephone directory, found the number she needed, and dialled.

On Tuesday morning, Sadie went back to work and André drove her into Stafford. She had insisted on having his name added on her car insurance policy, and it did make sense. André decided to drive straight back to The Gables. Polly had told him that she was going to be out, that she'd arranged to see an old friend, and that meant that for the first time since the day he had guiltily trespassed, he would have the chance to be alone in the house. He would be able to relax, to quietly absorb the atmosphere of his old home, and he was hoping that perhaps then...

'Who is it that Polly's meeting?' he asked, as he glanced over his shoulder to check which turning to take when he drove back.

'She didn't say,' Sadie said, 'probably an old school friend.'

'She's a lovely girl. You brought her up well, Sadie.'

She didn't reply and he glanced curiously at her averted face. But then she was indicating a small boutique a few yards away. 'That's the one,' she said, and he drew up outside.

'I'll pick you up at six, then?' She nodded and after getting out, walked briskly away.

When he let himself back into the house André paused in the hall, looking up at the staircase, at the polished banister, wondering whether as a boy he'd ever slid down to bump into the carved balustrade at the bottom. Then slowly he walked from room to room, just as he had before. But now it was different. He knew that he had a right to search along the bookshelves, to take out books and browse through them, felt free to run his fingers along the wood of the furniture, to open drawers. Not to pry, never that, but just to see if there was anything, some remnant of his childhood, some trivial object, that would trigger a memory, however small. In the kitchen he found a small ball of string at the back of a drawer, and held it in his hand, rolling it around in his palm. He'd always liked string, had often irritated Nicolas with his insistence on unravelling lengths that had wrapped parcels, and winding them into small balls. 'Waste not, want not,' he'd said, and now he wondered from whom the saying had come. It was probably his other grandmother, the English one, who Polly had told him she was named after. Apparently she had died when he was ten years old.

Immersed in his thoughts, when the knock came at the back door, it startled him, and he opened it to be faced by an elderly man. He was wiry, stooped, and despite the warm weather wore a shabby tweed cap. André waited. The man peered at him. 'They said you'd got a beard.'

'Who did?'

'Folk in the village – it makes you look different.'

André hesitated. 'I'm sorry, but are you someone I should know?'

'They said that as well – that you'd lost yer memory, like. I'm Fred, the gardener – yer gonna 'ave forgotten me!'

André frowned. 'But I've met the gardener, he's called Harry.'

'Oh, he's nobbut a youngster. He hasn't been 'ere five minutes. I worked for yer father for thirty-five years.' His tone was proud.

'Oh, I see. Well, please come in, Fred.'

'Oh no, I won't if yer don't mind. I've never bin inside yet, and I don't intend to start now. But I wouldna mind a chat.'

'In that case I'll come outside.' André shook his head in perplexity. It seemed ridiculous that the man wouldn't come into The Gables. Surely the days had gone when such lines were never crossed? But then, he thought as he followed the old man slowly along the patio to the bench, old habits die hard.

Fred lowered his thin frame and André sat beside him. 'I remember you,' Fred said, 'when you were a little 'un. Always climbing the trees, you were. Yer were a right little devil.'

André smiled.

Fred went on, 'It's a bit of a turn-up this, you not being dead; an' after all this time, an' all.'

'You sound different,' André said slowly, 'from other people I've heard talking.'

'That's cos I'm a Potteries man. Born and bred in Longton. I only moved 'ere cos me wife didn't want to leave 'er mother.'

'Oh, I see.' André smiled. This chap was a right character. 'So it's all round the village, is it?'

'Polly told Mrs Booth, and that woman's got a right gob on 'er.'

André laughed. 'I haven't met her yet. She was supposed to come yesterday, but apparently she was ill.'

'You will,' Fred said darkly, 'not that she 'asn't bin good to Polly, everyone knows that.'

André frowned, not sure what the old man meant, but he was rambling on again.

'I can't believe you don't know me. 'Ere, let me take this off.' Fred removed his cap to reveal a shiny bald pate. ''Ow about that, then? I was always bald, 'ave bin since I was in me twenties.'

André stared at him, and an image suddenly flashed into his mind of this man's hand taking his own, pushing one finger into soft earth. He said slowly, 'You used to show me how to plant seedlings.'

'That's right! You had yer own patch of ground, down there.' Fred beamed at him with delight. 'There, you do remember!'

'Fred,' André said suddenly. 'How would you like me to buy you a pint?'

'Now that,' Fred said, getting up with difficulty, 'is an invitation I won't refuse.'

And so both men walked slowly into the village and into a small pub. André and Nicolas had been into it before, but it had stirred no memories. The landlord was a newcomer and the interior had recently been refurbished, although not, as Fred said, for the better, complaining that it had spoilt the atmosphere. André watched in amazement as the old man lifted his pint glass, licked his lips and without pausing for breath, poured his beer straight down his throat. He wiped the froth from his mouth and looked across the table expectantly. With a grin, André got up and went back to the bar.

This time Fred only sipped at the beer and André said, 'You must have known both of my parents.'

'I did that. Yer mother was a lovely lady, even if she was a Froggy. And yer father was a gentleman. I always got a bottle of whisky and a cigar every Christmas.'

André smiled. 'You're the first person I've met so far who can remember my mother.'

Fred glanced keenly at him. 'Well if you don't mind me saying so, yer'd get a lot more people remembering *you* if yer shaved that beard off. You don't look a bit like the lad I remember – apart from yer eyes.'

As André listened to the old man's distinctive voice reminiscing about the old days, he suddenly began to experience a few flashes of memory. How Fred had whacked him on the bottom with a branch after he'd stamped on some plants in a temper. The infinite patience he'd shown in explaining the names of flowers; how he'd taught him to care for his own small garden.

Fred gazed at him. 'Don't worry, lad, it'll all come back to you.' He leaned forward, and whispered, 'Is it true yer don't remember yer wife?'

André nodded. 'I'm afraid so.'

Fred looked down. 'Hmm.' he said. And that was all. André's eyes narrowed. He surveyed the man before him, sensing his discomfort. Now why would Fred, previously so garrulous, suddenly clam up?

'What did you mean, Fred,' he said curiously, 'when you said that Mrs Booth had been very good to Polly?'

'Well, she had ter be, didn't she, once that governess had left.'

'Oh,' André said slowly, 'I see what you mean.' He frowned. He didn't, but he intended to find out. However, he had no intention of questioning Fred. He intended to go to the source.

48

While André was sitting in the pub talking to his father's gardener, Polly was at the home of her grandfather's closest friend.

Cedric Black, seated opposite her in a chintz-covered armchair, was listening intently to her account of the past few days. His keen, intelligent eyes beneath their grey, bushy brows widened in shock as he realised the amazing implication of what she was telling him. Then, when she eventually drew to a close, he stared at her, his plump face creasing into a wide smile. 'My dear, I'm so very pleased for you. This really is the most astonishing news. It almost makes you believe in miracles.'

'I know,' she said. 'I just wish...'

He nodded in sympathy. 'I'm sure you do. And I do too. This would have meant the world to your grandfather.'

'I wanted to see you,' Polly said, 'not only because I wanted to tell you myself, but also because I need your advice.'

Cedric gazed at her. He was still bemused by what he had just heard. It was a shock, but an inspiring one. And now, unless he was mistaken in his assessment of John Merton's granddaughter, he thought he had an inkling of what was troubling her.

'Is it about the will?'

Her eyes met his. 'Yes.'

'And...?'

'It doesn't seem fair as it stands. We both know that my grandfather wouldn't have left everything to me – The Gables, all of his assets – not if my father had been alive.'

Cedric began to pull on his left ear lobe, a habit he had when concentrating. 'That's possible.'

'Mr Black, you know he wouldn't have done. And you're the executor. You handle all my financial affairs.'

'That's true. I do.' He hesitated. 'Have you mentioned this to anyone else?'

She shook her head.

'Not to André – or even to your mother?'

'Not to anyone.'

'Good. It's perhaps best to keep it like that, at least for the time being.'

'I just know,' Polly said, 'that I'm going to feel

402

awful when my birthday comes in November, when I legally inherit everything.'

'Tell me,' Cedric said. 'What do you know of André's circumstances? Is he a wealthy man?'

'I've no idea,' Polly said slowly. 'All I know is that he works as an administrator in a Paris shipping company. He and his son, Nicolas, live in an apartment in Paris, so that could mean anything.' She looked at him. 'But it doesn't make any difference, does it? As the only son, surely he must be the legal heir.'

Cedric was non-committal. 'I'm no legal expert. As you know, I was a banker. But what I'll do is consult Richard Knight, the solicitor who handled the will, and come back to you.'

'Thank you.'

Cedric said quietly, 'You say your father has no memory of Sadie. Does he know that she left you with John when you were a baby? About the way she lives?'

Polly shook her head.

'Then when he does find out, and these things always surface eventually, I think your mother is going to find life very difficult. How are things now between you?'

'Better,' Polly admitted. 'If it wasn't for her…'

'Men friends?' he prompted.

She nodded, '…plus the fact that she was missing for most of my life, there wouldn't be a problem. Even so, I think we're beginning to understand each other.'

'Have you decided on what course of action to take when November comes? You're released then of any obligation towards her.'

Polly shook her head. 'I've just kept putting off thinking about it,' she admitted. 'And now,' she shrugged, 'I've no idea what's going to happen.'

'We'll wait and see what Richard has to say,' Cedric said. 'It's no use worrying about things until we know the facts.'

'I just want to be fair to Dad,' she said, and smiled at him. 'I still can't believe it. Can you imagine how I feel – having a father after all these years!'

He smiled at her and couldn't help a pang of envy. 'He's a lucky man, Polly.'

'Once we've sorted this will business, you must come to dinner and meet him. You'll be able to fill him in on lots of details about his life before the war. After all, you knew my grandmother too, didn't you?'

'Oh yes,' Cedric said quietly, 'I knew Emilie.' He looked at Polly. 'I loved her, you know.' Polly stared at him in astonishment. 'Neither she nor John ever knew, of course.' He ran a hand over his balding head. 'I can't believe I told you that. I must be getting old.'

'I'm glad you did,' she said softly. 'Is that why you never married?'

He nodded. 'You're very like her, my dear.'

Polly smiled at him and said softly, 'I know.'

That evening Nicolas rang from Paris and after André had spoken to him, he passed the telephone to Polly and went back into the kitchen to pick up a tea towel and begin to dry the dishes.

'You don't have to do that,' Sadie protested.

'I'm not a guest,' he pointed out. 'Why

shouldn't I help?' Then he smiled, 'I've left Nicolas talking to Polly. I had the distinct impression that he wanted me to get off the line as soon as possible.'

'Had he any news?'

André shook his head. 'No, there were some letters, but nothing of any real interest.'

So far he hadn't mentioned meeting the old gardener either to Sadie or to Polly. And that was because he was still thinking about Fred's cryptic comment. André could understand the benefit of a French governess to Polly, particularly when she was under school age. But why, he wondered, once the Frenchwoman left, had Polly needed support from the cleaning woman? There was also the matter of the marriage certificate. He glanced sideways at Sadie as he dried a fork. Was there anything else she was keeping from him?

It was the following evening that Sadie at last phoned Babs to give her the news. Polly and André were watching TV when she came back into the room. 'She's so excited,' she said, 'that she wants to come up. Either that, or we could go to Hereford. And you know, André, it would be really good for you to see her again. It might bring back all sorts of memories.'

'I'd like to think so,' he said, 'but if I can't remember you then it's not very likely that I'll remember our bridesmaid!'

'It's worth a try,' Sadie said. 'In any case, you'll like Babs. You did, didn't you, Polly?'

'Yes, she was lovely.' But Polly was watching her father. 'Anyway, this amnesia's a funny thing, isn't it? You can never tell how it's going to work; who you'll remember and who you won't. Isn't that right, Dad?'

André glanced sharply at her.

'I went to see how Mrs Booth is this afternoon,' she said. 'She's got a lousy cold, so I told her to skip this week. But she was, as usual, a mine of information as to what's going on in the village.' Her eyes challenged him.

'I suppose she told you that I met the old gardener, Fred?' André admitted. 'He came and knocked on the back door yesterday morning.'

'Apparently, you remembered him.' Polly frowned, at a loss as to why her father hadn't mentioned it.

Sadie gazed at her husband. 'You remembered him?' she echoed. 'Why on earth didn't you tell us?'

André shrugged. 'I forgot,' the white lie came easily. 'Yes, there were odd patches that I remembered; mainly from when he used to let me help him in the garden when I was young. We went and had a pint together at the pub. Or at least, Fred had two.'

'You're lucky you got away with only two!' Polly grinned. 'I used to like Fred, he made me laugh.'

And then, André thought, why not bring it up now, when they are both here? After all, there's probably a very simple explanation. He had no intention of raising the matter of the marriage certificate, though, not when Polly was in the room.

'Fred did say one thing,' he said slowly, 'that puzzled me.'

'What was that?' Polly said.

'About how good Mrs Booth has been to you, Polly – particularly after your governess left. I wasn't sure what he meant.' He looked at his daughter, only to see her dart an uneasy glance at her mother.

André frowned. He turned to his wife. 'Is there something I should know?'

Sadie was almost in a state of shock. How could it have come out of the blue like this? And suddenly, as she looked at them both, Sadie, for the first time, realised the enormity of what she had done. 'I *was* going to tell you, André,' she said. 'It just never seemed the right time.' She took a shaky breath. 'The truth is that I didn't stay at The Gables after Polly was born. Not after the first twelve months. I went back to live in London.'

'But I thought Polly grew up here?'

'She did.' Sadie forced herself to meet his questioning eyes. In a low voice she managed to find the words, to confess what she knew might destroy his respect for her for ever. 'But without me.'

André stared at her with incredulity. He swung round to face Polly. 'Let me get this right. I know you spent your childhood deprived of your father. Am I to understand that you spent your childhood deprived of a mother as well?'

Polly could only nod in misery. She was finding the unfolding scene unbearable. There had been so many years when she'd lain awake at night, often in tears; hurt and resentful that her mother took little interest in her. She'd missed so much the softness and warmth that she'd seen her friends enjoy. And yet now, to see the look of stark unhappiness on Sadie's face...

407

'Sadie. I'd appreciate it if you could explain. How could you let such a thing happen?' André's voice was full of controlled anger.

Polly, already tense, felt her chest tightening. For most of her life she'd wanted to know the answer to that question; one that had, during the past few months, often hovered on her lips. Silently she watched her mother, painfully aware of her distress, her apprehension. But the time had passed for secrecy. Sadie had no choice but to answer her husband and Polly realised, with a sick lurch of her stomach, that at last she was going to learn the truth.

49

In the drawing room, the atmosphere was tight with tension. Bewildered, André stood before the fireplace, yet his eyes were hard and accusing.

Polly sat in one of the armchairs.

Sadie faced them. Her palms were damp with perspiration, her mouth suddenly dry. 'Is there any chance of a drink?'

André went over to the sideboard. 'What would you like?'

She flinched at the ice in his voice. 'I think a brandy might help.'

Silently he poured out a measure and handed it to her. Sadie raised it to her lips and then cradled the glass in both hands. For one moment she stared down at it and then said slowly, 'I was nineteen, André, when I first left London to come to live at The Gables.' She paused. 'I hated it from the very first moment.'

Polly stared at her. Hated it?

'But knowing that your father was grieving for Emilie, you wanted to be able to see both of us on the rare occasions you could get leave. And it made sense to get away from the air raids. So I stayed. But I never settled. Your father was out at business most of the time and I missed city life too much. When the telegram came from the War Office and I saw the words "believed killed", something died inside me.' She turned to gaze at Polly. 'Three weeks later you were born.'

The silence in the room was tangible.

'You were a fretful baby,' Sadie said in a low voice. Polly noticed that her hands were beginning to tremble. 'Always crying, always difficult to feed. And no matter how hard I tried, I couldn't seem to feel anything for you, not love, not pride, not any of the things a new mother is supposed to feel.' Sadie looked up and her eyes met those of her daughter. 'It went on for months,' she said quietly. 'The doctors called it a severe case of the "baby blues". Eventually your grandfather got a nurse in, and I was glad of it. It relieved me of any responsibility, you see.'

Sadie took another sip of the brandy. Again there was only silence in the room. 'It was very hard on your grandfather. He had his own grief to cope with. My depression, my uselessness as a mother, totally bewildered him. In the end, he said, "I think the best thing you can do for that baby is to go back to London and have a complete break." And so I did.'

'And never came back.' Polly's voice was almost a whisper.

'And I never came back.'

And now André spoke. 'You mean you abandoned our child?'

'It was hardly abandoning her, André. She had a grandfather who adored her, a capable nurse and a comfortable home.'

'Don't split hairs, Sadie. She was your child, not my father's.'

'And when you came to see us,' Polly said, 'did you never think of staying? I mean, I can try and understand why you left in the first place, but surely when you felt better?' An image came to her of Sadie, perched on a chair, smiling through bright red lipstick, chain-smoking, talking gaily, and leaving within hours.

'Oh, you did come to visit, then?' André's voice was full of sarcasm. 'You did remember you had a child?'

'I could hardly forget.' Sadie raised her eyes to his, flinching at the coldness in his eyes. 'And I can't explain why I didn't come back, not in a way I could make you understand. Somehow, time just went on...'

'You mean you preferred your life in London!' Polly's tone was flat. 'Didn't I mean anything to you?'

'Of course you did.'

'But obviously not enough to be a proper mother to me,' Polly said, and they could both hear the misery in her voice.

Sadie stared at her, and then suddenly felt an

overwhelming sense of shame. She thought of the small girl staring at her with eyes she had thought hostile and now realised had been full of hurt. Sadie had always gone back to London with relief, telling herself she wasn't needed. Had she simply seen what she wanted to see?

'I've told you,' she said quietly, 'I'm a very selfish person.'

André stared at her, appalled that he could have married such a woman. He thought of Gabrielle, of her protective love for Nicolas, her sadness that she could never have another child.

'I think I've heard enough!' He stared down at Sadie for one brief moment then began to walk stiffly out of the room. She called after him in desperation, 'André...'

Polly turned to see her mother in tears. And then silently she followed her father.

André was in the breakfast room when Polly found him. He was standing before the fireplace holding a photograph of her as a child. 'How could she do it?' he said in despair.

'I've asked myself that many times.' Polly sat by the table.

'What I don't understand is – why is she here now? And you seem to get on so well. What changed things?'

'My grandfather died.' She looked up at him. 'Do you mind if I explain about that another time?' She hesitated, 'Dad...'

'Yes?'

'About Sadie...'

'That's another thing,' André said, still seething

411

with anger. 'I wondered why you called her by her Christian name. Now I know.'

'It's just that ... I think perhaps if you knew what her childhood was like...'

'Whatever it was, there's no excuse for what she did.'

Polly told him everything she knew. Of the poverty, of the father Sadie had adored and lost when she was twelve. 'She was left to the mercies of her mother, who sounds a horrible woman. She not only neglected her, but also brought men...' Polly's voice trailed off as, with horror, she realised that she'd said too much.

André's eyes narrowed. 'Brought men...? Go on, Polly. You might as well tell me all of it.'

Polly fought panic. She must be very careful what she said. After all, she had promised Sadie...

'Apparently,' she said, 'her mother frequently brought men back to the flat, a very small flat with thin walls. It was a way of earning money. I think you can imagine what effect that had on a young girl.'

Horrified, André stared at her. 'She actually told you this herself?'

Polly nodded. 'I know it took a lot of courage for her to tell me. What I'm trying to make you understand is that she never had a role model – as a good mother, I mean.'

André was struggling to reconcile the picture Polly had drawn of Sadie's background, with the poised and normally confident woman he'd seen during the past two weeks. Eventually he said, looking at Polly's flushed face, 'Knowing all this made a difference to you, Polly?' he said.

412

'It did help me to try and understand her better.'

André looked at his daughter. She seemed so mature for her age – possibly, he thought, because of being brought up by John Merton, a man he was beginning to have enormous respect for.

'I hated her for years, you know, and I think part of me will never forgive her.' Polly looked up at him. 'Isn't that a terrible thing to say? But since she's come back, although we've had our differences – we still have – I really have become very fond of her.'

André didn't say anything. Instead he gazed down at the floor. Polly decided to leave him alone.

'I think I'd better go back,' she said, 'and see how she is.'

50

The following days were ones of tension. André spent much of his time in John Merton's study, a small room at the back of the house that had rarely been used since his death. It was there that he came to know the man who had raised him, the man to whom he owed so much gratitude, who had taken his own place in his daughter's life. Through the businessman's papers, André realised what a fine brain he had, what a strong sense of social justice, and hoped desperately that one day his memory of him would return. He avoided his wife as much as possible.

Sadie carried on with her normal routine, baking, working alone in the garden, going to the boutique. But inside she was a total mess. Because not only could she see contempt in André's eyes, she had to live with the dread of him finding out how she'd been living all these years. And the refrain constantly running through her mind was that she was going to have to tell him. Should she do so now and get the whole unpleasant business over with? Or would she be better to wait until he'd calmed down, had adjusted to the shock of what he'd just learned?

Polly had been bitterly hurt by what her mother had said; that she'd never been able to love her, not even as a baby. But hadn't she always known that? And wasn't she now at an age when she should just accept it? She knew that her parish priest would, as with any disappointment or injustice, advise her to 'offer it up'. Polly preferred the old proverb, 'If life gives you lemons, make lemonade.' And that was what she was determined to do. The last three years had shown her that it was possible to mend fences, even while never forgetting what had happened in the past.

Now she found herself in the role of diplomat, keeping the conversation going during mealtimes, trying to smooth over any awkward silences when they were all together. So when Cedric Black phoned her to suggest another meeting, it was with relief that Polly eventually escaped to drive into Stafford. And she couldn't help hoping that when her parents were alone in the house, they might – as Sadie had previously said – sort things

414

out between them. No matter how painful it was.

It was Sadie who raised the subject. After Polly had left, she walked slowly to the drawing room, hovered for a moment in the doorway, and then crossed over to where André was reading the morning paper.

'Can we talk?' she said. Her voice was hesitant.

He glanced up from his armchair. 'I'm not sure we have anything to say.'

Sadie went to sit opposite. She waited a moment then said, 'That's not true, André, and I think you know it. You don't remember anything, do you? About how we met, how we came to get married?'

André laid down his newspaper. 'I know what the date was on the marriage certificate, and I know that Polly was born five months later. I'm assuming that's why I married you. I can,' he said in a hard voice, 'think of no other reason.'

Tears sprang to Sadie's eyes. 'That's very cruel, André.'

'Is it?' he said. 'Don't you think you were cruel in what you did to Polly? Even if your childhood was one of neglect, did that mean you had to deprive your own child?'

Sadie stared at him, and he said, 'Yes, Polly told me. I think she was trying to find excuses for you. But I'm afraid I'm made of harder stuff, Sadie. I find it almost impossible to forgive you.'

Sadie seized on the word 'almost', and a tiny flicker of hope flared inside her. But then she saw the bitterness in his eyes. She said quietly, 'I think it's time you knew how we met, what sort of girl

415

I was then, and what sort of woman I am now.'

André became very still. 'What sort of girl you were? What exactly do you mean?'

Slowly, her eyes fixed on his, Sadie described that first evening in the nightclub. She told André of his depression after his mother's death, the concern of his crew. How he had gone back to her cramped bedsit and how, like so many before him, he had turned to her for comfort. 'I made no secret of what I was,' she said. 'You knew perfectly well. But as I told you then, I never took money, not from anyone. I want you to know that right from the first moment you touched me, André, it was different. I loved you from that very first night. I never stopped loving you,' and now her voice became almost a whisper, 'I still do.'

But André could still hear the words, 'I never took money; not from anyone...'

'I didn't sleep with anyone else after that – I couldn't,' Sadie managed to continue. 'So when I found out I was pregnant, I knew the baby was yours. My first thought was to ask you for money for an abortion. I never expected you to offer to marry me.' She gave a wry smile. 'You were a man of high principles, just like your father. He even refused to come to our wedding, hoping you would change your mind.'

She saw the question flare in his eyes and shook her head. 'No, he never knew about the other men. He just thought you were making a terrible mistake. But he relented afterwards. He was a wonderful man – I owe him a lot.'

André had never doubted that he was Polly's father; one only had to look at her resemblance to

Emilie to see that. He tried to imagine the young man he would have been in 1941, fighting in a war, unsure of how long he would live. And suddenly he understood why he'd married Sadie, why he'd wanted to protect the only child he might ever have.

'This depression you say I was suffering from...?'

'Everyone said I brought you out of it,' she said. 'But I want to be honest with you, André. You never loved me, not really. I had hoped that in time ... but unfortunately we weren't given that chance.'

André looked at her, knowing that was one thing that Sadie hadn't needed to confess. She was being completely frank, no matter how painful ... but then he felt a sudden rush of anxiety.

'Polly doesn't know, does she? About the way she was conceived?'

Sadie shook her head. 'No, and she'll never hear it from me.'

'On that, at least, we're agreed.'

'I'm sorry, André. I know this must all have come as a shock to you.'

'That's putting it mildly!' André got up from the armchair, and walked over to stare blindly out of the bay window. He tried to reconcile the woman who had shown such sensitivity towards him, whose company he'd come to enjoy, with the image she had just painted. And the fact remained that she was still legally his wife.

Sadie reached out to take a cigarette from the silver box on the coffee table. With a trembling hand, she lit it and inhaled. She looked at the rigid set of André's shoulders, saw the way his hands were clenched at his sides, and leaned for-

417

ward, perched tensely on the edge of the leather chair. She knew there was one more question to come. She didn't have to wait long.

With his back still to her, André said in a tight voice, 'You said earlier – "what sort of woman I am now". Do I take it that you mean…'

'Yes.'

He swung round, his expression one of incredulity.

Sadie had no intention of apologising. She never had, and never would. 'I enjoy sex. It's as simple as that.'

'It's as simple as that,' he echoed. Then his eyes narrowed. 'You haven't brought men back to The Gables? Not with Polly under the roof? For God's sake! You're a mother! But I forgot,' and his voice was like a whip, 'that doesn't mean much to you, does it?'

'That's not fair, André. I may have been a poor one in the past, but now…'

André felt utter despair. Polly had been exposed to *this?* 'Damn you, Sadie. Damn you for sullying this family.' He held up a hand as she began to protest. 'No, don't say another word. Although you've been honest, I'll grant you that.'

Sadie was beginning to feel sick, but she still had to persist. 'There's one last thing, André.'

'My God, don't tell me there's something else!'

She shook her head. 'No, I've told you every-thing. But as far as Polly knows, we met at a party held at a nightclub. And I want to keep it that way. Let's not destroy her illusions about us. The story must be that I only "went off the rails" after I returned to London.' Sadie rose and, keeping her face averted, said in a strangled voice, 'I'm going to make some coffee. I need something to steady my nerves.'

André watched her leave the room, knowing that she was close to tears. At the moment he was too full of anger and disgust to care. And yet, he thought as he turned away and lit a cigarette, her last statement revealed that she did feel something for Polly. It was just a shame that it came twenty years too late.

51

When Polly arrived home, there was no sign of Sadie. André was sitting on the sofa in the drawing room smoking, and judging by the number of stubs in the ashtray had been doing so for some time. He turned to face her and she was shocked by his haggard expression, the misery in his eyes. 'Sadie's told me everything, Polly.'

Polly's breath caught in her throat. 'What exactly has she said?' She went to sit beside him.

'There's no need to try and be loyal. I know all about what sort of woman she is, the life she's been leading.' His voice was harsh.

'I'm glad she's told you,' she said quietly. 'It had to be done. But it must have been very hard for her.'

'It wasn't very pleasant to listen to either!'

There was a short silence then André gazed at her, his eyes full of bewilderment. 'How on earth can you live with it?'

'What choice did I have?' Polly felt her throat close, deeply upset to see him so unhappy.

'And how did you find out?' André said, 'I can hardly imagine she announced it when she arrived.'

Polly became very still. She had no intention of telling him about that horrendous night, of the mix-up of bedrooms, the naked man trying to climb into her bed. 'Just circumstances,' she said with a shrug. 'I've had to learn to accept that it's the way she is.'

'Better a bad mother, than no mother at all, I suppose!' André turned his head away, staring blindly into the distance.

'I know one thing,' Polly said with desperation, 'it will all stop now. Sadie's promised me that, and I believe her.'

André didn't answer. He couldn't believe he was having this conversation, one that in any decent family would never arise.

When the day of the wedding arrived, Polly left early to dress at Anita's house. As she drove away from The Gables, she was more worried about the atmosphere between her parents than she was about being a bridesmaid. And now that Anita had invited them, how would they cope in public? But then once she arrived at the bride's home, it was all excitement, last-minute panic, and she had to concentrate instead on calming Anita's nerves and reassuring her that she'd chosen the right veil.

Back at The Gables, André was standing before the heavy oak dressing table thoughtfully knotting his tie, relieved that Polly had confessed she'd been teasing about morning dress. A few days before he'd finally made the decision to shave off his beard, his apprehension about the scars proving to be unfounded as most had faded and were almost undetectable.

Sadie was already waiting downstairs in the hall, elegant in a navy dress and jacket trimmed with a white spotted collar, and matching cuffs. Her white hat, set at a slightly rakish angle, was a frilly confection of tulle. She watched André descend the stairs, thinking yet again how handsome he looked without his beard, and so much more like the man she'd fallen in love with.

'You look lovely,' he said with sudden sincerity.

'Thank you.' Sadie smiled, 'I think we both scrub up well.'

Despite himself he had to smile. He'd forgotten what a good sense of humour she had – there had been little sign of it recently. But then he'd been so trapped inside his anger, he'd given scant regard to how Sadie was feeling.

As he stood in a pew at the back of the ancient church, André watched his daughter walk with dignity behind the young bride. Polly looked stunning in a long peach dress, her glossy brown hair crowned with a headdress of fresh flowers. He felt so proud, so full of what he realised was becoming a deep and protective love. Sadie, beside him, felt her eyes prick with tears. She had become, to her annoyance, rather emotional since André's return.

Later at the reception, held in a large marquee at the back of the bride's home, she and André stood slightly apart with their drinks, and then to

Sadie's consternation, she saw George approach.

'Good to see you, Sadie,' he said. He turned to André and held out his hand. 'George Eldon, Mark's father. I can't tell you how delighted I am about the news.'

'Thank you.' André shook his hand.

'I haven't seen Mark anywhere,' Sadie said.

'He's away with some of his friends from university,' George said, 'it was all fixed ages ago. They've gone camping in the Dordogne – do you know it, André?'

As the two men talked, Sadie gazed around the marquee with unease, but couldn't see any other man who might cause her embarrassment. Two middle-aged women did turn and glance in her direction but she simply stared challengingly back at them, amused when they swiftly looked away. But later she was relieved to see their place names were at the end of one of the long tables – safely away from curious eyes. And gradually, in the enforced social situation, she and André managed to give the appearance of being on the best of terms.

It was not until after the speeches that Polly was free to come over to them. 'I had my hands full with those two little ones,' she laughed. 'One has been sulking, and the other was sick with excitement – fortunately after the service.' She turned to her father. 'Have you seen anyone you know?'

'Not really. One man came up to me and said we used to teach at the same school, but I couldn't remember him.'

'I was thinking that we might invite him to dinner,' Sadie said.

André smiled at Polly. 'We were so proud of you, weren't we, Sadie? You look beautiful.'

Polly looked at them both. Was she imagining it or had the ice between them melted – at least for today? 'Thank you,' she said, 'I just wish Nicolas could have been here. As soon as Mark's back, we're going over to see Ruth about the Paris trip. I can't wait to tell them the news.'

The following Sunday afternoon, Michael struggled to open the front door to Polly and Mark and at the same time to control his young Westie, who was frantically jumping up at the visitors. Michael scooped him up in one arm and led the way into the small sitting room.

Bridie, having cleared the table after Sunday lunch, had left the dishes to soak in the kitchen sink and was reading the *Universe*. Sean was reading the *News of the World*, a contrast not lost on Mark who hid a grin. Maria and Teresa were sitting on the settee looking sulky. They had, she later found out, just been reprimanded by their father for using bad language.

Ruth came forward with delight to kiss Mark. 'Polly's got something to tell you,' he whispered.

Ruth saw the excitement in her friend's eyes, saw her glance quickly around the room, and said hastily, 'Come on, there's something I want to show you upstairs.'

Michael watched them go. 'She hasn't really, it's just secrets,' he said in disgust. 'Girls have always got secrets!'

Mark laughed. Polly had told him the dramatic news in the car. Mark knew of the rumours surrounding Sadie, but he'd just ignored them; people were always tittle-tattling about something. But now, with the return of her husband, he couldn't help wondering how things would turn out. It couldn't be easy, either, to find yourself a married couple after twenty years apart.

'How did the camping go?' Sean put down his paper.

'Brilliant.' Mark grinned and began to recount a few amusing anecdotes, particularly one about himself and a wayward goat, and soon even the twins were giggling.

Meanwhile, Ruth was listening with astonishment to Polly's news. 'You mean that straight after we dropped you off that night...?'

Polly nodded. 'Sadie took me into the dining room and told me. Then I went into the drawing room – and there he was.'

'It's wonderful, Pol.' Ruth leaned over and hugged her friend. She began to dab at her eyes. 'Look at me, I've gone all emotional!'

'You can imagine how I felt.'

'As for Sadie...!' Ruth put her hand to her mouth. 'Oh, my God – how's your father going to feel when he finds out?'

Polly hesitated. 'Actually – and this is just between the two of us – my father knows. Sadie told him.'

Ruth stared at her. 'Gosh, that must have been hard – for both of them. And...?'

'I honestly don't know what's going to happen.' Polly's eyes clouded. It was a question that was constantly on her mind.

Ruth gazed at her with sympathy. 'Never mind,'

she said. 'You've still got the divine Nicolas.'

'He is, isn't he?' Polly grinned at her. 'Eyes off, you've got Mark.'

Ruth began to finger the coverlet on the bed. 'Hopefully, I have.'

'Listen to your Aunt Polly and stop worrying. I've told you, it's too soon to even think of a proposal.'

'Maybe he will in Paris?' Ruth's tone was wistful. 'I suppose I'm just afraid of losing him, Pol. After all, I'm no great catch, am I?'

'Rubbish! Those days have gone, Ruth. It's the sixties for heaven's sake.'

Downstairs, Mark was watching Michael trying to train Whisky to sit on command, and realising yet again how much he enjoyed being with Ruth's family. During the camping trip to France, his two friends had flirted outrageously with girls on the campsite. But he hadn't been tempted; Ruth was too fine a girl to cheat on. We'll see how Paris goes, he thought. People always say that going on holiday with someone can be a 'make or break' situation.

He turned with a smile as the two girls came back into the room, then as Polly told everyone her good news, he and Ruth escaped to the kitchen. Offering to wash the dishes in this house was often the only way they could get time on their own.

52

The week before Polly was due to leave for Paris, she went into the drawing room hoping to find her father alone. 'I wondered whether I could have a word,' she said.

André looked up from his writing pad. 'Yes, of course. I'm just making a few notes before I go down to the Foreign Office. I thought they might like to know what I learned about the address on my identity card. Or rather,' he said grimly, 'about what happened to the people who lived there.' An image flashed into his mind of the old woman with the shopping basket, of her anger and bitterness. 'Sorry,' he said, 'you wanted to talk to me?'

'Do you by any chance remember someone called Cedric Black?'

André slowly shook his head. 'I don't think so. Why?'

'He was my grandfather's closest friend and the chief executor of his will. I'd like you to come to a meeting with him. The solicitor will be there too.'

André frowned. 'What's this all about, Polly?'

'I just think it isn't fair that The Gables and everything will come to me. It wouldn't have happened if Grandad had known you were alive.'

André looked down at his writing pad. So that was it. He'd wondered what the situation was.

'Everything's in trust for me until I come of age in November,' Polly explained. 'I was only fourteen when the will was drawn up, and it made Sadie my legal guardian.'

'And she agreed to it? To leave London and come up here?'

Polly bit her lip. 'He increased her allowance – considerably.'

André stared at her. 'What do you mean – her allowance? You mean all those years, he...?'

Polly nodded. 'I think he felt he had to step into your shoes. He was always a man who took his responsibilities seriously. Please, you will come, won't you?'

'If you want me to, then of course I will.'

The meeting was held on a day when Sadie was working. When Cedric Black opened the door he came forward with hands outstretched. 'André!' His face alight, he took André's hand in both of his own, and shook it vigorously. 'Only now can I really believe it. This is a red-letter day and no mistake.'

Once inside the house and in the sitting room, André glanced around at the typically English furnishings, at the leaded bay window overlooking neat lawns, at the polished oak block floor. Then suddenly he saw an ivory chess set displayed on a low table; the pieces were of Roman design, the largest about five inches high. He looked at the shrewd blue eyes of the genial man before him, then again at the chess set. His eyes narrowed. A second later he said hesitantly, 'You taught me to play chess. I'm right, aren't I?'

'You certainly are!' Cedric was obviously delighted. He moved away as the doorbell rang. 'That will be Richard.'

'Gosh, Dad, that's amazing,' Polly said.

André was elated. Maybe the longer he stayed in England, the more of his memory would return. He turned as Cedric ushered in a tall, bespectacled man, saying, 'André, this is Richard Knight. You would have known his late father.'

'Good to meet you, André,' Richard smiled. 'Hello, Polly. Are you keeping well? Off to your first teaching post soon, I hear.'

'That's right. I'm fine, thank you, Mr Knight.'

'Shall we go into the dining room?' Cedric led the way into a pleasant, sunny room and they took their places around an oak refectory table. André had hoped that in this room too he would find something familiar, only to be disappointed.

Richard opened his briefcase, took out a folder and placed it before him. 'First of all, André, I take it you have proof of your identity?'

André described the documents he had, including his birth and marriage certificates. 'I'm sorry – I never thought to bring them with me.'

'If you need further clarification, I can stand as a formal witness,' Cedric said. 'I've known André since he was born.'

'Good. So I suggest with your permission, Polly, that I acquaint André with the terms of his father's will.'

A few minutes later, there was a short silence in the room. Polly glanced warily at her father, but André's expression was impassive.

'I have gone into this unusual case very carefully,' Richard said. 'But I'm afraid legally there's no provision for the will to be changed. John Merton was of sound mind when it was drawn

428

up and it's watertight. In law, the fact that André has reappeared after a twenty-year absence has no relevance.'

André leaned forward. 'I want to make it clear that I'm not making any claims. I came here only because Polly asked me to.'

'We understand that,' Cedric said.

'Is there nothing I can do?' Polly protested.

Richard gazed thoughtfully at her. 'We'd have to be careful about the tax implications, but once you're twenty-one, you can do what you like with any money your grandfather left you.'

Polly stared at him, at first unsure what he meant, and then her face lit up. Of course! She could do nothing about The Gables, but maybe she could transfer shares – at least do something!

'There is one thing you might like to consider, Polly,' Richard said. 'If in November you were to make your own will, which I would have advised anyway, then you could name your father as your beneficiary. As it stands at the moment if anything happened to you, everything would go either to any children you had, or to named charities.' He smiled, 'Not to your husband. Your grandfather was very careful to ensure that you didn't become prey to fortune hunters.'

'That sounds good advice,' Cedric said. 'Do you feel happy about that, Polly?'

'Yes, of course.'

'André?' Richard gazed across the table at him, 'Is that agreeable to you? It's best to get things sorted now, while you're in England.'

André recognised the fairness and good sense in what the solicitor suggested. 'I agree,' he said slowly, 'but I think a safeguard should be added. If Polly did die before me and I'm named as the main beneficiary, then provision should be made in the will for any children she might have.'

'Yes, of course.' The solicitor closed the file and inserted it back into his briefcase. 'Well, I think we've covered everything.' When offered coffee he said, 'No thank you, Cedric, I must get back to the office.'

Once back in the sitting room, André went over to the chess board, and picking up the figure of the queen, held it reflectively in his hand. It was cool and smooth to the touch, perfectly balanced. He placed it back on its square. Yes, the memory was there. He knew this room, he knew this man. So why in God's name, couldn't he remember his parents? Was he only ever going to be able to remember the living? And if so, then why on earth couldn't he remember his own wife?

And then he suddenly realised that during the meeting, Sadie had hardly been mentioned. And remembering the clause in John Merton's will, André realised that in November his daughter would be facing a very difficult decision. And, he thought grimly as he went to join the others, so will her father – although my own decision needs to be made even sooner than that.

As the weeks had gone by, and the area became more familiar to André, small snippets of memory were beginning to return, although mainly just feelings of déjà vu. Whenever he went to Mass with Polly, different parishioners would come up to welcome him, saying that they'd known him since a child. A few offered their condolences on the death of John Merton three years earlier.

'It's a terrible tragedy,' one kind-faced, elderly woman said, 'that he didn't live to see this day. After your mother died, I used to cook for him up at The Gables, you know – especially when he entertained business guests.'

'I didn't know,' he said, looking round as Polly came to join them.

'Hello, Mrs Dunne. Isn't it wonderful?'

'It is that, Polly,' she beamed. 'Well, I must be getting back; I've got the joint in the oven.'

'Do you remember her?' Polly said, as they went out to the car.

'I'm not sure. The problem is that people are a lot older now.'

'It's a pity that the parish priest is new,' Polly said. 'It would have been Father McKenna when you were young. But we could easily find out where he is now.'

André, who had been told that he used to be an altar boy, nodded. 'Good idea.'

Polly turned the ignition key and turned to smile at him. 'Right,' she said, 'now to the Crown for lunch and a surprise for you.'

Startled, André glanced at her, but she shook her head and put a finger to her lips. 'You'll just have to wait and see.'

When, with Polly still teasing her father, they went into the bar lounge it was to see Sadie sitting with a dark-haired woman of about the same age. She stood up as André approached, stared at him wide-eyed, and then her lips curved in a delighted

431

smile. 'André Merton! I just can't believe it! It really is you!' She came forward to kiss him while Sadie and Polly watched.

'I'm sorry...' André glanced helplessly at Polly, who came to his rescue.

'It was a bit of an experiment,' she explained. 'To see if you recognised her. This is Babs. You know, Sadie's friend – the one who was her bridesmaid?'

'Yes, of course. But I thought you lived in Hereford?'

Babs said, 'I drove up this morning. So you don't remember me?' She shook her head in bewilderment. 'That's really weird.'

'Isn't it?' André turned to Polly. 'What would you like to drink?'

'I'll just have an orange juice, please.' Polly watched him go over to the bar and turned to the others. She scooped up some peanuts from a dish on the table. 'Well, that's a disappointment – him not knowing you, I mean.'

'I never thought he would really,' Sadie said. 'After all, he didn't know me, and I was married to him.'

'I know. But that was at the beginning. I'm sure his memory is getting better.'

Sadie said, 'What we're hoping is that if Babs and I bring up the old days, talk about people we all knew, it might trigger something off.'

'It's certainly worth a try. How long are you staying, Babs?'

'Just a few days,' Babs smiled at her. 'It's good to see you, Polly. You're looking lovelier than ever, it must be this young Frenchman Sadie's been telling me about. There's nothing like romance to

432

put a sparkle in a girl's eyes.'

Polly laughed. 'I'll be seeing him next week.'

But Sadie was sitting frozen with shock. Because standing before the bar, chatting to the barmaid, was a tall thickset man whose profile confirmed her worst fears. It was Rupert Evans – the man who had blundered naked into Polly's room on that terrible night; the man Sadie had hoped never to see again. She glanced swiftly at her daughter but fortunately Polly had her back to him and was talking to Babs. With rising panic Sadie looked over at the bar only to tense as Rupert turned to glance casually over his shoulder. She saw a flash of startled recognition as his eyes met her own, and then he turned away, but not before she'd seen an ugly flush stain his cheeks. Seconds later he drained his glass, thrust it back on the bar and strode out of the room. With a trembling hand Sadie lit a cigarette, shaken by the guilt she'd felt, the fear of discovery. And it was several minutes later before she was able to relax and breathe more easily.

During the meal, André was quiet, listening to the women, watching their faces. He was curious about Babs. She was the only person, apart from Sadie and himself, who knew their whole story. And she must know of the way Sadie had lived since. And yet she'd remained friends with her. And then as he watched the animation in her face he began to relax and enjoy her company. She was like a breath of fresh air, and he decided that her errant husband was a fool to have left her for a younger woman.

The following day, Sadie took Babs off for the

day to visit some of the factory shops in the Potteries. Babs wanted to impress her 'widower', as she called him, with a new dinner service. As they drove along, she talked to Sadie of her hopes. 'If he eventually proposes, I'm going to say yes,' she said, 'although I must be mad to take on more kids. But I think we could make a go of it.'

'How do you feel about Jimmy these days?'

Babs turned away to stare out of the window, 'Still pig-sick, to be honest. But I've had to accept it. And why shouldn't I build a new life too?'

'Absolutely – you go for it, girl,' Sadie said. 'You do love this Bernard, though?'

'Not in the same way I loved Jimmy. But there's different kinds of love, aren't there? He's a nice guy, Sadie. And I liked being married, being part of a couple.'

So did I, Sadie thought, then smiled at her friend. 'I hope it all works out for you, Babs. I really do.'

At The Gables, it was one of Mrs Booth's days. André had struck up a friendly rapport with the bustling cleaner, and going into the kitchen said, 'I'm about to make myself a cup of tea, would you like one?'

Doris beamed at him. 'I wouldn't say no. That's what I like to see, a man who can make himself useful. Now my Ernie, he'll sit in an armchair for hours waiting for someone to brew up for him.'

André smiled. 'I got used to fending for myself after my wife died.'

Doris bent down to get some polish out of the cupboard beneath the sink, hoping she'd been

434

better than the one he'd got now! Straightening up, she said, 'It's been wonderful for young Polly, your coming back.'

'Thank you.'

Doris gazed at him. 'But are yer stopping?' she said bluntly.

Startled, André turned to her. 'Sorry?'

'Are yer going to stop – here at The Gables? I'm very fond of Polly, she's almost like one of my own. But she misses her Grandad, anyone can see that.'

André slowly poured out the tea. It seemed inconceivable that this cleaning woman felt she could ask him the question that so far nobody else had. But then he reminded himself that she wasn't just an employee, Mrs Booth had shouldered some of the responsibility that should have been Sadie's. And he was profoundly grateful for that.

'I can't answer that question, Mrs Booth,' he said. 'It depends on a lot of things.'

Aye, she thought, as after taking the cup and saucer from him, she watched André leave the kitchen. I can just imagine what one of them is as well!

The following day, Sadie had to go to work so Polly took Babs into Stone. The day was cloudy with a hint of rain, and after strolling up the High Street, with Babs frequently peering into the windows of shops to see the prices, Polly suggested they go for a coffee.

It was while they were sitting by the window, with Babs smoking a cigarette and Polly indulging in a slice of coffee cake that at last she felt able to talk about what had happened recently.

435

'I suppose you know,' she said hesitantly, 'that Sadie told my father – about everything?'

'Yes, I do.' Babs blew out a stream of smoke. 'How is the situation between them? From where you're sitting, I mean.'

'Better than it was,' Polly admitted. 'Things were pretty gruesome after he found out.'

'It's hardly surprising.'

'Babs?'

'Yes?' Babs gazed warily across the table at her.

'You know when my mother came back to London, the time when she left me as a baby?'

'Yes?' Babs narrowed her eyes.

Polly began to fiddle with her teaspoon. 'When she got over her depression, what did she do? In London, I mean? Were you still around?'

'Not all of the time. I'd married Jimmy by then. But Sadie and I kept in close touch. Why?'

'Well I've been wondering. Wouldn't she have had to do some war work or something?'

'You mean she hasn't told you? Now isn't that just typical of her.' Babs stubbed out her cigarette in irritation. 'Honestly, I despair of her sometimes.'

Slowly Polly replaced her china cup in its saucer. 'So she actually did do something?'

Babs regarded her. 'It still hurts, doesn't it – her leaving you behind? Well, I'm not surprised – I've never been able to understand it either. Not so much initially; after all, she was ill with depression. But afterwards...'

'I know.' Polly gave a slight shrug.

'Sadie did a great deal,' Babs said quietly. 'As soon as she was well enough, she volunteered to

436

be an ambulance driver. And she stuck at it, despite it being dangerous. I know she was in some sticky situations at times. Your mother did her bit, Polly.'

Polly stared at her. 'Why on earth didn't she tell us?'

'Sadie's got this odd way of thinking. I've seen it countless times. She'll never say anything that sounds as if she's boasting or making excuses for herself.'

Polly picked up her handbag and took out her purse to pay the bill. 'I'm going to tell my father,' she said. 'It might help him to see a better side of her. He probably thinks she was...'

'I'm not saying she was an angel,' Babs said, 'Sadie will be Sadie wherever she is. But there's a lot there to be proud of too.'

Later, Polly spent some time in her bedroom. She was supposed to be sorting out her clothes for the trip to Paris, but instead found her mind returning to what Babs had told her. Polly remembered newsreels and films she'd seen of terrifying air raids on London. Of bomb damage and distressing scenes of victims found and survivors being rescued from the rubble. To drive an ambulance, Sadie must have risked her life many times and seen horrific sights. And yet she'd never said a word. I think, Polly thought with confusion as she took out a dress from the wardrobe, that I must have the most complex mother in the world.

53

It was the evening before Polly was due to leave for Paris. In the large, clinically white bathroom, Sadie was luxuriating in a cloud of scented bubbles. She was looking ahead, planning. The relationship between herself and André was now one of reasonable harmony, due mainly to the wedding, which had broken the impasse between them. But she was no fool; she knew that there were still times when André would look at her with contempt, even anger. But there were other times when, suddenly glancing up, she would catch him off guard. And if she knew anything about life, she knew about men. Despite himself, her husband was attracted to her. And Sadie clung on to that, it was her raft, her lifeline. Not yet, not even for some time, but she was hoping that one night André would welcome her into his bed. Not her own, that would be a ghastly mistake; she always took great care to keep the door to her bedroom closed. If there was one thing she did know it was how to please a man; but most of all she longed to experience again the joy of sex with a man she loved. It still amazed her that her love for André had never faltered; it was as strong now as it had been all those years ago.

And, Sadie thought as later she wrapped herself in a fluffy white towel, with Polly away in Paris next week, she and André would be forced to spend more time alone. If nothing else, maybe she could charm him into at least liking her more...

Paris was all that Ruth had dreamed of. From the moment she saw the Eiffel Tower and the Arc de Triomphe, she was enthralled. She was even excited by the modest hotel, the same one that Mark and Polly had stayed at previously. The two girls were sharing a room and as soon as they arrived, rushed to open the shutters, to breathe in the garlicky smells, the scent of tobacco, to listen to the noise of the traffic. Polly looked out at the city, feeling a sense of excitement at the knowledge that Nicolas was somewhere out there. She was both longing to see him again and yet a little bit apprehensive. Would he still find her attractive? Would they still both feel the same about each other? Nicolas could even have met someone else, deciding that he didn't want to be tied down to a girl who lived in another country. And who could blame him? she thought nervously. After all, he was young, handsome and had all of Paris to choose from.

'What time are we meeting him?' Ruth said over her shoulder. She was unpacking her case and deciding where to put her things.

'Eight o'clock at the famous café with the burgundy awning!'

'Gosh – it's like something in a film,' Ruth said. 'The heroine returns to the scene, that sort of thing.'

Polly laughed. 'It is, isn't it?'

Ruth flopped down on the soft bed. 'I wonder,' she said dreamily, 'what will happen this week.'

Polly glanced at her. 'Why not just enjoy yourself and have fun, Ruth.' She was at a loss to understand why a sensible, clever girl like Ruth felt so insecure. It could only, she thought, be the wretched class thing. 'Come on,' she said, 'forget all that, let's decide what we're wearing tonight.'

Later, Nicolas sat at a table outside the café and glanced at his watch; he was early, impatient to see Polly again. To his regret he'd been unable to take time off from work, but was hoping they could meet every day for lunch as well spending each evening together. It had been strange these past few weeks, living alone in the apartment. Then he glanced up, saw the three of them approaching, and his gaze slid past Mark and Ruth to Polly. Her face was alight, her brown hair swinging, her lissom body outlined in a white linen shift dress. Nicolas knew in that one second that his feelings hadn't changed; the same feelings that had prevented him from even looking at another girl. He moved swiftly forward to kiss her on both cheeks then held her close against him. 'I've missed you,' he whispered. He turned to greet the others and with smiles they joined him at his table.

'Is this the one?' Polly said eagerly.

'This is the one. And Papa was walking along in that direction. You see? He had just gone by when he heard you laughing – and that was how it all started.' Nicolas was caressing her with his eyes.

'I take credit for all of this,' Mark declared. 'If I hadn't told a brilliant joke that made you laugh, Polly, none of this would've happened. You would not have a French boyfriend, you'd never have...'

'Oh shut up, Mark.' Polly was watching Nicolas as he gave the order for their drinks to the waiter.

'And,' Nicolas turned to wave a hand towards the interior of the café, 'the table in the back by the wall is the one where Oliver Sands and his friends were sitting. And that changed the course of history!'

They laughed. 'Has your father told him what's happened?' Ruth said.

Polly shook her head. 'Not yet. He did phone but there was no reply. He was probably on holiday. But I know he intends to.'

'I thought we'd eat at a little restaurant I know,' Nicolas said, 'it's very traditional – I think you'll like it, Ruth.'

'I can tell you all now – I absolutely refuse to eat snails or horsemeat!' Ruth stared defensively at them.

Nicolas laughed. 'I think French cuisine does have a little more to offer.'

And there was a lot of laughter that evening. With romantic music being played by a strolling accordionist, they sat in the soft evening air beneath a blue and white striped awning, and enjoyed not only a delicious meal, but shamefully copious amounts of wine. Ruth wrinkled her nose. 'What can I smell?'

'It's the ambience of Paree, my dear!' Mark grinned, 'In other words – Gauloise cigarettes.'

'Well, I like it.'

'Would you like to try one?' Nicolas offered her his cigarette case.

Ruth was tempted; she didn't smoke, but hadn't she come away to gain new experiences?

441

She reached out to take one, but Mark held her wrist. 'Not a good idea, sweetheart. They're too strong – they'll make you feel ill.'

'He's right. I'm sorry, Ruth, I'd forgotten you were a non-smoker.' Nicolas put the case back in his pocket.

'We haven't got any vices, have we, Ruth?' Polly said. 'In fact, you're dining with two perfect ladies.'

Mark nudged Nicolas. 'Sounds boring – shall we try and find a couple of others?'

'Don't you dare, Mark Eldon! In any case, you speak for yourself, Polly. I'm actually a femme fatale. I've just been waiting to come to Paris to prove it!' Ruth tucked her hand in the crook of Mark's arm and gazed meaningfully up at him.

He gazed down at her. It was only the wine talking, of course, but he glanced quickly across the table to see Polly watching them. Maybe it was just as well that the two girls were sharing a bedroom.

'I love it.' Polly's exclamation of delight when she first saw the apartment filled Nicolas with relief. As before when he'd returned from England, it had seemed small compared with The Gables. And yet he thought she was right; situated as it was overlooking the small square with its chestnut trees, it did have a certain charm.

Polly turned and went over to the dresser, picking up an ornate framed photograph. A slightly plump young woman gazed out at the camera with a sweet, calm expression. She was dark-haired and neatly if not fashionably dressed. 'Is this your mother? She looks kind.'

Nicolas smiled, 'Yes, she was.'

'Do you have any other photographs?'

Nicolas went to the dresser and from a drawer took out an album. 'I can't promise any of myself lying naked on a rug, though,' he grinned.

'Now that is a pity!' She came to sit beside him at the dining table and he showed her other photographs, of his grandparents and their farm, of himself as a boy, of her father – younger, and not always looking as well as he did now. 'It took a long time for him to completely recover,' Nicolas said.

'Yes, I can see that.' Polly looked around, imagining it in the winter, with the stove heating the room. A comfortable home and, she would imagine, a happy one. What a tragedy it was that Gabrielle had died so young. And yet if not, she would have discovered that she'd been 'living in sin' for twenty years, and the complicated situation between Sadie and André would have been even worse.

'It seems stupid that you should have to pay to stay in a hotel when there's a perfectly good room here standing empty.' Nicolas went to put the album away.

'But then Ruth's parents wouldn't have let her come.'

'Parents,' he shrugged. 'Don't they realise that there will still be lots of opportunities ... after all, you can't be there all the time.'

'I know. What do they say, "Love will always find a way"?' Nicolas laughed. '*We* don't need a chaperone,' he said. 'Papa casts a long shadow.'

Polly stared at him, and then began to laugh herself. 'He hasn't warned you...?'

Solemnly Nicolas nodded. 'Are you sorry?' His eyes teased her.

Polly wound her arms around his neck. 'I'm not sure,' she said, 'why don't we find out?'

54

It was raining when they arrived back in England.

'Typical,' Polly said as she began to descend the steps from the aircraft. 'Just look at those grey skies.'

Mark was quiet, as he had been all day. While the two girls had chatted on the flight, he'd immersed himself in a thriller, or at least had tried to give that impression. In reality he had been deep in thought. And that same evening he waited until his father was enjoying a cigar and then said, 'Dad ... about Ruth.'

George glanced across at him. 'Yes?'

'You do like her, don't you?'

'I think she's a fine girl, why?'

Mark said, 'I think I'm going to ask her to marry me.'

George tensed. 'Have you considered all the aspects of this?'

'If you mean the difference in class and religion – yes, of course I have.'

'And you're prepared for any children you might have to be brought up in the Catholic faith? They'll insist on that, you know.'

'I think so, Dad. To be honest, as long as they're

brought up Christians, I'm not too bothered which church they'll go to. As for the class thing, I think Ruth and I are strong enough to cope with any problems.'

'Yes, I think you probably are,' George said thoughtfully. He hesitated. 'Forgive my asking, but this has nothing to do with Paris, has it?'

Mark knew exactly what he meant. 'I respect her too much for that.' But he also knew what had happened, or rather nearly happened, the night before. After a romantic dinner alone, and a dreamy stroll along the banks of the Seine, he and Ruth had gone back to the hotel to find Polly was still out with Nicolas. It had seemed the most natural thing in the world for Ruth to come to his room, for them to stand on the balcony to bid goodbye to Paris. The temptation of the bed behind them had been impossible to resist; just to lie down together, to touch and kiss; even to begin to make love. And that love had come so near to being consummated...

'And you feel you have known each other long enough?' George continued to probe. 'It is less than a year, you know?'

Mark nodded. 'Yes, we have. And I don't want a long engagement either.'

George's eyes narrowed. He gazed for a moment at his son, then he gave a slight nod. 'Well it's not as if you can't afford to get married. There's the money your mother left you; that would give you a decent deposit – unless, of course, you'd consider living here?'

Mark gently shook his head. 'Thanks for the offer, Dad.'

'I can't say I blame you,' George smiled at him. 'Okay, Mark – you have my blessing. Of course, she may turn you down,' he added with a grin.

'I don't think there's much danger of that.'

'I think your mother would have approved too,' George reflected, 'I think she and Ruth would have got on very well. Felicity always admired intellect.'

When Polly arrived home she was dismayed to be met with an empty house. There was a note on the kitchen table: *Hope you had a good time. We've gone down to London, back about eight. Love, Sadie.*

Polly took heart from the term 'we'. Surely that sounded as if everything had gone well while she'd been away? She lugged her suitcase upstairs, deciding to unpack and have a long soak in the bath. And she spent many minutes lying in the scented water, just dreaming, remembering, and already longing to see Nicolas again. He'd promised to fly over in about six weeks, but it was going to seem like an eternity.

Later, going downstairs in her dressing gown, Polly made some cocoa and was about to pick up her mug when she heard the front door open. She went into the hall. 'Hello, gadabouts!'

'Look who's talking.' Sadie came forward and gave her a quick hug, while André followed to kiss her on both cheeks.

'How's Paris?' he said.

'Fabulous! And Nicolas isn't so bad, either.'

He laughed, 'I'm glad to hear it.'

'I'm for a gin and tonic,' Sadie said, putting down her handbag and going into the dining room. 'Anyone else?'

'Not for me,' Polly said. 'I'm on the wagon for a bit.' She fetched the mug of cocoa and went to join her. 'Why have you been down to London?'

'Your father was going to the Foreign Office, so I thought I'd take in a matinee.' She offered André a brandy as he came in to join them, but he shook his head.

'How did it go?' Polly asked him, curling up in an armchair.

'Fine, it was very interesting.' André yawned. 'I'll tell you all about it tomorrow. Sorry, I'm really tired. I think I'll go to bed.'

They both watched him leave the room, then Polly said, 'I've got a present for you.' She took out a small, prettily wrapped parcel from the deep pocket in her dressing gown.

'Why, thank you!' Sadie untied the silk ribbon and with delight took out a Hermes scarf. 'It's lovely, Polly.'

'I got it in the Galeries Lafayette. You should have seen Ruth,' Polly said, 'she was like someone in a sweetie shop without a purse!'

'Oh, that's a pity. Couldn't Mark have...?'

Polly nodded. 'I tipped him the wink, and she'll find a little surprise in her case when she gets home.' She gazed at Sadie, then said quietly, 'Nicolas took me to their apartment.'

'What was it like?' Sadie had often wondered.

'A typical Paris home, really. It was in a small square, on the ground floor, and very comfortable. It seemed strange, trying to imagine Dad living there all these years.' Polly hesitated, but she knew Sadie would want to know. 'I also,' she said, 'saw a photograph of Gabrielle.'

Even the name to Sadie was like a blow. She looked up at her daughter and her voice was low as she asked, 'What sort of woman was she?'

Polly described the sweet-faced woman in the photograph, and Sadie listened with an almost morbid curiosity. She still found it painful to think of André being married to someone else. She tried to drag her thoughts away. 'So,' she said, 'how did things go with Nicolas?'

'They were fine.'

Sadie smiled at her. 'Come on, you can do better than that.'

'Well, we still feel the same, if that's what you mean.'

'It was. And I'm very pleased to hear it, Polly.' And Sadie meant it. She liked seeing the happiness in her daughter's eyes. She liked Nicolas too, but that didn't prevent her from seeing the value of such a relationship. What better way could there be for her to forge an even closer link with André? Then she glanced at the silk scarf again, at the distinctive pattern, the subtle shades of blue, and ran her fingers over its softness. She was touched that Polly had thought of her. 'Thank you again for this. I appreciate it.'

Polly smiled at her. 'So, you've asked me about Nicolas. How have things been here, between you and Dad?'

Sadie became thoughtful. 'I honestly think they're improving. In fact, we've had quite a good week. I'm trying really hard, Polly.'

'Has he remembered anything else?'

Sadie shook her head. 'Not really. But you know

that poem, "The Highwayman"? The one André remembered? He found out at the Foreign Office that "ribbon of moonlight" was his password, the one he was to use to identify himself to the Resistance.'

'Ever likely it struck a chord!' Polly exclaimed.

'It was also suggested that he might try and get in touch with some of his old crew – those who made it. I'm going to ask Babs to contact Jimmy, to see if he's in contact with anyone.'

'Good idea.' Polly stretched. 'Well, I think it's about time I went to bed.'

After she'd gone, Sadie lit a last cigarette. Her main concern now, one that was beginning to dominate her thoughts and fill her with dread, was the fear that André might leave. His visit to the Foreign Office accomplished – what was there now to keep him here? She'd taken every opportunity, while Polly had been away, to charm, to entertain, to be good company, knowing the value of laughter in a relationship. Her aim had been to portray an elegant, assured woman, and she had only once given in to temptation and worn a revealing, if ultra-feminine blouse. And to her satisfaction she'd seen her husband's eyes drawn more than once to the glimpse of her breasts.

And so she was stunned when the following day André told them that he'd decided to go back to Paris. 'As soon as I can get a flight,' he added. 'It's unfair to expect the company to give me any more extended leave.'

Polly stared at him in dismay. Sadie was still in shock.

André said, 'You'll soon be immersed in your

teaching career, Polly. In fact, you're going into the school tomorrow, I believe?'

She nodded. 'Yes, to meet the staff and prepare lesson plans.'

'And your mother has her part-time job. It's time I took up my life again.'

'But you'll be coming back?' Polly said desperately. 'You could come over with Nicolas at the end of September.'

He smiled at her. 'We'll see.' He was avoiding Sadie's eyes. It was not only because of his work that he'd decided to leave. André needed to get away from The Gables, to be in his own familiar environment. Only then, distanced from his wife, could he begin to think dispassionately. There was so much confusion in his mind. He knew he would never be able to forget the shock, the disillusionment he felt about Sadie. But he'd also learned something about himself. He would never have imagined that he was the sort of man to pick up a girl in a nightclub and casually father a child – even if there was a war on.

55

Once André was back in Paris, the two men quickly settled back into their routine. But André knew it would never be quite the same again, not now he knew that he had been born and educated in England and had fought for his country. He also had a daughter over there – and a wife.

Nicolas too had changed. He was still the light-hearted young man who worked hard and enjoyed his social life, but he was becoming more thoughtful, more mature. To be expected, of course, as he approached his late twenties, but to André it was obvious that Nicolas was in love with Polly. This was no mere flirtation. Letters went back and forth and the young couple spoke weekly on the telephone. And as their relationship developed, André knew that some sensitive issues would have to be dealt with. But first, he needed to consult his daughter.

A week later, a letter arrived back from her.

Dear Dad,

Thank you for your letter. It is a difficult situation, isn't it? In fact, I was going to ask you the very same thing. So far, I've managed to avoid Nicolas finding out that Sadie left me as a child. At first I suppose I didn't want to prejudice him against her, and then it just hasn't arisen. But it's bound to at some time and I don't mind at all if you feel the right time has come to tell him. About the way she lived her life – I'm not sure. I have to confess that it does worry me that once he knows, he might see me in a different light – after all, I am her daughter. But, of course, no matter what happens between us in the future, Nicolas will always be part of our family. And families shouldn't have secrets from each other. Perhaps talking to him about it all might even help – 'a trouble shared, etc.' May I leave the decision to you?

We are both fine, I'm enjoying teaching and have some delightful children in my class. Not that I don't have a couple of difficult ones as well, but I regard

451

them as a challenge.
  Sadie sends her love, and so do I,

  Polly
  x

André gazed down at the letter, appalled to realise that Polly felt herself tainted by Sadie's behaviour, or at least feared that Nicolas or any other man might think so. No young woman should have to carry that burden, certainly not a daughter of his.

It was Friday evening, when they were both relaxing after dinner, relieved that the busy week was at an end, that André said, 'Nicolas, I want to talk to you.'

Nicolas glanced up at him from his armchair, his eyes narrowing as he saw André's serious expression.

André said, 'It's about Sadie.' He told Nicolas of the traumatic scenes in the drawing room; how he'd discovered that Polly had grown up without the love of a mother, that Sadie had confessed how she'd lived her life since she'd been widowed. He made no mention of how they'd met or the circumstances of their marriage.

Nicolas listened with growing disbelief. He had spent many hours in Sadie's company, had come to like and respect her. That she was an attractive woman was undeniable, but he'd never imagined... 'Papa,' he said with some embarrassment, 'I don't know what to say.'

'You can see why I've found it difficult to tell you.'

Nicolas was thinking with sadness of a lonely

452

little girl in that large house. 'Poor Polly,' he said. 'And yet she's never said a word.'

'I don't think she's one to seek sympathy.'

'It must be awful for her, people knowing that her mother – I take it that people do know?'

'Polly thinks there may be a few rumours, yes.' André hesitated, 'Nicolas – I hope this won't affect the way you feel about her?'

For a moment Nicolas stared at him with perplexity, before saying slowly, 'You mean that because her mother is ... of course not! Is that what Polly's afraid of?'

'I think so.'

Nicolas slowly shook his head. 'That's absolute nonsense,' he said. 'And I shall tell her so. You know I'm still finding it difficult to believe all that you've told me about Sadie.'

'She's a very complex woman, Nicolas. Apparently she volunteered to be an ambulance driver during the war – and that takes a lot of courage.' André reflected on how Sadie had tried to explain why she hadn't told them.

'I think it was just pride,' she had said. 'As I've said before, I never make excuses for what I am. As far as telling John was concerned,' she tried to be completely honest, 'I think I was afraid that if he knew, he'd expect me to do the decent thing again and come back here.'

André looked up as Nicolas said, 'Papa, do you mind if I ask you something? As your wife, Sadie is your next of kin. But now, considering what you've just told me and what I know of your father... I can't help wondering...' Then his eyes narrowed, 'He left his estate to Polly, didn't he?'

453

André nodded. 'Yes, he did. And now she knows I'm alive, she feels guilty about it.'

'It's hardly her fault.'

'I know. Anyway, apparently the will can't be changed.' André told him what had been decided at the meeting with the solicitor.

'Tough luck,' Nicolas said. His expression became thoughtful. 'I wish she wasn't,' he said suddenly, 'going to be rich, I mean.'

'That's not her fault either.' André rose. 'Would you like another cognac?' Nicolas shook his head, instead lighting a cigarette.

André poured himself another drink with a sense of disquiet. He would have preferred the subject of the will not to have been raised, at least not yet. Even as a small boy Nicolas had been fiercely independent; he was like Gabrielle in that respect. When André turned, glass in hand, it was to see the younger man staring moodily into the distance. Instead of joining him, André decided to leave him alone with his thoughts.

It was half-term, and on Friday evening, Polly waited on the platform at Stafford station trying not to shiver in the chill autumn breeze. At last she saw the train pulling slowly in and began to scan the windows of the carriages. It was with a profound sense of relief that she saw both men alight. Only the previous night Nicolas had phoned to say he wasn't sure whether André would be well enough. She hurried along to eagerly kiss Nicolas, and then turned to her father. He held up a hand. 'I'd hate you to catch my cold.'

'It's wonderful to see you both!' She led the way

out of the station and to the car, with Nicolas's arm draped around her shoulders as he smiled down at her. André, glad of his warm scarf, followed, thinking how happy, how *right* they looked together. But he was still worried. Nicolas had never mentioned Polly's inheritance since that night, but André knew him too well to believe that it didn't occupy his thoughts. And he had to come to his own conclusion. As I, he reflected as he climbed into the back of the car, have had to come to mine.

Sadie had wangled Saturday off, and had carefully planned this long weekend. Serene and yet desirable was the way she wanted to greet André – she'd refused to accept he might not come – and was wearing a straight navy skirt, with a pale blue cashmere sweater. And, of course, pearls with matching small drop earrings. The Gables too needed to play its part, and was filled with fresh flowers, the larder stocked with delicious food. Now, as she waited by the bay window in the dining room, she was overjoyed when she saw André get out of the car.

Whether because of the journey, or perhaps it would have developed anyway, André's sore throat rapidly worsened. Sunday found him confined to bed; Sadie – guiltily delighted to have the chance – only too willing to nurse and pamper him.

'You don't have to do all this,' he told her.

'Yes I do,' she said firmly, bringing him yet more hot lemon and honey. 'We don't want it turning into flu.'

'Neither do you want to catch it.'

'I won't. I never get colds.' And it was true,

455

Sadie was rarely ill. 'Anyway,' she said, going to sit on the chair by the window, 'the more I'm up here, the more those two downstairs can be on their own.'

André leaned silently back against the pillows while Sadie revelled in seeing him in striped pyjamas; looking, she thought lovingly, not only handsome but also vulnerable.

André was wishing that Sadie wouldn't sit with her legs crossed like that. Gracefully outlined against the window, smiling so affectionately at him, how could any man not feel an effect? He tried to distract his thoughts by wondering exactly what was going on in the drawing room.

Polly and Nicolas were lying entwined on the sofa, her head on his shoulder, his fingers idly playing with her hair. Since Nicolas had arrived, they'd spent every possible moment together, that morning driving to Barlaston Downs, enjoying the autumn tints, the clean fresh air, and again frequently finding themselves in each other's arms. She gave a sigh of content and snuggled even closer.

'Polly,' Nicolas said at last. 'I suppose you know that Papa told me – about Sadie?'

'Yes, he wrote to me.'

He kissed the top of her head. 'It was a shock, of course, but it doesn't make the slightest difference.'

'Honestly?' Polly said quietly.

'Honestly.' Nicolas hesitated, 'But I hadn't realised that you're going to be a wealthy young woman.'

'Oh, I see,' she twisted round to look up at him.

'So you're thinking of marrying me for my money, are you? And then bumping me off! Well, Nicolas Giscard, my grandfather was there before you.' Polly briefly explained the terms of the will.

'Damn! That's ruined all my plans!' Nicolas grinned.

Then Polly saw his expression become serious. 'You're not telling me that it bothers you?'

'I'm a very independent person, Polly,' he said quietly.

She stared at him in dismay. Surely... 'You mean,' she said tentatively, and not without some embarrassment, 'that if at some time in future we decided to get married, my having money would put you off?'

'I earn a good salary, Polly, but I couldn't match...' Nicolas waved a hand at the room, 'all this. And I wouldn't want to live off my wife.'

'But it wouldn't be like that,' she protested. 'I'm going to make over some of the money to Dad, shares and things.'

Nicolas didn't like to ask her what was going to happen in November – about The Gables and Sadie. There were, he reflected, so many strands to the situation, involving the future lives of all four of them.

Instead he said, wanting to be honest with her, 'One problem is that I don't think I could live anywhere else but Paris. Not and pursue my career.'

'I know that,' Polly said. 'But I love France, you know I do.' Then she swung her legs off the sofa and stood up. 'Don't you think we're running ahead of ourselves a bit?'

'Probably,' he said, but they both knew it wasn't

457

the truth. Polly was totally in love with Nicolas, and if he'd proposed at that very moment, she would have willingly said yes, at least with her heart. But John Merton's wise counsel had ingrained caution in her. A year, she thought, we need at least a year before either of us makes a decision.

Nicolas too was sure of his feelings. He'd had lots of girlfriends in the past, but there had never been anyone serious. What he felt for Polly transcended any flirtation. He loved just being with her; their easy rapport, their laughter together. But there were still difficulties to overcome, and Polly was right – it was far too soon to try and plan ahead.

André's day in bed had proved beneficial, and he came downstairs on Monday morning. Polly glanced at him once or twice over breakfast, thinking that he not only looked pale, but seemed very quiet.

Sadie too was watching her husband. She sat with the others as they ate their bacon, eggs and warm oatcakes – even Nicolas had succumbed – smoked her cigarette and waited. Something was in the air, she could sense it.

Half an hour later, they were all in the drawing room, Sadie on the sofa with her magazine, Polly next to her and content to gaze at Nicolas as he read the morning paper.

André finished his cigarette and stubbed it out in the glass ashtray. 'There's something I want to discuss with you all,' he said.

Three pairs of eyes glanced up. Sadie immediately tensed; Polly was curious, Nicolas glad that it was all going to come out into the open.

'I've been thinking very seriously these past weeks,' André said. 'As you all know, recent events have completely changed my life. And I have to face the fact that I can never be Jules Giscard again. So my decision has to be – do I now try to become André Merton?'

Sadie found herself so full of tension she could hardly breathe. Did this mean...?

'It will be a bit of an experiment.' André hesitated, 'Polly, how would you feel about my coming to live at The Gables? To give time for my memory to return, I think it should be for at least a year.'

Polly's smile was wide. 'You don't need to ask, you know I'll be thrilled to bits!'

'I've already been in touch with the education authorities to see if I can teach again,' André told them, 'and apparently there shouldn't be any problem, particularly as I've been giving private lessons all these years.'

Polly turned to her mother. 'What about you, Sadie – isn't it great?'

'You all know how I feel about André,' she said in a shaky voice, 'but I can't really say anything about this...'

They all stared at her and then Polly and André glanced at each other in consternation. Polly suddenly realised that Sadie was in an impossible position. Guilt flooded through her. She'd been so involved with Nicolas and the children in her class, that she'd completely forgotten that November was looming. She reached out for Sadie's hand. 'You must know The Gables is now your home, that I want you here as much as I do Dad.'

Sadie was so moved that she had to blink tears from her eyes. Unable to speak she could only gently squeeze Polly's hand. And then she looked across at André. But although he gave a small smile, his expression was inscrutable.

Polly watched her parents, saw the plea in Sadie's eyes, the wariness in André's. And so they had one year too. And she tried to imagine the four of them seated here in the drawing room at the end of that time. It's in the lap of the gods, she thought. I certainly can't predict what the situation will be.

56

Paris, September 1963

Polly was reflective as she strolled alone towards Montmartre. It was a lovely day, with a slight breeze rustling the leaves on the trees; their early autumn tints forecasting the winter to come. Nicolas was hoping to meet her for lunch at one of the cafés – although, as he was due to interview a politician on the Algerian situation, he'd warned her that he might be late.

She chose a table in the sunlight and, after ordering a soft drink, sat for a while surveying the now so-familiar scene. Her trips to Paris had been numerous over the past months, sometimes just a weekend, in the summer holidays even a fortnight. Was it because of her genes, she wondered, that she felt so at home here? And she thought of her father living all those years in Paris, finding it natural to believe himself to be French, and now rediscovering his English roots.

There hadn't been any startling leaps of memory, just tiny ones. André had expressed it as small windows occasionally opening. But his recollection of Sadie had never returned. Thinking of her mother, Polly smiled to herself, remembering how as soon as Sadie knew that André had decided to return, she'd called the decorators in. Her bedroom was ruthlessly stripped of curtains, carpet and even the cherubs. It had become a haven of magnolia, with a brand-new bed, pale blue curtains and carpet, and charming flower prints. Polly hadn't been able to detect a splash of pink anywhere! And no longer did her bedroom door remain closed. A smile curved Polly's lips, an almost exact replica of the small secret smile she'd seen on her mother's face six months ago.

And after that, there had been a marked change at The Gables. André, who was teaching French at a private school, was involved with his pupils and gradually making friends. He had also begun to relax. It was only when Polly heard him laughing one day with Sadie in the drawing room that she realised how serious he'd always seemed.

'Papa was never what you'd call "the life and soul of the party",' Nicolas told her when she remarked on it, 'I suppose you'd describe him as more of a "thinker".'

Sadie's sense of fun would be good for him, Polly

thought. She was still hugging the knowledge to herself that her parents had decided to try to build a future together at The Gables. It was, she supposed, inevitable that there would always be a shadow on their relationship, but Polly only knew that Sadie was happier than she'd ever seen her. André had insisted from the beginning on taking responsibility for all of the household expenses. 'I not only have my salary,' he said firmly, 'since your twenty-first birthday, I also have financial security. The house itself may belong to you, but I think you've been generous enough, Polly.'

And now her thoughts turned to her own future, and it was then that she saw Nicolas – striding along, his light brown hair ruffling in the breeze. He saw her and waved, then before sitting opposite leaned over and kissed her. 'Busy morning?' she said.

'Very – it was interesting, though.' He smiled at her. 'How about you – did you have any success?'

She nodded. 'Yes, I did. I think I've found the perfect one. It's spacious, in a delightful area, and if we each pay half we'll be able to afford it.' She looked across the table at him, 'Will that satisfy your sensitive pride?'

He smiled. 'You know we've sorted all that out.' He leaned towards her and took her left hand in his own. 'Do you still think you made the right choice?'

She looked down at the sparkling square solitaire. 'I love it,' she said, 'almost as much as I love you.'

The publishers hope that this book has given you enjoyable reading. Large Print Books are especially designed to be as easy to see and hold as possible. If you wish a complete list of our books please ask at your local library or write directly to:

Magna Large Print Books
Magna House, Long Preston,
Skipton, North Yorkshire.
BD23 4ND

This Large Print Book for the partially sighted, who cannot read normal print, is published under the auspices of

THE ULVERSCROFT FOUNDATION